The Knicker knocker

by

George Donald

Snow dropping:
In some areas of Glasgow, a slang term for the theft of washing from the clothes line.

Chapter 1 - Tuesday

The early morning sun promised another hot June Tuesday as Lesley got out of the drivers' door of the patrol car and adjusted the weight of the utility belt on her waist. She inwardly groaned at the thought it needed another notch pierced, then burped and again tasted the microwave curry meal for two she had eaten alone last night, thinking maybe after all that it hadn't been such a good idea. She rapped her knuckles on paint peeling door.
"Missus McGuigan," she called, banging again but on this occasion with her fist. "It's the police. You phoned us. Open the door please."
Lesley could hear shuffling on the other side of the door and took a step back, her hand instinctively caressing the handle of her expandable baton while turning her head slightly and staring in turn at the wooden hoarding that the council's call-out joiner had temporarily hammered into place over the front window of the mid-terraced house. She turned her head further to glance back at the patrol car and at her partner, seeing the lazy bugger cat-napping in the passenger seat of the car. She turned and took an involuntary step back as the door squeaked open on un-oiled hinges and a pale face stared out at her through the crack in the door.
"What you wanting?" asked the elderly woman, her eyes narrowing as they adjusted from the dark of the hallway to the light.
"Missus McGuigan?" she asked and then saw the woman's shoulders slump as she nodded, "You phoned the station about the broken window?"
"Come away in, officer" the woman replied in a low and world weary voice, opening the door to permit Lesley entry.

"I'm Constable Gold," she said, removing her uniform cap and squeezing past the woman who was dressed in her nightgown, a faded pink robe, her grey hair tied loosely in a ponytail and smelling strongly of cigarette smoke.
"Through here," said the woman, leading Lesley into a front room, "and mind your feet, hen, there's glass everywhere."
The room was dimly lit by a single bulb dangling overhead, the walls covered by faded floral wallpaper that was at least thirty years out of date. The couch and two side chairs was a stainless steel frame covered by a yellow plastic vinyl, with some red coloured scatter cushions providing a vivid splash of colour and like the wallpaper, decades out of fashion. A large and outdated television sat crookedly on a corner table and a mahogany sideboard and coffee table completed the furniture set. Dust mites danced in the fetid air or at least Lesley hoped they were dust mites.
A heavy set, unshaven man in his early thirties wearing crumpled navy blue coloured pyjamas sat slumped on the chair nearest the open fire, his hair dishevelled and holding his head in his hands. He didn't look up when the two women entered and Lesley thought she heard him quietly sobbing and her nose wrinkled at the strong smell of stale urine that hung about him. Even though it was the middle of the summer month, two electric bars were lit and exploded heat into the already stuffy atmosphere of the room. Lesley could feel a rivulet of sweat coursing its way down her spine, but was uncertain whether to attribute it to the heat in the room or the previous nights curry washed down with the half bottle of red wine that combined to protest in her stomach. Her attention was taken by the large and splintered shards of glass that lay beneath the boarded window.
"What's the story here, Missus McGuigan?" she asked, reaching into the pouch on her belt for her notebook.
"This is my son Billy," sighed Missus McGuigan, her hand stroking the man's head, "he's got learning difficulties, hen. People round here don't understand, because he's such a big laddie. They call him names and things. Awful names and now this," her free hand reached for her throat as her voice broke.
Lesley waited a few seconds, allowing the older woman to compose herself.
"The kids, they're the worst and the parents don't do a bloody thing about it. Danes Drive used to be such a nice place to live at one time, but now? Knightswood has become the dumping ground for the council," she spat bitterly. "Used to be that you needed to know a councillor to get a house here, but they days are gone. All the shite of the day getting houses round here now," her complaint turning into a whine.
"The window, Missus McGuigan," Lesley patiently reminded the woman, panicking slightly as for one horrible instant, she thought her stomach was

about to erupt and a wave of nausea swept through her. She swallowed hard and tried to concentrate on breathing through her mouth.

"Oh, aye, the window," the woman sighed again and turned to stare at the debris. "Some bastard heaved a brick though it during the night, about three o'clock," she replied. "I heard the crash and them laughing when they run away."

"Them? Do you know who did it, then?"

Missus McGuigan shook her head. "No, I didn't see them," she admitted, then her eyes widened and her nostrils flared. "But it was them out there, them sods …."

Her voice choked and she stumbled backwards, feeling with her hands for the other chair. With her free hand, Lesley helped the older woman to sit down and asked, "Can I get you a glass of water?"

"No, you're all right, hen. I'll be fine."

"You've had trouble here before then?"

"You're not a local polis?"

"No, I've just started here from the Maryhill office. This is only my second day in this area."

"Well, Constable … Gold, did you say your name is?"

"Aye, Lesley Gold."

"Well, Constable Gold, You'll get to know me and my boy here. We're well known to you people down at your Garscadden office on Great Western Road with the bother we get from the bastards round here. It's my Billy, you see. Because he's a wee bit different, they can't understand that. If they're not picking on him for being slow, they're making fun of him, calling him names. Paedophile was the latest, a few weeks back because he likes playing with the kids, but he's just a big kid himself, so he is," her voice broke into a sob. "He doesn't know any different and now this."

Lesley's eyes began to mist with tears, but not at the sorry tale. The overpowering smell from the son and the churning of her stomach combined to nauseate and she knew she needed to throw up. Forcing herself to smile, she asked if she could pop into the toilet.

"Up the stairs hen," Missus McGuigan replied, then eyes squinting asked "Time of the month, eh?"

Lesley clenched her teeth and could only nod as she hurried from the room, scrambling as best she could to the top of the uncarpeted stairway, then pushing open the door to the small bathroom. She barely had time to lift the grimy toilet seat before her stomach discharged its contents in a thick and foul smelling, yellowish fluid. Her stomach heaved twice, three times and she vomited again, shaking at the exertion. She snatched a handful of toilet tissue from the roll and after dabbing at her mouth, threw the tissue into the bowl and pulled the handle. A thin stream of water worked valiantly at flushing the vomit away and she had to wait till the cistern refilled to completely cleanse the bowl. Ignoring the throbbing in her head, she glanced in the mirror that hung crookedly above the small sink. The pale, drawn face that stared back was framed by black hair, collar length but held back by a chequered hair band, that highlighted her ivory clear skin and steady grey eyes; not a beautiful face nor plain either, but strong and though she would never see it in herself, an honest face. Lesley could never quite understand why men found her attractive and she thought her nose to be slightly crooked, but something about her appealed to the opposite sex and for that, she wryly grinned, she was grateful. And it's not my figure, she again grinned to herself, aware that she was carrying at least just over a stone too much for her five foot eight inch frame. Taking a deep breath, she run the tap and doused her face with ice-cold water and reached for the hanging hand towel, but quickly withdrew her hand, grimacing when she saw some unidentifiable stains on it. Again she tore at the toilet tissue and used several sheets to mop her face dry, throwing them into the bowl then flushed them away. Her bladder needed emptying too, but the thought of exposing her backside to the grimy bowl made her shudder again and she decided she would hang on till she returned to the office.

From her pocket, she brought out a pack of spearmint gum and popping one into her mouth, opened the door and made her way back down stairs.

"Feeling better, hen?" Missus McGuigan asked and from the knowing look in her eyes, Lesley guessed the woman had heard her vomiting and probably suspected it was morning sickness. Aye right, she thought, a fleeting vision of the two-timing bastard flashing before her eyes.

"So the window, Missus McGuigan, one or more of your neighbours' broke it you think and you also think it's because they don't like your son here?"

"Don't like him? They hate him," she replied and her shoulders slumped, but such was the venom of the statement that Lesley wondered about the woman herself, how she really felt about her son.

"Do you get any support? From the social work, I mean?"

"Aye well, he's on their register and once a week a bus comes and takes him to a rehabilitation place, they call it. Try to teach him things, like woodwork and basic cooking, you know? But it's not really any use. Billy can't concentrate for more than a few minutes. And of course there's the disability allowance they palm me off with. I get money for keeping him here instead of getting him put into one of them adult homes. It's cheaper for them that way, you know?" she said, the despondency evident in her voice.

Lesley didn't really know, but nodded anyway and hoped to hell this wasn't going to drag on, that she could finish taking the report and quickly get out and into the fresh air.

"Why didn't you call us during the night, when it happened I mean?" she asked.

"What would be the point? The bastards had run away and besides, I'm not going to speak up against anybody, am I? I mean, I can't give you a statement or anything, it would only mean more trouble for me and Billy. I've got to live here, you know," she huffily replied. "The only reason I'm telling you now is that the council joiner said I had to report it for the crime number, so that I don't get charged a call-out fee."

Lesley sighed and nodded. It wasn't the first time she had encountered this type of call. It took but a couple of minutes to note the details and after promising to later phone the crime number to her, briefly considered offering to assist the woman in clearing up the glass. However, her stomach again rebelled at the thought of spending another minute in the fuggy room and closing her notebook she shoved it back into the pouch and turned to leave, but stopped at the front door and turned towards the older woman.

"Missus McGuigan, you said earlier when I arrived that the kids round here call your son names and you also said 'and now this'. What did you mean by that?"

"Oh, it's the latest name they're calling him. Some of the women round here have had their underwear stolen from the washing lines overnight and they're blaming my Billy. They're calling him a knicker-knocker. The thing is, my Billy's never out after eight at night and it's just an excuse for these sods to have another go at him."

She was walking back towards the patrol car, conscious of the twitching curtains that hid the furtive eyes that watched her when she saw the over-weight and apparent irate woman hurtling down the path from a nearby house to intercept her.

"What, are you not going to arrest that pervert then?" the woman hissed at her.

In the car, Lesley saw her partner's head lolling back, obviously asleep and unaware of the pending confrontation. "And you are?" she calmly replied.

"I'm the woman that's paying your wages and I want that thieving bastard taken away and shoved into a mental hospital where he should have been put in the first place!"

It briefly occurred to Lesley to draw her baton and smack the arrogant cow across her smug face, but common sense prevailed and instead she took a deep breath and grimly smiled. "By that thieving bastard, madam, am I to assume you are referring to Mister William McGuigan of that house over there?" she indicated over her shoulder with her thumb, "and I'm also to assume that you have evidence of some wrongdoing by Mister McGuigan and that you will provide me with the necessary statement?"

"Don't try to bamboozle me with your fancy polis talk," the woman sneered. In her late forties Lesley thought as the woman drew herself up to her full five foot one inch height, arms folded across her massive bosom. "We all know it's him that's stealing our underwear, so it is."

Lesley later wondered why she just hadn't choked back her response or maybe instead choked the cheeky bitch, but couldn't help herself and leaned forward till her own nose was mere inches from the woman's. "Well, I've seen Billy McGuigan pal and he's some size of a lad, so he is, and I reckon if it was him that stole your knickers, they'd never fit him because they'd be too fucking big!"

The woman was aghast and her face turned from shocked white to angry red. "And another thing," snarled Lesley, leaning even closer towards the woman so that their noses almost touched, "I saw where you live, so if I get another call back here about the McGuigan's getting any kind of hassle from you or any of your cronies, yours is the first door I'm putting my foot through, understand?"

"You …you …" stammered the woman, pointing her shaking finger as Lesley turned away towards the drivers' door of the car. "You!" she screamed, "I want your number!"

Lesley sat in the seat and slammed the door shut, then wound down the window. "My number's nine, nine, nine so just ask for me or Constable MacDonald," she cheerfully called out through the open window as she drove off.

As Lesley steered the car along the rutted road, her partner wearily rubbed at his face as he awoke. "Is that you done? Did you get the details?" he asked.

"Aye Morris," she replied, concentrating on the road, "I got the details. Time for a cuppa I think and by the way, you might be getting a phone call."

Chapter 2

Paul Hardie stared at Janice as she shrugged into her bra, her long blonde hair spilling across her shoulders, his eyes taking in the curve of her breasts as they grew taut against the cotton fabric when she clipped it at the back. "You'd better get a move on lover boy," she said over her shoulder, pulling on first the dark tights then the black, knee length skirt up over her shapely thighs and zipped it closed. She turned towards him, her face registering her curiosity. "Won't your wife wonder where you've been all night?"

"I already told you," he replied, stretching his arms wide as he lay back on the dishevelled bed, "she thinks I'm at a work conference in Edinburgh. I told her that I'm in line for a promotion and I don't want to piss off the boss by refusing to accompany him to the conference. Said it would probably be an all night thing," he grinned at her.

"I know you said something last night about it," she grimaced, "but after the second bottle of wine and what we got up to, a lot of it went out of my mind." She twisted her mouth, and reached for the crisp white blouse, her head down concentrating on buttoning it at the front then tucking it into the skirt. "Well, at least the part about the promotion is correct. Anyway," she stood up and slipped into a pair of short heeled black, patent shoes and began dragging a brush through her hair, "like I said, we can't arrive together at the office, so you better get your arse in gear. I'll drop you just after I come off the motorway at Bothwell Street and that will give you a five minutes walk to the office, okay?"

"Gotcha," he replied and sighed as he swung his legs over the side of the bed and stood naked. "Don't suppose we've got time for a …." he teased her as he took hold of his semi erect penis in his hand.

"No, we haven't," she sharply responded, "and I'm leaving in ten minutes whether you're ready or not," she called over her shoulder as she pulled open the bedroom door and went toward the kitchen.

He exhaled nosily and rubbing at his mop of thick, collar length fair hair, walked into the small, compact en-suite, turning on the shower and reaching into the wall cabinet for the shaving items he kept there. Rubbing at his jaw, he stared into the mirror, wiping it clear of moisture as the small room became enveloped in steam from the shower. This is the life, he grinned at himself. A good looking girlfriend, a flat without a scrub of grass that constantly needs cutting and no bloody wife whose sole topic of conversation day in and day out is that bloody class of kids of hers.

Through the open doors, he could hear the electric kettle whistling.

Fiona, he thought and again exhaled. She'd take the news badly. There would be tears and snotters, but he had his own life to live. He couldn't stay married to a plain, mousey thing like her that considered a weekly trip to the pictures or a pub the highlight of her life. Anyway, he thought, it wasn't his fault that she had let herself go from the pretty little thing she had been to what she is now. Six years was long enough to be tied down to her he had already decided and besides, he grinned as he lathered his face, his half share of the sale of the house would set him up nicely for a flat in the west end of Glasgow and particularly if the promotion comes through. Maybe somewhere near to Byres Road where there is a bit of life about the place. Maybe even persuade Janice to rent out this place and move in with me, he mused, deftly running the razor round his cheeks.

"Have you not even showered yet?" said the voice behind him then the playful slap at his backside, "Coffee's waiting for you in the kitchen, so please Paul, get a bloody move on."

"Two minutes," he shouted out as Janice retreated into the bedroom to apply her make-up then he stepped into the shower, adjusting the thermostat to a tolerable level.

In the bedroom Janice, her hair now tied back into a severe ponytail, carefully dabbed the deep red lipstick pen at her fulsome lips and then smacked them together before dabbing at them lightly with the tissue. Her glance in the mirror took in the bed behind her, the covers thrown back and the crushed pillows. Her eyes narrowed and shoulders slumped slightly as she stared into her own blue eyes, suddenly uncertain of her feelings for Paul. Sure, the last three months had been exciting, but him being married constantly put a damper on their relationship; unable to mix socially with colleagues and afraid of being seen together in public and meeting in all sort of way out places. On more than one occasions she had considered ending it, but softly smiled. She had to admit he was good company and the sex was good too. Besides, she argued to herself, the word was he would be soon promoted and his new income wasn't something to be sneered at either. If only he could get rid of that bloody wife of his.

The subject of Janice's thoughts, untidily dressed in pink faded pyjamas and an oversized, creased, brown corduroy dressing gown, was just then searching again for the slip of paper. Fiona was certain that before he had left for work the previous morning, Paul had said he'd written down the name and phone number of the Edinburgh hotel and that he'd left it on the small, dining room table. She twirled her lank, dull hair between the forefinger and middle finger of her left hand as she shoved aside the school jotters she had been marking, the text books and a dozen other files, her eyes scanning back and forth for the elusive slip of paper. The few people she associated with at school, not really friends, she admitted to herself and her parents both long dead, limited who she could call and her brother in Australia; well, he hadn't been in touch all year so it was pointless telling him about the news that so excited her. Paul's mobile phone had been on answer mode all last night and she guessed, as he had said, that the meetings must have gone on all evening. He's right, she sighed as she recalled her husband's moans; this isn't so much a dinner table as an impromptu desk. She sat down heavily on the creaking chair and looking about her at the scattered magazines and newspapers, clothes drying on the radiators, full washing basket in the corner and again promised herself not just to tidy the small house, but get Paul to check the loose leg on this chair she thought, as she idly patted at her stomach. She stared thoughtfully through the back window across the small, untidy rear garden, to the service lane that ran behind the mid terraced houses. A faint glow rushed into her cheeks and she smiled. In the kitchen, the radio announced the eight o'clock news and she jumped up, realising she hadn't yet washed and needed to change for school, wondering if she had anything clean and ironed in her wardrobe. Making her way into the small kitchen, she remembered she hadn't emptied the washing machine or washed the dishes again and sighed. Oh, well, too late now Fiona told herself and promised it would be more chores she would attend to when she got home that afternoon. The news was just ending and, distracted as she half listened to the latest developments in the middle-east, she decided on a cup of tea and some toast before she went upstairs to the bathroom.

Nobody ever took much notice to Frederick Evans, at least, not unless they wanted him to do something or sniggered behind his back. Not that he really cared, for after all, having worked at Dawson's now for most of his working life, Frederick had become almost inured to the put-downs and veiled insults. Well, almost. None of the staff, none of the three hundred or so who were employed in the large shop in Buchanan Street in the city centre, from the manager to the part-time school kids who helped out at the weekend, remotely suspected just how much Frederick hated them; hated them all. Well, maybe not all of them. Jennifer Farndale, who worked in the staff canteen was nice and sometimes when her supervisor wasn't looking, she'd slip him the extra sausage or a larger dollop of potato and their eyes would meet and he knew, just knew that she liked him. He didn't care and it didn't matter to him that she was so skinny, that she wore thick glasses and it annoyed and upset him when he listened to the young girls from the other departments poke fun at Jennifer, the painted hussies from the fashion, lingerie and cosmetic departments who thought of themselves as a cut above the rest of the store girls. His knuckles turned white as he clenched his fists, an overpowering rage coursing through his own thin frame.
"Mister Evans, hover, hover," the voice behind him cut into his thoughts. Automatically, he reached up and straightened the suit jackets on the rack. "Can't have the clients thinking we are not there for them, can we Mister Evans?" The men's department floor manager, Robert Hamilton appeared at his elbow, unconsciously preening himself on the stand alone mirror next to the rack of suits, one hand smoothing down his jacket lapel and picking at a hardly visible thread while the other gently stroked the pencil moustache. "Remember, Mister Evans, we at Dawson's always pride ourselves on customer service, so let's be attentive and hover, hover and be ready to serve, eh?" and with that final comment, Hamilton minced off to catch some other unfortunate unawares. Hover, hover. Hamilton was never done telling his staff how his wife had recently bought him a flight on a helicopter as a birthday treat and the man now considered himself some kind of aviation expert. The fool!

Frederick stared at his retreating back. How he loathed the man and wryly enjoyed the younger staff's nickname for Hamilton. Bumptious Bob he was called behind his back. Frederick relaxed now that Hamilton had gone, wondering how long he could suffer another day working here. Over twenty-five years of servitude, twenty-five years of listening to the moans and whines of Joe Public, arguing about sizes, prices, styles, colours. Twenty-five years, day after day. And always at the beck and call of an ungrateful shower of … of … He couldn't believe how angry he had recently become and with no one near to see him, leaned into the soft fabric of the hanging suits, pressing his face against a sleeve to halt the tears that threatened to engulf him. Hamilton's promotion two months previously, he inwardly fumed, should have been mine. I've worked my balls off to impress, did all the shitty jobs that they asked of me and how am I repaid? The Johnny-come-lately had been at the store for less than a year and already he was promoted. Of course, the management said they had brought him in to encourage sales, put a bit of drive into an already overworked men's department staff and admittedly, sales had gone slightly up, but that was because of Frederick's hard work, not his! It's just not fair, he inwardly raged. He closed his eyes against the throbbing in his head as he envisaged what lay in the small, cardboard box that he had hidden behind the water heater in the cupboard in his room at home and smiled softly. Frederick swallowed hard and decided that tonight, if the weather held as it surely must, he would add to his collection. Taking a deep breath, he used the flat of his hand to smooth back his thinning, sandy coloured hair and glanced at his watch. It was almost time for his early morning break and, he smiled again, maybe an extra sausage from Jenny. He'd take his mobile phone with him and smiled in anticipation. All those hours of practise at home had paid off. He would sit and pretend he was using the phone to play one of the games loaded into it and no-one would suspect what he was really doing, using the camera to video those young tarts who regularly sat at one of the middle tables, preening themselves. He sighed with pleasure as he recalled the hours of film he had transferred to his computer, but more because as smart as the bitches thought they were, they never, ever suspected.

Lesley Gold steered the patrol car into an empty bay at Garscadden Police Office and thought that after a visit to the female toilet, there was nothing she needed more than a mug of hot, sweet coffee.
"Just nipping to the loo for a jimmy riddle," said her partner, Morris MacDonald, over his shoulder as he climbed from the passenger seat. She decided to sit for a moment and catch her breath, watching him make his way across the yard, punch in the code on the wall, then pull the door open and disappear into the dark of the rear corridor. Damn, she thought as in

frustration she tightly closed her eyes, what's that bloody number again and getting out of the car, had no option but to walk round the side of the office to the front entrance. As she pushed open the heavy glass doors, a voice called out from behind the Uniform Bar, "What's up, your majesty, tradesman entrance not good enough for you?"

Jinksie Peterson, the red-headed diminutive civilian bar officer, smiled at Lesley then turned to the tall, well-built postman who was bent over and shuffling the morning mail across the public counter. "Thanks Andy, see you tomorrow morning," said Jinksie and turned away to separate the mail into the dookits beside the counter. The postman nodded and averting his gaze, stood aside to let Lesley pass by, ignoring her cheery "Morning" as he made his way out the door.

"What's his problem?" she frowned at Jinksie.

"Andy? Aw, he's just a bit quiet and kind of keeps himself to himself."

"That's some scar on his chin and his neck," she said. "Been a bad boy, has he?"

Jinksie screwed his face up. "Don't know how he came by the mars bar, but if he's employed by the Post Office, he's not supposed to have a criminal record, is he?"

"Not sure," she shook her head in response. "So are you going to buzz me through or what?"

"Aye, sorry," he said, releasing the electric catch on the access door. "Forgot the rear door code?"

"Got told it once, but I can't remember it," she yawned as she entered Jinksie's hallowed ground.

"Here, I'll write it down for you," he said, scribbling the number on a piece of paper and handing it to her.

Thanking Jinksie, Lesley made her way along the narrow corridor to the women's locker-room at the rear of the office and was almost there when a head popped out of the sergeant's room.

"Lesley, just the woman I want to see. Got a minute?"

Pete Buchanan, the Community Patrol Sergeant beckoned with his thumb towards his office.

"I'll be right with you Sarge," she replied, "got to take a comfort break first." His face screwed in puzzlement till she added, "Need to pee," and almost laughed when embarrassed, he quickly looked away.

The locker-room was empty and after emptying her bladder, Lesley washed her hands at the bowl and stared blankly into the mirror above the sink. Her soft, grey coloured eyes betrayed her hurt, but most of all, surprised herself at the intensity of her anger. "Bastard", she vehemently whispered to herself, the memory so very painful and raw, and with her of all people. She let out a long sigh and rolled her tongue against the furry roof of her mouth, mentally making a note to bring a toothbrush and paste with her tomorrow to keep within her newly allocated locker.

Splashing some water onto her face, she tore off a couple of sheets of paper towel, wiped her face and pulled at the small chequered band, releasing her jet black hair. Shaking her head, she used her fingers, to drag her thick locks of hair back from her face into a severe pony-tail and wound the band back on. Taking a deep breath, she did one final check in the mirror, replaced her utility belt on her waist and then made her way to Pete Buchanan's office.

"Ah, Lesley, come in," he smiled at her and gestured towards the chair on the opposite side of his desk.

"So, this is what, your second day with us?"

She smiled tolerantly, knowing that he was trying to be sociable, but right now the last thing Lesley needed was another patronising, "I know how you must be feeling, but…." lecture from a supervisor.

As she stared at him, she knew he must know why she had been moved from Maryhill office to Garscadden, what had occurred, the blunt warning she had received. Inwardly taking a deep breath, she decided to get it over with.

"Look Sarge we both know why I'm here. It's not a secret that I got disciplined and moved. All you have to know is I'm not a disruptive officer. I'll come to work, do my shift and not cause you any problems. It's already been made clear to me that my coat's on a shaky peg. If I mess up at all, I'm out on my ear, so you'll have no problem with me, okay?"

Pete Buchanan raised his eyebrows as he stared at her. This was not how he envisaged the conversation would go and if he was honest with himself, he was a little relieved that he didn't have to raise the subject, that Lesley Gold herself had herself issued the warning he had planned for her. With just under two years service left till he was out the door and his pension kicked in, the last thing he needed was a loose cannon in his tight little unit of a dozen officers.

"Okay, Lesley, you've made it clear where we both stand. All I need add is that if you keep your nose clean, you'll not have any bother from me. However, one fuck up and it's down to Maryhill office to see the Chief Inspector. Are we understood?"

Lesley nodded and rose to leave, but as she opened the door, Buchanan called to her.

"Lesley, look, as you said, it's no secret why you have been posted to this office." He raised his hands as if in surrender. "I know that the bother you got into wasn't of your making; that it was down to your fiancé …."

"Former boyfriend; he wasn't my fiancé," she curtly reminded him.

He grinned in embarrassment. "Former boyfriend then," he nodded his head in agreement. "Not that it's particularly relevant, but I'd like you to know that Mike Duffy and I used to be in the same shift when we were cops at

Stewart Street. For what it's worth, I thought he was a prat then and from what I hear, he hasn't changed any." He grinned again. "If I were you, I'd consider that maybe what's happened has been a lucky escape rather than a misfortune."

"Anything else, Sergeant?" she replied, not trusting herself to speak and eager to be gone from the sanctimonious bugger.

"Eh, no, go and have a cuppa or something. I'll let you know when the Inspector arrives. I understand he wants to welcome you to the office."

"Right," she nodded and closed the door behind her.

Buchanan sat staring at the door knowing that it hadn't gone well, that she had caught him wrong-footed and he shouldn't have started the welcome to the shift with a warning. Shit. He slowly nodded his head, angry with himself and reached for the bundle of paperwork in his in-tray.

Outside the door in the corridor, Lesley slowly exhaled, also angry that the initial meeting with her new shift Sergeant had gone badly. She wasn't that naïve and fully aware her conduct had landed her at this shithole of an office with a reputation, one that in her mind she didn't really deserve. All the preceding seven years good and exemplary work ruined in one sudden burst of anger. And all because of Michael Duffy, may he rot in hell.

"Hey, neighbour," the voice made her jump. Turning she saw Morris MacDonald, a stained white mug held in one hand, a half eaten sandwich in the other and a scowl pasted on his face. "I've just had a call from a wee woman that lives in Danes Drive. She was shouting some shite down the phone, something about me threatening to kick her door down and intends to report me to the gaffers. Do you know anything about it?"

Chapter 3

Fiona Hardie switched off the engine of the old Ford Escort and held the driver's door open with her right foot then turning to lift the stack of jotters from the passenger seat with her left hand, precariously balanced her handbag and plastic bag containing her lunch in the other hand. Carefully she tried to slide from the seat out of the car, then came to a sudden halt, realising that foolishly she hadn't unclipped her seat belt. The jotters tumbled to the floor of the car between her legs and the plastic bag fell to the concreted ground. Sighing, she unclipped the belt and still seated, squatted awkwardly between the seat and driving wheel as she rummaged for the jotters.

"Need a wee hand there Missus Hardie?" asked the voice, startling her and causing her to bang her head against the underside of the steering wheel. Jimmy Dunlop had been the school janitor at Durban Road Primary school for nigh on twenty years and had seen all sorts of teaching staff come and go, but this young lassie, he privately admitted, must be the most inept teacher he had ever come across. Still, he inwardly sighed, she was a nice wee girl, if a little dim.

"Oh, yes, thanks Mister Dunlop, if you wouldn't mind," she breathlessly replied, smiling at the stooped, grey haired man and handing him a pile of homework books. "I'm a little late I think."

You're a lot late hen, he nearly said, but didn't, and God help you with that dictatorial bugger Miss Jenkins, he thought as he grabbed the pile of books from her with one huge hand, extending the other to assist her from the car. Subtly, he glanced towards the main building and saw the torn faced Head Teacher standing at her window, watching as Fiona Hardie and the elderly janitor walked toward the main door. Jimmy didn't like Jenkins or her type and pointedly ignored her frosty stare. He wished he could somehow warn the young teacher to be on her toes, that likely she would get yet another rollicking from the martinet Head, but knew it would be useless. Missus Hardie was such an innocent and beyond advice and nothing Jimmy might or could say would alter the fact the young lassie was a disaster. He glanced at her as she cheerfully strode beside him, seeing her make-up looking like it had been applied by one of her primary three pupils and the front of her light blue coloured frock stained with some unidentifiable food material and her hair looked like it had been brushed down one side only. As they walked together, he glanced down and reminded himself the white lines that outlined the netball court needed repainted, half listening to her babbling on about some good news or such nonsense or other, realising she was blissfully unaware of the storm that awaited her. That decided him. He wouldn't just see the lassie into the building, but walk with her to her classroom and hopefully deter any ambush that awaited her in the corridor. He knew the bullying Head Teacher Miss Jenkins would relish the opportunity to bollock the wee lassie, but guessed she wouldn't do it in front of a common worker like him, whom she constantly reminded wasn't a teaching staff member. No, he thought to himself, she would then need to wait till later, maybe the lunch break. It might give her time to calm down a bit, but he knew in his heart that regardless of when it happened, poor wee Missus Hardie was in for it.

Pushing open the heavy glass doors, Jimmy smilingly insisted on carrying the books and plastic bag and continuing with the dizzy teacher to her primary three classroom where opening the door to permit her to enter, he saw the matronly teaching assistant Angela Paterson sigh with relief at Missus Hardie's arrival, albeit a lot later than the nine o'clock commencement for her class.

"Good morning, boys and girls," Fiona cheerfully chirruped, turning with a smile to relieve Jimmy of the jotters and bag. As the door closed behind her, Jimmy inwardly grinned at the loud sound of the childish response as thirty odd voices replied, "Good morning, Missus Hardie," then he decided the replacement bulb in the dining room could wait till after he'd had a cuppa and a chocolate digestive.

Janice Meikle smoothly rolled the red coloured Mini into an empty bay in the Cambridge Street car park and switching off the engine, rested her hands on the steering wheel and stared blankly ahead at the unpainted concrete wall. She had dropped Paul from the car just a few minutes earlier at the Bothwell Street junction, reminding him that it wasn't such a good idea being seen together in the office let alone outside. It worried her that he laughed at her concern. She unconsciously shook her head with the knowledge that should they be discovered, any office impropriety with a married man in the strait-laced company would be dealt with by her dismissal, while he likely would receive no more than a reprimand and probably knowing winks and good natured slaps on the back from his male colleagues for shagging her. Bloody unfair, she angrily slapped her hands on the wheel. Again, it occurred to her that they were taking too much of a risk, that her options were either to end their relationship and dump him or hope, as he frequently promised, he'd get rid of that mouse of a wife of his. But she'd been through this before. She inwardly sighed, remembering the mess she had left at her previous firm when her affair with the Sales Director had become public knowledge. Only the intervention of the Board, protecting the company name and the confidentiality deal she struck with the firms' management ensured she left with an excellent and unblemished character reference, though the messy and public divorce that ensued following her departure had threatened to identify her. As her old dad used to say, she had got out of there just ahead of the posse.

The digital clock on the dashboard reminded her she was running late. With a quick glance in the rear-view mirror, she daintily dabbed with the small finger of her left hand at a slight smudge of her lipstick and sighing, pushed open the door.

A young man dressed in workman overalls exiting an old black coloured Ford Focus three bays away cast an admiring glance and smiled at the long legged lovely as she gracefully slid from the Mini.

"Need any help there, doll?" he cheekily called out to her.

She smiled without replying and turning away, shrugged into her suit jacket and pulled at her blonde ponytail till it hung over the back of the jacket. Slinging the strap of her handbag over her shoulder, she made her way towards the exit in the knowledge that the guy would be watching her and deliberately wiggled her arse to tease him, inwardly thinking, in your dreams, pal.

Janice Meikle didn't just like, but craved the attention of men and with her lengthy experience of them, knew exactly how to demand their interest.

Midway through that morning, Frederick Evans rolled his eyes to heaven, gritted his teeth and fetched yet another dark coloured suit from the rack and decided the heavily tattooed young man, no more than a youth really, wasn't just uncertain - he was a downright cretin and shouldn't have been allowed out without some kind of carer.
"Sorry pal," the young man apologised yet again, "it's a funeral I've got to go to and I don't want to give myself a showing up, you know? Turning up dressed as if it's a dance, you know?"
"Of course sir, but as sir will likely be aware, black is traditional," stressed Frederick, unable to hide the pomposity in his voice, a voice that was high pitched, almost falsetto and had been cultivated by him since he was a young child. Frederick was proud of his voice and though it had been the source of much amusement to his peers during his school years that in turn led to bullying, he believed his voice to be cultured and a cut above the riff-raff he was unfortunately obliged to serve.
"Aye, I know that, I'm no stupid, pal," the young man scoffed, now irritated by the older man's attitude towards him, "but I'm no paying they fancy prices for a suit that I'll no be wearing to the dancing or functions, you know?"
"Of course sir," replied Frederick, his patience now wearing thin and again couldn't disguise the scorn in his voice as he replied, "Perhaps sir might consider a more fiscally appropriate purchase at one of the larger chain stores that stock off the peg clothing?"
"What does that mean?" the young man screwed his face, his eyes registering his suspicion that the skinny wee shite of a salesman was taking the piss.
"What Mister Evans means, sir," said the voice behind Frederick "is that perhaps sir might consider something in navy blue, perhaps a fine pinstripe that I believe will be appropriate for a solemn occasion as well as suitable for more social events."
The floor manager Robert Hamilton appeared from behind a rack of suits, smiling benignly at the young man. With a jacket held in his right hand and trousers draped over his left arm, he stepped in front of Frederick to face the young man and held the jacket open for the young man.
"Aye, well, I mean, you're the expert pal. If you think that might be all right," the young man hesitatingly replied, turning to slip his arms into the jacket sleeves.
"We at Dawson's pride ourselves in satisfying a customers every need and of course sir, your style is our business, isn't that correct Mister Evans," he turned to stare with steely eyes at Frederick, having helped the young man

shrug into the suit jacket, he deftly turned him towards a free standing mirror. "There now sir," he stood behind and patted the young mans shoulders, then stood back and cast a professional eye over him. "What do you think, Mister Evans? Now, isn't that just the most perfect fit?"

The young man, his attention taken by his reflection in the mirror as he posed in the suit jacket, nodded his head, unaware of the tension that now existed between Frederick and Hamilton.

"Aye, this is the biz," the young man agreed, turning back and forth to inspect himself in the mirror. "What about the trousers? Will they fit too?"

"Mister Evans," smiled Hamilton, "perhaps you will accompany the customer to the changing room and sir," he turned and smiled at the young man, "any adjustment to the trousers will of course be without charge and Mister Evans here will ensure they are completed and ready for collection within two working days. And of course sir," he smiled again, this time solicitously patting the young man's arm, "will also likely require a white shirt and appropriate tie for the sad occasion. Mister Evans?" he continued his professional smile, "perhaps once you have made the appropriate fitting details you might accompany the customer to the shirt department and attend to his needs? Maybe even consider some shoes to complement the suit?"

"Yes Mister Hamilton," Frederick dully replied, now thoroughly miserable, his face and neck reddening as he burned with shame.

"And once our valued customer has his needs attended to," the instruction in his voice clear and unequivocal, "might we have a quiet word?"

Frederick could only nod and watched as Hamilton walked off, then forcing his lips to smile, led the young man towards the male changing rooms. The combination of embarrassment and anger caused tears to bite at the back of his eyes. His hands clenched the material of the trousers as he fought to stop his body from shaking with hatred and not for the first time in his life, Frederick Evans wished for someone's death.

The three officers sat round the table, their uniform belts, caps and stab-proof vests discarded on the floor while they concentrated on their card game and half nodded in acknowledgement when Lesley Gold entered the small canteen. She dumped her utility belt and its attachments on the floor by the sink in the small canteen and filled the worn and bashed electric kettle, then asked who was for coffee or tea?

"Nothing for me," replied Morris MacDonald, slapping a card down into the pile on the table and pointedly ignoring Lesley, still undecided whether or not to forgive her for setting him up as the fall guy for the angry besom of a woman from Danes Drive.

"You Lesley?" asked the stocky, short blonde haired female officer.

"That's me," she nodded in reply.

"Pleased to meet you, I'm Dotty Turner. Dorothy being my given Christian name and I'll have a coffee. I like it black and strong, like my men."

"Tea for me please," said the skinny, younger officer sat opposite her, "with milk and two large sugars."

"And this wee wanker is my probationer, Alex Mason," Dotty nodded towards the younger of the two men. "Ten months in and thinks he's a real polis."

"How you doing guys," replied Lesley, grimacing at the state of the stained mugs sitting on the draining board. Gingerly, she held up a mug with distaste and asked, "Are we not in danger of catching salmonella or something from this place?"

"Are you kidding? The cops in this place couldn't catch a cold," butted in wee Jinksie, sneaking into the room behind Lesley and placing his Celtic FC mug down beside her own. "And I'll have a cuppa."

"That wee sod can hear a kettle filling at one hundred yards," grumbled MacDonald, who grinned and slapped a hand down on top of the card, shouting loudly, "Snap."

As she waited on the kettle boiling, Lesley shook her head. If the child's game of Snap was the sole source of entertainment at break-time, she'd consider bringing a book in with her. Glancing round the room, she saw the peeling paint, a down-at-heel notice board with out of date memo's and take-away menus pinned to it, some mug shot photographs sellotaped to the walls in no particular order and more worrying, a topless plastic bin that threatened to overflow and invade the already stained and mottled floor. A microwave oven sat forlornly on the stained kitchen worktop with a hand written notice stuck to the door that indicated it was not to be used.

Dotty saw Lesley glancing at it and explained the sign. "A couple of months ago, one of the night shift tried to dry out his Doc Martens in that," she nodded towards the microwave, "but forget about the wee metal eyelets for the laces and nearly blew the thing off the worktop. Hasn't worked since," she sniffed.

"Is there not a cleaner for the office?" Lesley asked, wrinkling her nose against the smell of fried food that seemed to permeate from the very walls.

"Used to be," replied Dotty, slapping a card down on top of the pile in the middle of the table, "but she got the jail a week ago. She stabbed her husband with a pair of scissors when they returned home after a night on the bevy in a pub in Byres Road, accused him of making eyes at the barmaid. Pity that," Dotty sorrowfully shook her head, "she was a nice wee woman."

If Dotty thinks a woman who uses a pair of scissors to stab her husband is nice, Lesley wondered, what would she consider to be a bad woman? She turned as Sergeant Buchanan poked his head through the door.

"Lesley, that's the Inspector arrived. He says he would like to see you in his office when you're ready."

"Right Sarge," she replied as he walked off, then turning to the room she said, "You guys will need to sort yourselves out with your own drinks," and made to walk out of the door.

"Here Lesley," Dotty turned in her seat, her eyes betraying her curiosity. "Are you the lassie that gave that Sergeant in Maryhill a sore face?"

All four faces stared at her as she stopped and turned towards Dotty and then took a deep breath. "It's a long story, but let's just get it settled here by saying the bastard deserved it."

Dotty grinned at her and raised her right hand in a fist. "Go on yourself, girl."

As she stepped into the corridor, Lesley smiled knowing that she had made at least one friend in her new office.

Inspector Frank Cochrane called out, "Come in," and looked up as Lesley pushed open the door.

"Ah, Constable Gold, please come in, sit down," he smiled at her and indicated the chair in front of his desk. "Okay to call you Lesley?"

She nodded, suspicious at the unexpected bonhomie. Was this a prelude, she wondered, to another warning that she was to behave herself while she worked out of his office?

Cochrane, a clean shaven, sandy haired, slim man looked to be no more than thirty and seemed to her like a gawky teenager compared to some of the grizzled Inspectors Lesley had previously encountered in her service. She guessed he was a high-flyer, one of the university graduates the police lured to the job with the promise of a fast-track promotion and glowing career, a job with prospects and full of promise before reality set in.

Cochrane leaned forward and flipping open a slim, buff coloured cardboard file on his desk, stared down at the single sheet of paper it contained. Lesley stared at the top of his head, noticing that already he was displaying signs of premature baldness. He sat back in his chair and again smiled at her. "I'd already read the report from your last Inspector, Lesley. She says that you're a good, hard working cop but inclined to be a bit heavy handed with suspects."

"Only if they deserve it, sir," she replied in a monotone voice.

"I'm also aware why you were posted here. You assaulted a supervisor, a shift Sergeant. Punched him to the face, I understand." He tapped the file with a forefinger. "This doesn't explain why and when I spoke with the Chief Inspector at Maryhill, he suggested I ask you. Is it something you might care to explain or was it personal?"

She frowned and her eyebrows knitted at this strange tactic and again she was suspicious, disbelieving that Cochrane wouldn't have been told of the reason for her move to the sub-office.

Cochrane sighed and rubbed his hand over his face. "Maybe I'd better explain," he smiled again at her. "I'm kind of in the same boat as you Lesley. 'Till a couple of months ago, I worked at police headquarters in Pitt Street in the Policy Unit, but there was, eh," he paused and scratched at his nose, "a slight disagreement with the Chief Inspector regarding a decision he made. It's probably of no real interest to you and I'll not bore you with details, but I ended up telling my boss he was a fucking idiot, if you pardon my French."

For the first time since entering Cochrane's office, Lesley smiled. "You're kidding sir, yeah?"

"No, it's a problem I've always had. Could never suffer fools, particularly fools that believe because they've achieved some kind of rank it makes them smarter and that fool, no names, no pack drills," he put up his hands in surrender and smiled in return, "was one of the many officers I've met in my brief and to be brutally frank, uneventful eight years in the polis who was obviously promoted to a level of incompetence. So what's your story then, do you want to share why you're here with the rest of us duffers in this," he waved his hands above his head, "salubrious outhouse?"

Lesley felt herself warming to her new boss, wondering if he was real, surprising herself that his honest confession had begun to earn him a little of her respect. Admittedly, albeit he seemed younger and had obvious roughly the same service than Lesley, her feminine intuition decided that Cochrane wasn't a threat to her, that she maybe needn't worry about looking over her shoulder as she had feared. Anyway, she reasoned, even though the officers present that night had been ordered not to discuss the incident, she knew the story was out and she was the talk of the steamie. She took a deep breath and shrugged her shoulders deciding that he'd be better hearing it, as it were, from the horses' mouth rather than the gossip that was likely to follow her to her new station.

"The Sergeant I ..." she hesitated and began again. "The Sergeant I punched. Michael Duffy. He and I were supposed to be an item. We'd been seeing each other for just over four months. He had separated from his wife, or so he had said," and then her voice betrayed her bitterness, "and like an idiot, I'd believed him, that she was to blame for the break-up of their marriage," she almost spat out then shook her head. "That said, believing he had separated before we started going out, I was convinced I wasn't the reason for the split, okay?"

Cochrane didn't reply, simply nodded his head.

"We'd talked about moving in together. He was intending renting his place out and moving in with me, or so we had planned. Then when I was on nightshift last week, out with my partner in Maryhill Road and walking past the Indian restaurant at the corner of Shakespeare Street, I saw them, him I mean, with her, the blonde bimbo who works as an analyst for the CID. The two of them, nice and cosy together in the restaurant, hands across the table stuff, you know? I was gutted. It was bad enough being two-timed, but with that bunny-boiling cow?" She stopped to catch her breath, the memory of that night still hurting, her hands wrestling in her lap under the desk as she softly exhaled. "I didn't say anything, not then. I was embarrassed, humiliated, maybe a bit numbed. My partner knew I was seeing Michael. He's a good guy and didn't say anything, just steered me away and walked me to a wee all night café. Got me a coffee and the next thing I know I'm in a panda car. My shift Sergeant was a decent sort and thought the best thing was for me to get away home. Anyway, I couldn't sleep and didn't answer Michael's phone calls the following day. I knew he was on late shift the next night and I would see him at the shift changeover time, my lot going on while his shift was finishing. I had just arrived at the office and gotten changed into my gear when he walked into the muster room. Seems that he'd heard from somebody, I don't know who, that I had caught him with the analyst and tried to talk to me about it. Jesus," she shook her head at the memory of that night. "There must have been at least a dozen cops in the room and the bastard tries to explain in front of them?"

Cochrane sat in silence, acutely aware that if he interrupted her, Lesley would likely clam up and instinctively guessed she needed to talk.

"I was upset and didn't want to talk to him. I remember trying to push him away. Then, because I'm not prepared to listen to him, he grabs me and pulls me close, then whispers so that nobody could hear him that it's my fault he shagged her, that if I hadn't put weight on, if I hadn't gotten fat," her voice now full of vehemence. She shook her head and almost shuddered at the memory. "So I lost it sir, punched him. Right there and then, in front of a dozen cops."

"Must've been some punch," Cochrane drily remarked, "broke his nose I hear."

Lesley could only nod, feeling unaccountably better now than she had in the last week. "Aye, but I've no regrets other than I wish I'd got a couple of more punches in before I was hauled off him."

"One thing puzzles me. The Chief Inspector said that it wasn't in the public interest to charge you with assault, that after the debacle a month ago when it was all over the media about the three cops who got lifted for brawling in that pub in the city centre, another assault case would only undermine public confidence in the service. I understand where he's coming from on that point, but he also mentioned there was what he called mitigating circumstances. Care to enlighten me?"

Lesley slowly nodded. "He was probably referring to some domestic issues that I'm currently experiencing, some personal issues sir."

Cochrane stared at her then faintly smiled. "Okay, I'll not press you, but if there's anything you need to talk about or anyway I can help, let me know. Right that said, let me now be formal and tell you that I've three rules, Constable Gold. If you get drunk or do something stupid when on duty, I'll do my best to support you. If you get complained about for doing your job, I'll definitely do my best to support you. If you steal or commit a crime or in anyway try to kid or con me, I'll be the first in line to have a go at you, understood?"

Lesley nodded.

"So, Lesley as far as I'm concerned as of now you're working for me. That means you've a clean sheet and from what I've heard about your work, I'm pleased to have you here, so welcome to the shift."

Fiona Hardie dismissed her class for lunch and watched as Angela Paterson cheerfully led them in double file from the classroom into the corridor and then towards the dining hall. Turning her attention to the jotters, she absent-mindedly reached for the plastic lunchbox on her desk, but clumsily spilled the sandwiches it contained to the floor. "Drat," she said out loud and knelt to sweep the sandwiches back into the box, using a tissue to wipe the floor. She didn't hear the door open and startled at the appearance of a pair of legs in front of her.

"Not joining us in the staff room for lunch, then Missus Hardie?" asked the imperious voice of her Head Teacher, Gwyneth Jenkins.

"Oh, Miss Jenkins," she smiled up at the older woman, then using the desk, levered herself to her feet. "I'm a little behind in marking these jotters," she indicated the books on her desk, "and thought I'd get them done during lunch."

To anyone who cared to listen, Gwyneth Jenkins boasted that she modelled herself on the Head Teacher from her own primary school years in the late sixties. Intolerant of anyone not within her own profession, she had dedicated her life to her own advancement and, it was widely rumoured among her peers and staff, at the cost of personal happiness. Her overbearing attitude towards colleagues who had since progressed in the education profession had earned her a number of enemies and bitterly, she realised the small primary school over which she now so forcefully ruled was the final chapter in her less than illustrious career. Living alone and almost friendless, her life was the school and if she was unhappy, by God she would make someone suffer for it. Her gold rimmed glasses perched on the end of her oversized nose and the small broken veins in her cheeks betrayed her one weakness, the secret she did not realise that was open to many. Her mint breath could not fully mask her fondness for Scotland's primary export of which she habitually kept a half bottle in her lower left desk drawer, convincing herself it was for medicinal purpose only.

"Perhaps it's just as well we're alone, Missus Hardie," she almost snarled at the younger woman, "as I wish to have a quiet word with you. About your deplorable time-keeping, among other things," she added.

"Ah, yes, about this morning," began Fiona whose stomach was now churning, but got no further.

"I'm speaking, Missus Hardie. Kindly refrain from explanations till I'm finished," Jenkins hissed in reply.

Since Fiona's first day at the school some eighteen months previously, Gwyneth Jenkins had intimidated her. A skinny five foot nine inches tall, she towered about the diminutive Fiona and with her prematurely greying hair piled in a knot on her head, it added a further two inches to her imposing height. Now, standing before Fiona dressed in a deep purple coloured crew neck sweater and heavy pearl necklace, knee length tweed skirt and tan coloured brogues, her hands tightly clasped in front of her, she at last had the young teacher where she wanted and didn't intend losing the opportunity to have her say.

"Frankly, your time-keeping is deplorable and this morning was the seventh occasion this month you have been late for class. Because of your tardiness, an unqualified classroom assistant was thrust into the position of …."

"But Angela, Missus Paterson I mean, is a very capable …"

"Do not interrupt me!" Jenkins leaned forward as she screeched in reply, their noses almost colliding and little bobbles of spit striking Fiona in the face. "As I was saying, Missus Paterson had to stand in for you …" she stopped and stared at Fiona, her eyes running up and down the length of the younger woman's dress. "Look at you. Slovenly, too I see. My God, you can't even arrive clean and tidy. Besides everything else, I have lost count of the number of times I have had to attend your classroom because of your failure to exercise any control over your pupils. You are a disgrace to this profession."

Shocked, Fiona could only stare wide-eyed in return and slumped back against the desk, her hands feebly feeling for then holding the edge for support, her legs shaking and for an instant she worried they would not support her.

"Well, Missus Hardie, I've had enough of you. I'm officially informing you that I will be submitting a report to the council education department and recommending that your tenure at this school be terminated forthwith. Do I make myself clear?"

Fiona couldn't trust herself to speak and could only nod in response. With a final, scornful look, Jenkins turned and throwing the door open, stomped from the room.
Fiona stumbled round the desk and her body shaking, slowly sat down and rested her head on her forearms as she sobbed uncontrollably. In the corridor, Jenkins stopped and listened, smiling with satisfaction as the sound of the distraught young teachers crying reached her then satisfied she had achieved her goal, walked towards the staff room, unaware of the presence of the old janitor who stood holding a box of light bulbs and watching through the open door from the darkened cupboard.

Chapter 4

Frederick Evans hardly saw or heard any of his fellow staff members as the large store went through the daily process of closing, the departments routinely shutting down for the day and the till drawers being carried by the sales assistants to the security office. The hubbub of chatter echoed through the emptying store as the assistants lined up at the security office window to check in their cash drawers, each drawer being sealed in preparation for the following days checking and accounting by the finance department. Standing there in the queue among his colleagues, the drawer held tightly in his hands, Frederick's mind was spinning and still smarting with the memory of his confrontational meeting within Robert Hamilton's office. To stand there and be lectured by that…. but even in his mind, the words failed him.
"Outrageous behaviour Mister Evans and particularly from someone who has worked at Dawson's for all these years. Outrageous! To treat a customer in such a shoddy fashion, it beggars belief."
Hamilton had made him stand before his desk like some errant schoolboy while he ranted at him. Him, who had so faithfully served the store for all those years, but the cruellest cut for Frederick was that Hamilton served notice that he was placing Frederick on a formal warning that one more incident and he could expect to be dismissed.
"Are you going to stand there all day, Freddy boy?" the deep voice broke into his thoughts. Blinking rapidly, he realised he was now at the front of the queue. The security officer Peter Wylie stared curiously at him as he reached for the cash drawer Frederick held, while the young female assistants behind him giggled at his tardiness.
"Wee bit of dementia there Freddy boy?" grinned Wylie as he sealed Frederick's drawer and handed him the receipt chit.
Frederick glowered at Wylie, desperate to retort but a response failed him, then angrily and almost with childish petulance, hissed, "Don't call me Freddy!" Snatching the receipt from the amused Wylie's outstretched hand

and face burning, he stormed off, ignoring the giggling teenagers behind him. Some day, he vowed, he'd get them. Get them all. Make them pay for their insults. Bastards! He walked to the male locker room in the basement, avoiding the staff who hurried past him and oblivious to the curious stares of some that thought that Weedy Evans from the Men's Department seemed a little distracted.
Not one of those who saw Frederick could have guessed at the hatred in his heart.

The early shift now concluded, Dotty Turner was in the female changing room shoving her stab proof vest and utility belt into her locker and chatting to some late shift officers when Lesley Gold entered. "Me and some of the boys, Alex, Jinksie, Morris and Pete Buchanan are going to the bowling club just off Anniesland Road for a wee aperitif, if you want to join us, Lesley," she asked.
"Thanks Dotty, but I'm behind with the washing and ironing," Lesley replied, feeling a little guilty at the lie. "The early shift gives me the opportunity to catch up. You know what it's like."
"To right I do," grinned Dotty. "I've two kids and I'm on my own, so it's a lot easier to deal with when I've had a wee snifter."
"What ages are the kids?" replied Lesley, shrugging out of her vest and unsnapping her equipment belt.
"Angie, my girl's ten. She's at primary and a right wee madam, so she is. My lad Iain is fourteen, going through the change at the minute."
"Sorry, the change, what's that?"
"Aye, the change, well, that's what I call it. My Iain doesn't know if he's a wee boy or a young man. Thinks I don't know about the porn magazine he's got hidden under his mattress," she softly laughed.
"How do you deal with that one then?" smiled Lesley.
"I don't. I just ignore it. He's no different to any other youngster, going through the angst of his teenage years. He's a great wee man so he is. We get on really well and he's a good help in the house, particularly when I'm on late shift or nightshift. I mean, I don't leave them alone or anything like that. No way," she crossed her hands over each other. "My folks are great too. They'll sleep over if needed, so I'm luckier than most, I suppose. I've got great support," she grinned into the cracked wall mirror, pursing her lips as she deftly applied lipstick and smacking them together.
Lesley smiled at Dotty's back and it occurred to her that the cheery woman seemed to be one of life's fortunate's, those individuals that no matter what life threw at them, they always had a half full pint of milk.
"Maybe another time, for that drink I mean," said Lesley, waving cheerio as she pushed through the door into the corridor.

Alex Mason, a bright green coloured blouson jacket over his police issue polo shirt, stood leaning against the wall. "Dotty still in there," he sighed with the impatience of the male gender.
"Putting on her war paint, so you had better watch yourself Alex," grinned Lesley.
The civilian bar officer Jinksie appeared from his office as Lesley made towards the back door.
"Not going for a drink then doll?" he smiled at her.
"Not today, wee man. Maybe another time when I know we'll not get barred for you being underage."
"Aw, hey, that's below the belt," he pretended to complain.
"See you," waved Lesley as she pushed through the door and walked to her car parked in the rear yard.

Lesley drove her Toyota Yaris south towards the Clyde Tunnel and joined the city bound expressway that in turn led her to the eastbound M8 motorway. Twenty minutes later, she exited at junction 9 and then made her way to her house in Bredisholm Terrace in Baillieston. She stopped the car outside the small, semi-detached bungalow and resting her hands on the steering wheel, prepared herself for the visit. Her mother Peggy had seen her daughter's car draw up and had the front door opened, her right forefinger against her lips as a smiling Lesley made her way up the narrow path, noting the grass again needed trimmed and mentally comparing it to the neat and tidy garden it had once been. She made a note to herself that on her next day off, she would come down and attend to it.
"Hello love," her mother quietly greeted her, extending her arms and hugging her daughter to her. "Just finished then?"
"Second day at my new office," Lesley whispered with a nod and gently closed the door behind her before following her mother through to the small kitchen where sighing, she drew out one of the two chairs under the small pine table and sat down. She didn't fail to notice the bags under her mother's eyes and how tired she looked. "Is he sleeping?"
Her mother nodded in reply as she filled the kettle from the tap. "Another bad night I'm afraid. It was the nurse's day off and heaven knows, the poor woman doesn't get that many. She left a contact number if things got too bad, but fortunately the stronger medication seems to have helped, so I've been able to cope."
Lesley thought her mother seemed more than usually down and expressed her concern at Peggy's loss of weight. "What about Linda," she added, "has she visited?"

Peggy Gold, standing with her back to the sink and her arms folded across her bosom, shook her head. "You know how it is with a wee one," she said, "and then of course she's working now."

Lesley raised her hands and turned her head to one side. She had heard all this before and wanted to scream out, yes she's working part-time while I'm doing shift work and am here every other day, if not more. It infuriated her, her sister's lackadaisical attitude towards their father's terminal cancer and yet her mother and father still excused their younger daughter's selfishness. She was about to retort, but decided against it, knowing that it would upset her mother even more and difficult though it was, kept her mouth shut. Her mother sensed how upset her daughter was and decided to change the subject. "So, this thing between you and Michael, it's really over then?"

"Dead as a Dodo," Lesley replied, grateful that she wasn't again getting into it with her mother and determined more than ever to have it out with Linda, whom she ought to be shouting at. Peggy turned to pour the boiled water into the silver polished teapot that she set on the cooker to brew and she watched as Peggy milked two mugs.

"He two-timed me, Mum. All the while telling me that he loved me, that he wanted us to be together, get married even and the bastard was seeing a lassie from the office behind my back." She felt the tears bite at the back of her eyes and knew that her mother was the one person she could really confide in, that nothing she said would go further than the kitchen walls. She couldn't help herself and twisting her fingers helplessly in her lap, lowered her head as she began to gently weep, conscious her mothers arms were wrapped protectively round her shoulders, a sheet of kitchen roll pressed into her hands. Her tears fell, but Lesley didn't know if she cried in self-pity or shame that she had been so easily fooled.

Her mother handed her a tissue and she wiped at her eyes and her nose.

"For what it's worth, Lesley, I never liked him anyway," said Peggy. "He just seemed too smarmy to me."

Lesley laughed through her tears. "Is smarmy really a word?" she asked then suddenly both were giggling.

"Thanks darling," her mother smiled at her, "I needed a laugh. Just a pity that the subject was your break-up with Michael, but to be honest, I didn't feel he was right for you."

Bringing both mugs to the table, Peggy pulled out the other chair and sat down, then said, "So tell me about this new office? Do you know any of your new colleagues?"

"No, not one and as for the office, it's the same old, same old, only a different location. I'll get used to it. One of the cops there, a lassie called Dotty seems to be okay and I've just got to know the other guys on the shift by name, so time will tell I suppose."

"Peggy, Peggy?" a voice called out and was followed by a rasping cough. Both women leapt to their feet and Lesley followed her mother into the hallway. At her mothers backwards hand signal, she stopped just outside the door of the largest of the three bedrooms, now used as a full time nursing room for Thomas.

"Okay, Tommy, I'm here darling," she heard her mother say then add, "You've got a visitor."

"Is that you Linda?" her father asked, the pleasure evident in his voice.

"Eh, no dad, it's me, Lesley," she heard herself say, acutely disappointed that her father should first ask for his younger daughter, the one who rarely visited.

"Oh, aye, come away in then hen," she heard him gasp his reply and forcing herself to smile, entered the darkened room, the only light coming from a small beside lamp. The air was lemony fresh, a pleasant aroma arising from the yellow coloured scented candle that burned within a glass jar on a low table in the far corner. Her father lay in the centre of the double bed, his prematurely white hair framing a pale face, his cheeks sunken and eyes almost translucent. The covers reached to just below his chin, though his arms lay on the outside of the quilt cover and even though it had been just two days since she last saw him, Lesley noticed her father seemed even more shrunken, his arms thin and wasted. An oxygen bottle stood to one side with the mask and tubes draped across and within handy reach if required."

"So you're not taking me to the dancing tonight then?" she grinned at him, the old joke between them.

"Maybe tomorrow," he wheezed and tried to smile. "Going to work or just finished?" he half nodded at her uniform polo shirt and cargo pant trousers.

"Just finished early shift," she smiled at him.

"Suppose you'll be seeing that big lump of yours later on then. Tell Michael I was asking for him," he gasped, his voice turning to a whisper as he added, "I like that big guy. He'll be good for you. About time you got yourself settled down and gave me some grandkids, like your sister."

Her mother stared at Lesley, the warning obvious in her eyes. *'Don't tell him, he can't cope with that kind of news.'*

Lesley again forced herself to smile at her father and settling herself gently on the edge of the bed, took hold of his right hand in hers, aghast that even though the room was warm, how cold he was to her touch.

"Think maybe I'll have a wee nap sweetheart," he stared up at his wife and without looking, squeezed Lesley's fingers, then turned his head towards her, the pain of even that slight movement etched on his face. "My wee first born girl, never think I don't love you," then closed his eyes and was instantly asleep.

She sat there for a few minutes, staring at the wasted frame of her father, the man who chased his daughters round the park, who could so easily throw his girls high into the air and catch them giggling and squealing as they fell to earth. The man whom she knew loved her, but would never know how much he hurt her by constantly favouring her selfish, younger sister. The father she was about to lose without having the opportunity to have him walk her down the aisle. She felt her mother's light touch on her shoulder and nodded, quietly rising from the bed and tip-toeing out into the hallway where the smaller, slighter Peggy took her daughter's face in both her hands as she stared up into Lesley's eyes.

"It won't be long now Lesley," her mother's said in a choked voice. "You need to prepare yourself for that."

"Do you want me to stay over?"

Peggy shook her head. "No, there will be time enough when I might need you here, but right now there's nothing you can do. When the time comes," she paused and took a deep breath, "I'll want you to be available because there will be things needing done. In the meantime, get yourself home and I know it's useless me telling you this, but try not to worry about me. Your Dad's beyond worry now and I know you'll be concerned for your old Mum." She continued to hold Lesley's face in her hands as she said, "You're a good girl Lesley, always been a terrific daughter to us both. I know your Dad didn't always get it right, that sometimes he said things without thinking and that you might feel in some way he's let you down …."

Lesley tried to speak, to protest, but her mother gripped her face slightly tighter.

"No, Lesley, there's times I've wanted to butt in, tell Tommy he's wrong or mistaken, but I suppose I always hoped he would see the goodness in you, the marvellous daughter you truly are. As it was, he sort of took you for granted and for that I'm sorry. But one thing you must know, your Dad does truly love you and so do I."

She gently pulled Lesley's face down to her level and kissed her on the cheek, now moist with tears.

"Now, away home with you and get yourself a good night's sleep. I promise, if anything happens, you're my rock, so you get the first phone call."

Paul Hardie was not having a good day. His problems began when half way through the morning, the HR Director Colin Davis called him into his office and broke the bad news.

"Look Paul, I know it was suggested that you might be promoted at the next financial year, but I have to inform you that it won't happen. As you know, we lost a lot of customers last year due to the recession, companies going burst and others simply not being able to afford our fees, that sort of thing.

I'm truly sorry," Davis gestured with his hands, "and while I don't like the use of the word redundancy, the best I can offer is that if you are prepared to remain with the company, though unfortunately in a more junior role, we might be able to review and develop your position in the following year."
Paul was aghast. He had not just expected, but relied on being promoted, not just for the prestige and responsibility it offered, but for the substantial raise in his salary it would have brought him. His mind raced and visions of independence from Fiona, the new car and the flat in the West End disappeared. With a start, he also suspected that Janice Meikle would not be prepared to put up with the affair as it stood and likely dump him as fast as shit off a hot shovel. Certainly for the foreseeable future, he would be stuck in a loveless marriage with his wife. His mouth hung open and he literally dropped into the chair facing Davis' desk.
"As I said Paul, you might wish to review your position with us at Berkeley and Finch, perhaps consider an alternative company?"
"Are you suggesting I resign?" he almost choked.
Davis nervously shuffled a sheaf of papers on his desk. He disliked confrontation and hated this type of interview and it didn't help that he was at least three stone overweight for a man of fifty-five and in his vanity, wore a shirt a size too small and now the bloody collar was choking him, He was suddenly conscious that a rivulet of sweat now threaded its way down his spine. He took a deep breath to calm himself and slowly replied, "What I'm saying, I mean, what the official line is and what I have been instructed to tell you is that the company is down-sizing and the position of Accounts Manager will not be tenable within the next six months. I'm sorry Paul, but you have one of two choices. Remain with us at a reduced position within Accounts or seek employment elsewhere. Of course, should you decide to leave, we will work out suitable remuneration for the time served here…."
"You can't do this to me!" Paul slammed his fists down on the desk, causing Davis to flinch as for the first time in his life, Paul considered the awful possibility of being unemployed. "I've been working here for over seven years. I was promised promotion. I have plans, I worked very hard for the company and to be treated like this … this…" he repeated then slumped back in his seat, all life seemingly draining from him.
It occurred on hindsight to Davis that perhaps he should have had a colleague with him, that though Paul Hardie had never previously displayed any aggression, the guy looked unstable, like he was about to snap.
"Look Paul," he softly said and conscious that the thin trail of worried perspiration sneaking down his back was now a torrent, "perhaps you might wish to take some time to consider your choices. Go home, discuss it with your wife …."
"Her?" Paul snapped back "That idiot couldn't decide what day it is let alone

anything else," he sneered and then taking a deep breath, decided his failing relationship with Fiona had nothing to do with Davis. He swallowed hard and stood up from the chair, not conscious that Davis' immediately tensed and his eyes widened, suddenly aware of his vulnerability should he have to struggle with the much younger and unusually volatile Paul Hardie. To his immense relief, he saw Hardie's shoulders slump.

"Yes, sorry. You're right of course," muttered Paul. "I'll go now, if that's all right with you."

Much relieved that the distraught Accounts Manager apparently wasn't going to assault him after all Davis walked from his side of the desk and clapped Paul on the arm. "I'm sure that whatever decision you arrive at Paul, it will be the correct one. I'm so sorry that this has happened," he sighed as he gently propelled Paul to the door, "but we are all tightening our belts at this difficult time."

Still stunned at the news, Paul could only nod as he shuffled from Davis' office. Closing the door behind the younger man, Davis breathed a sigh of relief and flicking the intercom button, instructed his secretary to call his wife at home to break more bad news, that because of the financial restraints being imposed, there would be no new car this week after all. Instead, they would be stuck with the company Jaguar for another six months or, his eyes closed as he imagined her outrage, possibly even a year.

Paul was in a daze. Pale-faced, he quickly walked through the main office without acknowledging the occasional greeting from his co-workers, ignoring their curious stares and whispered comments as he passed. The route to his department took him through the typing pool and he stole a glance at where Janice sat typing at her desk with her headphones on, pointedly ignoring him as he passed. He couldn't decide if she was deliberately avoiding his gaze because she feared their relationship would become public knowledge or had heard of his demotion and possible redundancy. Either way, it didn't really matter any more, he miserably decided as he passed through the room, he was bound to lose her anyway. He opened the door to the small office he currently occupied and looked about him, then glanced through the window set in the wall to the dozen or so accountants he supervised, realising that if he chose to stay, he was about to join them in the large open office. They'd love that, he viciously thought and with a shudder recalled some of the occasions when he had wielded the big stick, refusing some or other request and sometimes just because he could. Opening the desk drawer, he withdrew the keys to the company Ford Focus, realising that the perks of having the car and the allocated parking bay in the basement of the building would also need to be surrendered, demoting him to travelling on the bus or using Fiona's rickety old Escort and then the hassle of parking the damned thing.

As he grabbed his coat, he still could not believe that his day had gone so badly.
He might have stayed where he was had he known it was just going to get worse.

Frederick Evans turned up the collar of his anorak and made his way through the evening crowds to Union Street to catch the bus home. Standing at the bus stop, he seethed at what he believed to be the unjust treatment meted out to him by his manager, Robert Hamilton and imagined a dozen ways to get even, all of which ended with Hamilton on his knees before Frederick, a broken man begging for his life.
The trip home on the crowded bus was uneventful and after alighting at his stop on Anniesland Road, a still angry Frederick hurried through the quiet streets, cheered only by the thought and expectations that the night's outing offered him. Arriving at Dykesbar Lane, he pushed open the gate of the semi-detached house and walking the path between the neat and tidy lawn, took a deep breath and inserted the key into the lock.
"Is that you dear?" called out his mother, poking her grey-haired head from the small kitchen to peer along the dimly lit narrow hallway and smiling at him.
"Yes mother, it's me," he sighed, wondering to himself who else would it be for after all, the only visitors we get was his mother's church social cronies arriving to play Bridge and that's only once ever other Friday. Unless, he inwardly smirked, you count the young Avon woman each month. His mother disappeared into the kitchen and hanging his anorak on the wall hook behind the door, Frederick pushed open the door into the small front sitting room and switched on the television. Settling himself in the large, floral patterned easy chair, his mother appeared beside him, a cup balanced on a saucer in her hand.
"A nice wee cuppa for my lovely boy," she gushed at him. "So, how did it go today, Frederick?" she eagerly asked as she stood by his side, "did you do what you planned and tell that nasty man Mister Hamilton what you thought of him?"
"Yes, well I had a word mother. Took him down a peg or two," he glibly lied as he sipped at the tea. "Told him in no uncertain terms that if he didn't change his attitude, I was out of there and going elsewhere, that Dawson's would lose my expertise."
His mother froze and a sense of panic rushed through her. "But you didn't give up your job, dear? I mean, you haven't resigned or anything silly like that?"
"Of course not," he scoffed. "But the ball's in their court now," he pompously inclined his head. "They'll have to smarten up and get their act

together if they want to keep me. Lose me and their Men's Department sales will dry up."

"That's my Frederick," his mother proudly and gently patted the top of his head, a gesture he hated but suffered for her sake.

"Dinner ready then?" he asked her.

"Oh, right, yes. On the table in two tics," she winked at him in reply and left to attend to the meal cooking in the kitchen, softly closing the door behind her.

Frederick's eyes narrowed and he unconsciously shook his head. The old biddy was getting worse, but he wasn't beyond lying to keep her happy, well aware that apart from keeping his own back room tidy, he didn't do a hands turn in the house. In that respect, his mother was the perfect house companion, but nearing eighty years of age, he wasn't certain how long she would remain so. In the recent past he had noticed little things that worried him, her forgetfulness, the lack of dusting in the front room, his shirts not as crisply ironed as they once previously were. The BBC Scotland news report turned to sports and he immediately lost interest, his mind playing again the scenario he so lately enjoyed, wondering how his life would differ if his mother died. The house, purchased from the council by his late father, would be his and Jennifer Farndale, the canteen server at Dawson's, entered his thoughts, wondering what she would look like without the thick glasses, becoming aroused as he imagined her in his bedroom, in her underwear, performing at his bidding as she willed him to do so. He conjured in his mind that Jennifer's thin frame hid a voluptuous figure and he longed to explore her body, convincing himself that she would be grateful for his attention to her. Frederick thought of her as timid and shy and knew he would like that in a woman; servility. He saw the front window curtains were closed over and closing his eyes, reached for his genitals, fondling himself through his trousers as he imagined himself and Jennifer in his bedroom, the things he would have her do for him, then startled at his mother's voice, calling him through to the small room at the rear of the house where they took their meals. Grinning self-consciously at his erection, Frederick switched off the TV and breathing deeply, decided that he would continue the fantasy later when alone in his room.

Chapter 5

Fiona Hardie couldn't remember getting through that afternoon or the concern that her classroom assistant Angela Paterson had shown her and who had hushed the pupils when they became rowdy, forcefully instructing them to be quiet, that Missus Hardie was feeling unwell and entertaining them as best she could until the 3pm bell had rung. She couldn't remember the cup of tea placed before her or being assisted by Angela and the kindly janitor, Jimmy Dunlop, who flatly refused to permit her to drive in her shocked state and then being helped into the passenger seat of Jimmy's old Volvo estate car. She couldn't remember arriving at the door of her small, two bedroom mid terraced house, of being helped along the garden path by the bemused Jimmy who saw her seated in the lounge and then left, quietly closing the door behind him. She couldn't recall how long she sat there, still wearing her coat and waiting for Paul to return home. Paul, whom she hoped to surprise with the good news, but now had to tell him that she was about to lose her job.

Janice Meikle was in the ladies toilet checking her make-up prior to leaving the office when the two women from the Accounts Department entered. Janice didn't like the stuck-up cows from Accounts who thought of themselves as somehow superior to the typing pool.
"… and the word is he's getting a desk among us plebs," she heard the dark haired one excitedly say as entering a cubicle, she raised her skirt and turned to sit down as she pushed the door closed.
"When does it take effect then?" the fair haired, older woman called out.
"Not sure," the voice from the cubicle replied, "but I heard sometime in the next couple of weeks and if you want my opinion, the sod deserves it."
The fair haired woman faced the mirror and ignoring Janice, began brushing her hair. "You're right about that, hen. It's about time that two-faced shit Hardie got what was coming to him," the woman said. "The sanctimonious bugger refused me time off the other week for a school appointment. Had to send my mother in my place," she added.
Janice froze, realising they could only be discussing Paul. Smiling, she turned to the woman and asked, "Trouble in the Department?"
The woman didn't turn, but leaned towards the mirror, concentrating now on plucking at an imaginary eyelash as she replied, "The supervisor, Paul Hardie. You've probably seen him around. Smooth looking guy that thinks the sun shines out of his arse. He's one of the middle management getting the chop because of the cuts."
A toilet flushed and the dark haired woman opened the cubicle door, pulling at her skirt as she exited and stepped towards a wash basin. "Couldn't happen to a nicer guy," she laughed without humour. "Hardie has stuck it to a few people in Accounts over the years and believe me," she smirked, "there are a few with long memories. That's if he decides to stay with the company of course. He'll not have an easy time of it down among us rank and file," she added as she run the tap. She glanced at Janice. "You're in typing, aren't you?"
Janice nodded and forced herself to smile.

"You'll likely be getting the memo to type up, those that are getting the push I mean. Might be worth knowing you for a heads-up, eh?" the woman suddenly smiled.

"Yeah," Janice coldly returned the smile, "We girls in typing can sometimes be useful," while thinking not in a million fucking years.

Walking back to her department, she realised that her plans had without warning taken a sudden nosedive. As she reached the door, it occurred to her that the decision regarding Paul Hardie had been taken out of her hands. No matter what happened to him now, he no longer featured in her future plans. He was dumped.

Lesley Gold parked her car in a vacant bay in the roadway outside the front close of her Victorian tenement building in Crathie Drive and walking to the entrance door, glanced up at the bay window of her first floor flat. The flat had been her home for almost four years now, her first major purchase and though it had needed a lot of work that in part was still ongoing, a real steal. She pushed open the heavy wooden door and made her way upstairs, her mind preoccupied and recalling her mother's admission, *'It won't be long now Lesley, you need to prepare yourself for that.'*

She picked up the few items of mail from behind her front door and made her way into the narrow, cabin like kitchen, dropping the mail onto the worktop as she filled then switched on the kettle. Still she worried about her mother. She loved her father, of course she did, she thought as she slowly nodded, but the reality was her father was soon to die and her mother would need Lesley all the more. Her thoughts turned to her sister and she savagely tugged open the fridge door then self-consciously grinned. No need to take it out on her own kitchen she realised. Milking a mug, she popped in a scoop of coffee and filling it from the boiled kettle, took it through to the comfortable lounge, wriggling herself into her favourite hand-me-down easy chair and slipping off her boots, propped her feet upon the small flower patterned padded stool, a gift from her Mum. Sighing with pleasure she sipped at the coffee and considered her mother's surprising opinion of Michael, that he was not right for Lesley, that he was too smarmy, her Mum had said. She softly smiled and to her own surprise, found herself agreeing.

Paul Hardie didn't drive straight home as he first planned, but to the Cambridge Street car park where he knew Janice made use of the company's agreement with the city council to obtain discounted parking for the staff. Driving slowly through the entrance, he wound his way round the narrow lanes till he found her parked Mini. A bay nearby lay empty and he reversed the Focus in and switching off the engine, reached for the 'Glasgow News' and settled down to wait.

Jimmy Dunlop winced and his face contorted, then he drew a deep breath as the stabbing pain in his back caused him to tightly clench his teeth. For the umpteenth time he was grateful for the long handled grabbers the Council issued that saved him having to bend over to collect the sweet wrappers and abandoned lunch bags scattered about the playground. Grabbing at the empty crisp poke, he placed it in the waste bag he carried and moved on. In fairness to the children he thought, as he collected another empty bag, on the whole they were well behaved and the teaching staff, if not their parents, drummed into them the importance of keeping their school clean and free of litter. Nowadays it didn't take him long to tidy the playground and usually by five o'clock he was at home in the janitors house by the front gate, his feet up and in front of the television and a mug of char in his hand. He glanced at the school gate where the few remaining children and parents were departing and then at the line of cars parked in a neat row outside the building's main doors. He slowly shook his head, knowing the Head Teacher Miss Jenkins would keep the staff there till four thirty on the dot. In his forty odd years as a school janitor, Jimmy could not recall having worked for such a nasty boss as her. Having completed almost twenty years here at Durban Road primary, Jimmy considered the last years with Jenkins in charge of the school as the worst of his career and he had already discussed with his wife the viability of taking the Council early retirement package before he ended up jailed for strangling the nasty woman. As much as Jimmy despised men who practised domestic abuse, he had to admit that if someone kindly murdered and buried Gwyneth Jenkins in the Argyll hills, he wouldn't complain. He inwardly smiled at his own description of her, a nasty woman. Brought up in a strict Glasgow Catholic family, Jimmy had adhered to the Faith long after his siblings had slipped off the narrow path and believed himself to have lived a good life. Through his teenage years, even during his short stint with the RAF, Jimmy prided himself that he had never said a bad word about any other human being and had always tried to find the best in his fellow man and woman. But Gwyneth Jenkins, again he shook his head, would try the patience of a saint let alone a humble man like James Dunlop.

As he moved about the concreted playground, he thought again of the wee lassie Missus Hardie and his mouth tightened as he recalled the verbal abuse she had suffered from Jenkins. Nobody should be made to feel like that in a working environment, nor any environment he inwardly corrected himself. He thought of Jenkins, the secret tippler, who adopted the moral high ground, but was immoral herself. He glanced again at the main building and played in his mind some way he could even the balance, bring the haughty Gwyneth Jenkins to book for her arrogance.

Frederick Evans opened his bedroom door a fraction and listened, satisfied his mother was downstairs in the front room and guessed she was again puzzling over the crossword in her weekly magazine while Radio Four played in the background. Quietly, he closed the door over and turned the key in the old fashioned lock. Switching on his laptop computer on top of the small desk, he fetched his mobile phone from his jacket pocket and plugged it into the laptop terminal. He scrolled down to the camera images and selecting that day's images, downloaded the video footage from the canteen into his secure file. That done and as a precaution, he deleted the video footage from the phone in expectation of his next filming session in the canteen. A few seconds later he opened the file and sneered in delight, watching the two young women as through the hubbub of sound recorded by the camera phone, they leaned across the table gossiping as they shovelled their food into their lipstick painted mouths. His eyes took in the women's bodies and sitting as they were, their tight, pencil skirts had rustled up their thighs, exposing to him their long legs. His breathing became slightly quicker and taking a deep breath in anticipation, he stood and opened the cupboard door and shuffling against the quilted jacket of the water heater, reached behind to grab at the cardboard box then carefully set the box on top of the single bed. Removing the box lid, he used both hands and almost with reverence removed the contents, while glancing back and forth at the laptop screen, then carefully set out the eighteen pair of woman's knickers on the bed. Once they had been spread on the quilt cover, Frederick stood back to admire them, hardly daring to breathe as he gently stroked each pair in turn. The cheap and functional plain white cotton knickers with the slightly torn hem that had been caused when he pulled them from the washing line, the black coloured pairs, one with the pink frills, the floral patterned knickers and his current favourite, the red coloured lace knickers embroidered on the front with a small pale heart. The size of the knickers didn't matter to him, what mattered was that all the knickers had been worn, reasoned by Frederick because they had been washed and hung out to dry. New knickers that could be purchased had no meaning for him because they were simply a shaped fabric. But these, he gloated over his collection, these had been worn, touching each woman's private and exclusive body part, their genitalia. Lifting the red coloured lace knickers, he rubbed them across his face and closed his eyes then shivered with pleasure at the thought of where they had been, touching himself with his free hand. He realised he was becoming aroused and breathing heavily, hurriedly swept the shoe box off the quilt cover to the floor and continued to run the lace knickers across his face as he lay, squirming down on top of the remaining knickers, he reached to unzip his trousers.

Janice Meikle inserted the ticket and her credit card into the machine then punched in the special code that permitted her the discounted parking fee. Head down and heels clicking on the concrete ground, she concentrated on returning her credit card to her purse and didn't immediately see, but heard the car door open, then Paul's voice call out, "Janice."

She felt her stomach lurch and forced herself to smile, remembering that after all, she wasn't supposed to know about his problems at work. Glancing quickly about her to ensure they were alone, she forced her voice to be calm and asked, "Paul, what are you doing here?"

He was quickly beside her and taking her by the elbow, steered her towards the Mini. "We need to talk," he said and like her, his eyes scanning the area around them.

Taking a deep breath Janice turned to him, determined not to let him into the car for fear that she would have trouble getting him back out of it again.

"Then talk, Paul. What's so important that you risk us being seen together?"

"I'm not getting the promotion," he said at a rush, his hands holding her by both elbows, "the bastards are talking about either making me redundant or demoting me to the Accounts office."

Janice's mouth was suddenly very dry. She stared at him, suddenly realising he was on edge, his forehead creased with worry and a thin film of sweat had formed on his upper lip. Maybe, she thought, right now might not be such a good time to dump him, fearful that he would overreact.

"Look," she tactfully said, backing towards the driver's door and withdrawing from his grasp, "This isn't the time or the place to discuss this," she continued to cast her eyes about her. "Go home, think about it and we'll meet, maybe tomorrow, eh?"

"Think about it?" his voice suddenly raised, "Were you not listening to me? They're fucking getting rid of me. What's to think about, Janice? All my plans, our plans …." He reached for her, but she backed off between the Mini and an adjacent car, her eyes wary and fearful at the change in his demeanour, worried at the expression in his eyes. He stopped surprised and stared at her with sudden realisation. "You knew, didn't you? You already knew," he loudly accused her. "Jesus Christ! You knew and you didn't let on!" his teeth now bared, his fingers flexing as he shook his head, the overwhelming urge to hit out at something.

"You all right there, hen?" the weary sounding voice startled them both.

An elderly couple, he laden with a shopping bag in each hand, she with one hand on the man's arm and the other at her mouth and stood with her eyes wide. The elderly couple both stared apprehensively at Paul and Janice from ten metres distance.

Paul, his face red with fury, was too wound up to respond and turning, stomped off to his car parked nearby, hearing Janice call out, "Yes, we're fine. Thank you, it's okay, really."
He didn't turn and walking to the Focus, heard her car door slam, then the squeal of tyres as she drove off. Getting into the Focus, he slammed his shaking hands against the steering wheel as tears of impotent rage bit at his eyes. The elderly couple passed the front of the Focus as they walked towards an old Fiat, the woman pale faced and staring straight ahead while the man glanced towards Paul, who avoided his curious gaze. He sat 'till the throbbing in his head eased and his breathing returned to some normality. Turning the key in the ignition, he decided that on the way home, a bottle of whisky might help settle his nerves.

Lesley pulled on the pale blue coloured tracksuit top and trousers, her hair pulled back into a tight ponytail and face devoid of make-up and stared critically at her reflection in the wardrobe doors' vertical mirror. Twisting back and forth, she narrowed her eyes as she examined her figure, sighing at the slight bulge at her waist where less than a year ago there had been none. She had long ago accepted she would never have her sister's model figure, more a nubile shape as her mother liked to point out, though Lesley knew her Mum was trying to make her feel better about herself. She sighed again and sat on the edge of the bed to pull on the light blue coloured training shoes. She didn't quite know what possessed her, this sudden urge to use the membership for the leisure club in Finnieston, a present from Mike. She hesitated from saying or even thinking his name, guessing that his grand idea three months previously of them frequenting the gym to get fit was likely a ruse to keep her weight down, rather than being honest and just telling her. Angrily, she tugged at the shoelace, wincing slightly as the nylon cord bit into her hand then more slowly tying the knot. They had used the gym on just three occasions, she recalled and the last time, he had spent more than half an hour discussing his diet with a pretty young nutritionist. She couldn't believe now how jealous she had been; an emotion she had never really believed herself capable of and yet that incident dissuaded her from returning. The more thought she gave that day, the more she realised that she had inadvertently sewn the seed of doubt, that her mistrust of Mike wasn't after all, misplaced. But his comment in the muster room about her weight had hurt her more than she was prepared to admit even to herself and it was that more than anything else that persuaded her she had better get something done about it. Lesley was no stranger to physical activity and prided herself that in her younger days she had run, played tennis and lived a healthy life. Standing now, she shook herself, annoyed that she had let her fitness fall off. Making her way into the kitchen, she threw back the cooling coffee and grabbing the

car keys, small sports bag and membership card, made her way to the front door. She could fool others, but knew in herself that the shift work aside, her irregular eating habits and lack of self-motivation were more to blame for her lack of fitness than anything Michael Duffy had done. Walking down the stairs, she tossed her head in defiance and inwardly made a promise.
New shape, new lifestyle and, grinning now as she pulled open the heavy wooden close door and strode into the darkening evening, feeling better than she had done for several days.

Janice Meikle slammed the front door behind her and leaning back against it, suddenly jerked forward to throw her handbag viciously against the closed lounge door. That Paul had surprised her in the car park was bad enough, but for a moment there, she had felt so vulnerable, afraid he was about to strike her. She hardly recalled the drive home, her teeth clenched so tight with shock till they had hurt. Paul wasn't the first man who had taken his anger out on Janice, her eyes tightly closed, remembering the relationship just a few years previously when her dalliance with a colleague had earned her a black eye from her then partner. She slipped off her shoes and leaving them at the door, made her way towards the bathroom, bending to pick up the fallen handbag from the floor, deciding that a bath was preferable to a shower in the en-suite. Running the hot tap, she let her fingers stroke the gushing water till it run hot then pushed home the bathplug, all the while her mind racing at the sudden break-up with Paul. Not so much a break-up, she grinned without humour, more a dump and me moving on, she thought. Slowly she slid off the pencil skirt over her hips then stepping from it, lifted it from the floor and cast it through the open door into the hallway and then shrugged off her blouse. Sitting on the edge of the bath, the steam enveloping her, she slid the tights down her firm legs, staring absently at them and enjoying the sensation as she lightly run her fingers back and forth along her thighs. She unclipped her bra and threw it with the blouse towards the skirt, then standing and balancing one hand against the wall, slipped off her underwear. She turned towards the wall mirror and rubbed at the mist with her knickers, leaving wet smudges. The mirror reflected her from just above her head to her thigh and turning she weighed both breasts in each hand, then pushed them upright and together and smiled. Her breasts had always been one; no she smiled at the mirror, two of her best assets. Paul Hardie might be gone, but Janice knew that it wouldn't take much to replace him and this time, she inwardly vowed, no fuck-ups. She vowed her next catch, regardless whether he was married or not, must have money, lots and lots of money.

Paul Hardie saw an empty parking place outside the small, general store located in the middle of a row of shops in Great Western Road and ignored

the angry taxi driver who tooted his horn when Paul suddenly and without warning, slammed on his brakes and stopped in the bay. Several passersby paused when they heard the raised voice of the taxi driver screaming from his cab at Paul, the torrent of abuse swept away as the taxi accelerated to speed through the lights at Byres Road. Paul wasn't a man used to confrontation and apart from a playground fight that he lost when he was just eleven years of age, he had never raised his fists in anger at another human being. But of course, the odd slap at Fiona didn't count, for she was, after all, his wife. The memory of his anger and sudden rage at Janice was vividly fresh in his mind. He looked at his hands, amazed they still seemed to be shaking and took a deep breath. Locking the car door, he strode into the small grocers shop and head turning, saw the alcohol displayed at the rear of the shop and selected a bottle of Bells.
"Bit of a head banger that guy," said the cheery young Asian shop assistant, nodding his head to the open door.
"What?"
"The taxi driver, pal. The guy that hooted at you, they think they own the road some of them wankers," replied the smiling young assistant, ringing the bottle through the till and pushing the small credit card machine along the counter towards Paul. He then glanced at him, his eyes curious. "You okay pal? You seem a bit …."
"A bit what?" angrily retorted Paul.
"Sorry," the young assistant was embarrassed and shrugged his shoulders. "I just thought you seemed a bit, I dunno, upset."
"I'm fine," Paul snapped back, his face taut with tension as he punched in his card number and irritably tapped his fingers against the top of the counter. The machine took a minute to register the sale as the assistant bagged the bottle and handed it over. Tearing the receipt from the machine, he handed it to Paul who wordlessly accepted it then left the shop.
"Not just the taxi drivers that are wankers then," muttered the assistant, shaking his head as he watched Paul climb back into his car and take off at speed.

Paul drove to the abandoned factory yard at Rothesay Dock overlooking the River Clyde. He was about to slow up to avoid the rutted ground damaging the underside of the car, but then remembered the car was soon to be handed back and with an evil grin, accelerated, deliberately aiming for the numerous potholes that abounded the area. Bouncing about in the driver's seat, he spun the wheel and came screeching to a halt. He glanced about him and saw the place seemed to be deserted. Almost guiltily, he fetched the whisky from the plastic carrier bag and twisted off the cork, then slowly tipped his head back to swallow, but then gagged when the fiery liquid hit the back of his throat.

What had seemed like a good idea at the time now, he reluctantly admitted, was foolish. He wasn't a drinker. Yes, in his teenage years he downed a few pints with the best of them, but conscious that his career had taken off, Paul had become a social drinker, preferring wine rather than beer and spirits. His career, he miserably remembered, that was now over.

"Stay or go, stay or go," he whispered over and over to himself in the confines of the car, his fingers tapping in rhythm on the steering wheel as he muttered under his breath while outside, the fading light turned to darkness. Staring into nothingness, he continued to mutter over and over, "stay or go, stay or go."

But the decision, he already knew, had been taken from him. He was not to decide his own fate. He had made too many enemies among those he had supervised, too many people who would not just be delighted at the shit situation he now found himself in, but would take the opportunity to rub his nose in it. As an accountant, he was realistic enough to know that any redundancy package he accepted would soon dissipate when the bills started rolling in. The recession had effectively slammed the door on many opportunities and there were far too many qualified peers out there competing for the few jobs that were available. Hands on the steering wheel he slowly lowered his head and leaned his forehead against his arms. Tears of frustration bit at his eyes and he wept, his body shuddering with the memory of his humiliation. It seemed to him then that all his plans, all his dreams and ambitions had come to nothing, that the life he had planned with Janice was gone.

He wasn't aware he had dozed off until he heard the voice call out, "Hey jimmy, you okay in there?"

He startled, suddenly conscious of the cold, as his head snapped up. Three youths, no, he saw in the dim light, two youths and a teenage girl were standing at the front of the car staring curiously at him through the front windscreen. All three were almost uniformly dressed in tracksuit tops, the boys wearing skipped hats. The girl seemed to be carrying a plastic bag in her left hand and holding a can of lager in her right fist. "You all right jimmy?" the voice loudly asked again. Paul saw that it was the taller youth who spoke, the youth who wore the light coloured baseball cap and who stood in the centre of the trio.

"Yeah," he hoarsely shouted back as he nodded his head, feeling suddenly apprehensive then repeated, "Yeah, I'm okay thanks."

The smaller of the two youths slowly walked towards the driver's door, the fingers of his right hand trailing on the bonnet of the car. Suddenly afraid, Paul reached down and pressed the button on the armrest that locked the four doors. The audible click sounded just as the youth reached for the handle. Without warning, the youth pounded on the door with his fist and shouted,

"Fucking poof! What you doing down here? Waiting on your fancy boy?" and hawked a globule of saliva onto the side window.

Frantically, Paul reached for the keys and turned the engine on. The taller youth kicked at the front of the car while the smaller youth continued to hammer at the window with his fist, his face contorted and snarling as he directed a torrent of vile abuse towards Paul. Without warning, the girl hurled the beer can and an explosion of liquid covered the windscreen, surprising Paul who now temporarily blinded. He shoved the car into first gear, but in his haste forgot to release the handbrake and stalled the engine. Panicking now, he restarted the engine and releasing the handbrake, stamped on the accelerator. The car shot forward and he had a sudden glimpse of a body falling from the bonnet. With shaking hands he turned on the wipers at fast speed and realised he was heading over the rough ground at speed straight for the River Clyde. In his haste he turned the wheel too sharply and the car slewed round, the engine racing in first gear as he continued to push down on the accelerator. He switched on the headlights as something noisily bounced off the metalwork of the car. Hastily he changed into second gear and drove rapidly towards the open gates, emerging with relief onto the side road that led to Dock Street and into Glasgow Road.

Chapter 6

Fiona Hardie needed to pee. Dazed, she blinked rapidly and glanced about her at the cold, darkened room, suddenly aware she was at home and sitting in her small, untidy lounge and still wearing her coat. She had fallen asleep in the armchair, and smiled at her foolishness. Her hands were like ice and even though it was a July evening outside and cool rather than cold, she shivered. The digital wall clock showed it was almost thirty minutes after nine. Strange, she thought, that Paul hadn't yet arrived home. Did he say he was spending one or two nights with his boss, she asked herself, then legs aching from the position in which she had sat for so many hours, balanced one hand on the arm of the chair as she stood upright. The evening sunset still shone brightly in the sky and she moved to close over the curtains and then switched on the main overhead light in the lounge. The sudden brightness again caused her to blink rapidly and she realised she had a headache. Reaching for her small, tan leather handbag that sat on the floor beside the armchair, she scrambled inside it searching for the small pack of aspirin. Leaning against the mantelpiece of the fireplace, she emptied the bag of her car keys, purse and a wad of receipts and placed them on the mantelpiece, frustrated she could not find the tablets. The small, square window at the rear of the lounge framed the dark from the unlit back garden and she moved to draw the curtains, stretching over the small dining table as she pulled them

untidily together until they nearly met, but not quite. Conscious that she still now badly needed to pee, she made her way up the narrow stairs to the bathroom and slipping off her coat, dropped in on the floor of the top landing before relieving her aching bladder. Her head felt worse and after washing her hands, she reached for the door of the mirrored cabinet to get some aspirin, then stopped and smiled, unconsciously rubbing at her stomach. The sound of the front door slamming caused her to continue smiling. Paul was home, her Paul.
"Fiona!" his voice called out to her and reaching for her throat as the smile died on her lips. Her feminine instinct warned her there something wrong.

Lesley Gold slipped out of the large, fluffy pink coloured bath-towel and one hand balancing her on the adjoining sink, tentatively dipped her toe into the steamy, perfumed water, simultaneously groaning with pleasure and pain as the ache in her thighs and back reminded her of her over-exertion at the gym. Still, she considered, painful or not she had enjoyed the session and was keen to get back into some kind of fitness regime, promising herself she would try to get there at least three times a week and in between times, slap leather off the pavements round the flat. Very slowly, she stepped over the lip of the bath and lowered herself into the water then sighed with relief as her backside settled on the bottom and she lay back, enjoying the sensation of the soothing heat about her body. She was glad she had taken that extra few minutes to light the dozen or so tea candles that scattered about the room, gave off a dim glow and added to the ambience. She thanked herself for the decision not just to be satisfied with the shower at the gym and grinned as she squirmed in the soapy water. Dipping a small face cloth into the water, she lay her head back on the inflatable rubber pillow and placed the cloth over her face. As she lay there, enjoying the songs of Adele's album '19' softly playing from the lounge, her thoughts turned to her father and his impending death. Dress it up as you like, she inwardly sighed; his time was near. She worried about her mother's reaction to the loss of her husband and Lesley had already made the decision that like it or lump it, her mother would have a lodger for a few weeks after her father died. No way would Lesley leave her mother to grieve alone and she had already prepared herself for move home for a time.
Lifting the cloth, she wiped at her face with it then let it float in the water. It had occurred to her to ask her sister Linda and her husband Alex to invite Mum to stay with them in their plush new home in Kirkintilloch, where they had two spare rooms, but Lesley decided if Linda wasn't thoughtful enough to extend the invitation herself, it wasn't up to Lesley to make the request and already guessed that Linda would expect her older sister to step in when her parents needed something done. For after all, she bitterly thought, haven't I

always? Cynically, she guessed it would suit Linda to have Mum stay for a few weeks; a handy babysitter cum domestic for the time she was there and the thought left her almost as quickly as it arrived and she inwardly regretted her bitterness. For Lesley, it wasn't a chore, being there for her mother and father. She loved them both and would willingly help or do what she could, but still it irked Lesley that selfish or not, Linda could do no wrong in her father's eyes.

With the thought of her father's poorly condition still in her head, the sound of her mobile phone activating in her bedroom with an incoming text message caused her to almost jump from the bath, suddenly annoyed she hadn't thought to bring it into the bathroom with her. Halfway out of the bath and dripping water onto the tiled floor, she stopped. She knew that her mother had only recently mastered the I-phone keypad, but preferred speaking with her daughter and certainly wouldn't text her with bad news. The message could wait, so humming tunelessly to the faint strains of Adele's song, with a smile she settled back down into the water.

The small bedside clock read just after eleven pm. Frederick Evans always prepared his night excursions or his visits, as he liked to term them, with the utmost care. Selecting a pair of navy blue cargo pants and black training shoes, he quickly slipped them on and then pulled on the black coloured polo short. The night was warm, but still, he would wear his customary Barbour jacket with the special, discreet pocket he had himself sewn into the rear lining. He checked that he had his mobile phone with him, just as a precaution he always thought, and patted at the pocket where he carried the thin, black coloured leather dog lead that he had acquired at one of his mother's church fetes. He believed should he ever be challenged that the dog lead would give him a degree of credibility and could claim he was simply searching for his runaway pup. Now dressed, he again checked his Glasgow A to Z map and studied the page he had selected for his nights activity. Frederick never liked to venture too far from the house and never, ever visited twice in the same area. The areas of the pages he had previously visited and marked with the yellow highlighter pen were now a no-go, as far as he was concerned and the weather usually determined if he drove or walked. Using his deceased father's old Ford Fiesta saloon car provided Frederick with a greater choice of area to select where he would visit and, if it should ever occur, the means to make a hasty getaway. But Frederick liked walking, slowly and unobserved and tonight, he decided to go on foot for his target area, as he liked to call it, was a mere twenty minutes walk. He glanced again at the page he had decided for this evening, just south of the Glasgow High School, between Anniesland and Jordanhill. During his Sunday morning walk, a habit that he had adopted before he visited an area and

which he called his reconnoitre, he knew the area to be populated with terraced housing, most of which had poorly lit or sometimes unlit lanes that run between the rear of the one storey buildings and with gates or low fences that gave access into the rear gardens. His only concern was dogs and at the slightest hint of one in a house, he gave the property a wide detour. Patting his inside pocket to ensure he had his wallet and with a deep breath, the excitement coursing though his veins as it always did, he readied himself to leave. Inwardly, Frederick fantasised to himself that he was going on a mission and this only added to his excitement.
Arriving downstairs, he popped his head into the small lounge and called out, "That's me off for my constitutional mother and I shouldn't be too long, so get yourself off to bed when you can."
"Have you got your key dear?" she replied, turning her head from the magazine to peer at him over her thick lenses.
"Yes, of course," he smiled through gritted teeth, wishing the old bat would just get herself off to bed and never wake up, then startled that the crass thought even entered his head. Guiltily, he pushed open the door and walked over to her, gently ruffling her grey haired head and leaning over to plant a kiss on top of it.
His mother reached a hand over to pat his arm, then said, "Be careful walking out there. There's a lot of they young hooligans creating mischief these days," she warned.
"I'll be careful," he assured her and waved goodbye, softly closing the door behind him.
At the front door, he glanced about him, feeling foolish at the panicked thought that anyone would be watching him. Taking another deep breath, Frederick Evans walked slowly along the garden path to begin his evening's excursion.

Fiona Hardie sat still, her hands wrestling with each other in her lap and stared in shock at the unlit gas fire that was set into the old fashioned tiled hearth. She didn't dare look towards the kitchen where she could hear Paul banging cupboard doors and the clatter of dishes.
"Are you ever going to get some fucking shopping done!" he shouted at her through the open door.
She flinched and tightly closed her eyes. She had come to accept that he had a bad temper when he was angry and he had often sworn at her, but never with such vehemence. On occasions, she remembered, he had even grabbed her by the clothing and pulled her about and once or was it twice or more, she wasn't certain, even slapped her face, but Fiona didn't complain because he always apologised and said he was sorry and besides, she reasoned, he was always correct. She was a sloppy housewife. But tonight he seemed

particularly agitated. Her pleasure at seeing him home had been swept aside when he began complaining about the untidy state of the house. She had tried to explain she had been busy, eager to tell him her good news and her offer to make him some dinner had been ignored. Then she saw he carried a bottle of whisky and thought that strange. Paul didn't normally like whisky, she had remembered. She had fetched him a glass, but when he saw the smudge on it, he had thrown it against the fireplace wall. She turned slightly to stare down at the shards of glass that he refused her to pick up. She heard the sound of a tap being run.

Paul strode into the small lounge and sat down in the easy chair opposite her, the whisky bottle in one hand, a glass half full of water in the other, then filled it from the bottle. She glanced towards him, seeing his tie loosened, but still wearing his suit jacket. Nervously, she decided to try some conversation. "Did you have a nice trip with your boss, Paul?"

He didn't reply, didn't even look at her, just threw back his head and took a long pull at the whisky.

"I had a nice day at the school," she began, smiling at first, but then she remembered and her face clouded over. No, she remembered then, she didn't have a nice day after all. Miss Jenkins, had rebuked her, but Fiona had difficulty recalling why. She watched as Paul refilled the glass and placed the bottle on the floor beside his chair, worried that he was drinking so much whisky without any dinner. She tried again. "Can I get you something to eat, Paul, Maybe some toast and spaghetti?"

"Toast and spaghetti?" he slowly repeated, staring wide-eyed at her, his voice rising with undiluted sarcasm, "Toast and spaghetti? That's what you want to make for my dinner? All day I've been working hard to keep and support you and you want to make me fucking toast and spaghetti for my dinner?" he screamed at her, standing now, the anger evident on his face and the liquid from the glass spilling across the back of his hand as he shook with rage.

"You slovenly cow, look at the state of this place! You can hardly keep yourself clean let alone this house," he sneered at her, looking about him at the dishevelled room, realising with a gut wrenching certainty that this was now his life and even this place might be lost to him if he didn't find a job. But for now, he turned to face Fiona, little globules of saliva trickling from the corners of his mouth. Shaking his head he turned away, a black depression settling upon his shoulders. For now, they would have to survive on her salary alone. He stumbled to the door and made his way upstairs to the toilet.

Frederick Evans walked slowly and turned into the dimly lit Munro Road, his eyes casting about him and ears alert for any sound, but the road was quiet and nobody was around. He glanced behind him, his nerves on edge but enjoying the sensation and fantasising he was on a secret mission. The few parked cars seemed to him to indicate the area was upper working class and though he spotted a few tattered posters that warned it was a Neighbourhood Watch Area, he suspected the residents were not as crime conscious as some of the areas council housing estates. At least, he almost giggled, he hoped so. Pretending to be looking about him for the mischievous, if fictional runaway puppy, he wandered towards the darkened lane that led behind a row of small, mid-terraced houses. In the darkness, he could just make out the sign attached to the end house wall which read Borden Road. Taking a deep breath and copying the tip-toeing presenter of the wildlife show he had recently watched, Frederick stepped into the lane.

Fiona shrunk back into her seat, watching terrified at the expression on Paul's face as he left the room. Slovenly, he had called her. Slovenly, she thought again, wondering why the word was so recently familiar. Then with a start she remembered. Miss Jenkins had called her slovenly just before she told her ….she raised a hand to her mouth and her eyes opened wide with horror. Just before she told her that she was going to have Fiona's contract terminated, that Fiona was to lose her job.

Frederick crept along through the darkness, treading lightly on the cobbled lane and pausing at each rear gate or fence. Some were too high to see over, but nevertheless he quietly tried each gate to see if locked or unlocked. At the fourth house, the high hedgerow hid the garden, but the gate was unlocked and cautiously he pushed it open, all the while listening for the gate hinges squeaking but more importantly, for sounds of movement or a dog. The dark of the night revealed that the washing line had items hung and left out overnight. As quickly as he dared, he sneaked at a crouch along the path only to find that the washing line was hung with shirts and tops, but no knickers. Disappointed, he retraced his steps and slowly closed the gate being him and exhaled softly then moved on to the next house.

Paul, one hand flat on the wall behind the cistern while he held himself with the other, glanced down into the bowl and watched himself urinate. The small, plastic flip bin beside the toilet was half open and spilled over with tissues and paper. He saw a rectangular box half sticking out from under the lid. Flushing the cistern and zipping his trousers closed, his curiosity aroused, he bent down to retrieve the box and stared at it with a sudden, chilled feeling.

It was at the eighth house with the low picket fence and half closed gate. There was no obstacle for Frederick to overcome and his spirits soared for even in the dark of the night and though the rope was propped up by a pole, he could see the washing line was bent with the weight of the clothing.

Paul stormed down the stairs, almost losing his footing and burst into the lounge, then screamed "What the fuck is this?" as he held the pregnancy testing box in his hand like a trophy.
Fiona could only stare and then smiled, knowing he would be so pleased. Maybe even a boy who would look like him, she thought.
"Well?" he advanced towards her.

Frederick startled at the sudden shout then relaxed. The voice had come from a house on the opposite side of the lane and as he peered toward it, he could see a hopper window open and light escaping through a chink in the curtains. One to avoid, he thought and turned his excited attention back to the light coloured panties he had just removed from the line. Another shout distracted him and he considered maybe he should be gone with his find. Taking a brief second to run the fresh smelling pants across his cheek, he reached round and lifting the back of his jacket, stuffed them into the secret pocket.

"I was going to tell you when you got home," she breathlessly replied, smiling even more, "give you a surprise. Isn't it wonderful?" she took a step forward, anticipating his joyful hug.
He stared at her with surprise. Was she that much of an idiot? What the hell happened to the bright, even vivacious young woman he married all those years ago? In a flash, the last three years run through his head, her lack of interest in her own grooming, her forgetfulness and her childlike naivety. He turned away, his mind refusing to come to terms with this latest blow to his plans, a child with Fiona. My God, he reeled, reminding himself of a drunken night some weeks previously when his sexual urge overcame his common sense and cheeks burning, recalled how he almost raped her. Now, living with or without her, he would pay for his stupidity and be tied to her forever. His back to her, he closed his eyes and quietly said, "You'll have to get rid of it."

Frederick crept back into the darkness of the lane, overwhelmed that as he was about to leave the washing line, he discovered a second pair of cotton knickers, admittedly large and faded, but still a treasured find. As he walked, he stuffed them into the secret pocket and glanced towards the beam of light that escaped through the curtain from the house from where the shout had come.

"I can't," she replied aghast and then in a low voice, forcefully said, "I won't. She stamped her feet, her fists tightly held by her aside. He slowly turned towards her with surprise etched on his face at her refusal and even with the whisky he had consumed, recognised that she was determined to defy him. Exhaling softly, he put his hands up and decided to try and reason with her, their eyes locked into each others. "Look, I had some bad news today, at work. I'm being made redundant. I'm losing my job, Fiona. We won't be able to afford a child on your salary alone. You must see that?"

Frederick, keenly excited at the double find of the knickers, decided to do something he had never before dared. With bated breath and eyes wide, he crept along the garden path towards the chink of light that seemed to summon him like a moth to a flame. Crouching below the window sill, he risked glancing into the room and reasoned that anyone inside the room who glanced at the window would simply see a dark wedge of blackness because their vision would be blurred by the light. As he peered through the window, he saw a slight figured, dark haired woman stood with her back to him and a taller, fair haired man standing facing the woman. The hopper window above Frederick's head was open and he guessed this was from where a few minutes earlier he had heard the shouting. As he watched, he could hear the man's voice, but speaking too lowly to make out what was being said. He saw the woman clench her fists and heard her reply to the man, but all Frederick could make out was the words, "I won't."

"My salary," she replied to Paul, the memory of Miss Jenkins threat searing through her mind. "I won't have a salary," she softly whispered. "I … I…" she tried to say.
Paul was confused. Won't have a salary? "What do you mean," he demanded of her, his face curious. "Fiona," he repeated, the anger building up within him, "what do you mean you won't have a salary? Has something happened?" he reached across and with his outstretched hands, pinned her arms against her body. "Tell me!"

Frederick almost fell onto his backside, then realising that this was something developing, with trembling fingers hastily withdrew his mobile phone from his jacket pocket and set it to camera mode. Crouching as close as he dare, he aimed the camera phone through the chink in the curtain and pressed the record button. The sound through the open hopper window was muffled, but the couple's raised voices continued to be recorded.

She stared back at him with defiance shining from her teary eyes, her mouth twisted in scorn at his suggestion they get rid of her baby, their baby. How dare he; her thoughts screamed at her. How dare Paul! From where, she could not say but some inner strength possessed her and teeth gritted, she said, "I've been sacked too," she hissed at him. The stark realism of their situation came crashing into her thoughts as the reality of her life and her marriage collided with sudden clarity. "Why should you care?" she continued to hiss at him. "You've never taken an interest in me, my work, my children," she tried to wrest herself from his hold, but he held her with a fierce grip and she couldn't break free. She couldn't say why, but the urgent need to get away from this man, this husband whom she had adored and loved without question, but had treated her with such disdain and indifference overwhelmed her and now she wanted nothing more than to hurt him.

Frederick held his breath till his chest almost exploded as he tried to breathe with short gasps, now kneeling, holding the camera phone with both hands and completely engrossed with the situation being played out before him,

"Besides," Fiona sneered up at Paul, "who's to say the baby is yours?" His face turned red with fury and he pulled her in close and bent down, his lips turned back as he snarled in response, "Of course it's mine, you dirty little bitch. What other man would have you? You even smell of body odour."
She felt his whisky sodden breath on her face and almost gagged, then forcing her left hand free, pulled back her arm and clenching her fist in her fury, tried to strike Paul on the face. He easily parried her weak blow and she struggled to scratch at his face, but again without much effort, he avoided her pathetic attempt and still holding her right arm with his left hand, took a half step backwards. An overpowering rage overcame him and with a sweeping motion, he brought his right hand across his body then quickly swung his arm forward and struck Fiona on the face with the back of his fisted hand. Her head snapped backwards and spun round. He saw her face register shock and her eyes widen as droplets of blood sprayed from her mouth across the gas fire. Almost in slow motion, he watched as her light body spun and fell against the corner of the tiled hearth and with horror, heard a resounding crack when her head struck the edge of it. Fiona came to rest lying on the carpeted floor, her eyes fixed open and staring at him in surprise, the blood seeping from her open mouth and slowly dripping down her chin onto the rug below.

Frederick, his mouth dry and the camera phone still held in his now sweaty hands, watched in fascination, but did not at that time realise the enormity of the situation he had just not just witnessed, but recorded.

Chapter 7 - Wednesday

The following morning dawned bright and sunny. Lesley Gold sleepily fumbled for the switch on the digital alarm clock and finally cancelled the irritating voice of the early morning radio presenter. Perhaps, she thought to herself, this rising an hour earlier isn't such a good idea.

Throwing back the covers, she almost jumped from bed before her aching legs and back reminded her that she wasn't yet fit. Carefully, she slipped into a clean, bright yellow tracksuit, pulled her hair back into a ponytail and pulled on the white socks and light blue training shoes. "Right," she said loudly in an attempt to bolster her own confidence, then grabbing her phone and keys opened the front door and theatrically wheezing, whispered, "Here we go then."

Three minutes later found Lesley pounding the pavements round the Partick area, trying to manage her breathing on the upward inclined north facing streets and breathing easier on the parallel south bound downhill streets. As she jogged, she thought of the text message that had arrived while she soaked in the bath the previous night. Curiously, the message again played in her mind: *I'm sorry, Mike xxx*

She hadn't responded and didn't intend to, but a part of her wondered if maybe she was being a bit hasty. Maybe he was sorry, she tried to convince herself. She thought of the blonde analyst she had seen Mike with that night and remembered the young woman's reputation as a bunny boiler who had previously boasted of affairs with a couple of the divisional cops, one of whom was married. Maybe he was a bit weak then she mused and I have to admit, she sighed and shook her head as she ran, I had let myself go a bit. As Lesley turned into Dumbarton Road, a Post Office van passed by and the driver, who seemed oddly familiar, gave her a curious glance before he turned away.

Her thoughts again turned to Mike Duffy and briefly she considered that maybe a text or even a phone call might not do any harm. Perhaps even give him an opportunity to explain, she unconsciously bit at her lower lip as she crashed into the pain barrier and a stitch cut across her midriff. Slowing to a fast walking pace, she held her side and with a rivulet of sweat coursing down her spine, decided that enough was enough. Glancing at her wristwatch she realised that twenty minutes today would suffice and she'd try tomorrow for twenty-five.

Arriving back at the tenement flat, Lesley had just unlocked her front door when the phone activated with a text message. She opened the screen and read: *Did you get my message? M x*

Persistent isn't he, she mused, but couldn't help smiling and throwing the phone onto the bed, stripped off to prepare for her shower before going to work.

Frederick Evans hardly slept all night, tossing and turning as the previous evening's events raced through his thoughts. As soon as he had returned home, he had satisfied himself that his mother was asleep and almost bolted to his room, locked the door and the stolen knickers momentarily forgotten, with shaking fingers turned on his laptop. Eagerly he had inserted the phone lead and created a new, special file then downloaded the argument and the … at first he baulked at using the word killing and satisfied himself in his own mind by describing it as the thing he had witnessed. Only now in hindsight, in light of what the man did, or rather, failed to do after the woman fell to the floor, did Frederick excitedly believe the thing to perhaps be something even more serious than he had at first thought.

Paul Hardie awoke and found himself lying face down on the bed in the larger of the two upstairs front rooms, the curtains drawn wide and the sun beating a path to one side of his face. His head ached and his throat felt as dry as a crocodile tear. He groaned and rolled over on to his back, rubbing a hand at the stubble on his face and grunted with surprise to find that he was still fully dressed, even wearing his suit jacket, though somehow one shoe had slipped off. Blinking rapidly, the bile threatened to erupt from him and he staggered to his feet, groping the walls with shaking hands as he made his way across the small landing to the bathroom, then plummeted to his knees as with force, he expelled the contents of his stomach. He continued to shake and experienced a sensation of choking as the bile again erupted, but this time as a yellowish, sickly fluid. He shuddered and with his left hand, knocked over the small flip bin and spilled its contents. Bleary eyed, he glanced at the bin, his eyes narrowing as with a sudden horror he recalled the events of the night before, Fiona falling and hitting her head. No, not falling, he hit her with his fist and turned to stare at his hand. "My God," he stuttered with a whisper, hardly believing the memory of it, "she's dead."
Panic-stricken, he realised she still lay downstairs and awkwardly pushing himself upright, he staggered from the bathroom, the urge to vomit forgotten as one thought raced through his head; he had to get rid of her body. In his eagerness to get down the narrow stairs, he tripped halfway down and tumbled in an untidy heap to the bottom, groaning as he landed with a thud. He lay there feeling sorry for himself and almost called out to Fiona to come and help him before again he remembered. Fiona was dead and he was the one who had killed her.

Nervously he pushed open the lounge door and almost immediately gagged. The lights remained on and the curtains closed, but the sickly sweet stench of Fiona's blood that had now dried, permeated throughout the lounge. He had no option but to enter and try as he might, Paul could not avoid staring at Fiona's body that lay draped across the carpet and the fire hearth. He had a vague recollection of trying to resuscitate her, but his pathetic attempt had been to no avail. He closed his eyes and wondered how he could get out of this mess, how he would explain to the police ….his eyes snapped open; the police. He glanced around at the blood stained gas fire and wall, finally staring down at his suit jacket that was stained with crusted blood at the front and on the sleeve where he had moved her. With disgust, he tore the jacket off and threw it away from him, watching it slide across the couch. The police would never believe this to be an accident. He guessed all they would see was a dead woman and her killer husband. They would want to know why I killed her and, if I try to tell them it was an accident, why then I didn't phone for an ambulance? He rubbed the heel of his hand against his brow and shaking his head in disbelief, asked himself, why didn't I call an ambulance? But he already knew the answer to that. He had punched her with his fist and killed her, no matter how he tried to dress it up. Fiona falling and striking her head was because of him. An ambulance crew undoubtedly would have summoned the police and right now, he would be sitting in a cell charged with her murder.

Paul shuffled forward and edged against the couch then with his eyes focused on Fiona's body, felt with his hands behind him and sat down. He decided before anything else, he must get his thoughts together. The wall clock said it was almost eight o'clock. He knew that after his meeting yesterday with the HR Director Colin Davis, nobody would expect him to come into work today, so that would give him some time to get himself together, to collect his thoughts and work out what he was going to do, but try as he might, he could not avert his eyes from Fiona's body. With an effort he stood upright and ignoring the throbbing pain in his head, went into the kitchen. The worktops were the usual messy mayhem and he inwardly cursed at his wife's slovenliness, then stopped, correcting himself; at his dead wife's slovenliness. He wasn't aware of shaking his head at the thought of the task that lay before him, but he realised with a bitter, gut-wrenching certainty it had to be done. Opening the one tall cupboard, he fetched out a variety of cloths and cleaning materials and a roll of large, heavy duty black polythene bin bags that with the various sprays and polishes, he wryly recalled that this had been another of Fiona's house cleaning ideas that never got off the ground. He took a deep breath and filling a bucket with hot, soapy water, carried it all through to the lounge. Disgusted though he was by the sight of Fiona's bloodstained body, Paul was more afraid of being discovered and arrested. He stripped off his remaining clothes till he stood in just his underpants, ripped off a half dozen of the black bags and began the grisly task of manoeuvring Fiona's body into the bags. He was fortunate that she was so slight and slim and though a certain amount of rigour had set in, he had little difficulty in covering her over. He shuddered with disgust when he moved her and saw that her bladder had released its contents and there was a patch that was now dried, underneath her groin. From the kitchen, he fetched a roll of ordinary, domestic sellotape and wrapped several layers about the pathetic bundle. That done, he glanced at the clock and saw that almost an hour had passed. His thirst overtook him and drawing a glass of water from the tap, finished it in one gulp and was pleased to see that his hands no longer shook. That done, he ripped off another plastic bag and into this went the suit, shirt and tie, socks and shoes, bloodstained or not, that he had worn and threw in his underpants. Now completely naked, he dropped to his knees, his eyes narrowed as he saw the strap of her tan coloured handbag that had been kicked to one side. Reaching forward, he drew it toward him and thrust it in the bin bag and then recalled Fiona's purse and the jumble of paper on top of the fire mantelpiece. The receipts and purse followed the handbag into the bin bag while the car keys were thrust into a kitchen drawer. He was about to tie the bag closed when he remembered there was just one more thing that he had to add and oblivious to his nakedness, made his way upstairs to the bathroom.

Returning downstairs, he checked the curtains were still drawn and having no fear of being overlooked, decided to continue going about his next task naked. It was while he was scrubbing the wall and hearth of bloodstains that he heard the letterbox at the front door rattle. The sound startled Paul and almost caused him to faint. He stopped what he was doing and holding his breath, listened intently for any further noise, but the sound of someone whistling and fading into the distance calmed him. The postman, he suddenly thought with relief. Turning his attention to the hearth, he scrubbed it clean of blood, only to notice that where he had scrubbed the hearth it now gleamed while the remaining tiles seemed dull by comparison. He gritted his teeth and inwardly cursed Fiona for her lack of domesticity that left him no choice but to clean the remaining tiles till they also shone. The small scrap of rug that sat in front of the hearth was also stained, but he saw to his relief the blood had not soaked through to the carpet underneath and with the rags he had used, threw the small rug into the black bin bag and then sat down on the carpet and rested his back on the couch. While the area now seemed to be clean, Paul had watched too many television cop shows not to know that regardless of his efforts, he would not be able to entirely clean the area of Fiona's blood. The superficial cleaning he had accomplished would certainly fool the casual check, but somehow he had to cause suspicion regarding her disappearance to be concentrated elsewhere. Pushing himself to his feet, he walked into the kitchen and filled the electric kettle, poured a generous amount of coffee into a mug and waited on the kettle boiling. From where he stood, he could see the shapeless lump that had been Fiona and the second bag with his clothes, the rags and rug. As he poured the water into the mug, his mind raced at how he would explain his wife's disappearance. Sipping at the coffee his brow furrowed as an idea came to him that in his mind seemed so simple, but would be difficult to disprove. He glanced again at the large and smaller black bags that sat together in the lounge. His problem now was when, where and how to dispose of them both.

Lesley drove into the rear yard at Garscadden office then as she opened the car door, heard the squeal of tyres and stopped to watch a black coloured Vauxhall Corsa turn into the yard at speed then come to a sudden, shuddering halt a few yards from her own car. Boy racer, she thought as she shook her head and then smiled when the probationary cop Alex Mason exited the car.
"Must cost you a fortune in brake pads," she grinned at his dishevelled appearance.
Alex returned her grin and courteously held the back door open which reminded her, she must learn the bloody security number. "Good night was it, at the bowling club I mean?"
He nodded and replied, "Dotty and Morris only stayed half an hour, but the barmaid's got a thing for me, so I was there a wee bit longer," he winked at Lesley.
"Thought that," she wrinkled her nose at the strong smell of spearmint emanating from his mouth.
Alex breathed into his hand. "Is it that bad?" he asked, sniffing at his palm as they trudged along the narrow corridor.
"Let's just say I hope you're the passenger this morning," she grinned again as she pushed her way into the woman's locker room door to collect her equipment and cap.
Dotty sat in the small canteen that doubled as a muster room, her hands cupping a mug of coffee and nodded as Lesley entered. "Morning," she growled.
"Late night?" smiled Lesley, dumping her gear in an untidy heap on the floor.
"No, I always get my sleep. Well, not unless one of the kids is ill or something. I'm just not a morning person and the early shift kills me," she replied.
Alex Mason pushed open the door and walking behind Dotty, ruffling her short, curly blonde hair. "Morning mum," he greeted her with a grin.
"If I was your mother," replied Dotty without turning, "I'd have drowned you at birth, you cocky little shit."

Pouring herself a coffee, Lesley didn't fail to notice that Dotty's nose twitched at the sudden smell spearmint in the air.

Sergeant Pete Buchanan followed Alex into the room, a folder held in his hand. "Morning guys and gals, there's a change of neighbours today. Morris will be a wee bit late in this morning, so Dotty, you take Lesley out in the car and show her around the area. Alex, you work at the Uniform bar with Jinksie," he narrowed his eyes as the young cop averted his gaze. "It might be prudent to keep you away from the public for a while, eh?"

"Right Sergeant," replied a suddenly formal Alex, while Dotty and Lesley suppressed grins.

"Dotty," continued Buchanan, "there's a complaint been phoned into the control room and passed through to Jinksie at the Bar. Get the details before you leave, but it's not urgent, so finish your coffee first."

"Sarge," acknowledged Dotty with some relief.

As Lesley shrugged into her issue stab-proof vest and utility belt, Alex reached to open the door, only to be called back when Dotty softly said, "Hold on there wee man. A word if you please," then turned and eyebrows raised with the unspoken hint, asked if Lesley wouldn't mind getting the details of the complaint from Jinksie. As Lesley left the canteen and closed the door behind her she smiled, imagining the ear-bashing the probationer was about to undergo.

At the Uniform bar, Jinksie greeted her and it seemed to Lesley that he too was a little bit the worse from wear after the previous evening's *small aperitif* at the bowling club.

"Morning," she returned his greeting with a smile, "hung one on, did you?"

"I'm not really a drinker," he replied, "but my problem is I keep practising."

"You've got a complaint phoned in?"

"Aye," he turned to the desk behind him to lift a slip of paper, "seems there has been a bit of snow dropping along in Jordanhill at 61 Austen Road. The tenant is a Missus McClafferty at that address, complaining about the theft of washing."

"Snow dropping?"

Jinksie smiled at her expression. "Snow dropping," he repeated. "It's an old Glasgow term. Means stealing washing from the line; you know, clothes hung out to dry?"

"I know what washing is, Jinksie," she retorted like he was some sort of an idiot, "I've just never heard it referred to like that. Snow dropping?"

"Aye, it used to be a regular thing when Glasgow was mostly a tenement city, but these days with clothes dryers and tenements getting pulled down left, right and centre, you don't hear much about it. Not unless it's a knicker-knocker, of course."

Lesley put her hand up, palm towards the small man. "Knicker-knocker I know. I've had occasion to deal with a couple since I joined," then took the slip of paper from Jinksie.
"Ready to go?" said Dotty behind her, suited and booted carrying her cap in her hand.
"God help the public with you two floosies out there," jeered Jinksie with a grin on his face, turning to receive the post from the large, scar faced man who with curious eyes, watched Lesley as she walked out towards the back door.

Chapter 8

As Constable Lesley Gold was collecting the complaint information from Jinksie, the civilian bar officer at Garscadden police office, Frederick Evans was closing the garden gate behind him. Never had he enjoyed a morning as he did today. With a buoyant step, he walked the short distance to the bus stop in Lincoln Avenue, his mind replaying last night's visit, the couple arguing and then the man hitting the woman, his wife presumably, with his fist. The woman falling and from what Fredrick could see, striking her head against the fireplace surround so badly that she seemed to be unconscious. He watched as the man performed what Frederick thought looked like some form of resuscitation, or at least his pathetic version of it, Frederick airily sniffed, recalling his own in-store First Aid training course some years previously. The man had sat back on his haunches, apparently having given up the effort at which time Frederick decided that enough was enough and had sneaked away before the ruckus attracted someone else's attention or the ambulance arrived.
He turned the corner and walked to the stop with its half dozen or so bleary-eyed, city bound passengers, coughing and grunting as they queued for the bus. He viewed them with contempt, living their dreary little lives and unaware of what he had witnessed. How they would look at him, if they knew, his chest almost burst with pride at his secret.
The bus arrived a few minutes later and, as he flashed his pass at the indifferent driver, he saw that a large woman was sitting in the seat he usually occupied. Scowling as he passed her by, he made his way to the rear and squeezed into a seat between a young man occupied with his mobile phone and a larger man who insisted on spreading his arms wide as he read the Metro. It occurred to Frederick to complain, that the large man was taking up too much space, but convincing himself it wasn't worth making a fuss, pretended instead that his attention was diverted to the young man with the mobile phone. As he watched, Frederick again recalled last night's recording,

savouring the images he had watched almost a dozen times. His thought's turned to how he might use what he had witnessed. No stranger to the Internet site You Tube, he considered uploading the images or even trying to sell them to a newspaper. The difficulty was that a newspaper might wish to know how he had come by such images and that, he quite definitely knew, could not be disclosed to anyone. Anonymously, he wondered? But then how would he be paid for the recording?

As the bus weaved its way towards Glasgow city centre, it turned and tossed its passengers back and forth, most of whom grunted and groaned with each sway; however, the slightly built man sitting at the rear was unaware of the passage of the journey, his mind pre-occupied by thoughts of how he might exploit the recording that now lay within a secret file of his laptop.

It had taken Paul Hardie the best part of two hours to clean not just the lounge, but the bathroom too. The smell of vomit hung in the air and, as he had done downstairs, he threw open the upstairs windows to clear the air, then stood for almost ten minutes in the electric shower, leaning against the tiled wall and silently cursing the fate that had landed him with this problem. Already, he had worked out a strategy in his mind to explain Fiona's disappearance and disposing of her black bin wrapped body. The difficulty lay with convincing the police, but he thought again of his own professional training as an accountant and decided if his story was to hold up, he must examine every small if somewhat insignificant detail with a scrupulous eye for details, much the same as he would examine a balance sheet.

"So, Dotty," began Lesley Gold, "how long have you worked at Garscadden?"
Dotty's eyes narrowed as she negotiated the patrol car round the corner into Knightswood Road. "Let me see," she bit at her lower lip, "I'm thirty-seven and I'm now in my sixteenth years with the polis. My oldest Iain, I think I told you, just turned fourteen and I think he was about two when I transferred over from Govan, so just under twelve years now."
"Longer than I've been in the Force," murmured Lesley, staring at a passing junkie who turned his head away at the sight of the marked patrol car.
"Are you saying I'm an old git?" Dotty turned briefly to stare at the younger woman.
Lesley laughed, realising Dotty was kidding and shook her head. "Woman don't get old, Dotty," she grinned in response, "we only get more mature, you should know that."
"Aye, some of us like a fine old wine and some like a rotten cheese," Dotty grinned back, concentrating now on the heavy morning traffic that was making its way snake-like towards the city centre.

"Are you happy working at Garscadden," asked Lesley, "I mean, it's not exactly the centre of the universe, is it?"

"Its okay and it's typical of working in the polis. Nothing ever remains the same. Cops and gaffers come and go and at the minute, the shift isn't a bad crowd and the gaffers are all right."

"What's with Morris MacDonald? I know he was with you at the club last night. Is that why he's not in this morning, a hangover?"

Dotty braked behind a lorry that spewed out a cloud of dirty oily fumes from its exhaust and scowled. "Never a traffic cop when you want one," she complained and to Lesley's amusement, completely ignored the opportunity to deal with it herself. In fact, Lesley realised that Dotty had just not answered the question about MacDonald, but deftly changed the subject. A short silence fell between them and Lesley sensed there was something Dotty wanted to say about Morris MacDonald, but decided to let her tell Lesley in her own time.

"So," Lesley shrugged, "I'm guessing from what you've told me, no man in your life?"

"Bugger took off within a year of Angie arriving. To be honest, I don't think I made it too easy for him. I had a spell of post-natal and took most of my anger out on him. Jim worked for the council planning department," she paused. "He still does I think. He's not been in touch for a while and apart from the regular maintenance money going into the account for the kids, I haven't any contact with him."

Lesley detected a hint of bitterness, but Dotty quickly added, "Not that I'm too keen to see him, but the kids miss him. No birthday or Christmas cards. His new girlfriend takes up all his time I guess and let's face it, would you want a guy who splits his time between his ex-wife and kids and you?"

For the first time, Lesley had a sudden insight and realised that was exactly what might have happened had she continued the relationship with Mike. Her brow furrowed at the thought and this morning's text message knocked at her conscience.

"Austen Road, Austen Road," Dotty mumbled to herself, "If memory serves me correctly, I think it's just off Chamberlain Road," she said, turning the patrol car left into a side street, then said, "Quiet wee bit here, normally," she muttered, then said, "Ah, here we are. What's the number again?"

Lesley glanced at the slip of paper in her hand. "Number 61, a Missus McClafferty."

Dotty stopped the car outside the mid-terraced house and switching off the engine, turned in her seat to retrieve her cap from the rear seat. "Here we go then, Constable Gold," she grinned as she pushed open the driver's door, "Let's see you in action."

For the first time for as long as he remembered and with a spring in his step, Frederick Evans looked forward to arriving at work. The secret of his night time excursion continued to excite him and with a grin, he greeted the bemused staff that stood with him with a smile as they waited in turn to clock in at the time machine located beside the security desk at the staff entrance, situated in the lane behind the great store.

Just ahead of him in the short queue stood Jennifer Farndale the kitchen assistant. He could see her fair hair tied and rolled into a tight bun on top of her bowed head and as she shuffled forward, holding her credit card size pass in one hand and a Dawson's shopping bag in the other, he watched as Jennifer inserted the pass card into the time machine and then pushed her way through the swing doors out of sight towards the women's changing room. He sighed with frustration, regretting he hadn't been a few seconds earlier then perhaps he would have been able to engage Jennifer in conversation.

"Come on, Freddy boy, move it," said the youthful voice behind him. Turning, he saw it was one of the painted hussies from the Perfume Department, grinning at him as she nudged her equally painted and smirking friend. With a lofty indifference, Frederick ignored the comment, inserted his pass card into the machine and then pushed through the swing doors. If she only knew, he inwardly smirked, that on any night he chose, she and her big titted slut of a friend starred on Frederick's computer.

"Come away in, officers," said the haughty Missus McClafferty, "and please if you don't mind, wipe your shoes. I've just hoovered the hall carpet."
The large woman was wearing a multi-coloured flowered dress and her greying hair tightly curled in rollers. The lavender perfume she wore barely masked the smell of sweat and as she led Lesley and Dotty into the small lounge, they couldn't fail to notice the damp patches under her arms. Lesley saw the room was beyond neat and tidy, the floral suite covered with Chintz cushions and a host of China ornaments abounding on the many small tables around the room. Privately, she thought it must be a nightmare to dust. Hands folded together on her bosom, Missus McClafferty turned towards them.
"Now, I assume you will take the report before the CID and the fingerprint people get here?"
Poker-faced, Lesley removed her cap and fiddled with her utility belt pouch, ostensibly fetching out her notebook but in reality, to give her time to retain her composure before she started giggling. Taking a deep breath, she smiled tightly and said, "I understand that there has been a theft, Missus McClafferty. Can you tell me what was stolen and show me …." but, she got no further.

"Yes, of course, the scene of the crime. I watch CSI, you know. I never miss it and I'm well up to date with police procedure," Missus McClafferty gushed.

Behind her, Lesley could almost hear Dotty's sharp intake of breath as she too desperately tried to control her laughter.

"Right, follow me officers," said Missus McClafferty, imperiously turning and marching towards the rear of the lounge where she opened a French door and led the way into the small, narrow garden. Lesley saw a clothes rope, still strung with washing and set at an angle on a line between two hooks cemented into the opposite six foot high walls that separated the house from its next door neighbours. At the far side of the garden she saw a small wooden picket fence and open gate. With a dramatic sweep of her hand, Missus McClafferty pointed towards the clothes. "There we are; the scene of the crime."

Lesley narrowed her eyes and slowly nodded her head as though in contemplation of the theft. "When you phoned in Missus McClafferty, you said there were two items stolen, it that correct?"

"Indeed it is. The culprit made off with two." The large woman hesitated then moved closer to Lesley and whispered, "Lower lingerie garments, you understand."

Swallowing with difficulty, Lesley repeated, "Two lower lingerie garments, Missus McClafferty?" only to hear Dotty behind her say in a loud voice, "The lady means knickers, Constable Gold."

Missus McClafferty, her face red, stood upright, aghast at Dotty's use of *that word* in public.

Ignoring Dotty's outburst, Lesley forced her face to maintain its composure and pencil in one hand and open notebook in the other, noted the relevant times and Missus McClafferty's details then asked her to describe the stolen items.

"Perhaps indoors, if you please," she replied then without a further word, walked past the officers into the lounge. Lesley followed her in while Dotty, her shoulders shaking with suppressed giggles, pretended to examine the clothes line and the small wooden gate at the back on the garden that led into the lane.

"Now Missus McClafferty, a description if you please?"

"Yes, well," relied the woman, glancing over Lesley's shoulders as she watch Dotty in the garden, "my daughter's lingerie, she works in a pharmacy, you know," she replied with a hint of pride, "they were light pink in colour. Not quite panties, more," she hesitated, uncertain of the name.

"A thong?" suggested Lesley.

"Yes, that's it," she agreed, her cheeks colouring, "a thong."

"And the second pair, please?"

"Mine. White coloured, cotton and M and S of course."

Lesley wrote the details in her notebook and as the large woman turned to peer through narrowed eyes at Dotty, Lesley glanced at her ample backside and thought it prudent not to ask the size of the stolen knickers, but briefly considered that it might be worth checking out the local chandlers at the docks to inquire if anyone had tried to sell cheap material for making sails. Snapping her notebook closed, she firmly said, "Right, Missus McClafferty. So, you didn't hear anything at all during the dark hours or early hours this morning and once again, the washing was left out overnight between the times you told me?"

"Yes officer, now, about the CID. I was thinking …."

Lesley raised her hand. "No, Missus McClafferty, I won't be involving the CID. This is a sensitive issue, the theft of lingerie and I don't wish you to be embarrassed by a lot of men asking you questions about your personal clothing. That's why our control room sent female officers, because of the delicacy of the call."

Over Missus McClafferty's shoulder, Lesley saw the now composed Dotty returning to the lounge. "As women together," she reached out and touched the older woman on the arm, "we understand these matters, so rest assured, I will do my utmost to track down the thief and I'll also ensure that during the dark hours, the local patrol car will take a turn round this and the nearby streets, just to keep an eye open on you and your home."

"Nothing for Scenes of Crime," interrupted Dotty, shaking her head, both thumbs hooked into her utility belt as she stood behind the large woman. Lesley was pleased that Dotty had almost immediately picked up on her handling of the situation.

The phone in Lesley's pocket chirruped with a text message, but she ignored it, considering if it would be unprofessional to answer calls while dealing with a member of the public.

"He must have worn gloves," suggested the now solemn-faced Missus McClafferty.

"Yes, that will be it," agreed Dotty beside her, who then turned to Lesley. "Right, Constable Gold, if you've finished here with our witness?"

That comment pleased the older woman and brought a smile to her face. She was a witness.

Back in the car, Lesley and Dotty waited till they were mobile and out of sight of the twitching curtain before Dotty commented that it was the first time she had seen an arse that size and wondered if it had its own post code. Lesley nearly choked laughing and that set both them off, giggling like schoolgirls.

Paul Hardie bundled Fiona's body into the small cupboard under the stairs and dumped the black bin bag containing the bloodstained clothing and rags on top of her. The door wouldn't close over till he pushed her feet further into the cupboard and exhaling softly, figured it was time for another coffee. He stared at the front door, a thought crossing his mind. He had already decided to get rid of the body that night and knew he could drive the grey coloured Focus into the darkened back lane and bring her body out through the garden, but the lane was overlooked on both sides of his mid-terraced house and from across the houses across the way. However, he chewed at his lower lip, if he parked the Focus outside the front door where the outdated street lighting was poor at best, there was just a few feet of front garden and he only had the short distance from the gate across the narrow pavement to the car in which he could probably dump Fiona's body into the boot within seconds. Anyone passing by would see him, but pedestrians in the small, narrow street were few and rare as they were, would likely be local residents. He stepped to the door and unlocking it, pulled it open with the intention of checking on his idea when to his horror, a marked police car with two female officers passed slowly by. Paul stared wide-eyed at the passenger who briefly glanced at him, before turning away to speak with the driver. Throat suddenly dry, he slammed the door closed and stared at his shaking hand, then startled when the house phone rang in the lounge. He hurried through and lifting the receiver, said "Hello?"

"Mister Hardie, it's Jimmy Dunlop, the janny up at the school, Can I speak to Missus Hardie please?"

"Eh, I'm afraid she's not here at the minute," he replied, acutely conscious his voice sounded nervous. "Can I take a message?" The name sounded familiar to Paul, though he was certain he had never met the man and supposed Fiona had mentioned him during one of her ramblings about the school.

"Aye, I was wondering if she was going to collect the car today." There was a distinct pause, then the gruff voice said "and I was wondering if she's feeling a wee bit better today?"

Paul thought fast, his plan coming to mind. The phone call was a surprise and couldn't have occurred at a more opportune moment. He smiled at his own cleverness and forcing himself to exhale softly, replied, "I don't really know, Mister, eh ….."

"Dunlop, Jimmy Dunlop," replied the gruff voice.

"Yes, of course. I'm sorry Mister Dunlop. I don't think we've met. As for Fiona feeling better, I can't really say, you see, I haven't spoken to her. She's …" he smiled again during his deliberate pause, "she's not at home. In fact, wasn't here when I got home yesterday. Was she unwell?"

"Not really unwell," was the cautious reply, the discomfort now obvious in the older man's voice, "more upset I think. I'm not sure if I'm the person to speak with, Mister Hardie. Missus Hardie wasn't feeling herself and I gave her a run home. Maybe when you see her, I'm sure she'll explain."
It sounded to Paul like the janitor was now anxious to conclude the call.
"I will, Mister Dunlop," he smiled at the handset, "and thanks again for your concern. Oh, and I'll get her to collect the car too."

Jimmy Dunlop replaced the handset and sat back in the old, worn, patched desk chair in his small, cupboard like room and with a calloused hand rubbed at his chin. He had phoned just to check the lassie was okay, knowing that no other bugger would call Missus Hardie. Well, aside from maybe Angela Paterson the classroom assistant. She wasn't a bad wee woman and never failed to stop and say hello. Jimmy grunted. He guessed most of the other teaching staff might also be more friendly, but were too intimidated by the Head Teacher, that besom Miss Jenkins, devil take her, who insisted there was a line between the teachers and the other staff that included not just Jimmy, but the school secretary, the cleaners and the dining room ladies. As he sipped at his tea, his thoughts turned again to the young lassie. Her man had said he hadn't spoken with her yesterday and she wasn't at home when Jimmy called. Curious, he thought that her husband hadn't asked more questions. But there's nothing queerer than folk, he shook his head and thought; "what goes on behind closed doors is between a man and a wife". Ah well, he stood up and finished his tea as once more he prepared himself to tackle the persistent tap that was leaking in the boys toilets.

Chapter 9

Lesley Gold hadn't paid any particular attention to the tall, fair haired man standing by the door who stared wide-eyed at the patrol car as they drove by, her thoughts at that time preoccupied by the text from her mother that informed her that Dad had a relatively restful night. She guessed her Mum knew this because she would have sat by his bed, dozing in the old armchair, but with one ear open as she attentively listened for any change in his breathing. Her phone beeped again with an incoming text message and glancing at the screen, she smiled. Her friend Helen Lang was finishing work earlier than usual that afternoon and suggested if Lesley was free for a girls catch-up, to meet that afternoon at their regular coffee haunt; the Broomhill café. Deftly, she typed in her finishing time and sent the text. Almost immediately, a reply text said Helen would be there and meet her in the café after Lesley finished work.

"You're a popular bugger," said Dotty as she concentrated on negotiating the patrol car round a delivery van.

"Long time pal," smiled Lesley, slipping the phone into the pocket of her uniform cargo pant trousers.

They drove in comfortable silence for a while, Dotty avoiding the main roads and driving south in the general direction of the dock area. "Sometimes get the teenagers and the jakeys hanging about some of the abandoned warehouses down here," she explained as she turned the car into the rutted yard beside the River Clyde. "I don't mind them messing around, but if they bring cheap wine or some blow with them, they might end up falling in the river and that means me having to do a report." She stopped the car outside a large derelict building that showed evident sign of disuse and neglect, glass from the broken windows littering the ground, the main doors lying wide open and hanging off their hinges. "Watch your feet here," cautioned Dotty as she entered the doorway, stepping gingerly round a pile of what looked to Lesley like faeces. Wrinkling her nose, she tip-toed after her partner.

The broken windows permitted daylight to stream through into the building and a quick, cursory search revealed nobody within, though the numerous empty bottles and litter indicated that the place was habitually used. Two old mattresses had been dragged into a dry area and it was evident from the prophylactic debris that activities included more than just drinking and smoking dope.

Dotty shook her head and turned to Lesley. "If I thought my kids got themselves involved in this kind of behaviour, I'd murder them," she said, a turn of phrase peculiar to the loving Glasgow parent.

"Who's got them after school today?" asked Lesley as they walked back to the car.

"My folks bless them," replied Dotty with obvious affection, then knitted her brow and slowly shook her head. "It's not too easy being a single parent and holding down a full time job, particularly with the shifts that we work. I've a pal who's a DS in the CID in headquarters. She's got two kids as well as a husband and often tells me that when she's finished her shift and gets home, that's when her real job begins." She started the engine and slowly drove towards the yard entrance.

"What about Morris?" asked Lesley, her curiosity finally overtaking her, "married or what?"

"Ah therein lies a story," sighed Dotty with some resignation, now on the road and concentrating on her driving, "and I suppose that you'll find out anyway. Morris' wife Susan has MS. She was diagnosed a few years ago, I'm not really sure when, but as the disease progressed she got profoundly worse, had to give up her job and then became housebound. I don't ask, but I think she's now bedridden. Morris is the main carer and spends his time away from work caring for her. No kids, which I suppose on hindsight is a God send for them both. Last night, he actually spent half an hour with us at the club before getting home to let the dayshift nurse away. He's a nice guy, is Morris and you seldom hear him complaining. Comes in to work, does his job and aside from getting his shopping, goes straight home to Susan. The gaffers are aware of course and I know they tolerate if not actually condone his lateness and sudden days off. As you'll probably know from your own experience," she sighed again, "some bosses are better than others." She paused as if gathering her thoughts. "That MS should occur at any time is a tragedy, but particularly when Morris is in the twilight of his career. I'm sure he had plans that didn't include caring for his terminally ill wife." Dotty stopped at a Give Way junction, though there was no traffic and turned to stare at Lesley. "We're a small team at the office and it's kind of an unspoken acceptance among the shift, Lesley, that if Morris is late or has to take time off, we try to cover for him. Like this morning, if you get my meaning."

Lesley knew that she was being tested, that any complaint or reluctance on her part with Dotty would be construed as her non acceptance of the status quo in the shift. She suddenly decided perhaps a little personal insight might go a long way to her being accepted as part of the team. "I'm sure you'll keep this in confidence. My dad has cancer. It's a question of time," she softly replied. "My Mum's at home and cares for him there. So you see, maybe I'm not as hard pressed as Morris, but I think I can understand some of what he's going through. Count me in."

Dotty's eyebrows raised at the admittance and with her left hand, softly squeezed Lesley's arm in understanding, then grinned at her and drove the car away from the junction.

Nothing Frederick Evans departmental manager said or did that morning detracted from Frederick's obvious good humour. To the amusement of his fellow assistants, his smiling "Good morning" caused much comment, ranging from the possibility of Frederick having had a lottery win to some unkind soul who suggested Frederick must have undergone a positive personality transplant. His manager, Mister Hamilton chose to believe it was his pep talk that caused Frederick's sudden change of attitude and wishing to continue the bonhomie, with a whisper suggested Frederick go a little earlier for his break. "Just to beat the queue" Hamilton winked at him. Frederick acknowledged the favour with a smile that was as cold as the hatred he felt for the man. However, arriving at the staff canteen, he was pleased to see that there were few colleagues about. He held his breath when he saw that the canteen assistant, Jennifer Farndale, dressed in a white kitchen coat, a black apron tied round her waist, her hair still tied in a bun and hidden under a light blue coloured hairnet, was behind the hotplate serving breakfast to a sullen faced hosiery assistant. Sliding the plastic tray along the counter, Frederick felt his throat tighten and catching his breath, decided the time was now. As the sullen assistant moved away, Fredrick nodded to Jennifer. "Morning, Miss Farndale, how are you today?" he asked, his voice a little higher than he meant it to be.

Jennifer was surprised and, caught unaware by Frederick's beaming smile, stared back. "Eh, fine thank you," she replied in an equally high voice, surprised that anyone in the sales side of the store even knew her second name. With her ladle in one hand and a plate in the other, she indicated with a shy smile the pans in front of her.

"Oh, eh, two sausages, an egg, some bacon and beans please," smiled Frederick, growing more confident, his throat a little less dry.

As Jennifer piled the plate with his order, he watched as she dropped three sausages onto the plate and looking up saw her conspiratorial grin. Placing the plate on his tray, she moved along with him to the beverages where he ordered a mug of tea. Drawing the tea from the large urn, she placed the mug on his tray then stood behind the counter and ringing the order through the till, had a quick glance about her before she charged him for just the tea. Frederick's eyes opened wide at the blatant and generous gesture as he fumbled the pound coin over to her. Jenny returned some coppers into his hand and, as their eyes met, he said in a rush, "If you've got a minute, might you consider joining me?" With bated breath, he stared at her reddening face till she replied, "I'll get one of the lassies to cover for me so I'll be over in a minute, okay?"

Frederick almost dropped the tray in shock, amazed at his daring and even more so at her acceptance. Trying not to hurry, he made his way through the rapidly filling canteen towards the rear wall and placed down his tray on the Formica topped table, he saw that his hands slightly shook. Exhaling softly, he sat down and arranged the plate and mug of tea on the table, forcing himself not to glance towards the serving area. As he reached for the cutlery within the plastic container in the middle of the table, Jennifer slid into the chair opposite. "I've only got a couple of minutes," she breathlessly told him. He was aware, rather than saw the interest their meeting had provoked, but had eyes only for her and was suddenly lost for words.

As if realising he was speechless, she said "Mister Evans, isn't it?" and was glad that he couldn't see how nervous she was, her hands twisting together under the table.

He nodded, then replied, "Frederick, please, Jennifer."

The seconds seemed like an eternity and turning her head towards the rapidly growing queue at the hotplate, she said, "I'll really need to go. By the way, I usually get called Jenny, just Jenny."

Frederick knew he had seconds to make his decision and taking one of the few chances of his life, breathlessly asked, "Would you go out with me? I mean, like on a date? Please?" Almost immediately, he regretted saying please, knowing it made him sound desperate, but his regret was cut short when grinning, she nodded and replied, "Yes, if you like," then was off, hurrying back to the counter. He watched with a half-smile as her thin frame weaved between the tables then saw the three young women at an adjoining table watching her and glancing at him as they laughed behind their hands. A chill swept through him, his mouth tightened and his knuckles whitened as he gripped the cutlery in each hand. It was then he remembered, he hadn't told Jennifer, or Jenny as she preferred to be called, when or where they would meet to go out.

The policewoman's glance had unsettled Paul Hardie more than he thought and after Jimmy Dunlop's phone call, he sat down on the kitchen seat and idly stirred at the coffee with one hand, unconsciously chewing at the nails of his left hand, a habit he had outgrown in his teenage years as his mind wondered at the horror of the murder and slightly panicked that the police might discover Fiona's body still in the house. He stopped stirring and chewing. Murder, no, not murder. He hadn't meant to kill her. It was an accident, his thoughts screamed at him. But again he knew that was not how the police would view her death. That finally decided him. There was no other option. He would get rid of her body as soon as possible, right away, today even.

Paul slowly sipped at the coffee and thought about removing the body from the house in daylight. He had noticed that most of the regular cars that parked in the street were gone and reasoned most of his neighbours would be at work. In the three and a bit years he and Fiona had resided in the quiet street, Paul had never bothered to socialise with his neighbours and the most contact he had was nodding or grunting a 'Hello' as he arrived home or drove off in his car. Having made that decision, he again considered his idea for disposing of Fiona's body when a memory struck him. Leaping from the seat, he raced upstairs and from the bottom of the cupboard in the spare room, pulled out a worn rucksack. Tossing the rucksack onto the single bed, he rummaged through the long forgotten compasses and maps until he found what he sought; the Ordinance Survey map of the Argyll forest area. He swept the rucksack to the floor and spread the map across the unmade bed, his fingers tracing the road route through Dumbarton towards the forested area of the west coast. As a much younger man, a then besotted Paul had joined a ramblers club for the purpose of pursuing a pretty young woman, but left after a few weeks when it was obvious that the girl had no interest in anything other than a platonic relationship. But during those short, summer weeks, he had participated in several long and, in his mind, boring rural walks through the Argyll forests during which on one occasion, he had fallen behind the others and almost tumbled from the beaten path down a narrow and overgrown ravine. The experience had left him frightened and impacted upon him on how vulnerable his life was, but still he recalled the words of the lead rambler who told him that had Paul fallen down there and become unconscious, nobody would have found him. He slowly sat down on the edge of the bed and lifting the map, stared hard at it. Now, his brow furrowed in concentration. It had been such a long time ago, but if he could only remember where the ravine was.

Lesley Gold and Dotty Turner had little to do that sunny morning. The knicker theft call preceded a 999 domestic disturbance that turned out to be a petulant teenager refusing to attend school with an equally petulant mother demanding her daughter be taken away by the officers and locked up to "teach her a lesson."
"Maybe shove them both into a bloody cell," whispered Dotty, who then with admirable patience explained to the irate woman that this was a parental issue and warning her against further misuse of the emergency service telephone number. The angry woman was not happy with Dotty's decision and as she was closing the door on the officers, threatened she would be taking Dotty's refusal to assist her further with a complaint to her superiors.
"I don't have superiors, madam," responded a poker-faced Dotty, "but if you wish to complain to my supervisors …" at which point the door was slammed in her face.
"Advice given to the householder," Dotty grinned into her radio as striding down the close stairs behind Lesley, she called in the result of the incident to the control room.
"While you're in the area," replied the female voice.
Dotty raised her eyes and noted a further call, this time to assist a social worker at a vulnerable person's home, but on this occasion, the grateful woman wearing the name badge 'Betty' simply needed the strength of the two policewomen to help her lift the stocky built, elderly man from the floor, where he had fallen from his bed.
"Has he any family?" Lesley asked the harassed Betty, guessing the slightly built woman wearing the Social Work issued tabard to be in her late fifties.
"Oh aye," she sniffed, "but why should they bother when the council's care in the community can send someone like me to cook and clean for him," she sniffed with ill-feeling then leaned over to gently pat the bedridden old man's hand. "Deaf as a doorpost," she continued and then turned to the man, her voice rising by several decibels as she almost shouted, "aren't you Willie?" The old man returned her nod with a toothless grin.

"He's not a bad old soul. Fought and survived a war and worked all his days when the shipyards were on the go, down at the Clydebank docks. Lost his wife a few years back, but I didn't really know her. I've been dealing with Willie now for," she half closed her eyes as she tried to recall, "Oh, nearly three years come this September. He's got two sons and a daughter," she nodded to a portrait photograph on the wall beside the open window of a younger Willie and smiling woman, his wife Lesley presumed, who stood behind two teenage boys and a younger girl who stared solemnly at the camera. "The eldest, he'll be in his forties now I think, he's a jakey and lives in some men's hostel in the city centre and only ever visits on Willie's pension days. I collect the pension, but I don't have the authority to stop Willie bunging the bast… excuse me, his son every time the bugger arrives. As for the other son, well, as I say I've been tending to Willie for almost three years and I've never met him. No telephone calls, no cards, nothing."

"What about the daughter," asked a curious Dotty, smiling down at the old man whose eyes were now fluttering as sleep began to overtake him and his eyes slowly closed.

"That'll be the medication," said Betty as she caught Dotty's glance at Willie. "The daughter," she shook her head and folded her arms across her chest. "Lives with her man and weans in some fancy house up in Newton Means. She was here for a visit just after Christmas. Doesn't bring her kids anymore because they don't like the smell in this house," her falsetto whine parodying a child's voice. "She brought him a card, a tie and aftershave," she shook her head. "I mean, look at the poor old soul. A new tie and aftershave?" she repeated, the disgust evident in her voice. "Fuck me, what was she thinking, that he would get himself dolled up and go out on the pull or something? If you ask me, they were gifts her man had no use for. The best thing she could have given her old dad here was her time, but you know how it is these days. Everybody is in a hurry."

Dotty listened to Betty's account of Willie's apparent abandonment by his children and wondered what might have caused such a rift. Dotty's own life experience had taught her there were always two sides to a story.

On the other side of the bed Lesley startled at the bitterness of Betty's words, suspecting there was something in the older woman's life that paralleled Willie's family situation. But the words provoked her thoughts about her own parental situation. Yes, she visited when the shifts permitted, but was she doing enough?

"Planet Earth to Lesley," Dotty's voice broke into her thoughts. Startled, she saw her neighbour nod towards the door.

"Sorry, I was thinking about something," said Lesley as they took their farewell of the smiling, if cynical Betty.

Back at the patrol car, Lesley radioed the result of the call to the control room as Dotty drove off from the tenement before speaking. "Penny for them," she softly said.

Lesley exhaled. "I was just thinking about my parent's, how my Mum is my Dad's full time carer. What life must be like for her, constantly there, watching the man she married, the man she loves," she corrected herself, yet wondering if after all these years that were still true, "slowly waste away and feeling so helpless."

As if on cue, her mobile phone indicated an incoming text message that she saw was from her Mum and simple read: *no change x*.

For Lesley and Dotty, the rest of their shift was relatively uneventful.

Jinksie Peterson sat the mug down on the desk in front of Alex Mason and grinned behind the young Constables back. Alex, both hands supporting his throbbing head, gratefully reached for the steaming hot coffee.

"Drink plenty of water before you go to bed, that's the secret son," Jinksie wisely told him.

"What, then spend half the night up at the loo peeing?" mumbled Alex, exhaling as he sat up and shook his head in a vain attempt to clear it. "I don't understand, I was all right when I woke up this morning," he groaned.

"Aye, maybe so, but remember, you were drinking that Pernod and that always comes back at you later in the day. Well, anyway, it does me," replied Jinksie.

"What comes back at you," repeated Pete Buchanan, striding into the small office at the back of the Uniform bar with a sheaf of papers clutched in his hand. He stopped and stared curiously at Alex. "You still suffering wee man?"

"Aye Sarge, I think that pie and chips I had last night in the club might have been off."

Jinksie turned quickly away, his shoulders shaking with mirth as Buchanan, working hard to keep his face straight, nodded in agreement. "Aye, you're probably right. I don't suppose it was anything to do with they four pints and two or three Pernod's you knocked back. Must've been the pie and chips," he mumbled as he dropped the paper on Jinksie's desk and walked back through to his office. He didn't need to make the young lads life any harder and guessed that Dotty Turner would have dealt with it in her own inimitable way.

Jinksie lifted the handful of papers Buchanan had left for him and was about to leave the Bar to file them when with sudden insight, he turned to the young cop. "Do me a wee favour Alex," he began as he handed the papers to the younger man, "take these reports to the stationary room and see they get properly filed away."

As Alex took hold of the papers, Jinksie retained his grip on them and staring at the young cop, smiled. "Shouldn't take you more than a couple of hours in that wee, comfortable, back of the office room, eh?"

Janice Meikle had made an extra effort with her make-up that morning and after much thought, decided to leave her freshly shampooed blonde hair loose about her shoulders. The crisp white cotton blouse and her best push-up bra revealed a tantalisingly amount of cleavage that she knew showed her breasts off to their best advantage. The black coloured pencil skirt tightened nicely about her bottom and was just long enough to excite the male colleagues she was certain would seize any opportunity to corner her on some pretence or other, just to engage her in conversation. As she strode about the office she knew the men's eyes hungrily followed her as did also, she suspected, at least one of her female colleagues. Janice was on the pull and her whole being cried out of her availability.
In her mind Paul Hardie was a distant memory. Now it was time for Janice to find herself another man.

Chapter 10

Frederick Evans was literally hopping from foot to foot as he waited in the lane a short distance from the rear staff exit of Dawson's, his eyes continuously searching for the departing Jenny Farndale, who he guessed would likely finish her shift about one hour after the canteen closed at two pm. Each time the door pushed open to disgorge one or more employees, he shrunk back into the shadow of the derelict loading bay, fearing it might be his departmental boss, Mister Hamilton or one of his assistant colleagues who must by now have heard he had left early, complaining of a toothache. The last thing Frederick needed was to be caught out in a lie. After what seemed an eternity, the door again pushed open and Jenny, her jacket slung over one arm and a carrier bag held in the other, walked towards him.
Frederick almost didn't recognise her at first, so used to seeing her wrapped in the canteen work clothes, but now here she was coming towards him, her hair down and loosely bound by a black coloured ribbon and wearing a light green sweater and bottle green skirt to below her knees.
He stepped in front of her as she approached and watched her shrink back in fright.
"I'm sorry," he gushed, "I didn't mean to startle you. I was waiting for you," he said, then realised he was speaking too quickly and forced himself to slow down. "You said you would go out with me but we didn't make any arrangements."

She stared wordlessly at him, but then to his relief, smiled. "I wasn't sure if you were serious Mister … I mean, Frederick. Sometimes, the guys in there," she nodded back to the store with her head, "can take the mickey, you know? Pretend they want to take me out and then they don't turn up."

His eyes narrowed. "They have done that to you?"

"Oh aye, plenty of times," she smiled shyly, "you think by now at my age I'd have learned my lesson."

"And what age are you," he smilingly asked, but still keen to know and gallantly added, "mid twenties?"

Jenny blushed and deciding to knock off a couple of years, replied, "Early thirties actually."

Frederick smiled with surprise, glancing at her worn face and thinking she must be nearer forty, perhaps forty-two. Over her shoulder he could see the door being pushed open and more staff emerging into the lane.

"Look, can we maybe go somewhere, get a coffee or something?" he asked, desperate now to move with her out of the path of the approaching curious faces and knowing the gossip that would result from their meeting. He wasn't prepared for the excitement in her eyes and as she nodded, he hurriedly stepped towards her and taking her bag from her arm, almost rushed her from the lane into the bright sunlight and towards Argyle Street. He risked a glance back into the lane, relieved to see that the approaching staff members didn't seem to be paying any particular attention to them.

His arm at her elbow, he walked Jenny through the crowd towards Union Street where he knew of a small restaurant located there, one flight up in a tenement building. Frederick risked a glance at her as she strode beside him and saw her for the first time as she was. She seemed to be a little older than he had first thought and even wearing flat shoes, judging her to be an inch taller than his five feet six. He hadn't before noticed her angular nose or how lank her dark brown hair seemed. However, he swallowed hard, none of these things really mattered because he, Frederick Evans, was taking a woman for a coffee. Jenny turned and stared at him, her pleasure at his presence so very evident in her smile. So engrossed was she that she failed to notice the tall, heavy-set man who bundled into her and almost knocked her thin frame flying onto the pavement. Frederick instinctively reached to catch her before she tumbled to the ground and without thinking, instinctively shouted after the man, "Kindly watch where you're going!"

The man stopped and turned, seeing the slightly built wee dick that shouted at him helping the skinny bird who had bumped into him and fists clenched, took a step towards them.

Wide eyed with fear, Frederick's first instinct was to run, get away as fast as his legs would carry him, but in reaching for Jenny she had seized hold of his arm and so there he stood, transfixed by the hatred in the large man's eyes.

As the man advanced towards them he glanced upwards into Union Street behind the wee dick and the skinny bird and saw a police patrol car in the line of traffic that slowly edged towards the junction of Argyle Street. He hesitated, knowing that if he battered the wee shite there and then, he was definitely going to get lifted and the last thing he needed was another appearance at court. Slowly he let his fists drop to his side and with one further growl, turned about and continued on his way.

Frederick, whose whole, terrified attention was taken by the large man, had no idea the police car had slowly cruised past and speechless, could only stare at the retreating man's back. Jenny, still tightly gripping his arm and now shaking with fright turned to stare at her hero. Never before had a man, any man, stood up for her. On the odd occasion, the very odd occasion she would wryly recall, when a man had taken her anywhere, it was usually for a drink in some out of the way shitty wee pub then back to his place for a quickie and then taxi fare as he saw her to the door. Well, sometimes the taxi fare, but not always and never was she asked on a second date. But now this, she continued to stare at Frederick. This man had not only stood up for her, but nearly got into a fistfight with a big, ugly bastard?

Her rapidly beating heart almost bursting with pride, Jenny was overwhelmed with immediate affection for Frederick and she inwardly thought but for the curious stares of the passers-by and had he demanded it of her, she would gladly have lain down and dropped her knickers for him right there and then. Had she but known, her hero could hardly speak, so scared had he been and wordlessly as he tried to control his shaking legs led her towards the close and the restaurant situated on the first floor.

Lesley Gold, a light blue nylon windproof jacket over her uniform polo shirt, steered her car into a vacant space in the small car park that served the row of shops in Broomhill Road. The cafe located in the corner was a popular afternoon drop-in for women and boasted a large selection of cakes and delicacies to complement the variety of foreign coffees it served.

As her eyes adjusted from the bright sunlight, she saw her long time friend Helen Lang sitting at a rear table and waving, weaved her way between tables to join her. As always, Helen looked the picture of health, her make-up expertly applied, thick auburn hair to her collar neatly trimmed. Apparently she also had come from work for Lesley saw she wore a cerise coloured blouse and two-piece skirted, deep red coloured business suit. The young waiter staring at Helen blushed when Lesley smiled at him as she passed by. Sitting down, she saw Helen had already ordered a pot of coffee and a selection of cakes on a stand sat in the middle of the table.

 "Coffee's fine, missus," she smiled at her friend, "I've started my new diet and fitness regime as of this morning."

Helen raised her eyebrows. "What brought this one? New man or are you just wanting to show that selfish git that you don't need him?"

"Nobody new, but I took a good hard look at myself and reckon I could do with losing more than a few pounds."

"Well, I won't lie to you. I think you're talking about maybe a stone, Lesley. Those love handles of yours are becoming a wee bit too obvious."

Lesley grinned and shook her head. Working as an office junior during her University years in the Insurance firm where Helen was then employed as a supervisor and treated Lesley almost as a daughter, though Helen was seventeen years her senior, the older woman had taken Lesley under her wing, counselled and advised her through the four years she was with the firm. Since then and despite the age gap, they had become firm friends and continued to meet when the opportunity arose and only her mother or Helen Lang would get away with a comment like that, she thought to herself.

"Well, you're right of course," she poured milk for them both into the china cups and watched enviously as Helen, whose figure never seemed to change from svelte, selected a particularly creamy cake from the display.

"How's your Dad?"

"I got an update text from my Mum a couple of hours ago," replied Lesley. "He's holding his own, but there's no doubt it's a question of time. It's Mum I'm really worried about. I had a call this morning, a social worker attending to an elderly man and it kind of brought it home to me that my Mum doesn't have the kind of back-up she deserves."

"That's not fair, Lesley," Helen gently scolded. "We both know that you get over there as often as you can. I'm certain Peggy realises that. My God girl, you're holding down a full time job and you're working shifts. When you're not out doing your job, you're shopping for Peggy or sitting with Thomas to let her get some rest. Don't be too hard on yourself," she reached over to pat Lesley's hand. "I'm absolutely certain your Mum appreciates everything that you do for her and your Dad."

A quiet silence fell between them for a moment and then Helen asked, "Heard from Mike?"

"Had a couple of text messages asking me to phone him, but I haven't bothered," she said. "To be honest, I'm not sure if I should or not."

"Your decision," responded Helen, but the indifferent tone of her voice made Lesley peer at her.

"What?"

"Nothing," replied Helen, but that one word convinced Lesley that Helen was desperate to give her opinion.

"Okay, out with it," coaxed Lesley.

"Well, it's not that I would ever interfere," but got no further when Lesley replied, "That'll be a first then."

Helen glared at her, but without malice, for she didn't want to hurt this young woman of whom she was so extraordinarily fond. "I didn't like him, never did. So there, over and done with."
Lesley shrugged and replied with downcast eyes, "Not that I ever guessed, the way you always gave him the evil eye."
"I never did such thing," protested Helen.
"Don't lie, you wicked bugger," Lesley suddenly grinned, "I saw the way you stared at him. If looks could kill, he would have curled up and died each time you saw him."
"Well, admittedly, maybe I had my reservations," responded Helen, slicing with a small fork through the cream cake and deliberately taunting Lesley as with a pink tongue, she licked at it and then purred like a cat.
Lesley ignored the taunt and said, "So why didn't you say anything to me, at least give me a hint about what you felt about him?"
Helen paused, searching for the right words. "It was a hard decision. Andy and I could see that you seemed almost besotted with him and we didn't want to burst your bubble." She raised her hands to quell Lesley's protest and continued. "Yes, I know, we go back a long way and I would never say or do anything to hurt your feelings, but we spoke about it and decided that it would be better if you found out about Mike in your own good time."
"But what if I hadn't found him out, Helen, what then?"
"Believe me kid, there was no way Andy and I were about to let you walk down an aisle with that guy, even if it meant risking our friendship. You know how much we both value you, how much I value you," she stressed as she stared with affection at Lesley. "I wouldn't let you ruin you life with a guy that I didn't trust or think was right for you."
"Oh Helen," Lesley sat back with a half smile on her face, "how could you possibly know what he was like?"
Helen chewed at her lower lip, her brow furrowed and decided they'd gone this far, so the truth would no longer hurt her closest friend. "Do you remember the second time Andy and I met with you and Mike, at the small restaurant at the bottom of Byres Road?"
Lesley nodded and experienced a sudden empty feeling in the pit of her stomach.
"Well, you were at the loo while Andy was up at the back with the waiter, settling the bill when Mike passed me a scrap of paper with his mobile number on it. I'm so sorry, Lesley. I should have told you sooner, but I just didn't want you to think …"
Lesley shook her head, realising the position Helen must have found herself in and softly exhaled. "It's not your fault Helen and yes," she wagged a finger at her, "you should have told me."

They sat in silence for a few seconds and then curiosity got the better of Lesley who asked, "What did Andy say, about the phone number thing I mean?"

Helen smiled. "You know what he's like. Nice guy that he is, he has a hell of a temper when he's roused. That's why we kept finding excuses to cancel when you were so keen to go out on another foursome. Took me all my time to stop him from calling you because he was determined you ditch Mike and right away."

That's Andy, thought Lesley, always the big brother looking out for me. "Well, Missus Lang," she said, "both you and my shining knight will be pleased to know that I have absolutely no intention of getting back with Mike. That's over. He let me down and proved he's untrustworthy. My God," she slapped at her forehead and exclaimed as if having a sudden revelation, "the floosie I caught him with. That was me, except when he was with his wife, I was the floosie."

Helen shrugged her shoulders as if no further words were necessary. Lesley had gotten the message. Mike Duffy was a dead end and she was better off without him.

"So," Helen said, her eyes sparkling with mischief as she leaned forward, her elbows on the table and her hands cradling her chin, "this diet and weight training thing. What's the real reason then?"

Paul Hardie prepared himself. The car was parked up right outside the front door and he had dressed in old jeans, a shirt that frayed at the collar and the walking boots that thankfully, he had never disposed of. His mouth was dry and his hands shook slightly and already he could feel the damp patches under his arms as he considered what he was about to do. For the umpteenth time, he sneaked a look from the upstairs bedroom window to the street outside, his eyes searching for any sign of the police or anyone who was paying a particular interest in his house. Blowing through his mouth, he went down stairs and opening the cupboard door, stared at the pathetic bundle that was once his wife, the woman he had married and promised to love and cherish. But Paul was beyond sentiment and now the bundle simply represented a threat to his liberty. He decided that the first thing he would carry out would be the bag with the clothing and rags. If anyone was to see him, he hoped they would simply dismiss his activity as disposing of some old rubbish. He almost grinned at that thought, that Fiona was some rubbish he was getting rid of so that he might again begin his life.

He lifted the bag from on top of Fiona's body and unlocking the front door, took a breath as he pulled it open. Hurriedly, his head down, he walked the few short paces to the boot of the Focus and with fingers shaking, unlocked the boot and raised the lid. He shoved the bag to the corner and almost closed the lid before remembering he would be better leaving it open, that he'd be carrying Fiona's body and it might be awkward getting the boot lid raised again.

Risking a glance about him and seeing nobody in the street, he returned to the house and from the cupboard, pulled out her body. Paul had never before noticed the nail at the bottom of the door jamb that protruded slightly from the frame. As he pulled at the plastic bag that enwrapped her body, the bag snagged on the nail and ripped at the side of the bag, causing Fiona's lifeless arm to flop out onto the floor. Paul squealed in fright and letting go of the bag, fell backwards against the opposite wall, striking his head with such force he saw stars. He sat for a few seconds, staring with horror at her arm then turned his head to the large rectangle of light that shone through the wide and open doorway. With haste, he scrambled to his feet and with disgust shoved her arm back through the tear into the bag. Unconsciously, he rapidly wiped both his hands down the side of his jeans as though the very touch of his dead wife had somehow contaminated him.

Taking a deep breath and careful of the tear, he lifted her body, surprised at how light she felt, then almost immediately the body began to slip from his grasp to the floor when he found it difficult to hold onto the shiny plastic. Now bent over, he folded his arms round her slim frame and with her body tucked under his right arm, awkwardly side-stepped along the narrow corridor towards the door. A quick glance indicated the street seemed to be clear and with more difficulty than he had imagined, he shuffled over to the car and then using both hands, dumped the body into the boot, reached up and slammed down the lid. Eyes wide, he slowly released his breath in a long wheeze and again risked a glance about him but still, the street seemed deserted of neighbours.

Though he could not know, Paul had been fortunate for nobody had seen him carry his dead wife's body to the car.

Frederick Evans, now calmed after his confrontation with the large man, was actually relishing the adulation being poured on him by the wide-eyed and adoring Jenny. The remains of the tea and cake sat before them while the blank-faced waitress hovered nearby, thinking that the price of a pot of tea and a couple of scones hardly merited taking up the use of a table for nearly an hour and particularly as the evening rush was about to start.

"Honestly, I don't know what would have happened to me if you hadn't been there Frederick," simpered Jenny, one hand at her throat, her eyes aglow as she stared with hero worship at her new beau.

"Well," he adopted an air of modesty, "sometimes these people need to be put in their place. I mean, if people like me don't stand up to them, they'll just get away with it."

In the short time since Frederick almost wet himself with fear, he had in his mind become the champion of all women, convincing himself that had the large man actually come within arms length, Frederick might have been forced to punch him and conveniently forgetting the only violence Frederick had ever before encountered was when being victimised at school, with the emphasis being on him as the victim.

"Well, I just think you are absolutely marvellous," Jenny gushed with a smile, making a huge effort to appear demure and succeeding only in highlighting the piece of raisin that had lodged in the lower part of her tombstone like teeth.

Frederick smiled back and almost pointed out the offending piece of fruit, but with unaccustomed gallantry, decided that he could overlook the issue. As he returned Jenny's smile, it occurred to him that she seemed somehow different from his memory of her behind the hotplate; a little … he groped for the words, more common than perhaps he had anticipated. Certainly, having now learned she was at thirty-seven years, older than he had first thought and her skin in the daylight was not as smooth as he imagined. Her hair too seemed a little greasy, but he finally admitted to himself, that was likely the result of working daily in the canteen. Nevertheless, casting a furtive glance at her breasts, they did seem to be slightly larger than her frame suggested and he felt himself grow erect at the thought of exploring them in the privacy of his room.

"Frederick," she grinned at him, wondering why he was lost in thought, "I was saying maybe we could go to the movies or for a drink or something? Only if you like, of course," she added, the tension in her chest almost hurting as she silently prayed and willed him to say yes.

"Will you be wanting anything else, then?" asked the waitress, having now decided it was time to move these two love-birds on and let her get on with clearing the table.

"Eh, no, thank you," replied Frederick, then raising his eyebrows, said to Jenny, "Shall we go?" as he stood up from the seat and reached behind for his jacket.

Jenny nodded, her smile fixed on her face and stomach churning, conscious he hadn't replied to her question. She also reached behind her chair for her jacket and as she turned back and stood up, Frederick took the jacket from her and held it wide to permit her to slip her arms into the sleeves.

Jenny was taken aback. Never before had a man held her jacket for her. Her surprise was compounded when Frederick said, "The movies, yes, if you like. Would tonight be too soon?"

She could hardly reply, the happiness sweeping through her and felt tears stinging at the back of her eyes. He wanted to see her again! She couldn't trust herself to speak and nodded, her eagerness shining from her.

"I never thought to ask, where is it you reside; live I mean?" he smiled at her enthusiasm.

"Nitshill, Pinmore Street, with my mum," she quickly replied, conscious she sounded too eager, but not really caring. After all, she had a date, a real date and with a man that liked her for herself; a man that had protected her. A warm feeling engulfed her and she had to physically refrain from throwing her arms about this smaller, skinny wee man and giving him the biggest hug ever.

"Right," said Frederick in an authoritative voice, enjoying the proprietorial sensation of taking charge, "let's get you to your bus and we'll discuss where we're going tonight," he said, taking her hand in his, the first time he had ever done so as they made their way to the exit.

And not even a fucking tip, scowled the waitress at their back.

Chapter 11

Dotty Turner shrugged off her uniform polo shirt and stepping out of the cargo pants, stood in the bedroom of her home dressed only in her bra, pants and thick, navy blue socks. She could hear her Dad in the kitchen downstairs, making her a coffee as he listened and hummed along to Rod Stewart playing loudly on the radio. She grinned. The old bugger wasn't aware he was getting deaf and refused to admit that the TV and radio were being played louder than ever each day. She sat on the edge of the bed, pleased for the few minutes she had to herself. She considered a shower, but decided to wait till her Mum returned from the school with the kids and once they were settled in doing their homework and her parents gone, she'd draw herself a bath and have a good soak before getting the evening meal ready. Her folks were off tonight to a show at the King's Theatre, so wouldn't be hanging about for their supper. Idly, she rubbed a hand across her stomach, pleased that at thirty-seven and after two kids, it was still reasonably taut. She stood and faced towards the wardrobe mirror and critically examined her body. At five foot four inches tall in her stocking soles, she reckoned she didn't have such a bad figure. Using both hands, she run her fingers through her short, blonde hair and with her hands on her head, turned left and right, then posed, staring at her body in the full length mirror. She smiled self-consciously at her reflection and knew that while she was still an attractive woman, there had been nobody in her life since Jim left. It wasn't that she hadn't been made a few offers, but usually when it was mentioned there was baggage in the shape of two kids, that soon scared off the would-be suitors and Dotty wasn't into any quick 'wham-bam-thank-you-ma'am' type relationship. One night stands might be all right for some, but not her. She reached towards the mirror, her thoughts in a jumble as with her forefinger, she stared and gently traced the outline of her face, wondering again where her life was going. There was one man she liked, no, not liked. Desired, wanted; perhaps even needed, but the admittance of even that simple fact caused her face to burn with an embarrassing shame and even in her wildest dreams she knew it wouldn't happen. She swallowed hard and reached into the cupboard for a clean tracksuit top and trousers as her father loudly called from downstairs that her coffee was ready.

Lesley Gold was just entering the close when her phone chirruped with a text message. She stopped dead and flipping over the cover, saw it was from Mike Duffy and read: *last chance, your choice*. Angrily, she deleted the message and in a fit of *pique*, opened her Contacts list and deleted Mike's name and number, wondering why she hadn't already done so. Wearily she climbed the stairs to her flat to prepare an overnight bag and collect a clean uniform for tomorrow's late shift. This evening, she had decided, her Mum and Lesley would share a take-away Chinese meal and work out a rota between them for sitting through the night with her father, knowing that it might enable her mother to get at least some sleep.

The old janitor Jimmy Dunlop walked quietly along the corridor, listening to the ranting from the head teacher Miss Jenkins as passing her office, he heard her tear a strip off one of her teaching staff. Behind him, he heard the door being snatched open and the teacher literally run from the office, her head down as she strode quickly by him, the unshed tears threatening to explode from her and ignoring his sympathetic face. He heard Miss Jenkins door close with a bang and continued towards his own little pokey office, shaking his head at the injustice that allowed a bully like Jenkins to lord it over others. His thoughts turned again to the wee lassie who had failed to turn up today, Missus Hardie. Such a quiet and lovely wee girl, he inwardly smiled; timid almost and so unsuited to working under someone like Jenkins. It occurred to him that maybe he might give her a wee phone, but when he had called this morning, her husband hadn't heard from her. Curious, he had thought then and hoped nothing was amiss. Opening his office door, he stared at the telephone. Shaking his head, he knew it would be viewed as inappropriate that he, the janitor, was making telephone calls to a member of the teaching staff and, his resolve failing him, deciding against his better judgement that it had better be left to the head teacher to deal with.

Paul Hardie drove with a knot in his stomach, the start of a tension headache and knuckle's white as they grasped the steering wheel. He regretted not taking the time to have a pee before he left the house and squirmed with discomfort in his seat. Now on Dumbarton Road, he drove with caution, maintaining a speed that kept the Focus slightly below the limit for the road and his eyes on the mirrors, constantly alert for any presence of police vehicles. He deliberately switched the radio off so as not to be distracted and scanned the road ahead for anywhere he might safely stop to relieve the pressure on his bladder. Anywhere he would not be seen and where the car would be within his sight.

A lay-by loomed ahead and seemed to be surrounded by trees, but as he gently braked and neared the lay-by, he cursed, seeing the group of young people who laughing, surrounded the old, hand painted and worn-out Volkswagen Beetle type people carrier. With a fist, he pressed at his lower stomach, trying to stave off the pain from his bladder. He hadn't realised that in his urgency to get to a loo, he had inadvertently increased his speed. He glanced in the rear view mirror and to his horror, saw some distance behind him, a flashing blue light. His eyes glanced down and he saw that he was travelling almost ten mile faster than the permitted speed limit and out loud, said "Oh God, oh God, oh God" over and over again. Again, he glanced into the rear view mirror and saw the vehicles behind him puling over to allow the ambulance …. He quickly glanced again. A fucking ambulance, he almost cried out with relief, the pain in his bladder for now forgotten. As the emergency vehicle sped past him, he wiped his brow, unaware he had been sweating and opened both his and the front passenger windows to allow a stream of cold air to sweep through the stuffy interior of the car. He laughed out loud, believing that good fortune was on his side, but still he slowed the car till it was under the speed limit and continued to the area that he had marked on the map lying beside him on the passenger seat.

Almost without realising, he was passing the turning for Renton and suddenly aware that still travelling on the A82, he was less than half an hour from his destination. Mouth dry, he forced himself to continuously check his rear view mirror, now obsessed with the thought that somehow the police had discovered his secret and were covertly following him. He was, he knew, being stupid, that there was no way the police could know what he did, but still the paranoia persisted. The lights of a speeding car appeared in the mirror and his heart sank, but as it approached he saw it to be without blue lights and passing, that it was an old style Volvo estate car driven by a middle-aged woman, her concentration on the road as she overtook him at speed. He passed the Balloch junction and knew the turning onto the B831 could not be too far ahead, unconsciously slowing the car as though anticipating the turn-off.

Frederick Evans's early arrival home flustered his elderly mother who patting at the fine mesh net covering her hair, apologised that his dinner wasn't ready. In fact, she added mournfully, she had not even begun to prepare his evening meal.

Waving her away with good humour and heading up the narrow starts, he shouted at her retreating back that he needed a clean shirt ironed for that evening, adding almost as a boast that he was going out on a date.

His mother stopped dead and slowly turned, a slow smile breaking out on her wrinkled face as his words suddenly struck her. He was going out on a date? She shook her head to assure herself she had heard clearly and turned with a smile to first prepare his meal, but then doubt crossed her mind and an icy chill swept through her old bones as the once more the forbidden thought occurred to her that it might not be with a woman.

Blissfully unaware of his mother's doubts as to his gender choice Frederick mounted the stairs to his bedroom two at a time, feeling rejuvenated after his afternoon tea with Jenny, but not that rejuvenated as he was wheezing by the time he reached the top landing. Closing the door behind him, he took the precaution of locking it, hastily pulling off his jacket and loosening his tie in his eagerness to again view the film he had recorded the previous evening on his camera phone. As the laptop powered up, he impatiently drummed his fingers on the desktop, thinking again of his meeting with Jenny. She would never now how frightened he had been by the large man's threatening behaviour or his overwhelming urge to run, to escape regardless of what happened to her. No, he smiled; he would happily continue to play the hero. Typing in his password, he watched the screen come alive, but thought of Jenny sitting in front of him at the café. Granted, she wasn't the raving beauty his imagination had conjured up from the distance in the canteen, but the thought of her rounded breasts excited him and he believed, with a little encouragement, she would be a very compliant woman. Turning his head, he glanced about him at the room, as if seeing for the first time the single bed and faded wallpaper, the old but serviceable dining chair, the solid, but outdated wardrobe and family portraits of long dead relatives. He sighed, for it was hardly an inviting room to bring her back to. She had said she lived with her mother and he wondered at her own accommodation, guessing that she would likely have her own room. But would he feel comfortable, would he even feel safe, carrying out his plans for her in someone else's home? She told him she lived in Nitshill, but he had no idea where that was, other than it was located somewhere south of the River Clyde. They had agreed to meet that evening outside the multiplex cinema at the top of West Nile Street and choose the film together, but he already knew what he wanted to see and had little doubt she could easily be persuaded to agree.

He turned his attention to the laptop and clicked on the file he wanted, typing in the password that opened it for him. Again, he watched the shaky images come to life and turned the volume higher to hear the argument. Mouth open and eyes wide, he watched the man strike the woman, his wife presumably and her fall to the floor and striking her head on the hearth. Then the man's half-hearted attempts to resuscitate the woman and his failure to get her to respond. The film ended abruptly and Frederick again considered what he had, his knowledge of the assault and he was still undecided how he might make use of the film. But that was for another day. Tonight he had a date and eagerly looked forward to the promises it held.

Lesley arrived at her parents' house and locking the car behind her, prepared herself for an argument with her mother. Having lived most of her life in the semi-bungalow, she looked about her and thought that Bredisholm Terrace hadn't changed much in the few years she had been gone, though Baillieston as a district had thrived and continued to expand. As Lesley pushed through the garden gate, the elderly next door neighbour gave a cheery wave from her window to the young policewoman. Lesley smiled back and turning saw her mother standing in the open doorway, arms folded across her chest and a scowl on her normally pleasant face.
"I hope that's laundry in that bag, Lesley Gold," she said, staring from the holdall to her daughter, "and you're not thinking about coming home to live, because frankly, I'm the alpha female in this house and I won't tolerate competition."
Lesley grinned as her mother stood aside to let her pass, then dropping her bag softly onto the carpeted hallway floor, turned to give her a hug. "How's he doing?" she asked.
"Same old, same old," responded her mother with a sad smile. "Come away in and I'll get the kettle boiled. Have you had any dinner yet?"
"No and I hope you haven't either, because I'm treating us to a Chinese tonight. Low calorie of course," she winked.
"So, what's in the bag then?"
"Thought I'd stay over, I could use the company. Is he awake?" she continued before her mother could protest.
But Peggy Gold knew her daughter better than Lesley did herself and slowly shaking her head, replied, "There's really no need, hen. I've got it under control and besides, you've got your work in the morning."
"Well, on that point I'm actually late shift, so it's a four in the afternoon till two in the morning, so there's no early rise, Mum. I'm thinking that we can share the nightshift sitting with dad, then I'll lie in late and you can get me up in plenty of time for the work and maybe even plan it so that I'm here at least one night a week, if that's okay with you?"
Peggy Gold bit at her lower lip as the tears welled up within her. Nobody could possibly know how tired she was, the constant worry and lack of sleep that threatened to take her sanity, let alone her health. She turned away,

embarrassed at her show of emotion only to feel her daughter's arms wrap themselves round her waist and Lesley's head lie against the back of her shoulder. She placed both her hands on top of Lesley's and they stood like that for a few minutes; mother and daughter united by a pending grief.
"Right then," Peggy said, sniffing as she wiped at her eyes, "away in and see your father and I'll look out the takeaway menu."
Lesley gave her mother's shoulder a reassuring squeeze and made her way into the dimly lit bedroom. Her father lay on his back, gently snoring. She quietly sat in the upright chair beside the bed and watched as occasionally, his right hand twitched and she guessed this was a reaction to a pain that eluded the many drugs his body endured. As she sat there, Lesley heard him moan softly and whether it was the atmosphere in the room or simply that she felt so helpless, watching her father slowly die or the betrayal of the man she thought loved her, she couldn't tell, but without realising, she was slowly rocking back and forth, her arms wrapped round her body and tears streaming down her cheeks.
Wiping her arms on the sleeve of her sweeter, she stood up and leaning over, kissed her father on his forehead. Thomas didn't stir at his daughter's touch and as quietly as she had entered, she left the room, leaving the door slightly ajar.
Placing the phone back on the cradle, Peggy had ordered food for them both and Lesley's holdall was now lying on the bed in the small back room that was formerly occupied by her sister Linda, before she married and moved out. Peggy now occupied the slightly larger second bedroom that had once been Lesley's and had done so for the several months since Thomas had been returned from the hospital as a terminal patient. The compassion shown by the McMillan Nurses who continued to visit, had been tremendous and the offer to place her husband in a hospice, where Peggy knew the care was second to none, was made with kindness and consideration for her own well-being. However, well meant as it was, she had insisted that Thomas come home to die and his primary care would be hers. Lesley respected her mother's decision, but it didn't stop her worrying about her.
While Peggy prepared the small kitchen table to receive their food, Lesley unpacked her uniform and nightclothes, grateful that her Mum had not made an issue of her tears, but simply allowed her to carry on and wash her face as though nothing were amiss. When she returned to the kitchen she saw Peggy standing by the kitchen window that faced onto the roadway, watching for the food delivery to head the driver off before the bell was rung and disturbed her husband.

Parked in a lay-by next to a wooded area on the B832 and not far from the B831, Paul Hardie checked the map again and stared out into the green

Argyll hills. It seemed that he'd been driving around now for hours, checking and rechecking the map and all the time conscious of the day slipping away from him. The last thing he needed was a curious police officer driving past and wondering why he was driving back and forth along the same route. He slammed his fist against the steering wheel in frustration, wincing as it struck the unforgiving moulded plastic. There was nothing else for it. He knew now he had been naive, that after all these years trying to find the path from the roadway that in turn led to the ravine, was foolhardy. Like or it not, he had to dump Fiona's body and soon, before the very thing he dreaded occurred; a passing patrol car. He leaned under the driver's panelling and pulling the lever, got out of the car and raised the bonnet. He ducked his head under as though inspecting the engine which gave him the opportunity to search the road to the front and behind, but right then there was no sign of any other vehicles. He dropped the bonnet and getting back into the car, drove the short distance to where he had seen a track turning off the main road and into the forest. Still, there were no other cars and he held his breath, fervently hoping his luck would hold.

The twisting track was more suited to four by four vehicles and the Focus bumped across the compacted, but rutted earth. The further he drove between the trees, the darker it got and as the track narrowed, he realised there was no way he could reverse the car the distance he had driven without colliding with something and would need to continue driving till he found some kind of turning point. As a hundred metres became two, then three hundred, an increasing sense of panic overtook him that he would get stuck, but just as he decided to stop, the sun shone through the tree line into a glade with a wide turning circle. Paul breathed a sigh of relief and switched off the engine. He wound down his window and listened, but apart from some birds, there was no noise. Gingerly, he stepped from the Focus and slowly and quietly, closed the door over. He stood still and again listened, but all he could hear, or more rightly, imagine he could hear was the thump of his heart. At the rear of the car, he popped open the boot lid and with an effort, pulled, then lifted Fiona's body from within and slung it fireman style across his left shoulder. Bending his knees, he crouched as he reached in then felt the plastic of the bin bags slide on his shoulder and with both hands grabbed at Fiona's body to gain a better grip. Again, he crouched and succeeded in pulling the bag with the soiled clothes towards him. Standing upright, he began to walk into the woods then stopping and turning, realised that no matter what direction he took, he had to negotiate with the body and the bag through the thick pine forest. Taking a deep breath, he started out and within a few metres, was winding round trees, stepping over logs and was already breathless. The light faded quickly as the canopy of branches above him formed an umbrella and he felt an uneasy sense of claustrophobic dread, as though the very forest

were watching him. He turned to look at the car to measure how far he had come and was disappointed to realise that through the trees, the car seemed to be no more than twenty or thirty metres away. If only he had brought a shovel, he thought, shaking his head at his lack of foresight.
Then he saw it, an uprooted tree that when falling, had displaced a lengthy grave-like trench where the roots had been torn from the soft earth before coming to rest against a sturdier trunk. He made his way across to the trench and dropping the bag to the ground, with an effort and almost gentleness, awkwardly knelt down and laid Fiona's body in the earth, then pulled the clothing bag towards him and placed it down at her feet. That done, he straightened up and searched for something to scoop the loose earth over them both, but finding nothing suitable, resorted to kneeling down and dragging the dirt across with his bare hands. As satisfied as he could be and still remonstrating with himself over his stupidity in not bringing a shovel, he kicked at the places where the earth had been disturbed and, as he had seen done in the movies, with a leafy branch swept the area left and right to hide any trace of the disturbed earth.
Paul threw the branch away and rubbing his hands free of dirt, exhaled loudly and headed back towards the Focus without a backward glance.

Frederick Evans had made a decision that tonight he would drive his father's old Ford Fiesta motor car into the city and after the movies, depending on how things went with Jenny he would consider offering to drive her home. That would probably impress her he smiled to himself as he knotted the tie and inspected himself in the bathroom mirror. Using the flat of his hand, he slicked down a rogue few hairs and satisfied, checked his wristwatch. Half an hour before he was to meet Jenny, then a thought struck him. What if she wants sex on the first night? Should he have bought some condoms? He sat heavily down on the closed toilet lid, a sudden apprehension seeping through him. The reality was that he had never actually done it. He swallowed hard, reluctant to admit that when it came to women and their needs, he was completely out of his depth. Of course, he knew what to do and all the pornographic magazines he had read and sex videos he had watched were more than enough to teach him the basics and after all, most women were gagging for it anyway. So why should Jenny be any different? Maybe after today he was on, what was it that young lad he had overhead last week in the canteen called it? A promise, the young reprobate had called it. Yes that was it, a promise. He glanced again at his watch wondering if he had time to call in at the supermarket on the way to the city and get some condoms, just in case. He stood up and decided he had better hurry.

Frederick found a parking space near the small supermarket among the row of shops on Great Western Road just along from the junction at Byres Road and locking the old car, hurried between the traffic, ignoring the irate motorist who angrily sounded his horn at the idiot that caused him to brake sharply.

Panting slightly, he pushed open the door and made straight for the shelf displaying the pharmacy and grooming items. Nervously, he pretended to study the rows of Paracetamol and stomach ailment remedies, confused by the different type of condoms that were displayed and then grabbed at a packet of ten. Face burning with embarrassment, he casually laid the packet down on the counter in front of the teenage girl who, intent on reading the magazine in front of her, hardly glanced at the condoms as she passed them across the electronic reader and said, "Eight pounds fifty. Will that be cash or card?"

"Eh, cash," replied Frederick, handing over a ten pound note and anxious to be gone, suddenly aware of the elderly woman who had mysteriously appeared behind him and who curiously looked over his shoulder.

The girl handed him his change and jerked back with surprise when he almost snatched the paper bag containing the condoms from her hand. Hurrying back across the road, he unaccountably found himself smiling at his own embarrassment. In the car, he opened the pack and switched on the interior light to read the instructions, annoyed at the small print and inwardly admitting it was time he purchased some reading glasses. However, it seemed to Frederick the wearing of a condom seemed to be pretty straight-forward and he was satisfied that he would easily cope, when the time came. After all, he thought, how hard could it be and then again smiled at his inadvertent pun, though it did occur to him that as there were ten condoms, maybe he should practise putting one on. He glanced about him, realising almost immediately that sitting in his car in Great Western Road perhaps wasn't the ideal location to experiment. The dashboard clock reminded him he was cutting it fine to meet Jenny and starting the engine, jerked the car out of the parking space. Frederick wasn't a confident driver and had blithely learned to ignore the impatience of other drivers who were often frustrated by strict observance of the road speed and his lack of road manners, his argument being that after all, he paid his road tax so he was just as entitled to use the road as anyone else. Arriving in Renfrew Street, fortune again smiled and he saw a car draw out and drive off from the rear of a line of parking spaces, permitting him to ease the Fiesta in without the need to parallel park the car; his driving nightmare. Again he glanced at the dashboard clock and saw that he was a few minutes late for his rendeavous. Making his way toward the cinema complex, the figure in the light coloured coat turned and waved towards him, the relief on

Jenny's face evident even in the fading light, from where he hurried towards her.

"I thought you weren't coming," she said in a little girl voice as she pulled a face.

"Traffic," he replied by way of explanation and heart thumping in his chest with the realisation that he was actually on a date, took her by her elbow as he led her toward the crowded entrance.

While her mother checked on her father, Lesley lifted the plates and scraping off the remains of the food, run them under the cold tap before placing them both into the dishwasher.

"How is he?" she asked, when her mother returned to the kitchen.

"Sleeping, thank God," sighed Peggy. "The McMillan nurse that was here today, Gill her name was, told me that his dosage has increased slightly so that's probably helped him a little. Cup of tea or a wee glass of wine?" she asked, turning towards the kettle.

"Tea after a curry, I don't think so," smiled Lesley.

Peggy returned her daughter's grin and reached into a lower cupboard for a bottle of white wine as Lesley fetched two glasses from the wall cabinet. They sat in comfortable silence, sipping at their wine.

"So how are you, after the break-up I mean?" asked Peggy

"A lot better than I thought I would be," sighed Lesley, then continued "I met Helen Lang today for coffee. She was asking after you and Dad and like you, wanted to know I was alright. Told me a few home truths as well, about Mike I mean. Cutting a long story short, there is no way I'll be getting together with him, if that's what you're worried about." She was uncomfortable lying to her mother and didn't have the nerve to look her in the eye because she knew that Peggy would not accept that her daughter, rightly or wrongly, might still have feelings about an arse like Mike Duffy; feelings that Lesley was trying to ignore by reminding herself of Mike's betrayal.

Peggy reached across the small kitchen table and grasped her daughter's hand in her own, squeezing it tightly. "Let's just say you were brought up to have a mind of your own and I knew that you would see through him in time. I'm just pleased it was before you ended up living with him or God forbid, married to him."

"So," Lesley slurped the last of her wine, "why don't I take the first shift to say, two or three and you get your head down for awhile"

"You'll wake me if anything happens?"

"Course I will," she scoffed with a grin. "You're the expert when it comes to dealing with Dad and his medication. Now, away to your bed, woman and I'll lock up."

Peggy stood up, wincing slightly at the pain in her back that had recently developed from her nightly vigils in the chair in Tom's room. She reached over and first gently ruffling her daughter's hair, leaned over to kiss Lesley on the top of her head. "Don't know what I would do without you darling," she whispered, blinking back the tears from her tired eyes as she turned to go to bed and her first restful night for some time.

Frederick led Jenny by the hand as they moved slowly with the crowd down the stairs and through the foyer of the multiplex cinema. Conversation was impossible in the hubbub of noise and it wasn't till they reached the pavement that he turned to ask if she enjoyed the movie?
"Great," she exclaimed, her eyes shining brightly and too embarrassed to admit the plot of the spy thriller was beyond her. She was unaware that Frederick had arrived by car and uncertain if this was goodbye for the evening. She glanced about at the people milling around her who, engaged with their own escorts and friends, ignored the shy couple. She wondered if she should suggest they go for a drink or coffee when he surprised her.
"Can I offer you a lift home, Miss Farndale," he smiled, having already practised the posh voice to impress her and guessed she wouldn't suspect he had a car.
Jenny's eyes widened and her heart beat a little faster as she realised that Frederick seemed to like her. She could hardly speak and nodded with such a huge and happy smile that even Frederick hardly noticed her bad skin or stained teeth. Gallantly offering his arm, he replied, "Well Miss Farndale, your carriage awaits you."
They skipped across the road between the traffic stopped at a red light. Frederick led Jenny to the passenger door at the pavement and holding the door as she manoeuvred into the seat, her coat fell open revealing a short black dress that rode up her thighs as she seated herself. He stared at her thin, bare legs, realising she wasn't wearing tights or stockings and as he turned his head, saw Jenny smiling at him. Closing the door, he swallowed hard and made his way round to the driver's door.
Jenny wasn't the brightest of young woman, but if her few experiences with men had taught her anything, it taught her that men were usually only after the one thing. In Frederick's stare she recognised his intention and had already decided that if giving in to him meant that he stayed longer than one date, then that was what she was prepared to do. Long ago she had resigned herself to the fact that she wasn't pretty and when any man showed even the slightest interest in her for whatever reason, Jenny was so grateful that her open eagerness was usually mistaken as a sexual invitation. To her secret shame, she believed that to keep a man interested she had to offer her body,

but to her continuing disappointment, it was never enough to keep a boyfriend for longer than one, or on the odd occasion, two nights.

The journey across the darkened city tested Frederick's nerve to the limit. He hated driving at night and the south side of Glasgow was to him, almost a foreign land. His knowledge of where Nitshill lay was a brief glance at a Glasgow A to Z map and the small, brightly coloured page offered no real clue. To his quiet and inward annoyance, Jenny was of no use. Her knowledge of the route to her home seemed to be confined to staring out from a bus or on occasion, a taxi window and he worked hard at retaining his irritability from showing. However, once again that evening good fortune smiled on Fredrick and after a few hesitant false turnings, quite by chance rather than skill he found himself driving eastwards on Cathedral Street where the sign posts indicated the route to the M8 motorway that he remembered passed near to Nitshill. With a sigh of relief, he followed the signs and negotiated his way into the correct lane, ignoring the flashing lights and sounding horns while muttering, "Bloody idiots, should watch where they're going."

In the passenger seat, Jenny sat quite still, sensing Frederick's nervousness and preferring to remain silent while he concentrated on the driving. Slightly more relaxed now he had a committed route, he again was conscious of the bare legs that sat next to him and within reach of his hand. Jenny's close presence and her scent in the confined space excited him and he felt himself become erect, causing him to squirm with a slight discomfort in his seated driving position. He considered at one point reaching for the gear stick and pretending by mistake, touching her thigh, but his nerve failed him and instead, settled for some polite conversation.

"So, is your mother at home tonight then?"

Eager to break the silence, Jenny replied, "Yes, she doesn't really go out a lot except maybe to the shops or to the bingo with her pals. She said she would wait up for me to get in," she continued and then thought maybe that admission was a mistake and that Frederick might not want to come in for a cup of tea or a coffee. She fervently hoped he would, for Jenny was childishly eager to show her Mum that she had a real boyfriend. Almost before she realised, the motorway turn-off for Silverburn Shopping Centre appeared and recognising this as the place where the taxis turned off, excitedly directed Frederick to Barrhead Road. Now confident of her location, Jenny directed Frederick first to Peat Road and then towards Nitshill, finally arriving outside her mother's upper cottage flat in Pinmore Street. As Frederick slowly parked the car, he couldn't but help notice in the headlights and street lighting that was still operating, that while some residents vainly tried to keep their homes neat and tidy, others indicated unkempt and littered gardens. Some of the privately owned houses had been recently roughcast, but others showed signs of neglect and he guessed the area seemed to have been forgotten in the Council's much publicised renovation scheme. Switching off the engine and headlights, he turned to smile at Jenny, who asked him, "Would you like to come in for something, tea or coffee maybe?"

In his mind throughout the afternoon, Frederick had already planned this moment, how he would follow Jenny to the door, accept her invitation to her room and there amaze her with his sexual prowess. Inwardly disappointed because he was now aware that her mother was waiting indoors, he decided that it was unlikely he would get much further than the lounge and making his glance at the dashboard clock obvious, replied, "Perhaps not tonight Jenny. We've both got early starts tomorrow morning." Turning towards her, his heart beating rapidly, he smiled and with a quick glance about him to ensure nobody was about, leaned sideways to kiss her and reached his slightly shaking hand towards her thighs.

Jenny was equally disappointed that she wasn't getting to show off her new boyfriend to her mother, but at least she could boast he had brought her home and excitedly met his lips with her own. Pulling her skirt up with her right hand, she opened her legs slightly wider and with her left hand guided his to between her thighs.

Frederick had never before kissed a woman and now here he was, awkwardly stretching across the narrow space, her small tongue surprising him as it darted into his mouth and tasting the popcorn he had bought her as her hand pulled his towards the secret area between her legs. His trembling fingers caressed her cotton panties and he became immediately erect, his chest tightening and his breathing more rapid. Jenny opened her legs wider as Frederick's inexperienced fingers poked at her and pulled at her knickers and she remembered from previous brief encounters that men liked to hear her sigh and say dirty things to them. She didn't normally swear and was uncomfortable using bad language, but equally, didn't want to risk losing her new boyfriend. Breaking free from his wet lips, she leaned her head against his ear and with a faltering voice, whispered the words that any other time would make her blush. In the darkness of the car, she thought her face must be red and glowing with embarrassment and felt a bit silly saying these things, but in their closeness was acutely aware of the effect it was having on him.

Frederick was astounded by her words and unable to restrain himself and to his shock, his body involuntarily shook as he experienced ejaculation. He was still for a few seconds then shamed, quickly withdrew his hand from the moistness between her legs and stared out of the windscreen, aware of the dampening patch in his underwear and suddenly grateful for the darkness of the car. They sat for a few embarrassed minutes in silence, then Jenny, mystified by his sudden change of attitude, finally asked, "Is everything alright?" terrified that she had somehow annoyed or offended him, that he no longer wanted her.

"Yes, fine," he snapped back with more forcefulness than he meant, annoyed with himself rather than Jenny, that his very first sexual encounter with a woman was over so quickly. Turning towards her, he could see the street light reflecting the hurt in her face and knew that if he had any hope of further sexual activity with Jenny, he had to get it right. Thinking quickly and taking a deep breath while forcing a smile, he began, "Look, I want us to be a couple, but not like this, in the car I mean. Perhaps you might come over to my place, say after work tomorrow?"

Jenny almost cried with relief. He wasn't dumping her and she hadn't blown it after all. Trembling with passion for this man who wanted to see her again, she could only nod and reaching across the seat, planted a wet, tear-stained kiss on his cheek before she opened the door and rushed from the car along the narrow path to her door. She heard the car engine start and turning to wave, watched as Frederick drove off, his face staring straight ahead. But she didn't mind, because now she had so much to tell her Mum.

Paul Hardie sat nursing a cup of coffee in the untidy kitchen, going over in his head again and again his trip to the forest. He thought about his actions, what he had done, afraid he might have left some small indication to where Fiona's body was buried or worse still, some small shred of evidence that indicated his guilt. He reasoned that the police couldn't possibly know of Fiona's death, not yet fully prepared to even admit that he had murdered her, but still the feeling of guilt persisted. Lowering his head into his hands he shivered at the memory of her falling, her head striking the tiled hearth and the noise it made. In a sudden fit of paranoia, he wondered about the bag containing the bloodstained clothing, panicking that if Fiona's body was ever discovered that he had overlooked some identifying marks on the suit, some small item in the pockets that might cause the police to realise it was he that killed her.

Perhaps it was the dark or perhaps it was Paul's feeling of lonely isolation or maybe even that a few short days ago his plans for his future had completely disappeared. Whatever the reason, a sense of foreboding overtook him and without a thought for anyone but himself, he began to rock back and forth in the chair, his selfishness manifesting itself in tears of pity that dripped from his chin to the floor below.

Chapter 12 - Thursday

Lesley came slowly awake then stopped suddenly and cringed as the crick in her neck made it acutely aware that any sudden movement resulted in a sharp pain.

"You were supposed to wake me," hissed her mum, dressed in a red coloured robe, her once dark hair now liberally tinged with grey, hanging loosely about her shoulders and a mug of tea in her hand.

Lesley weakly grinned in response and sat upright in the dimly lit room. Her bladder reminded her that she had slept through the night. Accepting the tea she decided not to argue with her Mum, but nodded towards the door and the kitchen. Her mother walked through the door and as Lesley made to follow, she turned towards her father and surprised, saw him staring at her. With a slow wink, he smiled and slowly closed his eyes to return to sleep. Lesley softly sighed, turned back and stooped over to softly kiss his pale, cold forehead, but he didn't again stir.

Peggy stood in the brightly lit kitchen with her back against the worktop, a pretend scowl on her face. The wall clock indicated it was just after seven am. The smell of bread in the toaster wafted through the air. "Well?" she demanded.

Lesley grinned and shrugged. "I've the rest of the morning to sleep before I start at four and we both know you badly need a break. I'm not going to apologise for worrying about you," she said, sipping at the steaming mug, "so I'll have a slice of that toast with marmalade, then you can pack me off to bed."

Peggy shook her head and smiled. "Thanks darling. I did need a good night's sleep and you're right. I've been thinking about what you said last night and if you want to stay over during the week, even for a night on your day off maybe, I'll be glad of the break."

The toast popped out of the machine with a zinging noise and the agreement was made.

Frederick Evans carefully combed his hair, his thoughts filled with last night's adventure and how he had become almost immediately aroused at the touch of Jenny's knickers and her sexy language. His invitation for her to visit him this evening excited him even further, for he had lain awake for almost an hour before rising, planning what he would do to her in his room. His mother's voice broke into his thoughts, calling him to breakfast and with a final glance in the bathroom mirror he jauntily skipped down the stairs. So wrapped up was he with thoughts of his plans for Jenny that the recorded DVD never crossed his mind.

Jinksie Peterson hung his coat inside his locker and yawning widely, popped his head into Sergeant Pete Buchanan's office as he passed. "Morning, Sarge. Kettle will be on in a minute if you want to pop through," he called out.
Pete Buchanan glanced up at the tousled headed Bar Officer and smiled. "Morning Jinksie, I'll be through when I've finished these shift sheets," he replied, then lowered his head as he tried to fathom out which officer was on duty at what time and the minimum cover he required to effectively patrol the station's beat. Sighing, he shook his head and privately thought while he didn't want to wish his life away, retirement was becoming an increasingly attractive option.
Through the wall, Inspector Frank Cochrane hung his cap on the hook behind the door and unbuckling his utility belt, dropped it on his paper littered desk and then stepped next door.
"Morning Pete, what's doing today then?"
"Morning boss," replied Buchanan as he glanced down at the handwritten summary from the nightshift Bar Officer. "Couple of cars screwed in Kintillo Drive over in Scotstounhill and an attempt made through the night at the golf clubhouse in Knightswood. There was a bit of a rammy outside Barney's Bar in Dumbarton Road that resulted in three arrested for breach and one charged with police assault."
"Police assault?" repeated Cochrane.
"Aye, it seems that young Chris McEwan, the probationer on nightshift got punched in the face and his nose burst. Nothing broken, but he'll need to be off for a few days while the swelling goes down."
"Anything else?" asked Cochrane as he nodded.
Buchanan grinned. "It seems we might have a knicker-knocker on the patch. Lady up in Austen Road reported two pairs of women's lingerie," he stressed *lingerie*, "got nicked off the washing line. I've assigned Lesley Gold the inquiry."
Cochrane looked thoughtful and then asked "Is that a common occurrence these days? I've never actually dealt with that kind of theft."
"It was more common when Glasgow was mostly a tenement population and the wifies used the backcourts to hang their washing out. These days, with washing machines and dryers, people more in a hurry to get their household chores done and, more particularly, the inclement weather, women are less inclined to hang their washing out to dry. I've only ever dealt with one case of theft of knicker-knocking, back a few years ago when I worked over in the Pollok area. I understand in parts of the city stealing clothing from washing ropes used to be called snow dropping, though I can't for the life of me understand why. Anyway, the case I got involved with was a guy who was married, two kids, good job, as well as his own house and never been in bother with us before. He was caught blagging women's knickers from a

common drying area in a block of these new built flats that are connected by corridors, you know the type?"

The Inspector nodded.

"Truth was, the guy wasn't a bad lad, just had this problem; an obsession really. Needless to say when he was caught, he was devastated. Not so much by being caught, but what he had been arrested for. When I went to check his address, his wife couldn't take it in, for she had no idea of his obsession. We discovered a cardboard box with about sixty or seventy pairs of women's knickers. All shapes, colours and sizes, hidden in his loft area. I know the detective that dealt with him requested the Procurator Fiscal send a warning letter, rather than put the guy through the court and suffer further ridicule. I heard later, that the guy's wife took the kids and left him. You could say the wife convicted him herself, Rough Justice style."

"Takes all types, I suppose," murmured Cochrane in reply as he turned away towards his own office, but stopped and turned back. "Before I forget, any word on Morris MacDonald coming back to work?"

Buchanan sat back and sighed. "I gave him a wee call last night at the house. His wife Susan isn't any better and the likelihood is the poor soul won't get better. Morris was a bit upset on the phone. I've known him a long time now and he is a straight guy, he wouldn't swing the lead or anything like that." he replied defensively. Buchanan paused, uncertain how to unload the bad news, then almost as if disclosing a personal secret, confided, "She's not got long now, Morris's wife. It's just, well, days probably and at best, weeks at the most I believe."

"Oh, I didn't know that," said a contrite Cochrane, uncomfortable discussing a man's personal life, a man he knew so very little about. "As for Morris being off long term," Cochrane hastily added, raising his hand in apology, "I wasn't suggesting anything like that. What I mean is, I know you're close to Morris and I'm quite happy that you act as the intermediary, the point of contact if you will, so if you're speaking to him again, assure him that he has my," then paused, "our full support. He's not to worry about being off. I'll speak with the boss at Maryhill and square it with him. If we can manage with the resources we've got, so be it, but if we need any more officers down here to lend a hand, I'll do what I can."

"Right boss," responded Buchanan, relieved that he no longer had to try and wangle time off for Morris and pleased that Cochrane was turning out to be a good guy after all. Maybe even good enough for Pete to comfortably hand over the reins when his time to retire arrived and fingers crossed, he inwardly thought, the sooner the better.

"One more thing," said Cochrane, "you mentioned Lesley Gold. How is she shaping up?"

"It's early days yet. I had decided that she would neighbour Morris, but with him being off I'll have to re-think. She was out neighbouring Dotty yesterday and young Alex was in the Bar helping out with Jinksie," wryly deciding that Cochrane didn't need to know the true reason for Alex's bar duties.
"However, Dotty is young Alex's tutor cop so I can't have them separated for too long. It might be helpful if I had a spare body down here in the event Morris is off longer than anticipated?"
"Leave it with me and I'll see what I can wangle, but in the meantime as you're stuck, I'm still capable of walking a beat so mark me down as a patrol officer," he grinned, "if I'm going to be stuck here with you lot for the foreseeable future, it's about time I was getting to know the area a wee bit better."

Returning to his own office Frank Cochrane thought that maybe he had been a little hasty, offering his services as a beat officer when his true job was managing his resources. Seating himself behind his desk, he glanced at the pitifully small items of paperwork he had to contend with and grinned as he thought of his resources. Two Sergeants, eleven constables and a dayshift Bar Officer who is a wannabe cop. The truth was, he had to admit, he was bored. His accelerated promotion to Inspector had meant he had served little time on the street, hardly out of his two years probation period before being assigned office jobs, then promoted to Sergeant and scurrying about headquarters or shuffling paperwork and all because of a bloody Degree in History. He wasn't stupid and knew the police required educated managers who were being schooled to one day replace some of the dickheads currently in situ. He inwardly sighed, but his fall from grace had certainly put a damper on his own career prospects; or for the time being anyway. He sat back and clasped his hands behind his head, suddenly relishing the thought of getting out of the claustrophobic office and into the fresh air. No, maybe putting himself forward wasn't the best managerial decision, working alongside the rank and file as it were, but as far as he was concerned, it was the right thing for him. He glanced again at the paperwork and decided that Pete Buchanan could deal with that. The wily old Sergeant was on this final countdown before retirement and wanted nothing more than to sit about the office, idling his time away and avoiding any incident or issue that might result in a future court appearance when he was retired, for Buchanan had made it clear when he retired, he was gone for good. No citations chasing him for months after he left. Cochrane sighed and smiled. Yes, that was what he'd do and when the late shift commenced duty at four o'clock this afternoon, he would spend a couple of hours with them before finishing for the day.

Paul Hardie decided not to shower or shave that morning and spent almost five minutes practising an anxious face in front of the bathroom mirror. He thought if he seemed to be worried or even distraught, his story might be just that bit more plausible. Rummaging through the washing basket in the bedroom, he fetched out a creased, unwashed day old shirt and donned that over his jeans. Again and again he went over in his mind the story he would tell, once more practising in front of the trusty old bathroom mirror. He wasn't certain how the police might react to his tale and to satisfy himself just one more time, went down on his knees to again check for blood staining on the hearth and wooden floor. Watching the TV detective shows had taught him that if the Forensic programmes were in any way accurate, his scrubbing the flooring clean wouldn't fool the experts, but a cursory check would probably pass or at least he hoped so.
 He checked his wristwatch and saw it was almost nine-thirty. Taking a deep breath, he glanced one more time round the small lounge and grabbing his car keys, headed for the front door.

Dotty Turner reversed the Kia four by four into her driveway and switched off the engine. She sat for a moment catching her breath. Running the kids to school wasn't just a chore, but when her shifts allowed it was a pleasure; or rather it was, once she had refereed between them as to who sat in the front with her. This morning, Angie had won while Iain sulked in the back and then jumped into the front when his young sister got out at the primary school.
"Can I go to the pictures tonight with my mates, Mum?" he had asked her and trusting him as she did, gave her consent if he agreed that his Grandfather would pick him up when the movie finished. Huffing and puffing as young teenagers do, he finally agreed.
It didn't take long, she inwardly grinned to herself, to work out that his 'mates' was the young dark haired girl who shyly waved and stood waiting for him when she dropped him off round the corner from the school gates. So taken with the girl was he that he hadn't noticed his mother didn't immediately drive off, but sat watching as he walked with the girl towards the school. She couldn't explain the tightening in her chest and unconsciously rubbed at it; not a pain, she realised. It was the realisation that her son, no longer her baby, was now growing into a young man and a handsome one at that. She smiled at her own thoughts, now grinning that she must be hormonal as she watched Iain and the young girl disappear from her sight. Starting the engine she pulled smoothly from the parking space and headed towards the house. As she drove, her thoughts again turned to her own life and she gnawed at her lower lip, a habit she had since childhood. During the course of her career, it had always been easy going to work and

she looked forward to the challenges that each day brought. Sure, she enjoyed a good whine, but who didn't in their job and admittedly, the good times far outweighed the rough side of policing. But the last couple of years had been difficult, day in and day out, maintaining a mask to hide her feelings from the one person that she really ached to tell how she felt. Taking a deep breath she knew that she could never, ever reveal those feelings. To do so would simply embarrass him and in the short time that he had left to serve, the last thing Dotty wanted was to make his life difficult; even if it meant that when he finally said farewell to the job, she did not get the opportunity to express those feelings, how she really felt about him. Reversing into her driveway she switched off the engine and sat for a moment, mentally torturing herself by imagining what might have been.

Jinksie read again the lengthy memo of issues he had typed out on the PC to the Chief Inspector requesting that top of the list be the appointment of an office cleaner and treated with some urgency. As he read it he thought that maybe he shouldn't have added the bit about wearing a gas mask at his desk because the layer of dust was becoming a health hazard then grinned; nothing wrong with a wee bit of humour he decided. A short rap on the public counter caused him to turn round and he smiled upon seeing Andy the postman standing there, a bundle of letters in his hand.
"Morning Jinksie, I didn't mean to startle you," said Andy, the soft voice contradicting the tall, sturdy man's physique, the scar on his chin and face prominently white in relief against his weather beaten features.
Jinksie stood from his desk and moved to the counter, curious that Andy hadn't dumped the mail as he usually did then headed out the door with hardly a word. "Needing anything signed, Andy?" he asked, conscious that Andy was staring over Jinksie's shoulder.
"Eh, no, just thought I'd say hello," the big man lowered his head to smile in return and turned to leave, pulling upon the door and standing to one side as a tall, fair haired man entered. Jinksie turned to the new arrival and thought the man seemed a little agitated, but that wasn't unusual. In his experience, most people were sometimes uncomfortable entering police stations, regardless of their purpose.
"Can I help you sir?"
"Ah, yes. My name's Paul Hardie. I think my wife's missing."
Jinksie stared curiously at the taller man, wondering at his dishevelled appearance. "You think she's missing?" he repeated, emphasising the word *think*. "How do you mean, you think she's missing?"
"Are you a police officer? What I mean is, a real policeman?" replied Paul. Jinksie, ginger haired and not renowned for his tolerance, drew himself to his full five feet one inch height, his face flushing and glared at the cheeky

bugger. "I'm the bar officer, sir. I can assure you I am fully conversant with the procedure regarding missing persons," he snorted, reaching for a pen and a Missing Person form. "Now, perhaps we'll start with your own details, eh?"
It took Jinksie a few minutes to establish Paul's personal details by which time his attitude had softened slightly, sympathising with the guy's obvious worry over his missing wife, a woman who, according to her husband, had never been missing before nor had any reason to leave home.
"What about means, Mister Hardie. Has you wife taken her purse, her handbag, any cash that you might be aware of, maybe her credit cards?"
"Certainly her handbag is gone and I suppose her purse. They're not in the house. As for cash, I can't really say, but she will have our joint account bank cards with her, of that I'm pretty sure," inwardly grateful that he had thought to chuck all these items into the plastic bag with the rags.
"Do you have any idea when she last made a withdrawal on the cards? Your bank will have the details if you give them a call."
"I'll do that when I get home," he replied, biting at his lower lip, his brow creased as though agreeing this was a good idea.
Jinksie was pleased with himself, filling the form out slowly and trying to show this guy that even though he wasn't a 'real policeman', he was as professional as any of the uniforms that passed through the office. H paused as he considered how to phrase the next question without adding to the man's already obvious worry.
"Has Missus Hardie, Fiona I mean, been upset or out of sorts in the recent past?"
"How do you mean?"
"Well, her behaviour. Has it been out of the ordinary? Has she any worries, personal or financial perhaps? Or maybe a family crisis or did something happen at work?"
Paul slowly shook his head, forcing himself to seem like the distraught and worried husband. "No, nothing like that," then as if suddenly remembering, reached into his jacket pocket. "The only thing is this, I found it in the bin in the bathroom if it's any help at all," as he handed Jinksie the empty pregnancy test box. "You see," he half smiled as though confiding a great secret, "we've been trying for a baby and, well, we had a lot of disappointments."
Jinksie turned the small cardboard box over his fingers. He had never really seen one before and stared at it with curious eyes. "The test thing, the thing that's supposed to be inside that tells if a woman is pregnant or not. Was that still in the bin with the box?"
"No," replied Paul, "I couldn't find it," he shook his head, knowing it wouldn't be found for that was the final item in the bin bag before he tied it closed. Suddenly he now wondered if it had been a mistake disposing of it,

that the suggestion Fiona had been pregnant might have suggested hormonal problems, that she might have been irrational.

"Do you know who the last person that saw your wife might be," asked Jinksie, his head down as he scribbled details on the pad.

"When I got home yesterday and she wasn't there, I thought maybe she had gone shopping or something. Then the janitor at her school, a Mister Dunlop phoned to ask how she was, that she hadn't been feeling very well and he had driven her home in his car."

Jinksie glanced up. "This Mister Dunlop, do you know him?"

"We've never met, though Fiona spoke about him several times. Said he was a nice man and was often very kind to her," smiled Paul, his mind alert and on instinct, believed he was providing the small red haired man as a possible suspect for Fiona's disappearance.

Jinksie noted the details then asked, "What about relatives. Does your wife have any family or friends she might visit in times of," he searched for the words, "personal crisis?"

"What you got here Jinksie?" said the voice behind him. He turned to find Pete Buchanan standing behind him.

"It's a report of a missing person, Sergeant. Mister Hardie here," he pointed with his pen, "reports that his wife hasn't been seen since late afternoon on Tuesday. Says that it is out of character for her to be missing," and passed the form across for Pete to read. Buchanan scanned the form and smiled at Paul. "What about a mobile phone, I take it you will have called her?"

"I tried several times Tuesday evening, during the day yesterday and last night and again this morning, but my calls went straight to the answer service and she hasn't returned any of them, the calls I mean."

His eyes flashed with panic and the blood drained from his face as mentally he tried to recall if the phone in the bag buried with her was off or had he left it switched on?

Buchanan had mistaken his pale face for concern for his missing wife and asked, "What about family or friends?"

"Both our parents are dead. I was an only child, but Fiona has a brother. He's been in Australia since he was a teenager and I can't recall the last time they communicated. They weren't, aren't I mean, close."

Buchanan nodded slowly and explained that when an adult went missing, there was usually a family or domestic issue that provoked the disappearance and the vast majority were soon returned home safe. However, if the circumstances dictated a police response, the inquiry would be closely followed up and in particular if there was a suggestion or likelihood the missing person or MP, as the police termed the individual, might be at physical risk or worst.

"How do you mean worst?" asked Paul, passing a hand across his face as though extremely worried, feeling very hot and desperate to get this over with.

Buchanan swallowed hard, realising that maybe he had said too much. "Let's not worry about the worst scenario till we learn more, Mister Hardie. However, is there anything that you believe could indicate your wife might harm herself?"

Paul turned to stare at Jinksie who on cue, held up the cardboard pregnancy test box for Buchanan to see. "Mister Hardie found this in the bathroom bin, Sarge. The thingy that it contained wasn't there, so there's no way of knowing if Missus Hardie took the test and if she did, what the result was. The other thing is," he glanced sympathetically toward Paul, "they were trying for a child and had some …disappointments."

"I'm guessing that your wife took these disappointments badly, Mister Hardie?" asked Buchanan.

Paul slowly nodded, increasingly excited that these two buffoons were swallowing his story as he had planned. "She said it was all her fault. I tried to tell her that it didn't matter, but she got more and more angry with each failure. She was very distracted these last couple weeks," he said, now growing in confidence as he told his story.

"Do you have a photograph of your wife with you?" asked Jinksie.

Paul startled, the one thing he had overlooked. "No, sorry, I didn't think. How stupid of me. It should have been obvious, but I just …."

"Don't worry about it," Buchanan raised a hand and smiled softly. "I'll send one of my officers up to your house later today Mister Hardie and I must also tell you they will need to take a look round the house."

Paul's eyes narrowed with suspicion. "I don't understand, why would they need to do that?"

"Don't get upset sir, it's just a procedure we have to follow in the case of a person who is reported missing. The officer's might see something you've missed and believe me, when for example it's kids that are reported missing, you would be surprised how many we find hiding in the lofts or under beds."

"Are you suggesting my wife …"

"No, of course not," spluttered Buchanan, wishing now he'd left the MP report to Jinksie, who with diplomacy had turned away to fidget with some papers, "but we've a set procedure to follow, one that we have to adhere to."

"Yes, well, I'm sure you have your job to do," Paul huffily replied, "but for now, what should I do?"

It took all of Jinksie's willpower to stop from grinning at Pete Buchanan's discomfort and decided to step in and save him further embarrassment. "I suppose you won't want to be working today, so it might be a good idea if you stop at home and sit by the phone, just in case your wife decides to contact you or wants to come home Mister Hardie and needless to say if there is any contact, let us know straight away. Oh and when the officers arrive for the photo, you might provide them with a recent photograph of your wife, if you don't mind sir."

"Yes," Paul softly exhaled, "that sounds like a good idea and of course, I'll look out a photo for you. Well, in the meantime, thanks for your time," he nodded as with a final stare at Buchanan, he turned and pushed through the swing doors.

"Fucked that up, didn't I?" sighed Buchanan.

"Big time, Sarge," replied Jinksie with a grin.

Outside in his car, Paul clicked the seat belt into place and with a final glance at the police office, drove smoothly away from the kerb, his stomach no longer churning and after a hundred metres, permitted himself a self-satisfied smile and then, to his surprised delight, thoughts of Janice Meikle came to mind.

Lesley Gold had a relaxing morning and after a midday grilled brunch courtesy of her mother, drove the short distance to the local supermarket with Peggy's shopping list. Idling between the rows, basket in hand she encountered more than a few neighbours who asked kindly after her mother and father. It pleased her that so many people thought well of her parents and she was surprised to find it brought a lump to her throat. Her twenty minute shopping trip took almost an hour. Collecting her groceries and piling them into the boot of her car, she made one quick stop at the local surgery where she spoke briefly with the family's elderly doctor, the redoubtable Findlay McPherson and then returned home where she found her father sitting up in bed, propped by pillows and being spoon fed some chicken soup by her mum.

"Nice that you stayed over darling," he greeted her as she bent to kiss his forehead. "Mum could probably use a break from her twenty-four hour vigil of me," he smiled.

Though she managed a smile in return, Lesley thought her father looked frailer than when she had last seen him awake and in her heart, knew that it would now not be too long before he faced his final journey. Final journey, she inwardly gasped as she stared at him. Even after all the months of the debilitating and insidious disease that ravaged his body, she couldn't bring herself to say it – death, as though the very word itself might bring forward his demise.

"Away in to the kitchen and put the kettle on and we'll have a coffee," her mother interrupted Lesley's thoughts, some inner sense warning Peggy that her daughter was upset at the sight of Tom.

Nodding a smile and without speaking, Lesley turned away to do as her mother asked, her fists clenched to distract the flood of tears that threatened to escape.

"She's a good girl, is Lesley," croaked her husband as Peggy wiped at a spill of soup from his chin with a paper napkin. "I've always loved her more than she knows. I only wish in some way I could make her believe that."

Peggy smiled at Tom, not trusting herself to speak, her God given honesty aching to tell him that if he hadn't so obviously favoured his younger daughter, there might not have been the undeclared resentment that she knew existed in Lesley's heart. But now, in the twilight days of his life and rather than upset him in his weakened condition, she chose to remain silent and instead, simply replied, "She knows you love her. She's always known."

Tom sipped the soup from the offered spoon and slowly nodded in agreement, choosing to believe his wife rather than make another issue of an old argument. "Is the nurse coming today? I've kind of lost track of time," he murmured.

"Later this afternoon," replied Peggy, dabbing at his mouth with a clean, white cloth. She set the bowl and spoon on the bedside table and continued to sit on the edge of the bed, her hands clasped together as she stared at her husband, his eyes slowly flickering as sleep once more overtook him. Her head turned slightly and her eyes fell upon the bottles of strong painkilling medicine that sat beside the soup bowl. Not for the first time had it crossed her mind that a simple mistake on her part might relieve the man she loved of his pain, his daily torment. A shiver run through her and she absent-mindedly stroked an escaped lock of hair from her forehead, She was tired, so very tired and almost on the point of exhaustion. Last night's sleep had taken the edge off her near state of collapse, but Lesley she knew couldn't be here every night, not with her shifts. Her thoughts turned to her younger daughter Linda. Again she stared at Tom, knowing in her heart that had he been more forceful and not given in to her every little whim, Linda might have turned out completely different and not become the selfish young woman she is. Peggy's pride forbade her from ever asking for help. If Linda, who found the occasional hour every four or five days to visit would for once, just make the offer to help, it would not just be gratefully received, but might go some way to break down the barrier that Peggy knew now existed between her daughters. With a feeling of guilt, she again stole a glance at the medicine bottles.

"Coffee's ready," whispered Lesley from the open doorway and startling Peggy, who nodded and rising from the bed, leaned to gently stroke her sleeping husband's cheek before leaving the room.

Hearing her gone, Tom slowly opened his eyes and with difficulty, turned his head as he too stared at the medicine bottles on the bedside table.

Chapter 13

Frederick Evans day passed quicker than he anticipated and to his surprise he sold two of the department's more expensive suits and both within one hour. "Very well done indeed, Mister Evans," a smiling Robert Hamilton patted Frederick on the shoulder, still in the belief that his pep talk had worked wonders for the man. "Before we know it, you'll be after my job," he laughed light-heartedly as he strolled away.

Frederick stared after him, a cold fury hidden behind the blank smile. Even the previous evening's tryst with Jenny and the quick sale of the suits couldn't diminish his hatred of the man or own belief that Hamilton had robbed him of the manager's job that was rightly his. He glanced at his watch and with a nod to a colleague, indicated he was off for his mid morning break.

The canteen was unusually busy and at first, he couldn't see Jenny and was unaware that she had seen him.

"Good morning, Frederick," she whispered as she stole up behind him, a tray piled with dirty crockery and cutlery in hands.

"Ah Jenny," he half turned, taken by surprise and smiled to see that unusually she wore make-up, albeit he thought slightly gaudy for a mere canteen assistant, "perhaps if you get a free minute?" he asked, nodding towards what he now thought of as 'their table'.

She nodded as she hurried towards the serving hatch and passing the tray through to a fellow assistant, felt her heart about to burst. Her boyfriend, she inwardly rejoiced; my Frederick. His name rolled about in her thoughts and smiling, Jenny sneaked a glance back to where she saw him in the queue at the hotplate, collecting his breakfast.

With hands clasped in prayer, Jenny begged her boss to allow her a few moments off to sit in the canteen, unaware just how much the elderly woman liked Jenny, who she considered to be a good worker and though not privy to details, guessed there was someone out there in the store who was showing the plain and shy wee girl some attention. "God forgive me", the woman thought, "I hope he doesn't break the wee lassie's heart". However, the woman's curiosity got the better of her and sneaking a glance through the serving hatch saw Jenny sitting with the wee skinny guy from the Gents Department, that guy Evans and her heart turned cold. "Of all the men in the store", she sighed, "it had to be that wee weirdo". Exhaling softly, she reminded herself that it wasn't any of her business and the elderly woman turned to get on with her job.

"So," Frederick passed the slip of paper to her, "you'll catch a taxi to my address tonight and I'll see you there about eight then?"

Jenny was too excited to reply and simply nodded, then slipping the paper into the pocket of her apron was uncertain whether or not to lean across the narrow table and peck Frederick on his cheek. The decision was made for her when he smiled and said, "Well, off you go then. Don't want people gossiping, do we now?"

He watched as she shuffled back to the kitchen area, seeing the sly glances as those seated about him turned their heads back and forth between him and the departing Jenny, guessing at their gossip. He wished Jenny was more glamorous, better looking, perhaps even one of the younger women who worked in cosmetics, but for now he had already decided, she would do for him to practise on and inwardly smiled at what he had planned for the manipulable Jenny this evening, in the privacy of his bedroom.

The janitor Jimmy Dunlop was wheeling the barrow of earth towards the football pitch goals where the constant stamping of schoolboy feet had created a slight dip when he saw the taxi turn into the gates and drive towards the car park. He stopped and settling the barrow down, pulled an old rag from his rear pocket to wipe at the bead of sweat on his brow. The tall, fair haired man who exited from the rear seat wasn't familiar to Jimmy and curious, he walked towards him, watching as the man approached Missus Hardie's car, already guessing who he was.

"Can I help you?" he asked.

"Ah, yes. My name's Paul Hardie. I've come to collect," then hesitated. "Are you Mister Dunlop?"

"Jimmy Dunlop, that's me," Jimmy nodded as he agreed. "How is your wife?"

Paul half smiled, once more adopting into the role of the worried husband. "I really don't know," he slowly replied, you see, Fiona, Missus Hardie," he corrected himself, aware now he was speaking to just a common worker, "wasn't at home when I got back the day you phoned and she hasn't been seen since. No contact from her whatsoever. I'm extremely concerned and I'm sorry to say I have had to report her missing, to the police."

Jimmy's eyes opened wide. The wee lassie is missing? "I'm very sorry to hear that Mister Hardie. Have you informed the head Teacher, Miss Jenkins? I'm sure she would like to be informed," he replied while in his heart knew the callous cow wouldn't give a toss and if anything, would likely be pleased to hear of her missing and give more reason for Jenkins to be shot of the young teacher.

The last thing Paul needed was to sit down and go through the story again with a middle-aged spinster, but decided it would not just be strange if he didn't report her disappearance, but might work to his advantage as the caring husband, trying to retrace his missing wife's steps.

"Yes, that's probably a good idea. Perhaps you could direct me to her?"

"I'll take you in there myself Mister Hardie, if you'll follow me," replied Jimmy, turning and leading Paul towards the main entrance.

Jimmy knocked on Gwyneth Jenkins door and without waiting for a reply, pushed it open. The first thing he saw was her seated behind her desk, bending down to the lower drawer, her face flushed as she snapped at him, "Really Mister Dunlop, you might have waited on my response. Is this urgent?"

Jimmy's nose detected the faint smell of whisky rather than the overpowering smell of the rose petal spray that usually hung in the air. It briefly occurred to him that had he opened the door a few seconds earlier, he might have caught her with the bottle to her lips, but instead simply said, "I have Mister Paul Hardie with me, Miss Jenkins. Missus Hardie's husband; he needs to speak with you on a matter of some importance. He's just informed me that his wife is missing."

He saw the panic cross her face and guessed that she thought that, after her treatment of the young teacher and the threat to sack her, Hardie might somehow hold her responsible for his wife's disappearance. From a flushed face, she suddenly went pale and waving her hand, asked the elderly janitor to show Mister Hardie in then asked Jimmy to also wait. Jimmy forced himself to remain impassive, guessing that Jenkins wanted a witness to Mister Hardie's visit and vainly hoping that if the husband turned violent, the elderly janitor would protect her. Yeah, as if, he inwardly smirked and then turned and asked Missus Hardie's husband to come into the room. Jimmy stood just inside the door before closing it softly behind him.

Her nervousness was apparent when she greeted Paul and invited him to sit down in the chair in front of her desk and began by asking if there was any word of his wife.

"I'm so very sorry to hear that Missus Hardie, Fiona," she smilingly corrected herself, "has seen fit to put you through this awful worry, Mister Hardie. How can we here at the school be of assistance to you?"

It didn't take long for Paul to learn that in the recent past Fiona had, according to Gwyneth Jenkins, been underperforming in her position as a teacher.

"Is that why you threatened to sack her?" he asked with more curiosity than vehemence.

"Oh, that is probably less than correct," blustered Jenkins, staring at Hardie and avoiding the old janitor's blank face. "I did try, very hard," she stressed, her hands flat on the desk, "to motivate, eh, Fiona, but the poor girl seemed, eh," she sought for the correct word.

"Distracted?" suggested Paul.

"Yes, that's it. Distracted," then decided to change tactic. "I presume that you reported her missing to the police? Have they any news for you?"

Before Paul could respond and almost as soon as she realised that he was no physical threat to her, that he had simply come to report his wife's disappearance and collect her car, Jenkins off-handedly waved her dismissal of Jimmy, suggesting that he had other duties to attend to.

When the door closed behind the janitor, Paul replied, "I've not long come from there," he nodded his head. "They're sending a couple of officers to my house to check …. I mean, to see if there's something that I might have missed," he rose from his seat and extended his hand, "so if you don't mind, I'll leave now and I'd better get myself home."

"Of course," replied Jenkins as she stood and shook his hand. "Please keep me informed if there is anything, anything at all that I can assist you with."

After Paul closed the door behind him, she sat heavily down in her seat and sighed with relief, smiling that what had seemed to be a problem, might now be a blessing. If that little idiot Hardie turned up floating in the River Clyde or something similar, it would be so much easier than sacking her and going through a possible tribunal. Perhaps even provide the school with an opportunity to fund-raise in Fiona Hardie's memory and, her mind considered the idea, if the media were to be involved, it could only serve to highlight her own leadership skills in steering the school through what she will describe as an awful tragedy. The education department must surely be involved and it could only increase her profile. Suddenly caught up with her own thoughts, it seemed to her the situation might after all present the chance for her long awaited promotion. Turning, she reached for the lower drawer then stopped. That old fool Dunlop had almost caught her and she sighed in irritation. Why she employed a secretary to announce or rebuff visitors, but who allowed any bugger to wander in, she didn't know. Standing, she straightened her black coloured pencil skirt and pulling down the hem of her navy blue blouse, decided that she would find out, inwardly smiling at the opportunity it provided to vent her displeasure.

Dotty Turner arrived in the rear car park at Garscadden office as Lesley Gold was locking her car door and turning, waved and waited for Dotty by the rear door.

"Forgot the number again?" Dotty grinned.

"I'll get there, stop hassling me," Lesley returned the grin and followed Dotty through the door towards the women's locker room. They just reached the door when Pete Buchanan popped his head out of his office. "Morris is still off on the pat and mick," he winked at Dotty, "so Lesley, you'll have a new neighbour for the first two hours, then it will be into the Uniform bar with

Jinksie. He finishes when your neighbour does, so you take over his duties till knocking off time, okay?"

"Sarge," they replied in unison and then glanced at each other, clearly puzzled as they wondered who was to replace Morris. Their curiosity was solved when they entered the small canteen and saw the Inspector sitting wearing his stab-proof vest and utility belt.

"I'm Morris's replacement for the evening and your neighbour for the next couple of hours," he smiled at Lesley, "so please, be gentle, dear heart."

"Just do as you're told and when you're told and I'll see you're all right," she quipped back at him.

Cochrane smiled, a little relieved that she didn't seem too fazed and any awkwardness she might have felt going on the beat with her boss certainly wasn't obvious. "I've collected our first call from Jinksie," he leaned up from his seat to pass Lesley a sheet of paper. "A woman reported missing, last seen in her house in Borden Road. We've to interview the husband in his house, have a look about and collect a photograph. That's a copy of the report."

Dotty, shrugging into her utility belt, stopped and turned towards the Inspector, her brow knitted in recall. "Borden Road? That's near to where we had the call yesterday morning, the knickers stolen from the washing line, Austen Road, remember? If memory serves me correctly, Borden Road runs parallel to Austen Road, with a lane separating the backs of the houses," then scowled as Alex Mason, his hair in disarray and carrying his utility belt and protective vest, barged breathlessly into the room. "Sorry," he gasped, his heart sinking when he saw the Inspector sitting there, blank faced and ignoring his lateness and knew that Dotty was again going to have him by the short and curlies.

"I'll bear that in mind, Dotty, thanks," replied Lesley to distract the other woman, whose eyes stared through young Alex, then said, "Right boss, when you're ready?"

Cochrane, eager to be out and about before the suddenly steely-eyed Dotty went off on one, threw the patrol car keys to Lesley. "As we're both relatively new to this part of the division, I'll let you drive."

Frederick Evans was in a state of high excitement when he arrived home that evening and forcing himself to be calm, informed his mother that later that evening he was having a guest over, that she was not to make a fuss, that he and Jenny …

"Jenny," his mother repeated with a huge smile, her hands clasped to her chest and thanking the Lord that all those prayers were at last being answered.

He held up his hands to forestall his mother's questions and simply told her that Jenny was a friend, a colleague from work with whom he was going to help with some computer work on his laptop. No, he told her, Jenny wouldn't be wanting any dinner or supper and no, there was no need to make tea, that he would attend to Jenny's needs, inwardly smirking at his own comment. His mother's disappointment was obvious and she asked, "Will I at least get an introduction, dear?"
"Of course, mother," he sighed at the old fool's obvious attempt to meet Jenny and then decided, maybe not a bad idea. It would put Jenny at ease if she thought she was being formally introduced and might make things go that little bit smoother when it came to ….he smiled and holding the old woman's hands, assured her, "Of course you will get an introduction. After all, it's your house mother and I wouldn't bring any old stranger in, now would I?"

Paul Hardie paced up and down in his small lounge, anxiously glancing at the clock and wondering when the police officers would arrive. He was annoyed with himself that he hadn't forced the small red-haired guy at the station to give a specific time, but reasoned that why would he? He had, after all agreed to the suggestion that he would be at home all day, awaiting any contact from his missing wife. For the umpteenth time he plumped one of the couch cushions and walked to yet another part of the room, studying with a critical eye anything that might indicate that the horror of Fiona's death had occurred here. As satisfied as he could be, he went to the kitchen and made more coffee. He considered some toast, but when he opened the greaseproof bread packaging he could clearly see the green mould on the crust and with some disgust, threw the bread into the bin. Curiously, he had no real appetite and guessed he was living on his nerves, that at some point in the coming days he would be ravenous. Again he glanced at his wristwatch and hands on the work top, exhaled loudly.
When, he impatiently wondered, would they come?

Peggy Gold opened the door to the McMillan nurse, surprised to see she was accompanied by the old and rotund Doctor McPherson, the senior practitioner from their local surgery, the doctor who as a much younger man had seen Peggy through her pregnancies and both girls through their childish ailments. Though in his late sixties, but still practising, Doctor Mac as he was commonly known now tended Tom during her husband's final days.
"Good afternoon, lovely lady," he replied in a booming voice as he smiled at Peggy and doffed his beaten and sweat stained Fedora, then handed the young grinning nurse his old worn leather medical bag, "and is that the kettle I hear boiling?"

Peggy laughed and led the old doctor through to the kitchen while the nurse slipped through to the bedroom to check on her husband. Filling the kettle, Peggy turned to find that McPherson had closed the kitchen door and taken off and hung his tweed jacket over the back of the chair upon which he sat. One thumb was hooked into the broad, bright yellow coloured braces as with the other hand he twirled with forefinger and thumb at his greying, but perfect moustache, a legacy to his days as a National Service RAF physician.
"Do you not want to check on Tom first, Doctor Mac," she asked, smiling with surprise.
"Oh, I'm not here to see Tom, dear lady," he replied. "No, I'm here at the request of a very pretty and charming young woman called Lesley, who very persuasively insisted I come personally and have a wee chat with her mum. A mum, I might add whom she is most worried about. Now, I know it's bad for a man my age, but can I have two sugars please and perhaps a biscuit wouldn't go amiss either and preferably a chocolate digestive, if you have one."

Inspector Cochrane read the copy of the missing person report while Lesley drove and decided to be upfront with her, that a little honesty might be not be amiss. "Look, Lesley, I've had too many office jobs of late and frankly, I'm not as clued up with MP's as you will be. What do the markers indicate, these coloured alert things?"
"They're indicators that were agreed in collaboration with the social services, boss. When Jinksie is posting the missing woman's details onto the Police National Computer, one of the first things he does is check her details to inquire if she is previously known to us, maybe either as a regular MP or perhaps there have been previous domestic problems involving her or at that address."
"Yes, I'm aware of that side of it and I presume her husband too will be checked?"
"Damn right, if you pardon me. Too many times the MP's I've dealt with have been unsuspecting women who found themselves living with a guy that initially seemed to be okay, then the battering starts. That's why all parties are checked where the details are available. In simple terms, the red, amber and green markers are an indication relative to the risk assessment for the MP. Red as it obviously indicates means the MP is at high risk from self-harm or perhaps there is something to indicate there might have been criminal activity, maybe previous domestic abuse. Amber less so and green where there has been no previous indication of risk to the MP or where the MP has not previously been reported as missing. In the case of young kids, it will always be red, no matter what the home circumstances are. You'll know yourself we don't take chances where children are concerned. There's been

too many weans have fell through the net and it's a cop's worst nightmare, dealing with a lost child who has no history of going missing."
Cochrane nodded as he said, "I'm reading here that Missus Hardie is a green, a primary school teacher who resides at the given address with her husband Paul. According to this, he's an accountant by profession."
"Doesn't count for anything, his profession I mean. I've locked up a doctor for battering his wife. Do the Hardie's have any children, sir?"
"None listed so I presume that's a no." He glanced up as Lesley turned into Munro Road. "Borden Road is about here, isn't it?"
"This is us here now," she replied. "What's the number again?"
"Number nineteen, there it is" he pointed towards the red coloured door.
Lesley smoothly stopped the car and switched off the engine.
"I'll let you take the lead on this, Lesley, as it's your beat," he told her, handing over the MP copy report.
"Sir," she acknowledged, wondering if this was some sort of test, if the Inspector wanted to see how she handled her inquiries. Unbuckling her seat belt, she glanced at the mid-terraced house and saw the upstairs curtain twitch. Here goes, she inwardly thought.

Alex Mason couldn't bear the silent treatment any longer. "Look, Dotty, I said I'm sorry."
"Sorry doesn't cut it wee man," she sharply replied, her eyes concentrated on the road ahead. "Your time-keeping is crap and worse than that, you arrive late on the very day the Inspector is going out on patrol with us. Bloody hell, Alex, either you want to do this job or find some other line of work. I'm pissed off covering for you, I mean, it. How many times now have we had this conversation? What's this, a half dozen or so times? Frankly, I've lost count," her voice becoming quiet. "You know that everything you do, all your balls-ups reflect on me as your tutor. My career parallels yours for as long as I'm saddled with you. You mess up as you frequently do and my ability as a tutor gets marked down."
He turned his head away knowing that no matter what he said, any excuse would only add petrol to the raging fire that was Dotty.
She wheeled the car into a lay-by and stopped then turned to face him, her eyes still blazing in fury. "You're my third probationer since I was appointed a tutor cop and believe me Alex, you haven't impressed anyone so far. If you think you will get through the two years probation by being late for your work, turning up smelling of booze and generally acting the idiot, think again young man. My monthly reports on you have so far have been less than average, simply because you fail to impress me that you want to do this job. I'm detecting a real lack of interest and not just in time-keeping and turnout. I can help you with the paperwork and teach you beat duties, but commitment

is something you have to bring to the table on your own." She shrugged her shoulders, realising that having brought him down, maybe it was time for a little encouragement. "On the plus side, you're bright, articulate and better educated than I ever was. What seems to be letting you down is an adolescent immaturity that you think of yourself as some sort of wide boy. You're what, twenty-four now? It's time you consider joining the adult world. You want to be respected and get on; well it's all down to you. You have a wonderful opportunity to make a career in the police if that's what you really want. I suggest that when you get home tonight, you sit for an hour and think about what you really want to do and if need be, discuss it with someone that you trust, your parents maybe or even a pal." She finished, a little breathless and saw that he looked a little shame-faced. Had he been her son, he'd be getting a belt round the ear, but Dotty knew she could only push him so far. "Right," she took a deep breath, "let's get to that call now."

Jenny Farndale, dressed in an old pink coloured dressing gown while waiting on the bath filling, stood in the kitchen doorway and excitedly told her mother that she might be out for the night, adding her boyfriend Frederick had invited her to his house in Knightswood and she might be staying over. The mother was similarly excited, having already married off one daughter and one son, but she worried about Jenny being the oldest and hated the idea her daughter might end up a spinster on her own. Missus Farndale discounted her second son who had taken to the drink and drugs and left for London years previously. Good riddance, she inwardly thought, recalling the violence when he was doped or drunk, the nights when the polis turned up at the door informing her of another arrest and not to mention the missing cash and jewellery he had stolen from both his mother and Jenny to fund his habit.
"So, you'll maybe be meeting his mammy then, love?"
"I think so," Jenny's brow furrowed, "but he didn't say anything about dinner or that. I've to be there for eight o'clock so I'd better have something here before I go, eh?"
"I'll get the oven on then. So, pie, chips and beans all right?"
"Great," smiled Jenny and then half laughed, "don't bother about the beans, though. You know what I'm like with them."
Her mother stopped and turned, a little hesitant about raising the subject but she was, after all, a woman who had seen off a drunk, violent husband as well as her equally violent son and was much experienced in the ways of men. "Listen hen, I know your thirty-seven now and not a wee lassie and you'll be spending the night there. Make sure he uses a johnny and if he doesn't then don't be letting him, you know," now clearly embarrassed, her hands twisting at her apron, "come inside you, okay? You don't want to be left with a bairn and without a husband, not at your time of life, eh?"

Jenny's face reddened, ill at ease that her mother should give her this advice and dreading that she already knew what sexual activity Jenny had already experienced. She inwardly sighed. If mum only knew the number of times she had ached for a child, even on occasion more than a husband and jealously guarded her secret longing when she visited her sister and brother, each with their young families. "Right, I'll not be long if you want to get the dinner started," she avoided her mother's eyes as she made her way upstairs to the steaming bathroom, her thoughts turning to the evening's meeting and occupied by the opportunity for happiness that tonight might bring.

Chapter 14

Paul Hardie pulled the door open as the two officers entered the small path, his face a practised expression of concern and forcing himself to sound breathless, asked, "Is there any word yet? Have you found her?"
Cochrane was about to reply, then remembered this was Lesley's call and took a half step, permitting her to enter the door in front of him.
"Mister Hardie," Lesley asked, then in response to Paul's nod, replied, "I'm sorry, there hasn't been any news yet. The Inspector and I are here to conduct the obligatory house check, see if there might be something that you missed and to collect a photograph of your wife."
"Of course, please come through," Paul replied, turning in the narrow hallway and leading them into the lounge. "Please, take a seat," he indicated with his hand, his heart racing in his chest and ironically,causing his body to shiver and adding to the impression that he was a man under extreme stress, though not for the reasons the officers believed.
"Perhaps in a minute," Lesley smiled, anxious to put the obviously worried man at his ease. "If you wouldn't mind, can I have a look around the house while the Inspector discusses the photograph with you?"
He had to convince them he had nothing to hide and gestured towards the door. "Please, go on. There are two bedrooms upstairs. Anywhere you like," his heart raced even faster with the thought that he might have missed something and he worried himself almost to the point of nausea. So frightened was Paul by what the cops might find that he got himself into such a state that he thought he might hyperventilate.
With a glance at the Inspector, Lesley made towards the door while Cochrane took off his hat and pointed at the couch, his eyes requesting permission to sit down.
"Yes, of course, please sit," said Paul, "I'll get that photo," and walked into the kitchen from where he called out, "Can I get you and the lady a cup of coffee or tea?"

"No, you're all right, but thanks anyway," replied Cochrane, declining the offer as his eyes played about the room, taking in the confusion of mess and what seemed to be an obvious attempt at tidying up.

"Here we are," said Paul with a half smile, handing Cochrane the photograph of a smiling young woman dressed in a yellow coloured summer frock, sitting on a large rock beside a shoreline, her hair blown by the wind away from her face, hands clasped together at her knees.

"How recent is this photo, Mister Hardie?"

"Eh, just over two years I think. It was taken by a friend on a school away day. My wife was, is I mean," he hastily added, "a school teacher at Durban Road primary school."

"Has she changed much since this was taken?"

Paul wanted to scream out, yes, she became a slovenly pain in the arse, but controlling his temper, smiled and replied, "No, her hair is the same colour, natural I mean and about the same length."

Taking his pen from his belt pouch, Cochrane wrote 'MP - Fiona Hardie aged thirty years, photo taken two years previously' then added that day's date and said, "I'll have this copied and returned to you."

In the larger bedroom upstairs, Lesley glanced about and saw nothing that indicated a woman who for personal or domestic reasons, had suddenly decided to leave her husband. The small cupboard disclosed what looked like a full wardrobe of female clothing, much of what seemed to have been stuffed erratically into the shelving or hung on coat hangers and most of which was needing ironed. The set of drawers didn't reveal any obvious absence of clothing or underwear and Lesley concluded that when she left, Fiona Hardie likely went in the clothes she wore. Her eyebrows knitted as her nose twitched and she sniffed twice, then she glanced at the unmade bed, puzzled at the sheets and quilt cover that seemed overdue for changing. Pulling at the edge of the quilt she lightly run her hand across the creased sheets and wrinkled her nose at the smell of body odour released when she pulled the cover back then stood upright. Something pricked at her feminine curiosity, something she couldn't quite grasp. It annoyed her that she couldn't place her finger on what the something was and sighed. Time would likely tell, she decided and seeing nothing further that attracted her attention or could add to the mystery of why the MP took off, made for the stairs. She stopped at the bathroom and again stepped in, seeing with distaste the rim round the bath that needed scoured clean and the small, toilet mat that personally, she would have binned a long time ago. Binned, she thought the word again and stepped on the lever of the small flower decorated bin that sat under the sink. The lid lifted and as Lesley peered down into it she saw the bin to be empty, nothing in it at all. Not even a plastic bag liner. Glancing about the bathroom, her eyes took in the usual array of women's toiletry

bottles and jars on the window shelf, sitting beside a few gents' scent bottles and a hair spray. Bits of wrappers and an empty pack of feminine shaving razors sat among the debris. Again, Lesley's intuition told her that something was amiss, but once more she couldn't quite decide what. Sighing, she lifted her toe from the lever and closed the bin lid, then made her way downstairs. It was as she was at the bottom of the stairs she paused when she heard the Inspector ask Hardie, "You must be awfully worried, eh? When was the last time you spoke with your wife?"
"Eh, Tuesday morning it would be. Just as she was leaving for work I think it was. I gave her a call, just to say hello, you know?"
"And I don't suppose that at that time you had any reason to suspect she might be planning to take off for whatever reason?"
"No, none at all," Paul replied, then feigning anger, continued, "Bloody hell, if I thought that there was anything wrong…."
"That's me done upstairs, sir," interrupted Lesley as she deliberately pushed through the lounge door to cut off Hardie's rant. Both men stared at her with Cochrane rising from his seat and placing his cap on his head, inwardly thankful that Lesley had staved off a confrontation with Hardie.
"If you remember anything, anything at all Mister Hardie," continued Lesley, "I'm Constable Gold and I'll be overseeing your wife's missing person report. If you feel the need to speak to someone, please give me a call at the station or if I'm not available, leave word and I'll get back to you."
Cochrane followed her out in the hallway and Paul closed the door behind them more forcibly than he meant to.
In the hallway, Paul leaned back against the closed door and stared at his shaking hands. When he heard the sound of the patrol car being driven off, he began to laugh loudly, but with relief not humour.

It was not until a few minutes had passed and Lesley had driven from Borden Road that the Inspector spoke. "Okay, Constable Gold, spit it out. There's something bothering you, isn't there?"
Lesley didn't immediately reply; her thoughts a jumble as she tried to work out what had provoked her instinct that though everything seemed normal in the house, it wasn't quite right. The feeling persisted that she had seen yet not recognised or overlooked something. No, unconsciously shaking her head as she drove, her lips tight together, it disturbed her that she couldn't quite put her finger on what she had seen.
"Lesley?" prompted Cochrane.
"Oh, sorry sir, I was miles away. What did you say?" she risked a glance at him.
"I said, something bothered, you didn't it? In the house I mean."

She exhaled as she braked behind a bus stopped at a red light. "You know the feeling you get, when you think you know someone, but can't remember their name? Or when you've seen a face or heard a tune or something like that?"

Beside her, slumped in the seat, his attention distracted by the young, smiling blonde woman who walked by the car, he replied, "The kind of feeling that wakes you at three o'clock in the morning, you mean?"

"Aye, something like that," she inwardly grinned at his blush when he realised he had been caught ogling the blonde. "Well," she continued, "there's just something I think I missed, something that was shouting out 'Here, look at this', but I just can't put my finger on it and it's bugging the hell out of me." The mobile phone in her pocket beeped a text message.

"You want to pull over and get that?" he asked.

"If you don't mind," she said as she steered the car through the green light and into a lay-by across the junction. Wrestling the phone from her pocket, a quick glance at the screen indicated it was her mother who had first typed not to worry then asked Lesley to phone at her convenience. She grinned at the message, knowing that her mother was a digital immigrant rather than a digital native and must have laboured for several minutes to type the message, rather than use the predictor facility.

"Not bad news I trust from the smile on your face?"

"No sir, my mum had her own wee visit from the doctor today, not ill-health," she quickly turned to assure him, "just a wee morale booster, so to speak."

"The wiles of women," he sighed, "who will ever understand you lot. Last week when I was in town getting myself a couple of new shirts, I was in the Buchan Street Centre and I bought my wife some perfume, a bit of a bargain to be honest, but the bloody price of it took me aback. Not that I begrudge her, but she throws it about like bathwater. I haven't the heart to tell her I bought it because it was on sale, but when she opened it, phew," he waved a hand under his nose. "I thought it was too overpowering and I can't stand the smell of it. Wears it every bloody opportunity now," he moaned.

He glanced at Lesley in surprise when she slapped with her hand at his arm "Well done, sir. That's it. The smell," then pulling the car away from the kerb, said almost as an afterthought, "That's what has been bothering me; that and the bin."

Prior to ending his shift for the day, a weary Jinksie Paterson sat at his computer and collated the data of incidents that had occurred within the Garscadden Sub-Divisional area for the preceding twenty-four hour period that included just over a dozen traffic violations, three disorder offences, a half dozen reported crimes that included the theft of Missus McClafferty's lingerie, one snarling stray dog – thankfully returned to a grateful owner –and the report of Paul Hardie's missing wife. Well versed in the procedure, the task took him a mere ten minutes and once completed, Jinksie checked and re-checked the information then forwarded it by e-mail to the Divisional Headquarters Administration office at Maryhill. Received there, an equally weary assistant added the e-mail to the Headquarters own and three other Sub-Divisional e-mail incident reports and in turn, forwarded the lot to the statistical office at headquarters as well as copying it to the Media Department, who would cherry pick any items from the host of e-mails delivered that evening. These selected items would be analysed and those deemed worthy of publication by the media, fed to the local television or newspaper groups for broadcasting or publication. Of course, anything relevant to serious crime would first be discussed with investigating officers as to what information might be released; these officers always conscious that *sub judice* would apply and nothing of evidential value be mistakenly released that might either hamper the ongoing investigation or when judicially examined at court, hinder the rights of an accused individual. The less serious items that were to be considered for press release were normally chosen to request the public assist with information in solving some minor crime.

Like any office in any business elsewhere, the Media Department had its pecking order and though administered by a senior police officer, was mostly staffed by civilian support officers, many of whom were far more qualified in media issues than the police officers who managed and supervised them. That evening, Chief Inspector Harriet 'Harry' Downes was having a bad ending to an already bad day. Head in her hands, she sat at her desk in the hubbub of the main office, staring at the paperwork in front of her, considering the many ways she could murder her husband and get away with it, all of which involved him on his knees begging for forgiveness. He had just phoned to tell her that not only had the useless sod reversed his new Kia four by four into the garage door, but getting out from the car in panic, slipped and done his back in and was waiting for an ambulance to collect him as he lay on the drive-way. Sighing, she glanced up as the young trainee assistant Sharon, who stood nervously by her desk. Forcing a smile, she asked, "What can I do for you, pet?"

"Ah, these e-mails that just arrived from the city Divisions. What do I do with them, print them off or …" The young girl's hesitancy indicated her youthfulness and panic. Harry couldn't help but smile and glancing over to another, more experienced assistant, called out, "Mary, give the lassie a wee hand, pet. I've a domestic emergency I need to get to," she said, reaching for her jacket and handbag, her thoughts already engaged in planning her route through the rush-hour traffic to the Victoria Infirmary.

Unfortunately Mary, or 'Typhus' as she was commonly referred to behind her back, was a poor choice and frowning as she watched Harry's retreating back, snapped quietly at the young girl, "Listen, you've been here long enough now Sharon to know what we give the newspapers, so have a look through and anything that catches your eye, local housebreakings, street robbery, anything you think they might print in their crime bulletin column, do the usual. Pick out three, four or five items and just type up a wee summary and the name of the officer or the office that's dealing with it, okay?"

Sharon nervously nodded, wishing instead she could revert to the early days when her main duties were making tea and coffee and running back and forth with errands. Turning, she sat at her lonely desk, willing the e-mails in front of her to go away or the fire alarm to activate and even considered a dead faint that would somehow get her out of this predicament. Taking a deep breath she slowly exhaled and gamely deciding that sitting there wouldn't help, began to read the first of the e-mails.

Almost twenty minutes later, her lips tightly pressed together, she nodded with satisfaction and pressed the button that e-mailed her summary to the Inspector, who sat in the corner desk idly chewing at his already bitten fingernails and called out to him, asking that he read over what she had typed and to authorise for press release. The young and ambitious Inspector absent-mindedly wondered if Downes would be back to work tomorrow or if her husband's unfortunate accident might offer the Inspector the opportunity to take charge of the department, at least for the day. He half listened to the wee lassie Sharon, who had recently started with the Department and waved a hand back, pretending to concentrate on a report in front of him. When Sharon's e-mail arrived on his monitor he hardly glanced at the summary before returning the e-mail to her with his name and the word 'approved' typed below.

The Inspector's misplaced trust in his staff's summarising of press releases was later to be the subject of a verbal scolding from his boss, Harry Downes.

The supervising reporter at the 'Glasgow News' crime desk put down the phone and glancing at the notes he had scribbled, smiled. The wee lassie Sharon at police headquarters, he decided, must be new because that lot never usually provided so much information. Setting the notes down in front of him he began lazily typing at his computer, frowning as he wondered why the police were so concerned that they needed to make an urgent appeal about a primary schoolteacher who had been missing for such a short time.

Paul Hardie sat slumped in the chair, worrying about the visit by the two police officers. He wasn't stupid and knew that the man, the Inspector, had sat with him to distract Paul from what the woman cop was doing upstairs. Twice he had checked every room as minutely as he could, trying to see the room from her perspective, but nothing seemed changed; nothing seemed to be different. They had left without comment and he had breathed a sigh of relief, but then paranoia set in. Had he missed anything? More importantly, did they suspect something? His mind raced and his right hand shook slightly as he nervously tapped out a rhythm with his fingers on the arm of the chair. He stood up and again glanced at the tiled hearth, his body giving an involuntary shudder, then supporting himself with his hands on the mantelpiece, knelt down and lowered his head, sniffing at the floorboards; nothing. With almost a sigh of relief he pushed himself to his feet and began to smile, a smile that turned to a grin and then found that he was laughing uproariously. What was he worried about? He had done it, reported his wife missing and the cops had searched his house. She would never be found and he was free and clear. But then another thought occurred to him, did they bug the house? The next hour was spent checking everywhere the female cop had been, but then he forced himself to be calm. What possible reason would the police have for bugging his house? As far as they were concerned, his wife was missing, not dead. All he had to do now was keep his head. In his mind, he guessed that in the days to come, there would be more police activity, maybe even an appeal for information. Smiling, his ribs now aching from laughing and a release of tension, he imagined there might even be a television appeal, he the worried husband appealing for his wife to come home, the sympathy that it would evoke. He burped as his stomach rumbled and realised that he was hungry, that he hadn't eaten for some time and striding into the kitchen stopped. Maybe treat myself to a take-away curry, he thought and a few cans too. That's what I'll do. I'll nip out to the shop and fetch one in. No need to hang about here, he almost grinned as he glanced about him, waiting for a telephone call that would never come.

Her bath completed, Jenny Farndale, sat naked under her old bathrobe at the worn and chipped wooden dressing table in the privacy of her room and with a careful hand, cleared a space between the bottles and lotions that littered the top. Resting with both elbows on the table top, she leaned forward to get that little closer to the mirror. Jenny wanted to impress Frederick and was taking extra care with her make-up, trying the different shades of eyeliner and unable to decide which one made her look sultry. With a sigh she sat back and stared at her reflection, knowing in her heart that she would never be as beautiful as the creatures that adorned the packets lying in front of her. She smiled as a thought came to her, remembering a conversation that occurred a few days earlier when in the privacy of the female staff room, the supervisor and the other kitchen staff had laughed and joked about what turned their husbands and boyfriends on. Jenny had at first sat shyly, listening wide-eyed and then joining the laughter as the lewd and crude comments had been passed between the women as each tried to outdo the others with their outrageous stories. But now, some of those stories and the things the women had got up to, or at least told each other they did, came back to Jenny and with a grin, she made her decision. Slutty she could do and rummaged in the drawer at the side of the table for the suspender belt that a former man friend had insisted she wore when she visited him. She hadn't worn the belt or the stockings since that time, the memory of his demands making her blood run cold and she shivered, recalling with inward shame the handcuffs he insisted she wear. Though it was four years since that time, she decided that tonight, wearing the sussies might distract Frederick from what bloody eyeliner she was wearing. Her eyes narrowed and lips pressed tightly together, she stared at her reflection. In two months she would be thirty-seven years old and had never had a steady boyfriend, at least not one that lasted more than a week or so. Her thoughts turned to the day when Frederick had saved her from the man outside the café in Union Street and unconsciously, she raised a thin hand to her throat. She had known from that time that no matter what he asked of her, she was his. She inwardly prayed that he felt the same for her. Selecting a blood-red coloured lipstick, her eyes wide and lips pursed, she again leaned towards the mirror. "Tonight, Jenny," she deepened her voice in mimicry of a popular television game show host, "you're going all out for the star prize! Tonight you're going for broke!"

Inspector Cochrane glanced at his wristwatch and said, "You can drop me at the office, please Lesley. That's nearly six o'clock and I don't get paid for extra hours," he grinned at her.
"Right sir," she replied and steered the car towards Garscadden.
"So, you think there was something fishy about the smell in the Hardie's house then? Ah, when I say fishy, I don't mean …."
"I understand, sir," grinned Lesley, then continued, "It just seemed so odd, the fresh smelling lounge and to be honest, from what I saw downstairs and upstairs, housewifery wasn't Missus Hardie's first career choice. That and the bin in the bathroom had been emptied, you know the type, one of they wee peddle bin things? It was clean as a whistle and suggested to me that there had been a plastic bag insert in the bin that had been lifted out. Why do that and ignore the bits of paper and things lying discarded on the shelf in the bathroom and on the windowsill?"
"What kind of things?"
"Oh, on the windowsill there was an empty pack of plastic razor blade things, that contains the blades, you know?"
Cochrane nodded.

Her eyebrows narrowed as she recalled and continued. "And on the shelf there was an empty Paracetamol box with the used blister foil pack beside it and the paper instructions from the box and a wee empty paper bag. Just rubbish, but as I said, why empty the bin and its contents and leave those things lying there? It doesn't make any sense."

"Perhaps they were put there after the bin was emptied and don't you think that maybe you're judging other people's cleanliness habits by your own? My wife is always telling me off for, as she puts it, leaving things at my arse."

Lesley smiled and voice dripping with sarcasm, nodded, "You're a man, so it's to be expected," but then she added, "Could be that you're right about me judging my habits against the MP's I mean, but it was the fresh air smell when I was in the lounge. You must have smelled it, as though one of they candle things had been lit. I mean for example, if I was expecting visitors for dinner, I would probably light a couple to get rid of cooking smells or leave one lit in the toilet."

It was Cochrane's turn to smile this time as he commented, "No need to explain that one."

"Aye, well, you know what I mean. And did you see the tiles on the fire surround? They were spotlessly clean, polished almost. That seemed to me to be at odds with the rest of the place. It was they wee things that just seemed," she hesitated, "like a complete contradiction of the state of the rest of the house, you know?"

"So you think Mister Hardie, knowing the polis would be calling by, decided to clean up the fireplace and get rid of some incriminating smell in his lounge?" he teased her.

Lesley drew the car to a halt within the rear yard and switched off the engine. Turning to Cochrane, she stared at him. "From your experience, sir, what's the one, strong sickly sweet smell that lingers after a day or two?"

Cochrane's eyes narrowed in thought and then it hit him and he wasn't smiling now as he returned her stare. "Blood," he softly replied.

Chapter 15

Cochrane, sitting behind his desk, all thought of going home now abandoned, slowly shook his head and said, "For heaven's sake Lesley, you can't go and accuse a man of doing his wife in on the basis of a scented smell, a clean toilet bin and a polished tile fireplace. There's not even enough to go to the CID and seek their advice. Those sods would laugh you out of the office."

"Okay sir, I know that," she replied, pacing in front of the desk, one thumb hooked into her utility belt and the other rubbing at her chin, "but you must admit, together these three things form a strange set of coincidences. A woman who reputedly has never previously taken off suddenly gets on her toes. Did he mention if he'd checked their banking arrangements, if his wife had drawn any cash since she was last seen?"

"No, there has been no activities on the account by her, no withdrawals at all. He believes whatever money she had in her purse is the total she took with her and before you ask, he has no idea how much that will be, but doesn't think it can be more than a few quid, twenty pounds at the very most. Apparently she never liked to carry much cash and usually paid for purchases with plastic."

She glanced at the copy report her Inspector had returned to her. "The report says she was driven home from school by the janny, that she had been feeling unwell or something. So the car must still be up there? Maybe there is something in the car that will indicate why she took off."

Cochrane shook his head. "Earlier this afternoon, Mister Hardie collected the car from the school. He told me that he had been right through the car, but there was nothing in it to indicate why his wife had left."

Lesley frowned as she continued to pace up and down; a habit that she had since childhood and believed helped her to think more clearly. She would have liked a look in the car herself, but didn't want to push it with the Inspector. He should have known better than to take the husband's word that there was nothing in the car, but his earlier admittance that he was out of touch with MP inquiries partially absolved him for making that error. "So, let's recap. She disappears, seems to have little money with her and doesn't take the car. That means having been left in the house alone, well, presumably alone, she must have exited and either walked away or caught a taxi."

"Presumably alone?" repeated Cochrane, his eyes narrowing.

"No suggestion by the husband of a third party, a boyfriend or anything?"

Cochrane blushed. "Maybe I should have searched upstairs and let you question the husband, Lesley. Sorry, I didn't ask that question."

"Don't be annoyed with yourself, sir. It's not an easy question to ask when a husband or wife report their spouse has gone away, for whatever reason. If Missus Hardie doesn't turn up within the next day or two, it's likely we'll be making another call to that address so we can probe a little deeper then.

"What about the question of her maybe being pregnant? Do you think that her hormones or something has kicked in? Perhaps the thought of being pregnant kind of," he hesitated, feeling himself sliding into unknown territory where women's hormones were concerned.

Lesley smiled at his discomfort. "You think all we women are ruled by hormones, sir? That we do daft things at a certain time of the month or during some events in our life?" she teased.

Cochrane raised his hands in surrender. "All right Lesley, I give in. I accede to your superior knowledge, both about women's hormones and your suspicions about the MP and her husband. So, here's what I think we'll do. I'll go home to my nice hot bath and dinner that Missus Cochrane will hopefully have ready for her hard working and embarrassed husband. You, on the other hand, take your piece break and then because you don't have a neighbour for the rest of the evening, I want you to inform the control room that I have instructed you to continue the inquiry on the MP. Take a car to Divisional HQ and make some copies of the photo of the MP," he leaned across the desk to hand it to Lesley, "and follow up what inquiry you can tonight. The school janny for instance, it might be worth having a word with him. Maybe you can also do a wee door to door, see if anyone saw the MP departing the house after the time she was dropped off. However, what you are not to do," he stressed as he stared into her eyes, "is re-visit Mister Hardie and batter him into any sort of confession. We might be totally wrong, his wife could be sitting at her friend's or in a hotel somewhere with a boyfriend, about to phone home to let him know she's fine. If any more visits are to be made to the Hardie house, it will be a double manned visit. Is that clearly understood?"

"Yes sir," Lesley quickly replied, yet pleased that the Inspector had permitted her to continue with the inquiry. "I'm late shift tomorrow, so I'll leave a short summary for you to read in the morning of how I get on."

"Don't bother," he wearily replied as he stood and shrugged out of his belt and vest. "Because Morris is still off, I'm changing my shift tomorrow. I'll be your neighbour for the evening, so I'll see you at four."

Lesley found Dotty Turner and Alex Mason sitting in uncomfortable silence in the small canteen and almost immediately realised there was a bit of an atmosphere. "Thought I'd join you guys for a cuppa before I get to work on the missing person inquiry," she said, handing Dotty the photograph of Fiona Hardie.

"Nice looking young woman. So, what's the real reason for her taking off?" asked Dotty.

"Nothing to tell really," replied Lesley, sitting in the chair between her two colleagues as Dotty handed the photo across to Alex. "She was taken home yesterday from work, she's a primary school teacher at Dunbar Road," she explained, "and her husband claims when he returned home from his job, she was gone and hasn't been seen since."

"Claimed?" repeated Dotty, her interest now peaked by Lesley's one word of doubt.

"Well, nothing to say otherwise, to be honest, just a few things that set my nose twitching."

Alex stared from one to the other, then said, "Women," and with that one word, stood and left the room.

"Had words have we," smiled Lesley.

"Let's just say he was told a few home truths and is in the huff."

"Oh dear, men and their sensitivities," she grinned and then related her suspicions to Dotty, realising the woman was no longer just a colleague, but quickly becoming a trusted friend.

The remains of the carry-out meal lay discarded on the table. His hunger now satisfied and a sixth can of lager opened and sitting on the mantelpiece, Paul Hardie was in a good, lager fuelled humour as he set the ironing board up in the lounge and switched on the iron to heat. Making his way unsteadily upstairs, he fetched his best suit and what looked like a clean shirt from the ironing basket and returned downstairs, missing the second last step and only just managing to grab at the wall before he fell to the floor, giggling at his stupidity. His mind was made up. Tomorrow he was returning to work and this time, he spat a globule of saliva upon the underside hotplate of the iron to test the heat, his mood now grim, this time he wouldn't cave in like some fucking office boy. He had accepted the dismissal of his position too easily and was ashamed about whining at the loss of his job. The HR manager Colin Davis would have a different man to deal with now. He would demand his job back or the company would find themselves facing a law suit for unfair dismissal. Working in the general office with the plebs? I think not, he savagely attacked the shirt with the iron, pressing down on it as though it were the very face of Davis himself. He burped and turned the shirt over, his thoughts filled with the argument he would make for reinstatement. And that reinstatement would present the opportunity to win back Janice, thoughts of her now filling his head. Yes, he grinned, she would be pleased to see him back and particularly now he didn't have a wife hanging about his neck. Of course, he pulled a solemn face as he turned the shirt to iron at the sleeve, he would explain that his wife for some unaccountable reason had left him, that he was concerned for her safety, her state of mind and had been so worried he had reported her missing to the police and it was their problem now. As far as he was concerned, the longer Fiona stayed away, he would tell her, the better it would be for Janice and him. He would accept people's sympathy, their regret that his wife had left him and he would continue to play the part of the worried and saddened husband, at least for a while. There would come a time he would come to accept that Fiona was not coming home and tell people, friends and colleagues that he must move on with his life and then he and Janice could openly live together. He wondered how long it must be before he could file for divorce and decided he would look into it, wondering how he went about citing Fiona's abandonment of him.

In Paul Hardie's drink fuelled mind, he was becoming the victim, the husband whose wife had cast him aside and those thoughts fitted in nicely with his future plans.

He glanced at the telephone sitting on the small side table by the fireplace and smiled. Perhaps he should phone Janice now, just to let her know he was coming back to work tomorrow, give her the opportunity to prepare herself to apologise for the harsh words she had used when they last parted.

Carefully, he set the iron on its stand and hands in front of him as he warily made his way round the narrow legged ironing table and sat heavily down on the armchair by the phone. Lifting the handset from the cradle, he pressed the buttons for Janice's flat number and listened as the call dialled.

"Hello?" Janice Meikles's voice was silkily smooth in his ear.

"Hi darling," Paul replied, "thought I'd give you a quick call just to …"

"Why are you calling me?" was the icy, hissed reply.

He was taken aback, then realised she probably didn't realise it was him. "It's me, Paul," he jauntily responded, "I wanted to …"

"I know who it is Paul," she again interrupted him, her voice low, "I told you, we're finished. Do not call me again. Lose my phone number, do you hear?"

His eyes widened in shocked surprise, unwilling to accept what he was hearing. He was about to make a response when he heard a voice in Janice's background calling out to her, "Who is it sweetheart? What's wrong? Is there a problem?" just as the line went dead.

Paul slammed the phone down into its cradle, his face pale as a vicious rage overcame him. He sat very still and unable to believe who he had just heard. The last time Paul heard the man speak was when he informed Paul that he no longer had a job, the voice of the HR manager, Colin Davis.

Lesley Gold finished her sandwiches and carrying her mug of tea, walked into the dimly lit and empty Uniform Bar. The front door of the office was now closed and any callers were instructed by a notice on the wall adjacent to the door to attend at Maryhill Police Office or in the event of an emergency, use the handset set into the wall under the notice that would connect them immediately with the control room at Maryhill. Or that's what it was supposed to do and was another item in Jinksie Paterson's list of complaints to the Chief Inspector.

With nobody about, Lesley didn't think that the misuse of a phone call would dent the police budget and settling herself at Jinksie's desk, dialled her parent's number and then listened as her mother answered.

"Hi mum, it's me," she replied to her mother's greeting. "Any change?"

"Nothing dear," she heard her mum sigh. "You got my text message, about Doctor McPherson?"

"Not angry with me, are you?"

"No, of course I'm not angry. Surprised when the old codger turned up on the doorstep, mind you, but we had a nice long chat and he scoffed most of my Abernethy biscuits, but it was a nice wee visit."

"Did he say anything? About you, I mean?"

"Well, I know you're at your work, so I'll not keep you on the phone, but he offered me a couple of day's respite. You know, the McMillan nurses come in full time for a few days and I get to go away, clear my head as it were. Maybe get some rest," she sighed again.

Lesley bit at her lower lip, already knowing the answer. "What did you say to that, mum?"

"I'd love to dear, but let's not kid ourselves. Your dad's got days, weeks at the most and every minute with him is precious. When the...." she hesitated, then began again. "When the time comes there will be time enough for me to get all the rest I need. That doesn't mean I'm not grateful for the offer and for you contacting the Doc. It just again tells me that you are one special girl, a daughter I am so very proud of."

Lesley felt tears forming in her eyes and used her sleeve to wipe at them. Not trusting herself to speak, she feigned coughing and then, more composed, said, "I'll need to go mum. That's me got a radio message," she lied without malice.

"Okay dear. You be careful now. Give me a wee text to let me know that you're home safe."

"Mum," Lesley sighed with exaggerated annoyance, "I'm a big girl now and I don't finish till two in the morning."

"Don't worry about that, her mother replied, "I'll probably be awake anyway. Goodnight darling."

"Night mum," Lesley's voice was almost a whisper as she returned the handset to its cradle.

She sat for a minute; her thoughts filled with her mother, the heavy burden she bore. Standing, she was about to turn towards the corridor that would return her to the back office when she saw the flash of bright yellow lying on the counter that separated the bar from the public side. As she stared and walked towards the counter she realised it was a bunch of yellow tulips and then found herself smiling as she lifted and sniffed at the dozen or so flowers. Curious, she saw that a small white coloured envelope was attached by a thin piece of string sellotaped to the wrapping and with a quick glance over her shoulder to ensure she was alone, opened the envelope. Removing the small card inside, she saw in neat and precise handwriting the words: *For the new police woman, kind regards.*

She smiled at the unsigned inscription and then it struck her and her head snapped up with understanding. Lesley was the office's new police woman. The flowers were meant for her.

The first call Lesley made was to Borden Road where she knocked on doors to right and left of number nineteen. The residents that answered were first curious, then surprised at her questioning. No, they invariably answered, none of them had seen Missus Hardie on the day in question. No, most of them added, they didn't know the young couple at number nineteen, though the elderly man who resided at number twelve took the opportunity to complain about the indiscriminate parking in the narrow street. The loudness of the television from the lounge seemed to strongly suggest the old guy was deaf.

"Look at that," he pointed with a shaky finger at a fire red coloured Mini car. "Bloody doesn't even live here," he whined, "comes every other day to visit the daughter at number eight. Why the hell doesn't he park outside their house instead of my house, the inconsiderate sod, bloody cheek he has. You lot should be doing something about that. I pay my taxes, you know."

Looking at the octogenarian, Lesley suspected it was well over two decades since Mister McMillan had paid any kind of tax.

"And him too," he pointed at a grey coloured Focus car. "That's him at number nineteen. Nineteen?" his eyes narrowed with suspicion. "Is that not the house you were talking about officer?"

"Aye sir," Lesley replied, trying to think of a way she could tactfully withdraw from the door. "So, you didn't see anything a couple of days ago, when Missus Hardie was reported missing?"

"Who's Missus Hardie again?"

Lesley sighed and thanking the old man, moved on. Half an hour later, she was no further forward and spent another forty minutes in Austen Road, but again without any success and decided enough was enough. She took a note of the doors where there was no response to her knocking to try again the following day.

The delivery of flowers occupied Lesley's thoughts as she drove to the Divisional Headquarters at Maryhill and surprised curiosity turned to rage when she decided the only sender who came to mind had to be Mike Duffy. Stopped at a red traffic light on Maryhill Road, she slammed her hand against the steering wheel and shouted, "Bastard!" with such force the elderly male driver stopped on the inside lane turned to stare at her. Face blazing with embarrassed shame, Lesley ignored his stare and committed the cardinal sin of boy racers by speeding through the amber light and performing 'Hollywood Tyres' as she screeched away.

Slowing as she approached the office, she turned into the rear yard and parked the car in an empty bay, deciding to sit for a moment to recover her composure. That done, she got out of the car and pushing through the security door, headed for the first floor where she knew that though all the civilian staff had gone home for the night, the administration offices would be unlocked to permit the duty late and nightshift bar staff to use the copy machines located there.

While working at Maryhill, Lesley had briefly been seconded to the Admin and was well versed in the use of the colour laser printer. She pressed the starter button to warm the machine up to copy Fiona Hardie's photograph. As the photograph passed through the machine and the dozen copies began to print off, a voice behind her said, "Thought it was you. How are you doing, Lesley?"

Mike Duffy stood in civilian clothes, his arms folded as he casually leaned against the door jamb. He still sported a yellowy bruising to his nose and she had heard that because of his facial injury, he was working indoors for a couple of weeks till the bruising healed.

"Michael," she nodded to him and turned away to avoid him seeing her red face. She swallowed hard, anxious to be gone.

"You never answered my text messages," his voice was almost accusing.

"I didn't see any need to reply. We're not together anymore. You and your blonde bird saw to that."

"She's not my blonde bird," he scoffed, but what infuriated Lesley was that he smiled.

"She had the hots for me, Lesley," he continued with a shrug. "It was her that was doing the chasing. I just took her out to dinner to explain that I wasn't available, that I was already in a relationship with you," he leaned off the door jamb and made to take a step towards her.

Lesley bristled, and raised both her hands to ward him off. She gave a half laugh and shaking her head, said, "And you think a bunch of flowers would win me back? You probably think of yourself as a right cocky bastard, eh?"

He stopped a few feet from her, his own hands spread out before him, a fleeting puzzled expression replaced almost immediately by an easy grin on his face that she had once found attractive. "Look, doll, I tried to say I'm sorry. You got the wrong end of the stick and," pointing a forefinger to the fading, but still visible bruising on his face, "I think you had more than enough compensation for any hurt you might have felt."

Both hands now flat on the copying machine, to stop them from shaking, she turned her head and stared him in the eye, her voice icily cold. "Listen to me very carefully, Sergeant Duffy. I neither want to speak with you nor do I want anything to do with you. If you don't immediately turn and leave this room I will scream the fucking place down and accuse you of improper behaviour towards me. I will tell anyone who listens that you tried to touch me and fondle me and to back it up I will punch, scratch, bite and claw you. I will count to three and …."

"The offices are empty, there's nobody on this floor. Who the fuck do you think will hear you, eh?" he sneered at her, his hand balling into fists.
"Do you want to take that chance, do you!" she screamed back at him.
He stopped and she saw uncertainty in his eyes. She knew she had won.
"You're off your head, you fat bitch!" he hissed at her.
"And you're a wanker," she quietly retorted as she turned back towards the machine.
She didn't watch him walk away, more sensed that he had gone. She felt numb inside, but a little better about herself.
Fat bitch, she almost smiled. Well, we'll see about that.

The private hire taxi driver turned to the young woman in the rear of his car and smiled. "Here you are then hen, number forty-six. That will be thirteen pounds sixty, please"
As Jenny Farndale rummaged in her purse for the fare, her stomach was knotted and she felt queasy. Her nerves were getting the better of her and her legs felt as if they wouldn't support her on the short distance from the taxi to Frederick's front door. As she handed the driver a ten and a five pound note, Frederick glanced from the lounge window and seeing the taxi stop outside, rushed to greet her at the door.
"Big date tonight, then?" smiled the driver, pretending to search in his leather purse for the change, a ploy he was well versed in and usually resulted in the customer telling him not to bother.
Right on cue Jenny said, "Keep the change," and pushed open rear passenger door. As she swung her left leg to exit the car, the short dress rode up allowing the driver to see a stocking top and flash of bare thigh and he grinned. The skinny bird was wearing sussies and somebody was getting his Nat King Cole tonight, he thought and then cast a glance at the thin man standing in the doorway. That must be the lucky bastard, he inwardly grinned again as he pulled away from the kerb.
"Did you find us all right then?" asked Frederick, aware that he sounded almost as nervous as Jenny looked.
"Aye, no problem, I just got a taxi straight here," she breathlessly replied as she laid the small bulging bag on the floor and turned to allow him to slip her three quarter length coat from her. When she turned back, he was astounded at the change in her. Her hair was freshly washed and shampooed and she wore it down, over her shoulders. It was obvious she had taken some time preparing her make-up and the blush of her cheeks accentuated the red, ruby fire of her lips. Sparkling earrings dangled on either side and she wore a dress of shimmering silver, so low cut that wearing her new bra, it exposed most of the top of her small breasts and pushed them out to their full prominence. The dress came down to a few inches above her knees and his mouth suddenly

dry, he saw it was zipped at one side and already in his imagination he was helping Jenny step out from it.

"You must be Jennifer," said his mother's voice from behind him. Turning, he saw Eunice with her hand outstretched, wearing an old, faded but clean apron and squeezing past him in the narrow hallway.

"Jenny," she nervously replied and took the older woman's hand and allowed herself to be led through the door at her side into the front lounge.

"Mother," Frederick tried to interrupt, his voice raised in impatience, but Eunice was not to be denied the pleasure of meeting her son's friend and a lovely young female one at that, she inwardly thanked God.

"Sit dear, sit," Eunice ushered Jenny to a comfortable old armchair.

Jenny settled herself onto the chair, her knees tightly drawn together and hands clasped on her knees to stop them from shaking, afraid that is she sat fully back on the comfortable deep chair she would expose more than her stocking legs. It occurred to her that Frederick must have spoken about Jenny to his mum and her heart leapt with joy. If he had discussed her with his mum, maybe he really was serious about her and this visit wasn't just about another one night stand that had so worried her, on the journey over here. Her stomach felt that it was turning somersaults.

Frederick surrendered and knew no matter what he said, he must allow his mother her ten minutes before he could get Jenny upstairs to his room.

To what seemed to Frederick to be an interminable length of time, Eunice droned on in her interrogation of Jenny, questioning where she lived, her family history, her job and even her holiday plans. Finally, unable to take any more, Frederick rescued her from Eunice's clutches and reminded his mother that both he and Jenny were going to do some computer work on his laptop, that she needn't disturb them. He took Jenny by the hand while with the other, carried her bag and led her upstairs.

At last alone in his room, he turned to her and with dry mouth and nervous hands, stroked both sides of her face. Jenny too was nervous and wondered if she should first take her dress off, but thought maybe as she always did with men, she would let Frederick take the lead. Kissing her he first smelled then tasted the fresh, minty toothpaste of her breath. As she made to wrap her arms round him, he gently took hold of her arms and walked her backwards till clumsily, her legs backed against the single bed. His breathing was becoming more rapid and he worried that just as he did in the car, he might again prematurely ejaculate.

Jenny wasn't certain what she should do. Her total experience of men was that there usually wasn't any foreplay. They wanted her undressed, lain down, sometimes saying to her and having her repeat dirty words to them and then wham, bang, thank you ma'am and when it was over, they usually fell asleep. Inwardly taking a deep breath, she stared into his eyes, gulped and said with a nervous voice, "Do you want me to take my dress off, Frederick?"

"Here, let me help you," he instantly replied with the realisation that all his hopes and anticipation were about to come true. Unbelievably, here he was in his bedroom, about to strip a woman of her clothes. With shaking fingers, he brushed aside her hands and unzipped the dress. Jenny raised her arms to permit him to pull the dress over her head and as he did so, he stared fascinated at her pale skin, the almost see-through material of her wired bra that was unable to restrain the sudden swell of her protruding nipples. He tossed the dress onto a wooden chair at the side of the bed as wordlessly, he stood back to stare wide-eyed and open mouthed at her.

Jenny was embarrassed at his attention and swallowing deeply, used both her hands to pat down her hair that had ruffled when the dress had been pulled over her head. The very sight of her standing there, in black coloured bra and matching pants, stockings and suspenders with her arms raised as she stroked back her hair seemed to disconcert him and fingers still shaking, he almost hesitantly reached out to stroke at her breasts.

Jenny blinked with intuitive understanding. Frederick was more nervous than she was and acutely realising that perhaps she was also more sexually experienced than him, took his right hand and placed it on the top of her left breast, feeling his anxiousness as she placed her hand on his and squeezed. Her experience had taught her that men liked to hear women moan and her eyes half closed, pretended a gasp of pleasure as she tightened his fingers on the softness of her skin. With sudden insight, she realised that for the first time in her life, she was in control; that a man who wanted and desired her was now at her beck and call, that she would lead him to bed and teach him what she knew and inwardly smiling, was beginning to relax and enjoy the novel experience.

"Why don't you take your clothes off too?" she coyly asked as reaching forward, she began to unbutton his shirt.

Less than five minutes later, Eunice Evans, standing silently at the bottom of the stairs, listened intently and upon hearing the creaking of the floorboards in Frederick's room, clapped her hands together in joyful, if quiet applause and with a knowing smile, walked towards the kitchen to make herself a nice cup of tea.

Chapter 16 – Friday

Frederick came awake before the alarm sounded, at first confused at the bare arm that lay across him then remembering it was Jenny. For the first time in his life, he was not alone in bed. He lay very still, listening as she gently snored. The morning sun entered the room through a crack where the blind and the wall met, lighting the room sufficiently for him to see the abandoned clothing that lay on the floor. With a start, he realised he was naked beneath the quilt cover and needed to get to the bathroom to relieve the pressure on his bladder. As quietly as he dared, he slid one leg, then the other from the bed and sat up. Slowly turning his head, he saw that Jenny, lying on her side in the narrow bed and turned towards him, still slept, her dark hair spread on the pillow, her mouth slightly open and shoulders bare, He grinned, recognising that she too was naked and as gently as he could, pulled the quilt down to expose her pert breasts. He felt himself respond to her nakedness, but thought first he should pee. Stifling a giggle at his good fortune, he snatched his robe from behind the door and crept from the room to the toilet. As he made his water, he smiled at the memory of the previous night and admitted to himself, Jenny was useful to practise with in the dark of his bedroom, but while he had been screwing her, his thoughts were of the girls from lingerie and make-up.

It was the thought of those young woman that again excited him and remembering Jenny's sleeping nakedness, returned a few minutes later to the room where he disappointingly discovered that Jenny was not only awake, but dressed in a clean, white blouse and sitting on the edge of the bed, pulling on a pair of faded jeans she had brought with the blouse in her bag. His previous evening's ardour was now gone and as he stared at her, he saw her for the plain Jane that she was, a thin woman with small tits, lank hair and bad skin.

"Morning," she shyly smiled at him and then she inwardly sighed, recognising in his expression the attitude of men who had previously used her. She swallowed deeply and stifled a tear and half expected him to say he had called her a taxi. But remembering the excitement of the previous night, of being in control while they made love, she surprised herself with her determination and silently gritted her teeth, vowing not this time; this time she would decide what was going to happen next.

"Ah, Jenny, good morning," he formally replied as if surprised to find her there. "Sleep well?"

"Not too bad. How about you, did you sleep well Frederick?"

"Ah, yes. Look, about last night …"

"I really enjoyed myself Frederick," she interrupted him. "You're an amazing lover," she faked a gasp, believing that was what he wanted to hear. "Not that I've had a lot of experience or anything," she hastily added, realising that confessing her previous sexual liaisons might hinder any likelihood of a further relationship with him and Jenny was determined that like it or not, Frederick *was* going to have a relationship with her. An overpowering sense of something she didn't quite understand took hold of her. Then, almost as if inspiration had jabbed a forefinger in her back, she recognised what was happening. She was in control, she had the power.

Frederick was stunned. Last night in bed he had been awkwardly embarrassed at his fumbling of her, shocked to find he had relied on her to guide him in their coitus. All the imagined plans he had for her, what he would have her do, her apparent shy submissiveness, had eluded him when his horror of failing her as a man overtook him.

She sensed that he was uncomfortable and standing to button the jeans, said, "Look, last night was just the first of a lot of nights together, if you're okay with that? I mean, you'd like that Frederick, wouldn't you? Me dressing up for you and doing things for you," she softly whispered as she moved closer to him.

"Yes, of course. Indeed. Yes, definitely," he replied, his voice almost a squeak and unable to avoid her piercing gaze, but she sensed that he was a little hesitant, a little uncertain.

"So," she inwardly took a deep breath, now standing inches from him. "I mean, after last night, our being together and everything. That's us official, isn't it? Going out together I mean, boyfriend and girlfriend. Like a proper couple?" She continued staring into his eyes, her hopes for her future dependent on his reply and decided that a little encouragement might not be amiss. Taking one hand in hers, she guided it to the swell of her breast and with her other hand, tugged at the drawstring and drawing apart his robe, gently probed with her fingers at his groin.

Wide-eyed, Frederick startled at her touch and felt himself become aroused. "Yes, of course," he quickly nodded in agreement as he gulped. "As you say Jenny, we're a couple."

Just as Frederick was experiencing Jenny's subtle touch, approximately one mile distant as the crow flies Paul Hardie was awakening with a blinding headache and a mouth that tasted of strong curry and stale beer. Groaning softly, he rubbed at his stomach and turned to see the curtains wide open. He pulled the pillow over his head to block out the stream of sunlight that poured through the window, deciding to lie on for a few minutes to gather his thoughts and then remembered that he had made the decision to travel this morning to work and confront Colin Davies. The thought of the HR manager's very name caused Paul to grimace with rage. Angrily he sat up and throwing the covers from him, swung his legs towards the floor. Moving too quickly, that was his first mistake. His stomach heaved and the bile in his throat threatened to erupt. One hand clasped over his mouth, he raced towards the door and the toilet and made his second mistake. Slipping on his trousers that lay discarded on the floor, he fell back heavily onto his rump, his hands instinctively pushed out behind him to break his fall. Almost simultaneously a jet of projectile vomit sped from him towards the doorway while at the other end the build up of flatulence exploded from him with a nauseous smelling roar. Helpless as his body convulsed, he could only sit and retch and fart as more vomit discharged from him, spraying across his torso and legs and onto the trousers and floor underneath him. To his horrified disgust, he was unable to prevent his bowls loosing. Now shaking from the exertion of clearing his stomach of food and alcohol, a faint sheen of sweat formed on his forehead. He sat in his smelly misery, staring dully at the sickening mess. All at once, the horror of his situation hit him; the death of Fiona, losing his job, Janice taking up with his bastard of a manager, Davies … and now this.

It started with a sob, then he began to softly weep, but not for Fiona, his murdered wife. No, Paul Hardie wept for himself and how hard life currently was for him.

Eunice Evans had arisen early, in fact, a full half an hour earlier that she normally rose to see her son out to work. She had hardly slept, her excitement continuing through the night that Frederick had at last found himself a girlfriend and she wanted to be there when finally they emerged from his room. Be there to show her pleasure that Jennifer had stayed overnight. She thought of herself as a God fearing woman and didn't really approve of pre-marital sex. However, she persuaded herself while trying to come to terms with her beliefs, beggars can't be choosers as her husband was fond of quoting to her and reaching for the frying pan from the cupboard, decided that where Frederick was concerned, she would accept a dalliance under her roof if the outcome resulted in him finding himself a wife. Besides, she half smiled with pleasure, the young lassie seemed a nice enough girl. She stopped and cocked her head to one side, hearing the toilet upstairs flush and with added fervour, began to set the cutlery down on the kitchen table. Maybe now he would get rid of those dirty magazines that he had under his bed and again smiled at her son's deceit. As if he could possibly keep a secret from his mother.

Morris MacDonald knelt beside the bed resting his elbows on the quilt cover as he held his dead wife's hand, oblivious to the sorrowful stares of the ambulance crew who stood solemnly behind him. They weren't heartless people, the two young medics and were not yet completely inured to death, but it had been a long night and this they had hoped was their last call; silently wishing that they could get this over with and return to the station to sign off duty and finally, home to their beds.

"Mister MacDonald," the young woman, a native of Aberdeen by her strong accent, tiredly but softly asked, "Is there anyone we can call for you, perhaps a relative or a friend maybe, eh?"
Morris hardly heard her, his eyes focused on Susan's pale, serene features, her eyes closed and her hair brushed just that evening by him, now spread about the pillow and framing her face; a face that was finally at rest and seemed to him to indicate her relief that at last she had given up the struggle against the destructive disease.
"No thanks. No," he repeated, his voice breaking and tears threatening to engulf him. "Not right now. There's family, yes, our families of course, but I'll take a minute or two with my wife, before I call them," he bit at his lower lip, the tears now running unchecked down his cheeks.
The young woman glanced at her colleague who almost with resignation, shrugged his shoulders and nodded in unspoken agreement. Bending down on one knee beside Morris, she placed her hand gently on his shoulder.
"Mister MacDonald … Morris. Why don't we just stay here a wee while with you, eh? Maybe get you a cup of tea, eh?"
"Really, I know you guys have to … look," he tried to smile at the young woman and failed miserably, "you've both been very kind," said Morris, his hand in the medic's as she helped him to stand He wiped at his eyes with the sleeve of an old sweat shirt he'd thrown on when he had phoned the doctor and the ambulance. Taking a deep breath, he slowly exhaled, glancing briefly back to the bed where Susan lay. "Before he left the doctor told me that he's left the," he paused, almost unwilling to say the words, "the death certificate. He has been treating Susan for a number of years now, so there's no doubt about the cause. I'll phone my brother and between us, we'll get the undertaker to call. It's the Co-op," he smiled, "so they've done this once or twice before and honestly," he reached out to touch the young woman lightly on the arm, "I'll be fine. Don't be worrying about me. You and the young fella there," he nodded to her partner, "get away home. I'm guessing you'll be past your shift time, eh?"
She nodded, surprised that with all the mayhem, blood and guts she had seen already in her short service that this quiet spoken, kind man, who wasn't previously known to her, could still evoke her emotions.
"If you're sure," she replied, not trusting herself to say more.
He run a hand over his face and nodded. "I'm sure, hen. Susan and I will be just fine till my big brother gets here. Honest," he smiled as he softly wept and said again, "We'll be just fine"

Frederick Evans stood at his usual bus stop, still slightly bemused with all that had occurred the night before. The thought that filled his head was that he was no longer a virgin. He had joined the ranks of other men and his chest

swelled with pride. The bus arrived and with good humour, he stood to one side to permit a pair of chattering, middle-aged women to board first, neither of whom gave the thin man a second glance. Frederick stepped on as almost immediately the driver pulled away and he moved along the aisle of the bus, swaying with the motion as the driver turned a sharp corner and almost fell into a seat beside a young man who gloomily stared from the window. As the bus pulled up at the next stop, the young man excused himself and shuffling past Frederick, headed for the door, Frederick saw the man had forgotten his newspaper that lay on the seat and was about to call out, but decided not to, that if Jenny couldn't get away from her canteen duties, it would give him something to read at his morning break. He wasn't a fan of the 'Glasgow News', but the container that usually held the 'Metro' was empty and after all, he thought, a paper was a paper as he stuffed it into his coat pocket.
His thoughts turned to Jenny and he smiled. She was far feistier than he had previously considered. Why, he inwardly grinned, she seemed almost more eager for sex than he was and though he hadn't actually planned any kind of relationship with her, it seemed for now she would be a willing partner in anything he wanted her to do and found himself blushing at the memory this morning of her taking him in her hand. That reminded him that he should discuss with her his wearing of a condom. The last thing that Frederick needed was her getting pregnant because, he thought with male bravado, she wasn't the type of woman that he saw himself being tied down to. But, he decided with overwhelming confidence in his newly acquired sexual ability, Jenny would do for now and until he found someone better looking and more suited to him.

The subject of his thoughts was at that time munching her way though her second round of toast with the inquisitive Eunice Evans, who secretly delighted in the thought that if Frederick didn't mess this up, Jenny might be her new daughter-in-law.
Eager to create a good impression, Jenny sat with the old woman at the kitchen table, answering all and any question put to her, listening to her rambling on about how wonderful Frederick was while assuring Eunice that her son was the man of Jenny's dreams.
It had been Frederick's idea that they should not arrive at work together, that it was nobody's business they were now seeing each other, that he would as usual catch his regular bus and pressing a ten pound note into her hand, instructed that Jenny call a taxi to convey her to the store. This would permit her another fifteen minutes to take some breakfast.
It never occurred to her that Frederick's apparent discretion was simply because he was embarrassed by Jenny's plain looks, that he feared the laughs and snide comments if his colleagues learned of his relationship with a

woman that none of them would ever consider dating. It had once been unkindly and without her knowledge, said of her by a teacher just before she quit school, that Jenny was as bright as a blackout. Had the woman realised that beneath the shy and put-upon exterior of Jenny Farndale, there existed a shrewd mind that while slow on the uptake, was far sharper than the teacher could ever have guessed. Jenny was, in the Glasgow vernacular, a 'scheme' born bird with an inherent astuteness and wariness evolved through the years from the living conditions in which she was raised.

As she sipped her tea and listened to the increasingly boring old lady, she inwardly smiled at the irony that having been shagged the previous night, she was still being handed her fare and told to get a taxi in the morning.

This time however, she shivered with pleasure as sneaking a glance about her, Jenny knew with certainty she would be coming back.

Behind closed doors in the media office at police headquarters, Chief Inspector Harriet Downes was going off on one, pacing up and down behind her desk as she stared at the subject of her anger, her silent and embarrassed Inspector.

"It's not the job of a wee lassie to proof-read the stuff that comes in from the Divisions, it's yours and you failed to do that, case closed," she seethed at him.

"I didn't read Sharon's summary properly, Harry," he tried to apologise, but Downes was having none of it. "I leave twenty minutes early, twenty fucking minutes and the place goes to shit."

The door knocked and still angry, she shouted out, "What!"

Typhus Mary opened the door a crack and conscious that she might get caught up in the fall-out of Downes anger, almost with a whisper said, "The Assistant Chief's office phoned down, Harry. He wants to see you at your convenience. I think it's about that item in the 'Glasgow News', the item about the missing teacher."

Lesley Gold didn't sleep well and awoke in the darkness of the room, slightly later than she had planned and feeling like shit. She yawned and stretched, then rubbed at her head, trying to convince herself that she was too tired to go jogging that morning, but yawning again, resigned herself to getting out of bed and slipped tiredly into her sweat shirt and jogging bottoms. By the time she hit the street she knew it was a bad idea, but remembered Mike Duffy's taunt of 'fat bitch' then teeth set grimly, took a deep breath and set off.

In her flat, her mobile telephone lay forgotten on her bedside table, buzzing as it activated with an incoming text message.

Chapter 17

The fall-out over the inclusion of the missing person item was not the worst thing that Chief Inspector Harriet Downes had to deal with in her busy career and the last thing she needed was a lecture from an old fart, well past his retirement date who stiffly reminded her of the protocol in place for tracing MP's. Downes, renowned for her loyalty to her staff, accepted the rebuke without disclosing the actions of the errant Inspector or the naivety of her young civilian assistant. Yes, she agreed, details of MP's should only be included in media items where there is a an immediate threat to life or of injury and where all reasonable effort has already been made to trace the MP has failed; yes, she agreed, the item was prematurely passed to the 'Glasgow News' and for that she apologised without reservation and finally, yes she again agreed, it will not occur again.

Dismissed from the ACC's office, she made her way back to the Media Department, determined to first have a coffee and then complete her application to be returned to the CID, where she bloody should be in the first place.

Morris MacDonald sat in the lounge with his brother Roddy, the lights on though it was daylight, but with the curtains drawn. Both nursed a chunky glass that contained a generous amount of Glenfiddich single malt.

"Aye, well, she's at peace now wee brother," said Roddy, his accent still strong and betraying his origin sixty years previously in the Western Islands where he had lived since he was a child. His occasional excursion to the mainland and in particular, to visit his only sibling was such a rarity he habitually felt an obligation to visit as many of Glasgow's hostelries during the time his visit permitted. However, on this sad occasion he had been telephoned the previous evening by Morris, who rightly surmised Susan was almost gone. Landing at Glasgow on the postal flight, Roddy arrived sadly too late to say his farewells to his beloved sister-in-law. His suitcase lay unopened and forgotten in the hallway.

Morris took a deep breath and exhaled softly before sipping at his whisky. "I've called the Co-op. They should be here shortly," was his reply. He turned to stare at Roddy, his cheeks ruddy and tear-streaked. "I don't understand why I'm feeling like this, as if somehow I'm relieved. Why do I feel this way, Roddy?"

The bearded giant that was the retired fisherman and life-long bachelor Roderick MacCallum MacDonald stood up and walked to sit on the couch beside his brother, throwing his bulging arm about Morris's shoulder. "Don't be silly, now wee man. It's only natural you should want what was best for your Susan. Have you not done everything for her these past five years? Did you not spend almost every hour you were not working, tending to the lassie?

No man, no husband could have done more. You loved her as she loved you and I tell you this, wee man. That woman would be very angry with you now if she thought for one minute that you were thinking you had not done right by her. And what a temper she had when she was worked up," he began to heartily laugh, "do you remember the time she hit me with the saucepan when I touched her arse, just after you two were married. God, if ever a woman loved a man, it was Susan loving you."
Morris began to laugh at the memory of the irate Susan, nostrils flaring and eyes bright who had come to know Roddy meant no harm, that he was the joker of the MacDonald family and the tease of all women.
The sound of the doorbell announced the arrival of the Co-operative undertakers. As Morris tried to rise from the couch, Roddy's strong hand stayed him as he firmly instructed, "Sit where you are, wee man, and drink your whisky. Susan was like a sister to me and this is my job now, my privilege and my honour to tend to her needs. There will be time enough for you to see her later, when she is as pretty as you remember," then more kindly as he took charge of Morris, added firmly, "now do as your big brother tells you and drink your malt."

Jinksie Peterson smiled and walked towards the public counter to grab the mail from Andy the postman. "How's it hanging big man," he grinned at Andy.
"Same old, same old," Andy smiled in return and then the smile on his face faded and turned to one of curiosity as he nodded to the waste bin at Jinksie's desk. "So you're not into horticulture then, Jinksie?"
"What?" Jinksie turned and grinned at the upended flowers that protruded from the bin. "Oh aye, they were there this morning when I arrived. Don't know what the story is or where they came from. I was going to rescue them, but I reckon that might not be such a good idea. Whoever put them there obviously had their reason so I'm not getting involved." As he stared at the mail, a thought occurred to him. "Wait a minute Andy, there might be a card with them and walked over to fetch the flowers from the bin. "Aye, there's a card here," he began to pull it from the envelope.
"Maybe that's not a good idea Jinksie," Andy interrupted, "whoever they were for might not…"
But he was too late. Jinksie read the card and laughed. "It says for the new police woman, so they must have been for the new cop, Lesley Gold. Don't know why she has dumped them though."
"Lesley Gold. Is that her name?"
"Aye, she arrived from Maryhill under a bit of a cloud," replied Jinksie, sorting through the delivery of mail. "I don't know the whole story, but rumour has it that she punched a Sergeant, an ex-boyfriend or something. She

seems a decent sort though." His eyes narrowed. "She might not have meant to throw these away, they look expensive. I'll keep them here on my desk and …." Jinksie turned back to the counter, but the front door was swinging closed and Andy the postman had gone.

Lesley Gold finished her run and slowed to a walk as she arrived at her close, the perspiration running from her forehead and trickling down her nose then onto her chin. Her legs felt unsteady and her chest heaved with the exertion of the final burst of speed in the last few hundred metres. Shaking her legs and arms to ward off cramp, she paced up and down outside the close for a few minutes before entering and making her way upstairs. She was knackered, her sleepless night and punishing run combining to exhaust her. Closing her front door behind her she grabbed a bottle of water from the fridge in the kitchen and decided to check her phone before hitting the shower. The text message was from her friend, Helen Lang suggesting another coffee date and asking for a call back to confirm. Lesley thought about phoning her mother for an update on her father, but decided first to get out of her sweat soaked clothes before she chilled and resisted the temptation to step onto the electronic scales, having already decided to wait till one week of exercise and dieting had passed. Stripping off naked, she walked into the bathroom and turned on then stepped into the shower, again grateful she had paid the extra money for the more powerful model. As the bathroom filled with steam, she turned back and forth, luxuriating in the force of the water that cascaded down onto her. While she soaped her body and shampooed her hair, she thought again of her confrontation with Mike Duffy, pleased that she hadn't succumbed to his patter, now recognising him for the sleazy man he was and grateful she had got out of the relationship in time. Funny, she thought, she no longer had that feeling of failure, but instead felt relief and smiled. Then it struck her. He had seemed surprised when she mentioned the flowers he had sent her. Why? She turned and arching her back to allow the flow of water to rinse her, used her hands to smooth her wet hair back from her face and smiled again. Simple, she realised. Mike hadn't sent the flowers at all, that's why he seemed surprised. But if he hadn't sent them, she brushed an escaped lock of hair away as her eyes narrowed, who did?

Frederick Evans day got off to a bad start almost as soon as he entered Dawson's store. His manager Robert Hamilton was coincidentally arriving at that time and beckoning Frederick to him in front of colleagues requested that after Frederick completed his morning break, he meet with Hamilton in the small office on the Gent's Department floor for, as Hamilton smoothly said, a little one to one chat. The nudges and knowing winks from the others about him didn't escape Frederick's notice. Wearily, he climbed the back stairs to the second floor and after hanging up his coat in the small cupboard that served as a cloakroom, made his way to the shop floor to begin his sales assistant duties, troubled by the thought of the meeting in a few hours time. His morning went slowly and the only customers he dealt with did not make a purchase; one woman almost dragging her husband away by the arm in annoyance at Frederick's disdainful lack of interest in assisting the husband with the purchase of a sports jacket. Frequently, he glanced at his wristwatch, urging the time to pass towards his allocated break time for the canteen and he would worry there about the meeting with Hamilton. He was in no mood for idle chatter with Jenny and already made the decision he would take the newspaper he had collected on the bus as a cover and maintain the pretence that their relationship continue to be a secret.

At last, at a signal from Hamilton, he made his way to the canteen on the top floor and was grateful there was no sign of Jenny whom he assumed must be working at the rear of the kitchen area. Purchasing a cup of tea, he ignored the breakfast items that were laid out, but not because he wasn't hungry. His stomach was turning somersaults, dreading the thought of the meeting in Hamilton's office.

He selected an empty table at the rear of the rapidly filling canteen and spreading the newspaper open on the table, pretended to read while his thoughts jumped back and forth as to the possible reason his manager wished to see him. He discounted the opportunity for promotion. That particular boat had sailed with Hamilton's appointment, he bitterly recalled. It must be his sales figures, he presumed. Admittedly, in the last few months, they had been poor, but he excused this by comparing the sales figures for the store as a whole, the recession having wiped out the boom years and the rise of cheaper clothing in the downmarket stores that were springing up around the city centre. Sipping at his tea, his eyes unconsciously began to scan the 'Glasgow News' seeing but not really taking in the stories and absent-mindedly turned the pages. It was on page five that he began to read a story about a city centre rape and the police appeal for witnesses. Frederick liked stories about rape. The sometimes sordid reporting of women's humiliations appealed to him and as he savoured the details, his eyes glanced at a headline beneath the report, of a missing woman from the Knightswood area. As he continued to read, his eyes narrowed when he saw the woman was named as Fiona Hardie who resided with her husband Paul and was a school-teacher by profession and missing from Borden Road, though the house number had been excluded. The police appeal indicated that at this time there were no suspicious circumstances and included the usual request that anyone having any information about Missus Hardie's whereabouts contact them forthwith at the number listed on the report.

He sat upright, his eyes narrowing and his curiosity aroused by the report and reading it a second time, wasn't certain but thought that Borden Road was near, if not actually adjacent to where he had been on his last visit at Austen Road. He smiled with pleasure at the memory of acquiring the two pairs of pants; the large ones and the thong. Frederick took private pride in that he could recall from where all his collection was obtained. Now, his brow furrowed, was it simply coincidence that a woman from the same area was missing? Could it possibly be related to the recording he had made of the man assaulting his wife? His imagination took over and he wondered, was it possible the assault had proven to be far more serious than he had at first assumed, that the wife had fled from the man when she recovered? A chill run through his body as his imagination continued to prod at him. Did the woman recover or did she, he hesitated to even consider thinking the word, die?

Frederick had not used his laptop for some days and not since he had begun his relationship with Jenny, inwardly smirking at the word 'relationship'. His thoughts turned again to the newspaper article and saw that it did not provide a house number for the missing woman, but he knew that he would have little difficulty finding the house again.

His meeting with Robert Hamilton for the moment forgotten, Frederick excitedly knew when he returned home that evening he would watch the recording again.

It was as she collected a pile of used dishes from the serving hatch that Jenny saw Frederick sitting at the table in the far corner, reading his newspaper. Distracted, her heart missed a beat and she was about to call out to her supervisor to request a few minutes break to join him when the teenage blonde girl, who she knew worked in cosmetics department, snapped at her, "Are you deaf, hen? I said, take this tray please," and thrust it at her, the dishes it contained sliding from it towards to the floor. As Jenny grabbed at them the uneaten food stuff slid from the plate onto her apron, staining the front with gravy. The girl turned to her friend and laughed, "Unbelievable. Where the fuck do they find these people, eh?"

Jenny's face was scarlet with embarrassment and turning away, she placed the tray at the side of the large sink of hot water. A hand landed on her shoulder.

"Don't let these idiots annoy you, Jenny," said her matronly supervisor, her eyes betraying her sympathy. "You're worth a dozen of them, so you are. Paint their faces and they think they are something, so they do. Just remember when the next time that wee cow comes in for her dinner," she lowered her voice as she grinned, "do what I do with these stuck-up bastards. Wait till they're not looking and spit into her food."

"Thank you for coming in, Mister Evans," Hamilton smiled at him. "Please, take a seat," he indicated the chair in front of his desk as head bowed, he pretended to study a report that lay in front of him, a report that Hamilton already knew almost word for word. His previous supervisory experience had taught him that if he kept silent for a few minutes, it would unsettle Evans, a man that he privately and intensely disliked and was keen to see fired. So much easier to handle a disgruntled employee, he inwardly thought, when he finally divulged why he had called Evans into his office.

The formal use of his surname surprised Frederick and it was with a feeling of trepidation that he sat down, his mouth suddenly dry and hands in his lap, he began to twist at his fingers.

Hamilton suddenly glanced up and staring Frederick in the eye, was pleased to see his nervousness as he smiled and said, "The sales figures for the last quarter have become available, Mister Evans. I regret to inform you that your sales seem to have plummeted. Frankly, they make poor reading and you fall far below the standard required by this prestigious store, let alone this Department. Is there any problem at home, have you lost your motivation or is it simply that the job bores you?"

The coldness with which the rebuke was delivered unsettled Frederick, whose tongue failed him and he could only stare back, feeling like a first year pupil being scolded by a teacher, an unpleasant experience he recalled from his past.

Hamilton placed both hands flat on his desk and slowly shook his head. "I have to say I'm not really that surprised. The way you spoke with that young man just the other day shocked me, a man with your obvious experience speaking to a customer like that. I haven't had the opportunity to fully assess your ability, but the figures here," he dramatically waved at the paperwork, "seem to indicate either you are just not trying or perhaps you have decided that this profession no longer suits you?"

It was typical of the man's arrogance, thought Frederick that he believed selling overpriced suits to unappreciative customers was on a par with professionals. He wanted to leap across the desk, take Hamilton by the throat and tear his windpipe out, shove his thumbs in his fucking eyes and press through to the back of his skull, kill him, kill him, kill him; all this in an instant of thought.

But he did and said nothing, just stared pale faced and speechless at the man who, after twenty-five years of unblemished service, was determined to get rid of him.

On the other side of the desk, Hamilton didn't expect the weasel of a man to hand his notice over right there and then, but given time, yes, given time and just enough digs at his pride, he fully expected Frederick to quit. He took no pride or satisfaction in the thought, but reminded himself that his first duty was to Dawson's and as the Departmental Manager his responsibility was foremost in presenting the customers with a first class service and his employer with a professional and motivated staff.

"You seem a little taken aback, Mister Evans," he said at last, glancing at his watch. "I know you already have had your early break time and it's a little early for lunch," he softly laughed and then, as though offering a favour, continued, "But perhaps you might consider going for a cup of tea. Just to digest what we've discussed, eh?"

His body shaking, Frederick was incandescent with rage, but could only nod, his defeat complete as legs unwilling to support him he shoved the chair back with a squeak on the linoleum floor and turned towards the door. He would have liked to have screamed something nasty, some afterthought that startled and humiliated Hamilton, but Frederick was not a quick witted man and so without a backward glance, he left the room leaving the door wide open behind him.

Dotty Turner, wearing her bathrobe and sitting on the edge of her bed, stared numbly at the handset as she slowly replaced it in the cradle sitting on the bedside table, the small towel in her hand and her short blonde hair still damp from the shower. Sergeant Pete Buchanan had been apologetic for calling her at home and she instantly knew from his voice that something was wrong, the fear of a mother as she clutched at her chest. It was Morris MacDonald's wife Susan, Buchanan had quickly explained, in the early hours of that morning she had finally succumbed to her illness.

Dotty sat staring into space, her feelings confused, relief mixed with guilt at the call. The guilt she felt that it was about Morris's wife and the relief it was not about her kids; that they were okay, nothing had happened to them. Poor Morris, she thought, all those years of putting his life on hold caring for Susan and now this.

Buchanan had phoned because he knew they had worked together for some years and believed she would appreciate the call, the heads-up. That and to warn her to expect that it might mean a change of shifts to compensate if they didn't get a replacement for Morris within the next few weeks. She realised that Buchanan obviously didn't expect Morris back for some time and there was even the suggestion that Morris might never return, being so close to his retirement. Five months, if her memory served her correctly. She clasped at her throat as an awful dread seized her.

The funeral aside, it might mean her not seeing Morris ever again.

Lesley Gold, sitting in the soft cushioned armchair in her lounge, nursed her coffee with the phone pressed against her ear and listened as it rang.

"Hello Miss Gold," answered Helen Lang in her ear. "Got my text then?"
"Yeah, how does this coming Saturday suit you? Say lunch in the city, maybe that wee restaurant in Byres Road opposite the Underground?"
"You buying are you?"
"What, with the salary you earn? No way Missus Cheery," she laughed, using her pet name for her friend. "If I recall, I got the bill the last time."
"Can't stop a girl from trying," Helen laughed back at her. "Okay, Saturday then. I'm just about to head into a meeting, so I'll see you there at the restaurant, say, twelve thirty? Oh, and before I go, how is your dad this morning?"
"I haven't phoned yet," she clutched at her throat with a pang of guilt, "but that'll be my next call. See you Saturday and give my love to your man."
"Save it for your own man, when you get round to finding one," Helen teased her and hung up.
That'll be the day, Lesley grimaced at the phone, and thought to herself if I do get round to dating anyone it'll be on my terms. I'm not having another Mike Duffy in my life, she grimly decided.
Her next phone call was to her mother, who sounded tired.
"He's just the usual, darling. You know how it is. Oh, and your sister phoned this morning, to see how your dad is," then immediately regretted mentioning it, knowing where Lesley was concerned, any mention these days of Linda was like using petrol to douse a fire. The flare up was almost instantaneous.
"Offered to come and let you have some time to yourself, did she?" was Lesley's icy response.
Her mother sighed on the phone, considering her reply. Telling Lesley that Linda was working part- time and she had a child to care for was a waste of time. They both knew that Linda had use of a childminder and that she was forever boasting of her leisure time that included the tennis club, swimming club and Women's Rotary duties. Excusing her for not being involved with her parents and in particular her father's illness was pointless. Linda just wasn't interested in anything that didn't improve or impact on her own life and that included her terminally ill father. Peggy Gold even suspected that her daughter was a little ashamed of her parent's humble background, now that she had moved into a higher social circle.
"You know how she is," was all that she could reply, sensing Lesley's anger through the phone.
"Yes, well," Lesley softly laughed, deliberately taking the edge off her voice for her mother's sake, "You've always got me mum."
Tears formed in Peggy's eyes, but whether from tiredness or shame at Linda's behaviour, she wasn't certain. "You're late shift again this evening?"
"Aye, but I'll be off for a couple of days on Monday, so I'll bring a bag …" her mother began to protest, but Lesley spoke over her as she continued, "No

arguments mum. Besides, I like spending time with you, so that's settled. Right, I've a shower to get," she fibbed, "so I'll away now and give you a call tomorrow. Remember mum," she added, "any news …."

"Don't worry. I know where to find you," her mother replied and then, the lump again forming in her throat, said, "Love you, Lesley."

"Love you too, mum," she smiled as she ended the call.

Paul Hardie, cleaned up and wearing one of his best suits, white shirt, striped tie and smelling now of a particularly pungent aftershave, looked every inch the young corporate executive he believed himself to be as he drove the Focus into the company parking area in the basement only to discover the bay previously allocated to him was now occupied by a dark coloured saloon car. Tight lipped, he angrily double parked the Focus, effectively blocking the saloon's exit from the bay and locked the door to prevent the Focus being pushed aside. The act gave him a small victory and made him more determined to see through his plan.

He hesitated at the lift door, deciding instead to take the rear, fire exit stairs to the fourth floor in the belief the time to get there would permit him further opportunity to practise his prepared speech to Colin Davis. At the company's staff entrance, he was relieved to discover his pass card and entry code of four digits had not been cancelled and pushing open the swing door, walked confidently to Davis's office. His route took him through the typing pool and he saw heads turn to watch him as he strode past. Janice Meikle, easily identifiable by her natural blonde hair tied in a ponytail. Seeing her colleagues staring behind her, she turned and saw Paul walking towards her desk. Her eyes widened and her mouth dropped open, but to her relief, Paul hardly glanced her way as he strode past. She instinctively knew where he was heading and grabbed at the phone on her desk, knowing it was already too late, that he would be in Colin's office before she could warn her new beau.

Paul arrived at Davis' office and ignoring the elderly secretary who, her face displaying her curiosity, raised a hand to stop him, her voice calling out, "Wait a minute please, you can't just …" but Paul was already pushing open the door and slamming it behind him.

Colin Davies was on the phone when Paul entered and stood up from behind his desk, his face deathly pale in the belief that Hardie had come to hurt him. "I'll call you back dear, I have something to attend to," he said, replacing the handset and praying to God that Hardie didn't realise it was Janice he had been speaking with.

"Paul, this is a surprise. Please take a seat," invited Davis, his voice strained and jerky. "Eh, what can I do for you? Come in to clear your desk have you?"

Paul remained standing, his eyes boring into the heavy-set man's eyes, seeing a panic there and realising that Davis was frightened of him. But Paul had no intention of hurting Davis, at least not physically. Casually, his hands in his suit trouser pockets, he smiled and commenced his practised speech.

"I want my old job back, Colin and you're going to make sure that I get it. There's a couple of things has happened since we last spoke and I thought you should be aware of them."

Davis inwardly sighed, relieved the younger and far fitter man was not punching him out as he had feared, sat slowly back into his comfortable desk chair. He clasped his fingers together and stared at Hardie. "Perhaps before you go any further, Paul" he spread his hands out, "you should know that the loss of your position in the company was a Board decision, not mine. I can't see how I can help you overturn that decision," he smiled, now feeling a little more in control. After all, even though Hardie was right, that he had the final say in the recommendation that the post be made redundant, what could Hardie possible say that would change his mind?

Paul smiled, confident that he had the fat bastard by the balls. "I'm aware that the company is very conscious of its status as an investor in staff policy and am I correct in saying that we currently sport the 'Investor in People' logo on all our company stationary, as well as advertising it on our website and other commercial outlets?"

Davis slowly nodded, uncertain where this line of discussion was going.

"How would it seem then, to our many customers in the world of finance, if I speak to the media and accuse the company of being responsible for my wife currently being missing," his voice raised as he settled both his hands flat on the desk and stared menacingly at Davis.

"What? Your wife is missing? What do you mean? How would that affect the company?" asked a bemused Davis.

"After I met with you, I phoned her," Paul glibly lied, "and told her of my dismissal. She informed me she was pregnant with our first child and was losing her job and in a state of panic, she fled from the house and hasn't been seen since. She's missing and the police are looking for her. God knows what she's capable of in her state of mind, a state of mind that was brought on by my unwarranted dismissal," he hissed though gritted teeth.

Davis blinked rapidly, knowing that the company couldn't possibly be held responsible for Hardie's wife's disappearance, but equally aware that if Hardie went to the press with such a story, regardless of whether it was true or otherwise, the adverse publicity that would result could prove to be a public relations disaster for the company. The old adage of no smoke without fire would apply and Berkeley and Finch had many rivals in the world of accountancy who would seek to take advantage of a situation like that. It quickly occurred to him if he could steer the problem away before it took

hold and become public, but with his own spin on the shabby issue, he could later present the threat to the Board as dealt with and possibly even be credited with thanks and thereby increase his own standing.
"So hypothetically Paul, let's for the moment say that what you threaten was even remotely possible," Davis smoothly replied, "but why should I even consider recommending your former employment status at this company be reviewed?"
"Investors in People, Colin," he sneeringly repeated as he shook his head, "yet I'm dismissed for no logical reason, or could it be there was a reason for my dismissal that had nothing to do with the company?"
"I don't understand," Davis's face betrayed his genuine puzzlement.
"Why Colin," Paul smiled as he played his trump card, "I was dismissed to stop me revealing to your wife that you're shagging the blonde typist, Janice Meikle."

Chapter 18

For Frederick Evans, the remainder of his shift at Dawson's Gents Department had passed in a daze, unaware that in a very short time he had become the subject of gossip among his colleagues. Most of the younger members of staff had been pleased there was a real possibility the abrupt and dislikeable Freddy Evans might be fired. However, a very few others, predominantly among the aged and more mature colleagues, worried that Frederick's dismissal signalled either a clear-out of seasoned staff to make way of an influx of younger blood or downsizing of the Department as a fiscal reaction to the fierce competition from nearby rival stores, successfully selling cheaper menswear in response to the economic climate. Either way, they quietly and worriedly whispered in corners; it bode ill for them all.
He couldn't remember travelling home. He didn't recall arriving at his house or his mother's puzzled greeting as he walked wordlessly past her to climb the stairs to his room and was oblivious to her deep concern that he might already have broken up with the young woman, Jenny.
Sitting on the edge of his bed, his coat still buttoned, it was the fading light and the chill of the night air that seemed to bring him to his senses. The shock of his managers' dismissal of all his efforts over the preceding twenty-five years had not just enraged and hurt him, but the possibility he might lose his job had sent him into an almost paralysing state of mind. Slowly, like a kettle coming to the boil, the anger within reached a fiery climax and unconsciously clenching his fists, his hatred of Robert Hamilton knew no bounds. His imagination was out of control as he envisaged the many ways he would hurt the man, belittle him and make him suffer for the humiliation he had forced Frederick to endure.

His chin lowered to his chest and tears of frustration escaped him as he sobbed. He sobbed for almost five full minutes, the feeling of helplessness overwhelming him. Finally taking a deep breath, he wiped his eyes with his handkerchief and stood, unbuttoning his coat and hanging it in the cupboard. His eyes glanced at the edition of the 'Glasgow News' that still protruded from the pocket and he remembered then, the article about the missing schoolteacher. His curiosity overtook his anger and switching on the laptop, he sat down, more composed and humming slowly as his fingers drummed at the desktop, waiting on the machine readying itself for his instruction. Clicking the mouse button onto his secret file, he opened the recording and watched in fascination again as the man he had recorded hit the woman with a closed fist, but this time the recording made more sense as he paid more attention to the man's apparent unsuccessful attempt to resuscitate the woman. This time, if his suspicions were correct and if indeed the woman in the recording was the missing school-teacher, Frederick saw the incident not as a possible assault, but as something more sinister and he startled. Was it possible that he had witnessed and inadvertently recorded the man actually killing his wife? It seemed so surreal, but the more he watched the recording, the more he convinced himself it was a distinct possibility that the woman who did not rise after falling to the floor, was really dead. As he watched he cursed himself for not waiting that little bit longer to record more.

He sat back in the chair, his mind racing with the possible opportunities that the recording offered him. If indeed it was as he suspected, there was no doubt that it was worth money, but how would he go about selling such a recording? Of course, he inwardly sneered that his civic duty demanded that he turn the recording over to the police, but to do so would invite all sort of questions as to why he was sneaking about private gardens at that time of the night. He was under no illusion the police would soon discover his hobby and likely find himself the subject of their inquiries into the spate of lingerie thefts. That undoubtedly would mean exposure and public humiliation and the subsequent investigation would surely result in his name being released to the Press. He shivered with anticipated fear at the thought of being not just being imprisoned, but losing his job and being unemployable in the future. The ridicule he would endure would be like nothing he could imagine, for though Frederick was a friendless man, he was not blind to the ways of men and guessed how society and men in particular would treat someone like him, someone who stole women's underwear. It did occur to him that he could post the recording anonymously onto the Web, but the media was consistently disclosing how successful the police were at tracing paedophiles and such people through the Internet and he immediately discounted that idea.

Posting the recording onto the Web?

It was then that an idea struck him, a thought so dangerously exciting that he almost dismissed it from his mind. However, taking a deep breath he excitedly decided that before he did anything else he must first confirm that the address where he had recorded the incident was the same as that of the missing woman, the school-teacher called Hardie. Typing the BT Residential phone number page into the search field of his laptop, Frederick waited a few seconds with bated breath. He bit at his lower lip and stopped typing, then deleted 'Fiona Hardie', guessing if there was a house phone it would probably be subscribed in the husband's name. He quickly re-read the newspaper article and typed in 'Paul Hardie' and 'Borden Road'. Almost immediately, the phone number for a Paul Hardie at 19 Borden Road appeared on his screen. He could hardly breathe, so excited was he at the ease with which his idea was taking shape. His fingers were shaking so much he fumbled the pencil as he scribbled the number down onto a scrap of paper. Next, he tore the cellophane paper from a blank DVD and inserting the disc into the laptop, copied the recording to the disc. He hadn't previously noticed or given it much thought, but was now pleased to see that on the left hand corner of the recording there appeared digits that displayed the time and date when the telephone camera recording was made. The disc popped out of the machine and he was about to slip it into the hard plastic case when a thought occurred to him. Standing, he walked to the small set of drawers and collected a clean handkerchief, then carefully wiped both the disc and the case clean before slipping the disc into the case and, giving it a final wipe, wrapped the case in the handkerchief.

He smiled in anticipation, for all that now remained was another nocturnal visit to Borden Road to confirm that the house located at number nineteen was definitely the house where he had made the recording.

Unusually for her, Lesley Gold was a little late arriving for work and almost immediately knew that something was wrong when she stepped into the small canteen. To Lesley's surprise she saw that Dotty Turner's face was red and puffy and thought she had been crying. Young Alex Mason looked distinctly uncomfortable. Catching her eye, he subtly nodded to the corridor and joined her there, softly closing the canteen door behind him.

"Dotty's a wee bit upset," he said in a low voice, "Morris MacDonald's wife died in the early hours of this morning. I think Dotty had known them for some years."

"Oh, that's sad. I didn't know Morris before I got here," replied Lesley, feeling uneasily guilty for the trick she had played on him a few days previously. "His wife had …what was the illness again?"

"MS. I don't know the full story but from what I've heard she was quite profoundly ill with it, I think," replied Alex. "Anyway, for the time being

Pete Buchanan has suggested that Dotty remains with Jinksie in the Uniform bar for the late shift and you're stuck with me," he suddenly grinned. "I think the Inspector was going to neighbour you, but he's away to visit Morris at home. Also, I've been through to the bar and spoken with Jinksie who says there's not any calls for us to attend, at the minute."

"Okay wee man," Lesley nodded, somehow relieved that she wasn't under the Inspector's eye tonight. "Get your gear together and I'll see you in the car in two minutes. I want to check with Jinksie if there's any word on that MP, the school-teacher."

"The Hardie woman you mean? There was a piece about her in today's 'Glasgow News'. An appeal issued by the Media Department at Pitt Street. I think it was asking that anyone with information phone the polis and it was our phone number here that was in the paper, here, at Garscadden I mean."

Lesley was puzzled. Appeals, in her experience, usually didn't happen till some time had elapsed; at least not unless there was some extenuating circumstances such as risk from physical harm, self-harm or mental health issues. Nodding, she pushed past Alex and made her way through to the bar. Jinksie was sitting at his desk, tut-tutting over an e-mail response from the Chief Inspector that took note of his concerns regarding the immediate employment of a cleaner and suggested in the meantime Jinksie find a brush, pan, mop and bucket and clean the bloody place himself.

"You don't look happy Jinksie," smiled Lesley and then stopped, staring at the flowers lying on his desk.

"Yours I believe," he lifted them towards her.

First hesitantly, then shaking her head at her stupidity, she almost grabbed them from his outstretched hand.

"Hey, steady on Wonder Woman," he grinned at her. "Who's rattled your cage or pissed you off so badly that they need to send flowers to make-up for it?"

"No idea Jinksie," she answered, a little contrite at her bad manners. "The card didn't give me a clue. I thought it might have been …" but she didn't continue with Mike Duffy's name, now believing in her gut that he wouldn't have been so thoughtful.

"So," his eyes narrowed with curiosity. "Someone anonymously sends you flowers. Do you think it's a mysterious stalker perhaps?"

"I should be so lucky," she quipped. "To be honest, I haven't a clue. I mean look at me, I'm hardly a glamorous looking woman now, am I?"

Jinksie stared at her, a half smile on his face and wondered if she was fishing for a compliment, then decided that though he had known her for a short while, it just didn't seem to be Lesley's style. "Listen hen, if I was a foot taller and not happily engaged, I'd be chasing you myself. Whoever has got the hots for you, I fully understand why. Look at you," his outstretched hands towards her as he grinned, "You're a babe. Don't tell me you look in the mirror and can't see what a good looking woman you are?"

Taken aback by the unexpected compliment, Lesley blushed and swallowed hard. "Right, moving on," she replied. "I was wondering if there was any news on the MP, Fiona Hardie."

"The school-teacher you mean?"

"Aye, that's her."

"Hang on, I'll check the PNC and see if there's any update. You know that her disappearance is featured in today's early edition of the 'Glasgow News'?"

"So young Alex was telling me, but I thought that the standing rule was unless there is some suspicious circumstances then MP's don't really feature in look-out's for what, a couple of weeks or so?"

Jinksie nodded in agreement. "That's been my experience. I don't know why this woman should be any different," then his eyes narrowed in suspicion, "or maybe there is something that we're not getting told?"

"No, it's not that," replied Lesley, her curiosity piqued. "If there was something suspicious, the CID would be all over it and we wouldn't be doing the legwork. No, there must be some other reason if she's in the newspaper."

It never occurred to either of them that a simple misunderstanding and youthful inexperience at the Media Department was the cause.

Lesley watched as Jinksie settled himself before the Police National Computer terminal and signing on, quickly typed in the information.

"Nothing so far Lesley," he shook his head. "I'll print you off what's there;s been. The dayshift made a routine call to the address about midday, but the husband Mister Hardie, the guy who reported her missing …"

"Yeah, I met him," she interrupted him.

"Well anyway, seems he wasn't at home. I take it you'll be calling up tonight sometime, see if she's back?"

"That's the intention, thanks Jinksie," she said as she collected the paperwork from the printer, and then with a smile, added, "If you can, shove those flowers into some water for me, there's a sweetheart."

As she walked away, Jinksie stared after her, one thought in his mind. Lesley was a right good looker, but just didn't seem to know it and ruefully considered that if the opportunity ever arose, then shook his head and grinned. If his Siobhan ever thought he was lusting after another woman, he involuntarily drew his knees together. His balls were just not worth taking the risk. His glance fell upon the flowers and staring at them, drew the small card out from its envelope and again read the message. Funny, the neat handwriting seemed familiar, but he just couldn't place it. Oh well, give it time he thought as he replaced the card.

Jenny Farndale returned home from work, one thought on her mind. Frederick's mother Eunice had said to call anytime, but eager as Jenny was, she thought it only right and fitting that Frederick phone her. He had both her mobile and her house phone numbers and sitting in front of the television, her mother quietly snoring in the other armchair, she waited patiently, watching the clock hands tick by and ready to fly out of the door at a minutes' notice. If only he would call, she thought. I'll give it five minutes, then I'll phone him, tell him I just called to say hello. Five minutes passed and still she sat there, clock watching. I'll give it another couple of minutes she decided, restlessly twisting back and forth in her seat.

I'll make a cuppa then call him, she instead decided. The kettle boiled and the tea was made, but still the phone remained silent. Her mother's snoring was now competing with the television.

Anxiously, she wondered was that it? Had he tired of her so soon? Her anxiety turned to anger as an unaccustomed cold fury raged through her. If he thought he was dumping her just like that, her nostrils flared, recalling how she had sensed his inexperience and her face flushed with shame at the memory, coaxing him to fulfilment using her breasts, her hands, her mouth; showing him where to touch her and praising his sexual prowess when in reality he had been naïve and bloody useless and not at all like the men she had been with before.

Impatiently she strode from the lounge and walked into the kitchen and sat down heavily on a chair, the life draining from her. He had seemed such an opportunity. She looked about her at the squalor of the small kitchen, inhaling the greasy smell of a thousand or more fat cooked meals and remembered the neat and orderly home of Eunice and Frederick. Admittedly, the décor was a little dated, but in her imagination she had transformed the house into the home she always desired. Even the little that she had seen of the area where they lived was far removed from Nitshill where nightly in her part of the housing estate, unruly teenage gangs roamed and the sound of police sirens was commonplace.

She rubbed tiredly at her face, recognising again a sense of abandonment and her lower lip trembled. The last few days had been the happiest she could remember, but now it seemed it had all been for nothing.

Colin Davies sat in his study in the large house in Newton Mearns, an increasing sense of foreboding gripping him. He rubbed at the ache in his chest and knew the curry was a bad idea. Paul Hardie's threat to expose Colin's relationship with Janice Meikle had, he inwardly admitted, scared the shit out of him. Try as Colin might, he could see no option but to give in to the blackmailing bastard and try to get him reinstated. But would that be the end of it? Would Hardie be satisfied with just his job back? If his earlier experience's of the type of man Hardie is was anything to go by, Colin didn't think so and rubbing at his chest wondered how the fuck he was going to escape from Hardie's clutches.

Downstairs, his wife sat engrossed in another of her television soaps while upstairs, he sweated blood that his new relationship with Janice could destroy not just his career, but wipe out all the years of pension fund and stock shares he had accumulated with the company and he was far too old to go looking for another job. That and the kicking his wife's lawyers would give him if she ever discovered his infidelity, for Colin's wife was no shrinking violet and was herself his mistress when he was married to his first wife. Discovery would mean divorce and divorce would mean yet another huge settlement for his wife and likely poverty for Colin.

No, he had no option but to give in to the blackmailing bastard and that also regretfully meant giving up the fledging affair with the smooth and supple bodied Janice. With a sigh and ruefully recalling the short but active time they had spent together, his decision now made, he reached for his mobile phone.

Frederick prepared himself as he would for one of his 'visits', but this time there would be no acquisition, as he liked to term it, of lingerie. This time, he inwardly smiled in his excitement, it was a 'recce'; a term he had heard used in a multitude of war themed films. Outfitting himself in dark clothing and his Barbour jacket, he also donned thin brown leather driving gloves then placed the DVD disc recording he had made into the hidden pocket of the jacket and patted at a side pocket to ensure the dog lead was there. "Number nineteen," he quietly muttered as if to reassure himself and checking his laptop was switched off, collected the car keys from the bedside table and made his way downstairs.

His mother heard the creaking of the floorboard at the top of the stair landing and popped her head out of the lounge door. "Off to see your sweetheart tonight, Frederick?" she coyly asked.

"Ah, not tonight mother, I'm just off for a small constitutional," he replied, "got a few things on my mind."

"Well, don't leave that young girl hanging about Frederick dear," then recalling a phrase she had heard one of her cronies utter, added, "Jenny's a keeper," though wasn't entirely sure exactly what that meant other than surmising it was supposed to encourage a relationship.

Frederick smiled and nodded at his mother's attempt at matchmaking. "I'll give her a phone when I get back," he promised and closed the door behind him.

The short drive to the area of Borden Road took him less than ten minutes through the light traffic. He parked his car in the same spot and ensuring it was locked, retraced the route he had taken those few nights previously, ignoring and being ignored by the few pedestrians that were about. He walked with a purpose in his step as his mind contemplated the action he was about to take. Arriving at the rear lane that separated Austen Road and Borden Road, he hesitated at the sight of a number of lights shining into the back gardens from the houses that backed onto the lane. This time, however, he had no need to enter any gardens and was confident that should anyone see him walking in the lane, they would merely assume him to be a man with a dog lead searching for a missing pup. Taking a deep breath he set off at a brisk pace, aware that loitering would only attract undue attention and counted off the houses on his left as he walked. His step slowed as he approached the back gate of the house, recognising the small garden and the window where he had made the recording and counted it as house number ten in the line of mid-terraced homes. He spun on his heel and quickly returned along the lane, counting again till he arrived at house number one and satisfied that the house he identified at number ten in his count would be house number ten when he walked along the front of the houses. That done, he made his way into Borden Road and first ensuring there seemed to be nobody about, walked along the line of houses, inwardly counting until he arrived at house number ten, but did not stop. His brief, excited glance at the door confirmed what he suspected. The red coloured plastic PVC door bore the number nineteen in black enamel figures and he also saw that a light was on behind the drawn curtains. Continuing his walk along the road, Frederick kept his head down low and at the end of the road, about turned and walked back towards number nineteen, his fingers grasping behind him inside the Barbour jacket at the secret pocket. Now was the critical time.

His mouth was dry as he nervously fumbled at the DVD case and almost dropped it in his haste to extract it from the pocket. Suddenly, he was at number nineteen and casting a quick glance about him, shuffled into the small path and in one fluid movement, dropped the case through the letterbox, and held his breath as he listened for it falling, but heard no sound and used his gloved fingers to gently lower the post flap.

Head down and without a backward glance, he hurried from the doorway and made his way back to his car.

Chapter 19

Paul Hardie sat in the armchair in front of the fireplace, a glass of whisky clutched in his hand to celebrate his success in forcing Colin Davis' hand. He had seen it on the fat bastard's eyes and in his sagging shoulders, his defeat evident and he knew Davis would cave in; that tomorrow or the next day, Paul would probably receive a call informing him that the Board had reconsidered and he was to be re-instated. He sipped at the whisky and coughed slightly as the fiery liquid burned at the back of his throat. Tonight, he joked with himself, he would have a couple of halves only and there would be no repeat of the state he found himself in this morning. Which reminded him, and sighing, placed the glass on a nearby side table and pushed up from the chair to stand. He had the washing machine to empty of his shit and vomit stained clothes and walking to the kitchen, had just pulled opened the machine when the doorbell rung. His heart almost stopped, but then he grinned in relief. Fiona's body was too well hidden for it to be discovered, if it ever would be. Nevertheless, his heart continued to race as he made his way to the front door and stared curiously at the plastic DVD case that lay on the mat at the door. Bending to lift the case, he continued to stare at it as he opened the door, surprised to see two uniformed officers, the dark haired woman from the previous visit but this time with a younger officer, a man, but not the Inspector.

"Mister Hardie, Constable Gold," Lesley smiled as she reminded him of her name, her nose involuntarily twitching at the smell of whisky, "I apologise for calling upon you at this late hour, but just wondering if there was any word yet from your wife."

It didn't occur to Paul to invite the police officers in and staring from one to the other, he shook his head. "Nothing so far, nothing at all and I take it because you're here you haven't heard from her either then? She hasn't been in touch with you people?"

"I'm afraid not." Lesley bristled at his description of "you people" and Hardie clearly didn't intend inviting them into the house, as she added, "Ah, this is my colleague, Constable Mason. We're here simply because in the early days of a reported missing person we maintain contact with the home to see if there is anything else that might have come to mind, any reason why your wife might have decided to go away without notifying you or anyone else?"

Paul shook his head. "Nothing has come to mind. I've racked my brain to think of a reason why Fiona might have left, but we were very happy together and as I said when I visited your office, we were hoping to start a family, so no. I can't think of anything else to tell you Constable."

Lesley nodded, yet her gut feeling was that something was wrong. The feeling wasn't anything that she could put into words or make sense of; an intuition maybe or even a woman's unexplainable, irrational and totally illogical belief that told her that the MP's husband was lying to her. It seemed to Lesley that Hardie was too relaxed, too confident and not as distressed as she dared hope a man would be if Lesley were suddenly and without explanation, to disappear from his life.

But suspicion wasn't proof and so she replied, "Well, thanks for your time Mister Hardie," and forcing herself to smile, continued, "its likely there will either be myself or other officers calling by to check if there is any word from your wife. I know that earlier today some officers tried to …"

She got no further. Paul's eyes narrowed, his confidence soaring as he realised that the police knew nothing; that these dumb bastards had no inkling of what happened. He abruptly interrupted her and said, "Come on now Constable is that really necessary? These visits I mean? After all, if my wife turns up surely you must realise that the first thing I'm going to do is contact you to call off the search. I'm hardly likely to keep it a secret now, am I?" his voice oozed sarcasm.

Lesley swallowed hard and could feel her face turning red and beside her, she could almost sense that young Alex was about to take an angry step forward. "Of course sir, you're quite right. I'm sure the visits might seem to be a nuisance, but what the regular contact does is assure you that we are still trying to find your wife and also to inform you of the result of any search we undertake. However," she forced herself to keep her voice level, "I will note your complaint and request that any disruption to your life be kept to a minimum."

Paul wasn't a stupid man and staring at her had seen her cheeks turn red and her nostrils flare. Tight-lipped, Lesley turned on her heel and walked away, closely followed by the bemused Alex.

He closed the door and realised almost immediately he had handled that badly and leaning his forehead against the cool PVC on the inside of the door, slowly rested his head against it, angry with himself for being so bloody confident. He had seen it in the cops' eyes, recognised that the woman wasn't stupid, that he had annoyed her and what shook him was her eyes betrayed her thoughts.

She was suspicious of him and for the first time since he had killed Fiona, Paul knew real fear.

The bathroom was a blanket of steam so thick the small, wall-mounted fan could not cope and the sound of its whirring rotor blades was more an irritant than an aid to circulate the vapour from the room. Janice Meikle could hardly see the door from where she lay in the bath, enjoying the strains of Emeli Sande's latest CD playing in the lounge, the music filtering through the partially open door. As she sighed with pleasure, it seemed the hot, soapy and fragrant water was easing away the aches of sitting all day at her desk and squirming with delight, lowered herself deeper into the bath so that just her face was visible, her blonde hair like a cloud of wispy tendrils cascading about her on top of the water. From the bedroom, she heard her phone activate, indicating a text message had been received but, she grinned to herself, right now nothing was worth leaving the bath. She slid her bottom backwards, her head and shoulders emerging from the water and sat against the warm enamel of the bath. Using her hands Janice swept her hair backwards from her face and reached for the scented soap, sniffing at it then running it round her neck and arms. With an almost sensual pleasure she ran the soap across her bosom, grimacing as her fingers caressed the small, yellowing bruise on the left breast around the nipple where that idiot Colin had squeezed too hard. That'll cost him a present, maybe a necklace or a bracelet, she smiled unashamedly at her mercenary use of her body. She guessed she had been bathing for almost thirty minutes and softly giggled when her stomach rumbled to protest its hunger. Tonight was her night, a chance to just indulge in some self-pampering with a delivered take-away meal and a bottle of plonk and not worrying about Colin's fat body crushing her onto the bed mattress. Stepping from the bath she grabbed the large towel from the heated rail and as she dried herself, thought about Colin. He hadn't been her first choice as a replacement for Paul, grinning when she recalled how after being confronted by Paul in the parking area, she had arrived at the office and bumped into Colin in the lift. He saw she had been upset, or rather fuming and she played on his pathetic attempt to calm her down, offering coffee in the small refreshment area. It had been easy to make him believe it was his idea they have dinner that very night to discuss her boyfriend issues and confess her failed relationship with the latest, though she hadn't named Paul Hardie and inferred it was someone who didn't work in the office. It had been so easy to blame the fictitious boyfriend for taking advantage of her, to pretend she had no idea he was married. Men, she shook her head and grinned as she towel dried it; so easily manipulated at the sight of tears and a flash of leg. After the meal, it hadn't taken much effort to persuade him to drive her home to her flat and once she had him in her bed, she knew he would want more. But more of Janice came at a price and she guessed the kind of salary Colin earned would make it worth her while keeping him happy. Besides, she had always fancied a promotion to private secretary and had allowed her imagination to outfit herself with a new wardrobe.

She wrapped the light blue coloured cotton robe about her and shaking her hair free, decided to let it dry naturally through the evening. Making her way into the small kitchen Janice pulled open the fridge door and fetched out the bottle of Sauvignon Blanc and poured a generous measure into the wine glass. Sipping at the wine, she rummaged in the kitchen drawer for the take-away menu and selecting her choice, dialled the number to place the order. It was when she replaced the handset she remembered her mobile phone had received a text and glass in hand, wandered into the bedroom to fetch the phone from the dressing table. Scrolling down, she opened the text and scanning the message, her jaw literally dropped as her eyes fluttered in shock. A cold fury coursed through her veins and she banged the glass down, the wine spilling onto the table. Again she read the message and snarling, pressed the green button to call the number, but her call almost immediately went through to the answer service. She didn't leave a message, but ended the call and sat down on the edge of the bed, her teeth gritted in rage. If Colin Davis thinks he can shag me and then fucking dump me just like that, she fumed, her mind racing as she thought of a way to get back at him, a way to revenge his treatment of her and get from him what she wanted, what she believed she deserved.

Frederick Evans could hardly contain his excitement as he got into his car and was almost overcome by the need to tell someone of how clever he was. With shaking fingers, he fetched his mobile phone from his pocket and dialled Jenny's number, forcing himself to be calm as he listened to the number ring.
"Hello?" Jenny answered with just a trace of slight hesitation in her voice.
"Jenny, it's me," he cheerfully said, "just thought I'd give you a call. Are you doing anything tonight, now I mean?"
For her part, the call surprised Jenny, wearing her pyjamas and sitting on her bed, her arms curled round her knees that were drawn up almost to her chin. She had convinced herself that Frederick had already tired of her and sobbed for almost an hour till there were no tears left to cry. "I was just about to go to bed, Frederick," she replied, then added "I didn't think you were going to phone."
"Not phone?" he repeated, "Why ever not? I thought we were supposed to be going out together, boyfriend and girlfriend," he teased her, still high on the excitement of his nights foray.
Jenny's heart leapt with joy and she blushed at all the hateful thoughts she had gone through during that evening.
"I was wondering, do you fancy coming over tonight?" he asked, biting at his lower lip, his breathing a little irregular as he waited for her response.
Her brow furrowed. Glancing at her bedside clock she saw it was just after eleven o'clock and knew in her heart Frederick had called because he wanted sex. However Jenny was, if nothing else, pragmatic and if being at Frederick's beck and call and getting onto her back for him meant the relationship was to continue, then she was prepared to accept that. She sighed and said, "I'll get a taxi and bring my work clothes for tomorrow," she replied, forcing herself to sound more cheerful than she felt.
"Great," he replied with delight, "I'll see you when you arrive."

Lesley Gold turned the patrol car into the back yard at Maryhill Police Office while Alex Mason in the rear seat fought to restrain the violently drunken man.

"Settle down, you idiot," he snarled at the prisoner who, though his wrists were handcuffed to the front, continued to struggle while he directed a string of expletives at the young cop.

Lesley switched off the engine and turning in her seat, shouted, "Hey you. For one, I don't take kindly to that kind of language from a man of your age who should know better. Would you use that kind of language in front of your wife or kids? Now settle down and behave yourself. You're getting the jail for a racial breach of the peace, so no matter what you say or do, it's not going to help you any, do you understand?"

Almost immediately, she knew she was wasting her breath when the man screamed back, "Fuck off you whore," and tried to butt Alex to the face.

With a resigned sigh, Lesley got out of the driver's seat and opening the rear door, pulled the middle-aged and slightly-built prisoner out by the collar and with Alex on the other side of the man, frog-marched him through the security door and into the Uniform bar where the Duty Inspector and civilian turnkey awaited them.

"Evening Lesley," nodded the Inspector as she turned a wary eye to the prisoner. "So what do you have here then?"

"The gentleman was committing a breach of the peace outside the Asian grocers at the Kingsway Drive row of shops Inspector. The shopkeeper refused to sell him any alcohol due to his intoxicated state…."

"There's fuck all wrong with me and that Paki's getting it, when I get out of here," interrupted the drunk as he struggled between the two officers.

"So we got a call and the man wouldn't take a telling," Lesley related as both she and Alex struggled briefly with the man, who tried to kick her.

"Wouldn't take a warning, would you?" Lesley continued and then turning to the drunk, pressed her shoulder against him, forcing him against the wooden bar to prevent him butting her with his head and taking some pleasure in the pain he experienced as the hard and unforgiving surface met skin, muscle and bone.

"You sir," the Inspector glanced angrily at the drunk, "are here for court tomorrow for a racial beach, racial threat and in particular your belligerent attitude towards my officers. So," asked the Inspector, her voice betraying her impatience of the drunk as she commenced the procedure on the computer, "who's the reporting officer?"

"That'll be me, ma'am," replied Alex, glancing for approval from Lesley who surprised, nodded her assent. It occurred to her that perhaps Dotty's pep-talk was working.

"Right," the Inspector glanced up, and nodded to Alex, "proceed with the charge, Constable."

Ten minutes later with the prisoner still both threatening and protesting, but now locked in a cell, Lesley and Alex sat in the reporting room while the young cop dictated the details of the arrest over the phone to a late shift typist.

Lesley, nursing a cup of coffee from the vending machine, indicated to Alex with her hand she was going to make a telephone call and made her way out of the room into the corridor.

"Hello mum, I know it's late but I figured you'd still be up and just thought I'd give you a quick bell, see how things are."

"Hi darling, no change," her mother replied. "Are you in the office?"

"Yeah, we've just popped into Maryhill with a drunk. I'm drinking the worst tasting coffee in the world while my neighbour does the report. Look, I was thinking of coming over tomorrow about lunchtime. Have a quick visit before I go on shift."

"No and no again," Peggy replied. "I know you don't finish till two in the morning, so have a lie-in and relax. There's no need for you to be running over here and as I've told you Lesley," she stressed her daughter's name, "I'll let you know if you need to be here, okay?"

"Okay mum," Lesley smiled at the gentle rebuke. "You win. Just don't forget I'm here, willing and able, Missus Gold; ready to serve at your call."

She could hear her mother chuckle and ended the call, staring at the phone and wishing there was more she could do. As she stared at the phone, a thought occurred to her and making her way into an empty office off the corridor, sat at a desk and dialled the internal number for Garscadden.

"Constable Turner, Garscadden office" the call was answered.

"Dotty, it's me, Lesley. Alex and I are just winding up an arrest here at Maryhill and then we're heading back to the office. Do you want anything brought in? Milk, chips, strong drink?" she joked.

"Vodka would be nice," sighed Dotty, "but you'll not go wrong if you bring milk in. The early shift will only complain if there isn't any for their tea."

Lesley paused, then softly asked, "Are you okay, hen?"

"I'm fine," replied Dotty, a little too quickly thought Lesley.

"Right then," she tried to sound jovial, "we'll not be too long. See you when we get there," and hung up. She sat for a minute, recalling earlier in the evening how upset Dotty had been. The death of Morris's wife can't have been that unexpected, she thought, her brow creased as she considered what seemed to be Dotty's obviously tearful reaction. Yes, she knew that Dotty and Morris had worked together for some years and yes, they seemed by all account to have been friends. Or is it, she dared to wonder, that they had been

closer than just friends or am I imagining something that isn't there? With a sigh she decided that really, it was none of her business.
"Ready neighbour?" said Alex's voice behind her.
"Ready," she nodded and followed him through the corridor to the rear door.

It had just turned midnight as Lesley and Dotty sat in the small canteen, both nursing a mug of coffee while Alex Mason took the opportunity to first update the MP log for Fiona Hardie and later, to find a quiet spot in the general office to study for his final probationer exam.
"How well did you know Morris's wife, I'm sorry, what was her name again?"
"Susan, her name was Susan," Dotty gloomily replied, "and I knew her, what, maybe five years? Well, when I say I knew her, I visited a couple of times and sat with her, usually when Morris was having some quiet time."
"Eh, quiet time? I'm sorry," said Lesley, "what do you mean?"
"When he wasn't working, Morris spent almost all his off duty time with Susan. He cared for her every need, be that bathing or," she hesitated, "cleaning her. He was her social life in that room. Now and again when my kids were with my parents, I would persuade him to go for a pint with his brother Roddy, when he visited or to watch a film at the movies or even out just for a walk by himself. I would sit and just talk with her, maybe read to her or something. That said, I didn't know her well and all I knew about her was what Morris would tell me. He used to say that Susan had been a very active woman. Hill-walker, sports, you know, into all sorts of things."
"No kids then?"
"No, no kids," she shook her head. "To be honest, I don't know if that was by choice or, you know, just one of those things. Anyway, when she was struck down by the disease it hit her very hard and really, from what Morris has said, it was just a question of time." She sighed and said, "I'm surprised that she lasted this long, poor soul."
They sat in quiet contemplation for a few moments and then Lesley asked, "Do you think he'll come back to work?"
Dotty shrugged her shoulders. "His time is almost in. He's down to a few months, so that might include his bereavement leave. Really," she softly exhaled as she glanced about her, "why should he come back? There's nothing here that's going to help him."
Lesley thought she detected a quiet sorrow in Dotty's voice and resisted the urge to ask her outright. Well, at least she tried to resist, but her curiosity got the better of her and finally she asked, "You really like him, don't you?"
Dotty's head snapped round and her eyes widened as she barked out, "What do you mean by that?"

Lesley immediately realised she had made a huge mistake and raising her hands defensively, said, "Sorry Dotty, I'm out of line with that remark. I apologise. I'm really sorry, honest."
Almost as quickly as she angrily flared, Dotty calmed down and biting at her lip, her shoulders drooped as she shook her head. To Lesley's astonishment, tears welled up in the other woman's eyes and turning to Lesley she asked, "Is it that obvious. Oh, God. Does anyone else know?"
Lesley reached across the table and placing her hand on top of Dotty's shook her head. "Look, I didn't mean to upset you. I don't know anything. I just got the feeling that, well, you know, that you might have liked Morris a little better than just as a colleague. I didn't mean anything by it."
Dotty nodded and taking a deep breath to compose herself, wiped at her eyes with her sleeve. "I've never told anyone, daren't even admit it to myself," she quietly began. "I've liked him for a long time now. Years even, but how do you tell someone who is dealing with the sort of issues he had? How could I possibly even hint that he's always in my mind? God, I feel like such a bitch. His wife dying and all I can think about, is me, me, me."
As if in realisation of the enormity of her confidence, she stared at Lesley and said, "You won't repeat this, will you?"
Lesley shook her head and smiled. "You're not the first woman to fall for the wrong or unavailable man, Dotty. Trust me. When I think of some of the boyfriends I've been with, I'm a past master at that."
The door burst open and Alex Mason excitedly said, "Control room have just given us a call, Lesley. Housebreakers at a pub in Great Western Road," then as they smiled at his enthusiasm, he stared from one to the other, his eyes narrowing in suspicion as he sensed something had been said and asked, "What?"

Frederick Evans heard the taxi draw up outside the house and was at the open door as Jenny walked along the narrow path. Awkwardly, he bent over to kiss her cheek and took her small bag from her hand.
"Who's there dear?" called his mother's voice from the top landing.
"It's all right mother, it's only Jenny," he replied, "go back to bed. We won't disturb you."
Jenny was thrilled when he said, "It's only Jenny." In her mind that made her acceptable in the house, that she wasn't a stranger here, that she was Frederick's girlfriend. Right there and then, no matter what he wanted of her, she would be everything to him, inwardly rejoicing as she savoured the words 'her boyfriend' and almost puppy-like, followed adoringly as he led her up the stairs.

Peggy Gold opened her eyes with a start, her back aching from too many hours sitting upright in the armchair. Her husband's breathing, so very regular, had been interrupted as in his sleep, he struggled to breathe. She watched as he coughed, unconsciously feeling his pain and raising one hand, smoothed at his brow.

"Oh Tommy darling," she quietly muttered to the sleeping man, "I wish there was something I could do for you, something to ease the pain. Not for the first time her gaze fell upon the row of medicine bottles neatly standing side by side on the bedside table and she gave an involuntarily shudder. Everything in her church upbringing railed against the thought, but still it persisted. Softly, she rested her head back on the pillow behind her and closing her eyes, again tried to sleep.

Paul Hardie sat staring horrified at the blank screen of the television, his hand frozen on the remote control. His mind couldn't, wouldn't accept what he had just watched, a recording of him punching Fiona and her falling down and striking her head. Slowly, as though his eyes drawn there, he turned his head to stare down at the hearth. His stomach heaved and he knew he was going to throw up. Racing to the stairs, he made it just in time to discharge into the bowl, his body heaving as his already delicate stomach once again turned inside out. He knelt by the bowl, his hands clasped on each side of the rim and stared down into the almost colourless phlegm, but he saw only the recording of him striking Fiona. He sat back, resting against the bath as his mind screamed at him, how could this have happened? Who had recorded him? Slowly, his body still shaking, he pulled himself upright and wiping his mouth with a towel, made his way back downstairs. He took a deep breath and this time standing, operated the DVD player. The recording repeated and as he watched, he turned his head towards the window and realised that it had been made from outside by someone standing in the garden. He shook his head as though to ward off the demons that now played with his mind. Snatching at the case, he turned it over and over in his hands, but it seemed to be exactly what it was, a clear plastic DVD case. There was no note; so whoever delivered the DVD, he wondered, what did he or she want?

He sat heavily on the couch as the recording finished. Was it coincidence the police were at the door when he discovered the DVD? Was it some sort of trick they were playing on him, trying to get him to confess before they arrested him?

Paul had no experience of the police, had never been arrested and aside from watching television programmes, both reality and fictional, had no real idea how they worked. He puzzled over the recording and reasoned that if the police were aware of it, they wouldn't fart about hoping for a confession, they would more than likely drag him from the house and question him till he

gave up the story and where he had dumped Fiona's body. But they didn't and that could only mean one thing; the police did not know of the recording. That left him with one conclusion. Whoever had made the recording delivered it to Paul to let him know that they knew what he had done and that knowledge wasn't just dangerous to him, but gave them a hold over Paul. The question though, remained.
What did he or she want from him?

Chapter 20 - Saturday

Saturday morning, like those days preceding, began bright and sunny and the inhabitants of the West of Scotland revelled in the unaccustomed good weather. Those fortunate souls not employed took advantage of their time off to enjoy the sun while the majority of those less fortunate and in particular those employed working shifts in the public sector or service industries, grumbled and groaned as they made their way to work. Not so, however, Frederick Evans, having now spent another joyous night in the arms of a woman, and who now believed himself to be 'Jack the Lad', That morning, Frederick quite literally skipped onto the bus with a grin. Of course, sex with Jenny wasn't the full reason for his good humour. No, Frederick had taken the first step in his plan to advance his career and gave a reassuring pat at the phone number written on the paper in his pocket and with which he intended later that morning to take the second step.

The subject of Frederick's plan, the increasingly worried Paul Hardie, awoke very early that morning shaking from a fitful sleep, the shirt and trousers he had slept in and the bedding soaked in his sweat. His sleep in the main comprised mostly of nightmarish dreams of him being locked up with a mob of vicious, but faceless criminals, all of whom pursued him through dark and endless corridors, soundlessly grasping at him as they sought to seek revenge for the killing of his wife. As he raced from them, Paul endured terror beyond anything he had ever known and though the hands were just inches from him, he was never caught. His panicked fear was that his flight seemed endless and nothing he could do would stop them from coming for him. Still shaking, he wearily pushed himself from the bed and made his way into the bathroom. Tiredly, supporting himself on the basin of the sink, he watched his stream empty into the bowl, his thoughts occupied by the DVD that had arrived the night before. Again and again, he wondered who could have made the recording. The half dozen times he had watched it gave him no clue, other than it seemed to be pretty amateurish and he guessed from the quality that it had been made with a hand-held camera or perhaps even a camera phone. In the darkness, he had stepped into the garden, standing at the spot by the window where the recording was made but a search of the overgrown grass under the window revealed nothing. He'd peered through the open curtains, but confirmed nothing other than that was where the recording had been filmed.

Now downstairs with a hot coffee in front of him, he sat at the small kitchen table and racked his brains to recall who might have delivered the DVD. Could it be a neighbour, he wondered. Did they mean to warn him? Was it someone who thought he or she was helping, but almost immediately dismissed that thought. Why hadn't they told the police, he thought and then countered that by guessing whoever had been skulking around the garden at that time of night must have themselves been up to no good. As for it being a friend, he wryly shrugged; the few he had occasionally kept in touch with from university were either too busy or too successful to bother with him and certainly wouldn't be hiding in his garden, watching him kill his wife. That just leaves someone who is playing some sort of game with me, he reasoned. Someone who wants me to know that they know what I did. Someone who is taunting me or, his brow creased could it be, that he or she wants something from me?

That's it, he sat bolt upright. They want something from me. Could it be money? No, he glanced about him and dismissed that almost immediately. The house was certainly bought, but the mortgage was held by the bank and the address, though a nice enough area could at best be described as upper working class and certainly not affluent, not by any means.

His coffee chilled and wearily, he ran a hand through his hair. Try as he might, Paul was no closer to guessing why the DVD had been sent and realised all he could do was wait. Wait, worry and wonder.

Colin Davies went to bed late on Friday evening and spent a restless night that got worse when at one in the morning his wife angrily told him to stop his tossing and turning and finally ordered that he get out and let her sleep. Reluctantly, he made his way through to the spare bedroom and climbed under the cold duvet, his mind occupied by thoughts of how Janice Meikle would receive the text message he had sent that quite literally, dumped her. Not well, he astutely guessed. The few hours sleep he managed was punctuated by nightmares during which he raced through an endless lane, being pushed this way and that by homeless and faceless down and outs as he sought a place of refuge. "Not here", they all screamed at him, "not here." He awoke with a start, his pyjamas damp with sweat and clutched at the ever-increasing burning pain in his chest. If ever a warning signal to watch his diet and give up curries was evident, it's this, he thought. Maybe need to lose a wee bit of weight too, he glumly considered, dreading the thought of attending a gym. But then again, he mused, lots of nice dolly birds go to these places nowadays and with that happy thought, turned and tried again to get to sleep.

On the other side of the River Clyde in the Yoker area, Morris MacDonald hardly slept at all, lying on his back on what was always accepted as his side of the bed. His hand trailed across to where Susan had once slept before circumstances forced him to turn the spare room into his alone while the master bedroom where he now lay, had become almost like a hospital room. He had worked at making the room a pleasure for her; the walls adorned with her camera club prize-winning photographs, the daily bunch of her favourite flower, pink tulips in the old and slightly cracked, but gaily painted vase he had bought her at the Barra's all those years ago when they were courting and every penny had been a prisoner.
She had joked that when her time came, it was to be a cremation and that she didn't want him trailing up to some chilly graveyard every week and catching the flu nor did she want a housing estate built over her in a hundred years. He agreed with some reluctance to her request, that he would have her cremated and had retorted that it would be a 'homer', that he'd buy a gallon of petrol and just have the ceremony in the back garden and the mourners could have a barbeque. For after all, he had joked right back at her, the price of petrol being what it was, why waste a good bonfire? Lying there, he smiled at the memory, knowing that probably the thing he would miss most of all was her inherent good humour, her sense of fun and ability to laugh at herself, even in the darkest of times.
"Oh Susan," he softly whispered. "What have you done? Leaving me like this, all alone," and lips trembling, turned his head and smiled sadly at the photograph on the bedside table at the lovely, dark haired woman with the laughing eyes whom he had loved and always would.

Tired though she felt, Lesley Gold was committed to her new fitness regime and forcing herself to rise early from bed, pulled on the tracksuit and training shoes. With the sun beating down onto her bare head, she pounded the streets round the Partick area then head down, turned from Dumbarton Road into Gardner Street, determined to run up the steep slope of the road. It was as she approached the junction of White Street she heard the voice call out, "Hello, ah, good morning, Constable Gold."
Lesley was surprised to see the postman and then noticed the red mail van parked at the side of the road. She stopped and breathlessly nodded, now recognising the scarred man from Garscadden Uniform bar and watched as he knelt at the bottom of the open post-box and finished shuffling the mail into a large, light grey coloured canvas bag, before closing and locking the

heavy door of the post-box. "Sorry," she gasped at him, hands on her hips as she tried to catch her breath, "I don't know your name."
He stood up and as he leaned against the post-box, she realised that he looked to be powerfully built and towered over her and, to her further surprise, saw he was blushing.
"Andy," he replied, "Andy Carmichael. I'm the post man that delivers the mail…"
"To the office," she nodded as she completed the sentence for him. "Yes, I know. I saw you talking the other day to Jinksie." Her breathing was a little easier, but an awkward silence had developed and with an inward start, it occurred to her that the big man was shy. "So, this is your mail round then?" she asked and mentally kicked herself for asking such a stupid question.
"Ah, no," he shrugged his shoulders, "I sometimes fill in when there's a colleague off sick or something. Jack of all trades, master of none," he shyly grinned at her, a nice grin she thought; his teeth white and even, the wide scar a light pale against his darker complexion.
"Right, well, ah, nice to meet you Andy," she grinned back at him and then nodded up the street. "Better get on the road before a chill sets in, eh?"
"Good idea," he continued to sheepishly grin at her and felt his face burn red under her scrutiny, then called after her, "and when you're running uphill, take shorter steps, count to yourself one, two, three, four over and over and watch your feet, that way the steep slope doesn't seem to be so daunting and you'll be at the top before you know it."
'Daunting', Lesley inwardly smiled; a curious word to hear from a postman. "Right, thanks," she replied as half turning, gave him a small wave and started to jog away.
Andy stared after her and exhaled with a soft 'phew' of relief then grinned again. It seemed that volunteering to take this route on hadn't been such a bad idea after all.
At the top of the hill, she stopped to again to catch her breath and then it struck her. The postman, Andy she corrected herself; Andy had called her by name. How did he know my name, she wondered?

Even the presence of his manager Robert Hamilton hovering about the floor couldn't suppress Frederick's sense of excitement that morning. He hummed to himself and worked away at the displays, dressing and re-dressing the mannequins, standing back and with a critical eye, tut-tutting to the other sales personnel when he judged that they had got something wrong and to their overall astonishment, joked with them and even good-naturedly, jovially slapped one on his back. His fellow staff members were amazed and whispered among themselves at the change that had come over old Freddy.

Robert Hamilton watched all this with bemusement, wondering if the chat he had with Evans had caused some sort of personality to emerge that previously had lain dormant.

For his part, Frederick played his role to perfection, becoming for the day the life and soul of the department, but through it all waited patiently for his morning break and the opportunity to slip from the store to the public telephones, situated just outside the store on the pedestrian precinct in Buchanan Street.

Equally excited that morning, but for a very different reason, was Jenny Farndale. Breakfast again with Frederick's mother was a drag; at least it had seemed so until the old woman said, "This is becoming quite a regular thing, isn't it dear?"

Jenny's heart had almost leapt from her chest she was so happy and once more allowed her eyes to wander round the kitchen, imagining how she would change things. New wallpaper for a start, maybe even new kitchen units and a tiled floor like she had seen in the pages of the home furnishing magazines she frequently read when travelling to and from work on the bus.

"You'd better watch your time, dear," the old woman reminded her, "we don't want to be late for work now do we?"

"Oh, no, of course, you're right," she had gushed and washed the remains of the fry-up down with the mug of sweet tea. Lifting the dishes, Eunice shooed her away. "I'm sure you get more than your fair share at work without having to wash them here, dear," she had smiled at Jenny. "Besides, I like the thought of having another woman in this house. Fredericks' woman," she teased and gently poked a bony finger into Jenny's ribs. "Now, away with you and get yourself ready and let me clear this place up."

Jenny couldn't know that the old woman's excitement was almost as high as her own. Eunice had many years previously almost decided that Frederick, if not totally asexual, was a contradiction, having found magazines in his room of the female form in all manner of poses, though he never seemed to take an active interest in women and now this, a living, honest to goodness young woman. Though admittedly, Jenny wasn't as startlingly lovely as some of the women in the magazines, nevertheless Eunice could now consider her son to be courting and she could hope upon hope, one day be married.

Blissfully unaware of Eunice's aspirations for her, Jenny obediently did as she was told and returned upstairs to Frederick's room. No, she smiled inwardly correcting herself, our room. Now dressed, she turned her attention to the bed, fluffing the pillows and pulling at the quilt, patting it straight with the flat of her hands. She stared at the bed and sighed. Frederick was a long way from knowing what it took to satisfy a woman, she softly grinned, blushing again at his demands the night before. She took a deep breath and

shoved her used underwear into her small bag, and glancing round the room, smiled again. This would be more suitable for his mother and we could have the larger room, she thought to herself. All it would take was time and some gentle persuasion from Jenny.
She didn't know it then and could not describe the feelings she was experiencing, but Jenny's previously inhibited confidence had begun to assert itself and glancing round the room, her eyes were bright as her mind worked overtime at the changes she intended for the whole house; changes that now she had her foot in the door, she was determined to make. All she had to do was keep Frederick happy and smiling tightly, made the decision that no matter what it takes, no matter what indignities she might have to undergo in the privacy of the room, that's what she had to do.

Paul Hardie stared aghast at the phone in his hand, the hum of the concluded call echoing through the earpiece. The man's sneering voice, had been brief, but so threatening that Paul couldn't quite believe what he had heard, his mind racing and with difficulty, trying to make sense of the short call.
"You will have received the DVD Mister Hardie," the man had said. "Interesting to watch, isn't it? Of course, you have a copy and I have the original recording. I could deliver a copy to the police, but that wouldn't suit either of us, Mister Hardie. By now you will no doubt have wondered why it was posted through your door and also why I haven't informed on you, what you did." The man had paused, as though deliberating and reading from a script. Paul, too surprised to protest, found that even had he tried, his tongue felt swollen in his dry mouth and simply listened as the man resumed. "It's a simple case of scratching each other's back, Mister Hardie. I want you to do something for me, something that will tie us together and no-one will ever be the wiser. Do this for me, this little thing and you will never hear from me again."
At last, gulping for air, Paul spoke and asked, "Who are you? What is it you want?"
"Who I am, Mister Hardie is of no concern to you, just as long as you remember that I know who you are and what you did," the voice again reminded Paul. "What I want is really very simple, Mister Hardie. I want you to kill someone for me."

Chapter 21

To the east of the city, while Frederick Evans malevolently uttered his demanding threat to Paul Hardie, Peggy Gold answered the knock at her door and admitted the smiling McMillan nurse.

"Sorry I'm a wee bit late hen," gasped the flustered, portly woman, "my last patient is a nice old lady, but a wee bit demanding," she said in a whispered voice as she laid her black medical bag down on the hallway floor and shrugged off her coat. "So, how was Thomas's night? My God Peggy," the nurse's eyes narrowed, "you're like a half shut knife. You look as though you need my TLC more than your hubby does. Right," she ushered Peggy in front of her through to the kitchen, "first things first. I'll get the kettle on, you go and have yourself a shower or even better," she beamed at the bemused Peggy, "run yourself a bath and have a good soak. Leave the door unlocked and I'll pass you a coffee in. How does that sound to you, hen?"

Peggy smiled and sighed, more than happy to be ordered about by the capable nurse. "Like luxury," she softly replied, then added "Thomas was a bit restless again, so I gave him some of the new, stronger medicine that was prescribed by Doctor McPherson and I've marked it on the chart. He's sleeping now, so…" but she didn't get to finish and was shooed off into the hallway by the determined nurse, who turned away to fill the kettle at the sink.

Peggy, grateful for the small respite time, collected her dressing gown and mobile phone from the spare bedroom, had one last glance into Thomas then closed the bathroom door behind her. While the bath filled, she dialled the number and listened to Lesley's voice requesting the caller leave a message. "Hello darling, it's me, mum," she said, hating having to speak into these damn machines, "just to let you know dad had a comfortable night and the nurse is here now, so I'm having myself a nice bath. I'll call you later. Love you."

She stared at the phone and sighed at the lie. It didn't do to let Lesley know that her father's night was awful and again wracked by pain; that through the night her mother was lucky to catch ten or fifteen minutes nap through each hour; that every gasp Thomas made had Peggy fearful that it was his last. She turned the taps off and liberally added a powdered solution for her aching back then testing the water, stripped off and cautiously dipped in a toe. The door was quietly knocked and a hand appeared holding a mug of coffee. Taking the coffee, Peggy whispered her thanks. The door again closed and she placed the coffee on the small stool by the bath, smelling the rich aroma that reminded her stomach she hadn't eaten since early evening yesterday.

It was later, while lying in the soothing bath that her jumbled thoughts betrayed her for, try as she might to resist the idea, once more the row of medicine bottles featured in her mind.

Frederick could hardly contain his excitement and was almost overwhelmed at the sense of power he derived when he had issued his instructions to the stunned Paul Hardie. He was pleased his voice hadn't faltered as he had feared it might, the practised speech almost word perfect and crushing the paper in his pocket, decided to tear it and flush it in the staff toilets immediately he returned to the store. It wouldn't do to be caught carrying details of a murder in his pocket, he inwardly grinned.

Walking through the Saturday morning crowd of shoppers, he again went over in his head his instructions to Hardie and they were, he was satisfied, quite unequivocally clear.

The store closed at five o'clock on Monday evenings in preparation of bi-monthly late opening for *'Special Friends'*; those privileged customers who held store cards and numbered in their hundreds, if not more. Dawson's feted these cardholders and, on production of their membership card of course, provided them with a finger buffet and a glass of wine as they strolled through the store, enjoying the special advantages the store permitted them behind closed doors while being offered bargains that were not normally available to the general public. It was, Frederick had to agree, all so civilised and none of the customers departed without at least one purchase; a financial coup for the store that also ensured slightly outdated stock or the end of season goods and clothing was cleared from the shelves.

At the conclusion of such a night, it was customary for each departmental manager to ensure their respective staff had cleared from the store before themselves departing. Robert Hamilton had made no secret of his intention after finishing work. Frederick had heard him boast to staff of his prowess at the billiard table and his regular weekly meeting each Monday evening with his friends at the snooker club situated above the pub in Stockwell Street. On one recent occasion, Frederick had overheard Hamilton laughingly telling a fellow manager that while making his way through the brightly lit railway station underpass from Argyle Street into Osborne Street, he was accosted by a drunk and recounted seeing the man off by the use of his umbrella. From the conversation, Frederick deduced the underpass was Hamilton's customary route to the club.

This underpass, Frederick had instructed Hardie, would be the best place for the murder to occur. Identifying Hamilton, he had smoothly confided, would be no problem; a fat man in his forties wearing a light tan coloured overcoat with velvet collar and carrying a black leather briefcase who would be passing through the underpass between nine-thirty and nine forty-five. Frederick didn't bother to mention an umbrella, believing that if the current fine weather continued as it seemed to be, Hamilton wouldn't bother carrying one. The details of how he accomplished the deed Frederick would leave to Hardie, but stressed he must ensure that he steal Hamilton's wallet that he should, he smiled as he recalled his instruction, dispose of the wallet and its contents as soon as possible after the deed. The killing should seem to be a mugging gone wrong, but best of all, Frederick assured Hardie, with no connection to the dead man, Hardie would never be considered a suspect in the murder. However, it had to be firmly stressed, that should Hardie fail to accept carrying out Frederick's demand, the police would either the next or following morning, anonymously receive a copy of the incriminating DVD. His last parting comment was a promise, that if on Wednesday morning. Frederick should read in the paper of a murder at the underpass, he would never again be troubled by Frederick

He had smiled as he imagined Hardie's blood running cold at the instructions and listened as the man stuttered and protested, but his pathetic attempt to appeal to Frederick had been pointless. What Hardie could not possibly know was that Frederick had too much riding on Hamilton's death. His ambition to succeed Hamilton and be promoted outweighed any other consideration. Pushing through the doors on the Buchanan Street entrance, he nodded insolently at the uniformed security officer, unaware of the slight shake of the head he received in return and the muttered word, "Prick" that escaped the man's lips.

Lesley Gold listened to her mother's message and read between the lines. It was always obvious to her when her mother was fibbing and trying to protect her daughter from the realities of living with a dying man and she resolved to call her mother when she had washed and dressed. As she reached a testing hand under the spray of water from the electric shower, her thoughts turned to the postman she had met on her run. A curious encounter, she grinned to herself, recalling the vivid scar that run across the guy's chin and neck and disappeared under the neckline of his shirt. Her natural curiosity caused her brow to furrow as she tried to imagine how he had come by the wound. From the brief glance, it didn't appear to be regular like some of the knife or razor wounds she had seen inflicted on victims and the width itself further suggested it hadn't been caused by a sharp blade. An accident maybe, she thought and continued to wonder as she stepped over the lip of the bath to bathe in the glorious hot, steamy water. Running the soap about her body, she glanced down and cast a critical eye at her waist. Lesley had determined not to weigh herself until the end of the month and fingers mentally crossed, hoped for good news. She thought again of the postman, Andy he said his name was and wondered how he had come to know her name? She stopped rubbing at her arms with the soap, her free hand slowly rising to cup at her mouth. Oh my God, a sudden further thought occurred to her. The bouquet of flowers; was it him? Did he send them to her? She grinned. Could it be that she had a secret admirer or, God forbid, maybe even her very own stalker? She couldn't decide whether to be pleased or worried. If anyone would know, it would be Jinksie, but he was now off duty till Monday. Ah well, she continued to soap her body, time enough to ask him then and for the time being dismissed the issue from her mind and began to hum to herself.

Morris MacDonald, accompanied by his brother Roderick, similarly dressed in a sober dark suit and black tie, spent much of that morning at the local Cooperative Funeral premises discussing arrangements for the service and cremation of Morris's wife Susan. The undertakers were not just professionally considerate, but treated Morris with a kindness and dignity born from decades of experience. Such was the compassion with which he was treated, his quiet reserve collapsed and tears rolled down his cheeks as his body shook uncontrollably. The younger of the two undertakers solemnly nodded to Roderick and left the office while the older man discreetly slipped out through a side door to complete the paperwork, leaving Roddy to console his distraught brother. The younger undertaker returned five minutes later with a tray upon which rested two cups of tea and a small plate of digestive biscuits that he wordlessly left on the desk before again leaving the two men alone.

"Take your time, wee man," said Roderick, rubbing at his brothers back as he offered him a clean linen handkerchief. "There's time enough to make the arrangements if you would rather come back another day."

"No, you're all right," sniffed Morris, dabbing at her eyes. "We'll get it done and that'll be it. Sorry, don't know what came over me," he took a deep breath. "Right, if you want to fetch the gentlemen in, we'll get on with it." Roderick nodded and at the door, indicated for the undertakers to return to the room.

The arrangements, much practised by the two men, took no more than fifteen minutes and shaking hands with the undertakers at the premises front door; the brothers stepped into the bright sunlight.

"Right," grinned Roderick, taking a deep breath and slapping his brother on the shoulder, "what you need wee man is a dram and a plate of soup inside you, so let's be finding a pub and for once, it'll be my treat."

Morris smiled at his brother's attempt to lighten the moment and was about to respond when the mobile phone in his pocket activated.

"Hello, Dotty," he unconsciously nodded into the mobile, "I'm pleased to hear from you."

"Morris, I just wanted to say," then she choked, unable to continue with the speech she had so laboured over.

He listened and heard her taking a deep breath then exhaling, guessing she was finding it difficult to form the words and before she could continue, said, "Yes, thank you, Dotty. I know you'll be thinking of me. Look, I'm with my brother Roddy. We have just visited the Co-op and made the arrangements. Susan wished for a Humanist service and cremation, so it will be this forthcoming Thursday, ten o'clock on the dot at North Dalnottar Crematorium. I'll be grateful if you might pass the word to the rest of the shift, if anyone cares to attend."

"Sure, of course. I'll do that. Look Morris, if there's anything I can do, anything at all," she gushed then almost in the same instant, froze, suddenly thinking my God, am I being too forthright, then hurriedly continued, "I mean, if you need anyone to be given a lift or that sort of thing."

"No, you're all right," he replied, completely unaware of her panicked concern. "I might ask one favour of you, though. I'm not sure if I'll be back after this Dotty. I might need to sit down and talk it over with someone and if you're up for it?"

"Yes, of course," she almost shouted down the phone. "Just give me a phone. Anytime Morris," she said and then repeated, "anytime."

He said goodbye and caught his brother's querying glance. "Dotty, one of the women I work with," he explained as he pocketed the mobile phone. "She's a very nice woman. You'll meet her on Thursday. Now, where's the nearest pub that does grub?"

Jenny's Saturday shift in the canteen was more hectic than usual, primarily because one of Jenny's lazier colleagues had taken her habitual 'sick Saturday' to sleep off the resulting hangover from the booze consumed the previous evening. Jenny didn't mind, her thoughts preoccupied by the burgeoning relationship with Frederick and the opportunity it presented for her to escape from her own parental bonds. Even the sarcasm of the young women who customarily teased her had no effect such was her good humour and excitement at her possible future.

"Missus Evans," she inwardly rolled the words round her head, "Missus Frederick Evans. Missus Jennifer Evans," she practised the title and name, "Mister and Missus Evans."

"What you grinning at?" asked her supervisor, her hands holding a tray full of dirty plates and cutlery, herself smiling at Jenny's good humour.

"Oh, you know, just thinking," Jenny mysteriously replied, unable to stop grinning.

"Well, mysterious yourself over to that machine and start loading this lot of shite into it," said the woman, handing over the tray to Jenny, her large bosom and belly rolling as she laughed, "then when you've done that, get yourself a wee break hen. You've worked like a Trojan today, so grab a cuppa and a sandwich. I think I saw that wee guy you're winching sitting at a table at the back of the canteen there," she winked, "but no fondling under the table, eh? I run a clean shop here."

Jenny blushed furiously and tried to protest she would do no such thing, but the woman waved a hand and continued to laugh as she walked away to serve at the counter.

It took her a few minutes to load the dirty items into the large dishwasher and pouring a mug of tea and grabbing a sandwich, hurried from the rear kitchen to the canteen. Frederick sat alone at a table in the corner, reading a newspaper.

"Hi," she breathlessly announced her arrival as she sat down facing him.

"Hi yourself," he good humouredly replied and still pleased with his handling of the telephone call to Paul Hardie. "So, got into work all right?"

"Yes, though how I made it after that huge breakfast your mother fed me, I don't know," she softly giggled.

He smiled tightly at her, appreciating that perhaps now wasn't the best time to tell her that her giggle really did irritate him. That and her teeth needed some long overdue dental attention.

"How's your day been so far?" she asked, sipping at the hot tea.

"Really quite good," he replied, grinning now as he recalled the phone call. How he ached to tell her, tell anyone, boast of his genius, how easily he had manipulated the man Hardie. Soon, Hamilton would be gone and he would be the obvious choice to run the department. Frederick Evans, Departmental Manager. Already in his mind he savoured the title.

"Frederick?"

He stared at her, saw the curiosity in her eyes. "Sorry, I was thinking of something else there."

"Me perhaps?" she replied, slipping off her shoe and rubbing at his lower leg with her foot.

He startled and snapped, "Not here Jennifer. Someone might see. It's just not appropriate."

Crestfallen, she quickly withdrew her foot and slipped it back into her shoe and sat upright, her eyes downcast.

He saw he had offended her and made an effort to smile. "Sorry, it's just that, well, you know. Sometimes people get the wrong idea."

"I thought we were supposed to be a couple Frederick?"

"We are, of course we are, my dear, but this is the work place Jennifer. It wouldn't do for me to be seen acting like a teenager, not when …" he stopped, aware that he had almost blurted it out, that with the pending and sudden demise of Mister Robert Hamilton, he expected to be promoted to the manager's position.

"So," she replied and seizing on his statement, leaned across the table and reached for his hand, "we are definitely a couple then?"

"Yes, of course," he lightly patted at her hand as he stood and then withdrew it to pat at his pockets. "Right, better get myself back. They tend to worry themselves if I'm not there to advise them," he smiled at his own self-importance."

With a slight nod of his head, he turned and walked away. She watched him disappear through the door and then saw that three tables away, four young women from the cosmetics department watched her, grinning as they leaned their heads together to discuss what they had just witnessed. Jenny ignored them, content that once again, Frederick had …. Well, maybe in not so many words, but otherwise declared his affection, if not love, for her. Yes, she inwardly grinned as she nibbled on her sandwich and sipped at the remains of her tea, things were looking up indeed and once more she allowed her mind to wander as she dreamed of living at Dykebar Lane and the changes she would make there.

Peggy Gold stared briefly at the incoming number on the screen of the mobile phone and sighed, closed her eyes and pressing the green button said, "Good morning Linda. How are you dear?"

"Morning mum," answered her youngest daughter, "just thought I'd give you a quick call and see how dad is, oh, and you of course."

"Of course," her mother repeated, mentally chastising herself for her cutting response. "Well, your dad isn't any better and we both know he won't get better, Linda. The McMillan nurse said …"

"Hold on mum," her daughter interrupted, "Okay darling," Peggy heard her say, "I'll see you later then. Kissy kisses."

"Sorry mum, that was Alex, he's just off to the golf. He has been invited to join the Kirkintilloch club. Isn't that wonderful?" she gushed. "It means that we'll be able to attend the dances and events and meet some pretty important people. And that won't do his career any harm, I can tell you. Now, what was it you were saying?"

"Nothing dear," Peggy sighed again, "nothing of real importance to you. Now, why was it you rung again?"

Her daughter either missed or ignored the obvious sarcasm, Peggy wasn't certain, and replied, "Well, only if you're able I mean, now that Alex is joining the golf club, there's a meeting of the Ladies Committee this afternoon. Just a tea and cake thing that I simply must attend and I wondered, but only if you're able," she repeated, stressing the word 'able' and then adopting a little girl voice, "can you look after your little grandson for an hour or two?"

Peggy was tired beyond explanation and wanted to rage at her daughter, tell her to look after her own bloody son, but instead simply replied, "Yes, of course I will. Drop him off when you like."

"Thanks mum, you're a star," Linda said and with a hurried cheerio, hung up.

Peggy stared at the mobile phone in her hand, close to tears. So much was happening in such a short time. She sat heavily down on the kitchen chair and took a deep breath, but then Thomas's croaky voice called from the bedroom and pushing herself to her feet, she used her hands to brush back her hair and with the heels of her hands to stroke the few shed tears from her cheeks, called out, "I'm coming, darling. I'll be right there."

Lesley Gold was over half an hour early for her twelve-thirty meeting with Helen Lang and lucky to get a window table in the already crowded and small, but gaily painted café. She idly stirred her coffee, staring out at Byres Road that was at its busiest on this bright Saturday morning, with both shoppers and what Helen referred to as 'The West End Crowd'; those locals who seemed to appear each weekend and simply meander along the vibrant road enjoying the sunshine, atmosphere and diversity of the area. Lesley, wearing the minimum of make-up, her hair tied back in a ponytail and dressed in a light blue coloured floral patterned blouse, short denim skirt and barelegged with open toed sandals, had left the flat early and walked from Partick to the cafe, enjoying the uncommonly fine weather as she breezed through the throng of people. As she walked she thought of her telephone conversation with her mother and listened with a heavy heart as Peggy assured her daughter that she was fine, that her father had a good night's rest and knew it to be a lie, but a lie designed to protect Lesley from the harsh reality of her mother's life. An unaccountable rage overcame her when her mother mentioned that Linda had phoned and though Linda wouldn't admit to it, Lesley quickly realised that the purpose of the call was to have Peggy babysit the toddler. The fury of her thoughts towards Linda disturbed her and she forced herself to calm down. She caught her reflection in the window and almost laughed out loud at her stern expression and then blushed, wondering what the other patrons of the café must think of her. She again glanced at the window and her attention was taken by a tall, well built man with cropped gray hair, wearing a red, plaid shirt, brown corduroy trousers and standing at the pedestrian crossing on the other side of the road, waiting to cross. The man was holding a small, fair haired girl's hand and as she watched the lights turned in their favour and they crossed toward Lesley's side of the road, the girl was skipping and looking up at the man who returned the girls laughter with a huge grin. He looked vaguely familiar and as they approached the pavement, Lesley suddenly realised it was Andy, the postman. Without thinking, she knocked on the window and waved and almost instantly wondering what the hell she was doing?
Andy glanced at the window and stopped, staring at Lesley. The small girl was puzzled and stared from Andy to Lesley, then back at Andy.

Lesley, committed now, was torn between leaving the café and possibly losing her table and made a quick decision. She beckoned for the two to join her, again wondering what the hell she was thinking.

Andy pushed the door, ushering the girl in front of him and made his way through the crowded tables towards Lesley. It didn't escape her notice and surprised her that a couple of well dressed women in their late twenties at a nearby table gave him the once-over as he passed them by.

"Constable Gold, eh, surprised to see you again so soon," he smiled as he towered over the table. "Hope you don't think I'm stalking you," he grinned, then his face darkened, "What I mean is I'm not, you know, stalking you or anything. I wouldn't do that. I'm not …."

"It was me that saw you Andy," she smiled at him, feeling her own face blush, "and my name's Lesley when I'm off duty, not Constable Gold. So, who is this lovely young lady," she turned away to face the girl dressed in the bright pink dress and cerise coloured cardigan who was shyly trying to hide behind his leg, one thumb slowly making its way towards her mouth as she stared curiously at Lesley.

"This is Evie," he replied, "my daughter."

So he's married, thought Lesley, curiously experiencing a sense of disappointment as for the first time she noticed the wedding band on the third finger of the hand that lay protectively on Evie's shoulder.

"I hope that we're not disturbing you, I mean, you're obviously expecting company," he indicated with his hand to the chair opposite Lesley.

"My friend Helen," she replied, "and she's always late. Timekeeping was never her biggest strength. Please, join me and I'll treat you to a coffee and you," she poked a playful finger at the little girl, "probably don't like ice-cream."

"I do," Evie protested, coming from behind her father's leg and smiling at Lesley, recognising the strange lady was only joking.

While the waitress fetched two coffees and a bowl of vanilla ice-cream for Evie, Lesley opened the conversation with, "Do you live about here?"

"We've a flat over in Kingsborough Gardens in Hyndland," replied Andy, smiling gratefully at the waitress who placed his coffee in front of him.

Again, Lesley was surprised at the woman's blush and thought that Andy must have something I just don't see.

"Are you a police lady?" Evie shyly asked, interrupting her thoughts.

"Yes, but only when I'm working. Right now I'm just Lesley. So, what about you, twinkle-toes? How old are you? Let me guess, forty-five?"

"No," Evie giggled, "I'm five, not forty-five." Her small face frowned and she looked at Lesley as though all grow-ups were really silly.

"Evie's five going on forty-five," whispered Andy as he leaned across the table. "Runs my life she does.

Lesley smiled and nodded, the aroma of a pine aftershave drifting towards her. A very nice smell, she decided. Her eyes narrowed and decided to take a wild guess, with tongue in cheek she stared at Andy to judge his reaction when she said, "I got the flowers."

His face turned red and he drew a deep breath. "I hope you weren't offended. I just thought, well, to be honest. I don't really know what I thought. You're not offended, are you?"

"Not in the slightest," she replied. "It was a lovely gesture, however," then she took a deep breath, "I first thought they were from a man I had just broken up with and, well, didn't immediately appreciate the gesture." Then she grimaced as she added, "Sorry."

She thought it might not be the time to mention that she didn't care to receive flowers from married men, but with his daughter sitting there, Lesley figured that she would be better having a word with Andy when they were alone and the sooner the better, she inwardly decided, before he gets any ideas that she might be keen to progress a relationship.

"Not to worry," he replied, the relief evident on his face. "The girl in the florist said yellow was from friendship. It's been quite a while since I've sent flowers."

"Don't you send them anymore to your wife?" she asked, keen to gauge his reaction to her question.

"Daddy, I need to go to the toilet," interrupted Evie, sliding from her seat. Andy half rose, but was waved back down by Lesley. "Let me take her to the little girl's room. You stay here and watch out for Helen my friend. You'll not miss her. She's very glamorous and will be looking harassed because she's late," she quipped.

As she guided the little girl to the small shared toilet at the rear of the café, Lesley thought she had done enough to warn Andy off. Yes, she admitted, there was definitely an attractiveness about him, scar or not. Locking the door for privacy, she waited in the small wash bowl area while Evie hesitantly closed over the toilet door to pee, but left it slightly ajar. It seemed to Lesley that while the little girl wanted to think she was all grown-up, she still needed the security of an adult outside the door.

"Are you still there Lesley?" said the small, timid voice.

"I'm here darling, don't you worry. I'll not leave you," she smiled as she reassured the little girl.

A minute passed then Lesley heard the cistern flush and the door opened, Evie with one hand on the handle and the other tugging at her skirt.

"Here, let me help you," smiled Lesley, "after all, we're all girls together aren't we?"

"Now I have to wash my hands," said Evie as she rolled up her cardigan sleeves and reached for the tap.

"Let's make sure the water isn't too hot for little fingers, eh?" said Lesley as she filled the bowl and pressed some liquid soap into the girl's hands.

Evie vigorously rubbed her hands together and stared up at Lesley, her eyes narrowed and curiosity written all over her small and perfectly defined face. "Do you like my daddy?"

"Yes, he's a very nice man."

"Even with that big cut on his face?"

"Even with the big cut on his face," agreed a smiling Lesley.

"Mummy didn't like the big cut on daddy's face." Her brow knitted and her mouth twisted in childish thought. "That's why she left us, I think."

Lesley stared with surprise at Evie's unconscious confidence. Mummy left us? She wanted to ask more, but her common sense prevailed. How the hell could she quiz a five year old on what sounded like her parents break-up? However, her feminine curiosity won the day and she bent down until she was almost face to face with Evie. "Do you live with daddy?"

"Yes, but sometimes I stay with grandma and granddad. They're nice to me and buy me sweets and chocolate. Do you like chocolate?"

"I love chocolate. If your daddy says it is okay, maybe you and I can share a bar, eh?"

Evie giggled and put her hands up to her mouth. "I'd like that, but we'd better keep it a secret," she whispered, "because daddy sometimes eats my chocolate and tells me it's the fairies that stole it, but I know it's him."

Lesley opened the door and with her hand lying gently on Evie's shoulder, guided her back through the busy café to the table to find Andy sitting with a bemused Helen who was shrugging off her designer jacket. With pretended anger, she chided Lesley, "So, I'm always late and look harassed am I?"

Andy discreetly coughed and hands apart in defence, smiled as Evie settled on his knee, her arms about his neck. "Sorry, but she is exactly as you described her, though maybe a bit more glamorous than you said."

"So I'm glamorous, eh?" Helen looked from one to the other. "Well, I might just forgive you, particularly as you left a handsome big man like Andy here to meet me."

"You'll have met then," replied Lesley, glaring theatrically at Helen as she settled into the spare chair.

"Look, I'll let you two get on with your day. Evie and I are planning to hit a few charity shops on Byres Road," grinned Andy, "where I understand we can pick up some reading material at bargain prices."

"There are no charity shops on Byres Road, my dear," exclaimed Helen, pretending shock and in a falsetto voice, "however, there is a selection of vintage establishments, so I'm certain this wee girl," she tickled a giggling Evie under the chin, "will likely cost her daddy a pretty penny or two."

Lesley and Helen watched then waved cheerio to Andy and his daughter as they left.

Helen smiled and her eyes alight with curiosity, narrowed as she asked, "Well, where have you been hiding that big hunk of a man?"

"He's not anybody I know," Lesley shrugged. "He's just the postman that delivers the mail to my office. I only got to know his name this morning."

"Might be just the man to take your mind off things, if you know what I mean," teased Helen. "So, what's new in your world?"

Lesley enjoyed talking with Helen who listened to her moans and whines without complaint, was neither judgemental nor patronising and would when asked offer sound advice on any number of issues that concerned her young friend. It was during this discussion that Lesley mentioned the inquiry that was bothering her, the missing school-teacher who might or might not be pregnant, and confided to Helen that Lesley believed the husband wasn't telling the police the full story.

"Is there no way that you can get him to talk?" asked Helen, a smile dancing about her lips. "I mean, don't you torture suspects these days?"

"Only if they're cheeky," Lesley quipped and then sat back against her chair and sighed. "No, the harsh reality is that we have to accept his version of events. Unless there's contradictory information or intelligence, what he tells us is what we act upon. That and my Inspector, nice man that he seems to be, has quite categorically told me not to put the man under any pressure. But," she hesitated, "I just don't know. I have this feeling," she gritted her teeth, "this unaccountable feeling that something's just not quite right about the whole situation. I mean," she leaned across the table to her friend, "when I was in the house, making the cursory check that we do in cases like this, the place smelled clean, yet to be honest, it was a tip. And the bin in the bathroom …."

"The bin?" interrupted a puzzled Helen.

"Yes, the bin. It was empty, but there were bits of paper and empty packets there. The bin had been cleaned out. It just didn't seem …. Normal I suppose is the word I'd use. I'm not making much sense, am I?"

"Frankly, no," replied Helen, "but if there's one thing I've come to respect in my life, its intuition and in particular, women's intuition. The husband, what does he do?"

"Works as an accountant I think, somewhere in the city, if memory serves me correctly. Something and Finch, I'm certain it is. I can't recall the first name of the firm."

"An accountant, well, that's interesting," replied Helen, her eyes narrowing and curiosity piqued. "What's his name?"

"Eh, Peter, no, Paul. Paul Hardie. Why, you don't know him, do you?"

"The name doesn't ring any bells," she pursed her lips and shook her head, "but don't forget, I might be employed in HR, but it's an accountancy firm I work for. Do you want me to ask about?"

Lesley bit at her lower lip. Taking Helen into her confidence was one thing and a complete no-no as far as the inquiry was concerned, but she trusted her friend and replied, "Only if you can do it very discreetly, okay?"

Helen smiled. "Mum's the word. I'll give you a call on Monday if I find anything out."

They parted just under an hour later, Helen to meet her husband and Lesley to travel home to prepare for her late shift that afternoon.

Several minutes of conversation passed before Lesley remembered and exclaimed, "Bugger! I promised Evie a bar of chocolate."

It was much later that evening that Lesley wondered why she hadn't told Helen, her best friend in the world about the flowers and meeting Andy that morning, when she was out running.

Chapter 22

Paul Hardie was sick with worry. He couldn't eat, couldn't sleep and shuffled about the house almost in a daze. Since the phone call, all thought of attending at the office and confronting Colin David had been the last thing on his mind. Savagely, he aimed a kick at the lounge door. How the fuck could everything have gone so badly wrong, he wondered? He didn't realise and wasn't conscious of it, but as he wandered about the house, he muttered to himself.

Time and time again behind closed curtains he watched the DVD, hoping for some indication or some clue as to the identity of the man that recorded him killing Fiona. He paused the DVD player, restarted it, paused again, but nothing indicated who the man might be. The voice on the phone had been worse than non-descript. Paul's training as an accountant had taught him that no-one had an elephant memory and note taking was a necessary tool of his occupation. He glanced at the notes he had scribbled on the pad in his hand and read: Is he Scottish? Opposite the question he had marked - most definitely. The next question written was - Is he a Glaswegian and he had written - more than likely. Against educated, he had written - certainly well-spoken, polite voice and a little high-pitched and marked a question mark against the word 'condescending'. Against age he had scribbled anything between thirty and fifty and that was pure guesswork. Phoning from? He guessed a busy street and thought he had heard music, possibly bagpipes being played in the man's background. A busker perhaps, he had written, and again marked a question mark against 'maybe calling from the city centre.' Tight-lipped, he shook his head at the little he knew of his blackmailer and threw the notepad onto the couch in disgust as he glanced at his wristwatch. His eyes narrowed as a thought occurred to him. The time the recording was made. He had forgotten about the time. When he had argued with Fiona, no, when he had killed Fiona it was sometime after midnight. Frantically, he operated the DVD player and watched as the recording commenced. There it was, the time and the date in the top corner and confirmed what he had thought, it had been after midnight or thereabouts when he had struck her. So, he wondered, biting at the nails of his right hand, why was his blackmailer wandering about in his garden outside his window at that time of night?

Grabbing a jacket from the small cupboard in the hallway he went out the front door and walked the short distance to his immediate neighbour at number twenty-one. He rang the bell and waited a few minutes, but there was no reply and moved onto the house at number twenty-three. There was no bell so he knocked loudly. The door was opened by a small, almost wizened woman who stared curiously at him.

"Hello," he smiled at the old woman, "I'm Mister Hardie. I live at number nineteen …"

"Yes, I know who you are," the woman smiled in return. "Your wife is the wee lassie that's gone away, isn't it. I'm so sorry. I hope everything works out for the best."

Paul was surprised at the woman's knowledge of Fiona's disappearance and nodded. "Yes, I'm sure she will, once she comes to her senses," he agreed, keen to carry on the deceit. "Eh, the reason I'm calling is that a few nights ago and last night," he hastily amended his story, "I thought I heard somebody wandering about outside my back lounge window. I was just wondering if you had heard anything at all, any noise outside your house?"

The woman shook her head and replied, "Sorry, no, but I'm that deaf. It's my age," she smiled again. Though it does sound a bit worrying someone might be prowling about at night. Have you contacted the polis Mister Hardie?"

"No, I thought I might ask some of the neighbours first," he lied, anxious to move on and half turned, but stopped when the woman added, "Though it might be that knicker-knocker that stole some of Missus McClafferty's washing the other night. I forget what night it was."

Paul's heart almost stopped and time seemed to stand still. Wide eyed now, he asked, "Missus McClafferty? Does she live here on Borden Road then?"

"No, over the back in Austen Road," the woman jerked a thumb over her shoulder. "I can't remember the number, but I think her house is one of those that back onto your house, across the lane."

He thanked her, unable to believe his luck. For the first time, it seemed that maybe, just maybe he had gotten a break. Quickly, he walked round the roadway into Austen Road and judging the mid-terraced houses that were directly opposite his own, knocked on number fifty-nine before being directed next door to McClafferty at sixty-one.

Agnes McClafferty, dressed again in a flowing, flowery dress that reached almost to her thick ankles, opened her eyes wide and she beamed a huge smile when she opened her door to the tall, fair-haired and handsome young man who introduced himself as Paul Hardie from across the back lane. She didn't disclose that though she had not known his name, she often watched him from behind a bedroom curtain when he was in his back garden; him and that stick-insect of a wife of his.

"I don't normally invite strangers in, Mister Hardie, me being a widowed lady," she pointedly said in a husky voice, hardly believing her good fortune and subtly pushing her breasts against him as he squeezed past her in the narrow hallway. His nose twitched with disgust at the strong smell of lavender that seemed to just outdo the smell of perspiration and almost made him gag. With his back to her, he didn't see her tug down the front of her blouse to expose a little more of her heavy bosom than was socially acceptable. "Please, into the lounge on your left," she instructed, her hand straying onto his waist as though guiding him. Following Paul into the lounge, she invited him to sit.

He flinched at her touch. He was no fool, realising she was making a pass at him and almost laughed out loud at her cheek, but first he had to humour her. Declining the offer of tea or coffee and even a sweet sherry, Paul explained again that he had heard someone prowling about outside his garden window late at night, some nights ago and again last night. "Did you hear anyone?" he asked.

"Oh my goodness," the heavy-set woman fanned with her hand at her pasty face, inwardly cursing that she hadn't yet applied lipstick that morning. "That must mean he's back again, the dirty bas … I mean, the rotten thief." Sitting on the edge of the settee, which was no mean feat for a woman of her extraordinary size, Agnes McClafferty recounted how three nights previously some "items of lingerie" had been stolen from her washing line. "I reported it to the police, of course. Two women officers it was that they sent, by the way. Didn't really think much of their attitude," she huffily commented, then smiled at him. "You'll of course know what I mean Mister Hardie, when I say lingerie garments?" she coyly smiled at him, her eyelashes fluttering like pigeons wings in a high wind.

He had heard enough. He had no further need to be nice to the old cow and stood up. "Aye, knickers I believe?" he crudely replied. "Thanks for that," then insolently added with a sneer, "and if they were yours," his disgust evident in his face that the old fat bird was making eyes at him, "I hope he brought a backpack to carry them in. I'll see myself out."

Stunned, Missus McClafferty could only stare as he walked from the lounge, then like an unleashed whirlwind, her size belying her turn of speed, she was up off the couch and reached the front door just as he opened it. "Well," she hissed at him, "you're no fucking gentleman either," and slammed the door at his retreating back.

Saturday, as far as Janice Meikle was concerned, was not a day of rest. Her strict regime that kept her body in shape and much admired by the male patrons, as well as at least one female customer, commenced with an early morning workout at the privately exclusive gym near the motorway at Arkleston in Renfrew, followed by a sauna and steam room session to tone her and finally, a relaxing light lunch in the small, but expensive cafeteria. It was here as she sipped at her mineral water, that she plotted her revenge against Colin Davies and inwardly seethed, for no man, or at least no man in his right mind, dumped Janice Meikle. Whether he guessed or not, Mister Colin fucking Davis was about to get his comeuppance and it would cost him, she inwardly grinned. Yes, she glanced about her at the extravagance of the cafeteria; it would most certainly cost him.

Across the city, the old school janitor Jimmy Dunlop had a relaxing morning; his wife gone food shopping while he sat on the garden seat outside the bungalow located just inside the locked school gates that were closed till Monday. Jimmy sipped at his tea and read the sports page of the morning edition of the 'Glasgow News'. Placing the paper down on the ground beside him, he pondered his retirement and his mind wandered and again he thought of the missing lassie, Missus Hardie.
He had read some days previously in the 'Glasgow News' of the police concern for her safety and well-being, but nobody at the school, other than the cleaners and the kitchen staff, who whispered among themselves, seemed prepared to discuss the missing woman. Bloody too scared of that witch Gwyneth Jenkins, he almost spat the name out. Shaking his head, he wondered how a cruel and arrogant woman like her could ever have the confidence of a school board to be in charge of not just children, but other decent, hard-working folk like most, if not all, the teachers undoubtedly were. He sighed deeply, his mind conjuring up a dozen ways in which she would finally get what was coming to her and just then, as though a spark had been lit, an idea came to the old man. An idea that was in itself so simple that he shook his head at his foolishness and wondered why he had never before thought of it.

Lesley Gold arrived at the rear yard of Garscadden Police Office a full twenty minutes early for her late shift and saw that already Alex Mason and

Dotty Turner's vehicles were parked there. Making her way to the female locker room, she grabbed her gear and pushed open the door to the small canteen.

"Afternoon troops," she greeted Dotty and Alex, both nursing a mug in their hands.

"Tea's on the brew," nodded Alex.

Dotty waved a sheet of paper at Lesley. "Afternoon, honey," she smiled. "That missing schoolteacher," then glanced at the paper, "Fiona Hardie. Inspector Cochrane's working out of Maryhill this afternoon. He asked if you and I could visit the husband and update the PNC if he's heard anything from her or got any further information."

Lesley took a deep breath recalling the confrontation with Mister Hardie the last time she had visited. "Right," she acknowledged, "so what about Pete Buchanan? Is he with us today?"

"He's doing paperwork at Maryhill too," interrupted Alex, "so I'm the odd man out. I've been told to stay here meantime and get my head into the books for my final probationary exam. However, most importantly, I've not got a piece in with me, so can you floosies bring me some chips in at the break?"

Dotty glanced at Lesley with narrowed eyes. "Floosies are we? I know what I'll get you, you little shit," and took a swing at him with the flat of her hand that he easily evaded. Lesley grinned and realised whatever difficulties they both had must have been patched up.

"I've a better idea," Dotty grinned at him, "I'll bring chips in for us all and you can pay," she said as she held her hand out for money.

With pretend reluctance, Alex handed her a tenner as she added, "and don't expect change."

It was later as Lesley drove the patrol car towards Borden Road the two women discussed the funeral arrangements for the forthcoming Thursday, for Morris MacDonald's wife Susan.

"Have you spoken with Morris, then?" asked Lesley as she concentrated on the evening traffic.

"Aye, briefly," sighed Dotty, one hand on her lap and the other massaging her forehead. "He had just left the undertaker with his brother Roddy. All he said was to tell everybody about the time of the service. He sounded okay, well, what I mean is as okay as he possibly could be, given that he has just lost his wife."

Lesley didn't reply, but thought that Dotty sounded a bit down. "You okay hen?" she cast a brief glance at her partner.

"No, not really if you must know. It's Saturday and every other bugger in the world is going out socialising for the evening, my kids are with my folks overnight, I'm working then going home to an empty house and my head

feels like Fred Astaire is doing a tap dance on it. What I'd give for a gin and tonic," she sighed.
Lesley couldn't help herself and grinned, "Can you keep a secret?"
"Given that you're party to my biggest secret in the world, that I fancy a man that's just been widowed, who better to take into your confidence," Dotty again sighed, but this time her curiosity was piqued.
"You know the postie that delivers to the office, Andy?"
"Well, I know who he is though I don't know him, not in the biblical sense anyway. Why? You got a wee thing for him and if you're about to ask me if he's a bit of all right, that big scar aside, I'd say aye. He's a bit of a hunk. So, carry on," she half turned in her seat to stare at Lesley with a smile on her face, "give me the rundown."
"I met him today, twice in fact. The first time when I was out running …."
"Don't remind me," Dotty interrupted, patting at her midriff, "I'll need to get myself out there as well."
"Do you want to hear this or not?"
"Aye, go on, then," Dotty grinned.
"Anyway, I met him again this afternoon before I came to work, in Byres Road when I was waiting on my pal in a café."
"You've got a pal? There's a first."
"Don't take the pee out of me," retorted Lesley. "He was with his five year old daughter. A cute wee thing she is. So, we got talking and guess what. He's the guy that sent the flowers to me at the office," she beamed, stopping the patrol car at a red light on Archerhill Road and turning towards Dotty. "I think he's got a fancy for me."
"I heard about the flowers. Did you not dump them in a bin?"
"Only because I thought that bastard Mike Duffy sent them," then in a few, terse sentences, related her encounter with Duffy at Maryhill Police Office.
"The bastard," snarled Dotty, her hands clenching into fists. "You're well shot of him, Lesley," she shook her head and then she smiled and playfully slapped Lesley on the shoulder. "Andy the postman sounds a better option. Good for you. Dump one and get right back into the game, hen. Mind you, if he's a got a daughter, does that mean there's a wife?"
Lesley wrinkled her brow and told Dotty of the brief conversation with Evie in the toilet. "I don't think so and I wasn't going to question the wee one."
"Quite right, play it cool," she nodded, "wait till you have his wean again on her own and squeeze everything out of her then," she joked. "So, where do you think you'll go from here?"
Lesley drove the car through the green light and face screwed in concentration, exhaled. "I'm not sure. I think Andy's a shy big guy, so I'll give it a couple of days and see what happens."

"Keep me informed Constable Gold. I need some romance in my life, even if it's somebody else's," retorted Dotty.
"Right, let's go and get the MP form updated from Mister Hardie," Lesley said, once again her thoughts turning to the missing woman and the husband that she suspected knew more than he was prepared to disclose.

"Daddy, that was a nice lady we met today, but I can't remember her name."
"Her name's Lesley," Andy Carmichael smiled at his daughter, who seated at the table watched as he pitched oven fish fingers and chips from the tray onto her plate and then the bulk of them onto his own.
"Does she catch bad people and put them in prison?"
"Hmmm, I think so," he nodded and replied, then sat opposite her at the small table in the kitchen of their flat. "Right, young miss, let me see you eat up all those fish fingers and chips and beans and we'll maybe talk about some chocolate mousse if you do."
Evie giggled and set to work, shovelling the food down and grinning with a mouthful of food at her father.
Andy picked at his meal, thinking again of the good looking police officer. It was by chance they had met that day, twice, he inwardly smiled and he was more than pleased that she had knocked the café window to attract his attention and even more pleased when Lesley invited him and Evie to sit with her. He had wanted to ask her then if she might consider going out with him, but somehow, the opportunity hadn't arisen. It had taken him a long time to get over Shirley's betrayal and his lack of confidence wasn't helped by the … he breathed in and unconsciously stroked at his neck with his free hand.
"Does it still hurt, daddy?"
He glanced up to see Evie staring at him, her eyes full of concern and he smiled. "No sweetie, it doesn't hurt. I was just thinking and didn't realise what I was doing. Now, eat up and when we're finished, we'll flush the dishes in the toilet to wash them …"
The little girl burst into a fit of giggles. "Daddy, you're so silly. Dirty dishes go into the dishwasher not down the toilet."
"Oh, that's right. Well, okay," he nodded as if that sounded a better idea.
"So, here's an idea," he whispered. "Finish your dinner and then we'll clear up, get our mousse and sit and watch some TV. How does that sound?"
Evie clapped her hands in delight and again set about demolishing her food.

Paul Hardie felt a glimmer of hope that though it wasn't much, he had learned something from the fat woman about his tormentor. The man was a common thief, a gutter-snipe prowler who sneaked through gardens at night, stealing from washing lines. The more he thought of it the angrier he became. He guessed the man must be relatively local. After all, he reasoned, who would travel any distance, to steal underwear? The more he thought of it the more convinced Paul was that the man must live close, perhaps even in a neighbouring street or road.

That a nameless, sneaky little shit who skulked down lanes at night would dare to provoke him into committing another murder? He paced the floor of his lounge, his body shaking with anger and forcing himself to be calm as he thought through all that he knew. He had a choice to make. He could either carry out the bastard's instruction to kill the man, whoever he was, or instead, bluff his tormentor. He sat heavily down on the couch, his mind working overtime. Paul would need to make the man believe that he would find him, that an anonymous voice on the telephone wasn't nearly enough to hide or save him from Paul.

He wondered about the man that his blackmailer wanted killed. What was his story? A fat man dressed in an overcoat carrying a briefcase and making his way through a lane? His accountancy training again came to mind, the need to make sense, to balance what he had learned. What connection was there to Paul's blackmailer, his tormentor? There had to be something; something that profited or benefited the tormentor with the man's death. Logic dictated that the tormentor and the intended victim must know each other and so, if Paul could identify the fat man, he might then be able to identify his tormentor and recover the original DVD recording.

Yes, he slammed a right fist into the palm of his left hand as a plan took shape in his mind. That's what he would do. He wouldn't kill the fat man like he had been told to do, but find out who he was. Now decided on a course of action, he realised he was committed to carrying out his plan and swallowed the bile in his throat at the thought, knowing that if it came to it, if his own survival depended on it, he might have to hurt the fat man.

Chapter 23

Dotty replaced the Airwave radio-phone in her belt and said, "Alex took a phone call from that woman who had her knickers stolen the other night, Missus McClafferty. Apparently she wants to see us, says it's important. Well, when I say us, I mean you."

Lesley turned the patrol car into Borden Road and smiled. "Don't suppose I can leave you in the car, can I? I mean there's no need to go provoking the poor woman again, is there?"

"What? And miss the fun? No chance. That's one call I'll be happy to attend. I'm guessing she's seen her knickers down the local park being used as a tent or something," then turning, unclipped her seat belt as Lesley pulled up outside number nineteen.

Lesley rattled the letterbox and stood back. Paul Hardie opened the door and stared at her before saying, "Yes? Have you found her?" The insolence dripped from his mouth and it was patently clear they weren't going to be invited into the house.
"Nothing yet, Mister Hardie," replied Lesley, forcing a tight-lipped smile, "We're just making the obligatory call to assure you that we're still making inquiry into your wife's sudden and unexplained disappearance and I'm presuming you have no further information for us?"
An awkward silence fell between them before Hardie shook his head and then exhaling loudly, said "Well, if there's nothing else then?"
"No Mister Hardie, there's nothing else sir," replied Lesley and then watched him slowly close the door.
"I really don't like that bastard," growled Dotty at her side.
"I not only don't like him," agreed Lesley as she turned to enter the car, "but I don't trust him either."
Dotty got into the passenger seat and closing the door, turned and said, "You really think he's lying about his wife's leaving then?"
"Can't prove anything, Dotty, but my gut tells me that he's not telling us the truth."
"Suspicion isn't proof, neighbour," she reminded Lesley, who started the engine and smoothly pulled away from the kerb.
"No, you're right. I know that, but still, it bothers me and I hate to think he's maybe harmed the woman."
Doty glanced sharply at her. "There's not been a suggestion of him having assaulted her," then paused and added, "or worse. Is that what's going through your mind, hen?"
"Dotty," Lesley half smiled as she shook her head, "I've absolutely no idea what's going through my mind. All I know is what my gut's telling me and it's telling me that man's a lying sod. Anyway, hopefully time will tell, so let's forget it for now and take a wee turn in to visit Missus McClafferty."

The short drive to Missus McClafferty's house took barely a minute. Lesley's knock was responded to by a slim, dark haired and attractive young woman in her late teens, the daughter they presumed, who smilingly invited them in.
"My mammy's up the stairs and will be down in a minute, if you'd like to take a seat in the lounge," she invited and then turned to walk towards the kitchen door while calling out loudly, "Mammy! The polis is here."
"Ah, before you go, was it you that lost the other set of underwear?" asked Lesley, already guessing the answer.
The girl smiled. "Aye, it was just a wee thong, no big deal," then lowered her voice, "you'd think it was the crown jewels the way my mammy's going on about it. If it makes the pervert happy, so what?" she grinned, then

whispered, "It's the nearest the sad git will come to getting into my knickers."

As the young woman walked into the kitchen, Dotty leaned towards Lesley and whispered, "Maybe he'll use the mothers knickers as a dressing gown."

"Ah officers, thank you for coming," said the voice behind them as the large woman swept into the lounge, wearing what seemed to Lesley to be full-length pink floral curtains and fervently prayed that Dotty would refrain from further stage whispers.

"I'm sorry to say that we've not found any trace of your …" started Lesley, but got no further as Missus McClafferty waved her hands to indicate that apparently wasn't of interest to her.

"No, the reason I asked you to call was because I had a visitor earlier today," she began, sitting in the armchair opposite the officers. She leaned forward with both hands clasped at her bosom to prevent her from toppling over onto the floor, her face flushed and for one awful moment, Lesley thought the large woman was about to have a heart attack.

"Mister Hardie. He lives across the back there, across the lane I mean, in Borden Road. He's the guy whose wife recently ran off. Do you know him?"

Lesley felt a chill of apprehension, and felt Dotty stiffen beside her. "Yes, Missus McClafferty. We're aware of Missus Hardie being reported missing. Do you have some information about her?"

"No, nothing like that," Missus McClafferty waved a hand in front of her. "No, but he was at my door today, asking about the thief, you know, the guy that stole my knickers?"

It seemed to Lesley that the large woman's vocabulary had dropped a pitch or two, as well as the lingerie now being demoted to common knickers. Missus McClafferty continued, "He said he had heard somebody prowling about on the night the knickers were stolen from my washing line and again, last night. Well, to be perfectly honest, I tried to be nice to the man, invited him into my home and even offered him a cup of tea or coffee…."

And I'll bet that's not all you offered him, you old tart, thought the cynical Dotty.

"…but what a foul mouthed bugger he turned out to be. I'll not demean myself by repeating what he said, but I was very upset," she sniffed.

"Did he mention anything about his wife, her disappearance?" Lesley asked, fighting the urge to get excited.

"No, nothing like that," she replied, shaking her head. "Just said that he had heard a prowler and asked me if I had heard him too, the prowler I mean. But of course I hadn't heard anything. If I had, I would have phoned you people, wouldn't I?" she sniffed again.

Seated beside her, Lesley felt Dotty bristle at 'you people', then said, "Do you happen to know Missus Hardie, have you ever had occasion to speak with her or anything?"

Missus McClafferty turned to face Dotty with eyes that bored through the smaller woman and replied, "No, I keep myself to myself, you have to understand, but I have seen her," she slowly admitted, "a few weeks ago. She was hanging out a washing and I was coming along the back lane from the shops with my messages, a wee skinny woman, sort of mousey in build; a bit like yourself officer," she tartly added. "We never spoke," she said and hands now settled in her lap, turned her head away from Dotty, dismissing the poker faced policewoman as she once more sniffed before adding, "I just thought you should know."

"Right, Missus McClafferty," said Lesley, quickly rising from the couch and eager to prevent her insulted partner from drawing her baton and beating the large woman to death. "That's been very useful. Needless to say, we'll keep this conversation between ourselves as we're still conducting inquiries into Missus Hardie's…. disappearance."

"Oh, aye, right you are then," replied Missus McClafferty, rising with difficulty to her feet, her eyes widening and pleased that the polis were taking her seriously. Well, the dark haired one anyway, she inwardly thought, ignoring the wee skinny blonde one with the red face, who seemed with hair like that to be a tart anyway and avoided even looking her in the eye. She followed them to the front door and watched as they got into the patrol car, waving at Lesley as they drove off and hoping the neighbours saw her doing her civic duty.

In the car, Dotty waited till they were out of sight before exploding in laughter. "That was very useful?" she parodied Lesley. "We'll keep this conversation to ourselves? My God, that woman will be on the phone to all her cronies before we've driven out of the road telling them she's a vital witness in a missing person inquiry. She'll be at her back window all night with binoculars, watching for him across the lane digging a grave."

Lesley grinned and then shook her head. "Here's hoping that you're joking," she quietly replied.

Jenny Farndale waited till Frederick exited the staff door and walked towards him, a smile on her face. It was unfortunate that just then some of the Cosmetic Department women were also leaving at that time and conscious of their stares, Frederick rebuffed Jenny's attempt to place her arm through his with a short whispered, "Please Jenny. Not in front of the staff."

Surprised and a little hurt, she was about to retort that like the women, both Frederick and Jenny were also staff, but the words failed her and embarrassed, she simply matched his quick pace along the cobbled lane that led to the nearby Mitchell Lane. When the women, heads together and intent on their own conversation had passed them by with barely a glance, Frederick turned unexpectedly and caught her hand. "I'm sorry sweetheart," he smiled apologetically at her, "but you know how those painted tarts talk. I don't want you to be the subject of gossip."

It was in her mind to tell him the two of them were already the subject of store gossip, but she refrained, still smarting from his rebuff in the lane. She had already guessed the real reason for his aloofness with her and it had nothing to do with gossip. She had thought that her lack of self-confidence had inured her to all sort of put-downs, but realising that Frederick was ashamed to be seen with her had been unexpected and taken her by surprise. The knowledge caught in her throat and blinking back tears, she could only nod as though agreeing. But that wasn't the end of it, as far as Jenny was concerned. As they strolled towards her bus stop in Union Street, she guessed that he would ask her to visit again tonight, knowing that it would simply be an excuse for him to have her for sex that because tomorrow being Sunday, the store was closed. It would likely mean that he would expect her to be at his beck and call through the next day too. But not tonight, she inwardly decided. Tonight, was her opportunity to remind Frederick that Jenny did not intend their relationship to be one-sided, that he must learn to appreciate her and if, as he had promised, they were to be a couple, then he must openly display that for others to see. All this passed through her mind and mentally preparing to challenge him, they arrived at the crowded bus stop. He turned and said, "Dinner tonight at my place, dear?" with a smile on his face.

Her courage and prepared statement failed her and all she could do was quietly mumble in reply, "Not tonight if you don't mind Frederick. I've got a headache," she lied, hoping that he wouldn't pursue the issue.

"Oh, my poor girl," he pulled her close to him, holding one hand and with his other, rubbing gently at her back. It seemed to Jenny that he was not only oblivious to, but also ignoring the curious stares of the passengers standing nearby. Had she got it wrong, she thought? Am I being to harsh? Is he really concerned and doesn't want me to be the subject of store gossip? Eager to give him the benefit of her doubt, she was about to respond and explain that perhaps later, when she felt better she might catch a taxi and come over to his house, but the opportunity passed her by for Frederick suddenly released her and said, "Oh good, here's your bus. Got your pass?"

She nodded, not trusting herself to reply as stepping onto the platform, he called out to her, "I'll give you a call later," and continued smiling as he watched her move along the aisle of the lower deck. He used his hand to indicate holding a phone to his ear and she could see his mouth forms the words, "I'll call you." The bus moved off and sitting in an aisle seat, she turned to see that he was walking off, his back to the departing bus and making his way through the crowds. A feeling of guilt overtook her and fumbling in her bag for her mobile phone, grasped it and was about to call him, to tell him she would come over tonight when it struck her; she sounded like a desperate woman. Jenny took a deep breath and made her decision, recalling her mother's old adage that absence makes the heart grow fonder. It might do Frederick some good to be without her for one evening, maybe make him appreciate her that little bit more. Settling down in her seat, she worried all the way home and prayed that Frederick would do as he promised and that he would call her.

Making his way through the Saturday evening shoppers, Frederick felt a little relieved that Jenny wasn't coming to his house that evening. Of course yes, he planned on her making more frequent visits to his room, but had already made the decision that he might first need to get some things in order. For one, though his laptop was password protected, he couldn't risk Jenny discovering any of his little secrets and in particular, the stolen lingerie in the box hidden behind the water heater in his cupboard. As he walked, he considered several better hiding places throughout the house for his prizes, but with some reluctance, decided that to be safe, he had better dispose of them. He inwardly grinned, realising that with Jenny now frequenting his bed, he had her to practise upon and no longer needed his prizes and his vivid imagination. Yes, he strode with confidence towards the bus stop, Jenny would do nicely for a while, at least till he achieved his ambition of snaring a better looking woman; perhaps one of those younger women in the cosmetics whom he would impress with his new position as departmental manager.
His thoughts turned again to what he had planned on Monday night for Robert Hamilton. The plan was foolproof. He was confident that Paul Hardie had little choice but to carry out Frederick's instruction. He would kill Hamilton, steal his wallet and nobody could ever connect the two men. That done there would be no need for Frederick to ever again contact Hardie.
At that time, Frederick would be in the company of Jenny, a real alibi who would truthfully swear that he was with her and could not have been involved in robbing and killing Hamilton.
He arrived at the bus stop in West Regent Street and joined the queue, his thoughts already turning to how he would receive the news of the murder of Robert Hamilton, his shock then humble acceptance of taking over first as temporary, then permanent manager and decided that tonight, in the privacy of his room, might be a good time to practise facial expressions of grief.
"Are you getting on or what," the harsh voice of the woman behind him, interrupting his daydreams and pointing to the open door of the bus that had arrived without him realising. Stepping onto the bus platform, he could not

but help himself grin. Everything he had hoped for, all that he had so meticulously planned was about to happen in just two short days.

Peggy Gold popped her head into the bedroom to ensure her husband was still sleeping and sighed with exhaustion. The 'hour or two' minding her daughter Linda's son was now well into it's fifth hour. The wee lad hadn't been too much of a problem and was well used to being dumped in front of a television. The quiet time, when Thomas was asleep, was time that Peggy needed to rest her weary body and the wee guy hadn't slept since he arrived and needed occupied for every minute he had been at the house otherwise he was bawling his head off and disturbing Thomas. She listened as a car drew up outside the house and glancing through the curtained window, saw Linda exit the driver's door and hurry up the path.

"Thanks mum," her daughter air-kissed at her mother as she rushed noisily into the lounge and lifted her son from his playpen, "sorry I was a tad bit longer than I expected. The shops were so busy today, it being Saturday."

"I thought you said you had a meeting with some ladies at the golf club?" her mother bristled.

"Oh, yes, I did, that was a wee bit earlier," her daughter blushed as she turned away from her mother, embarrassed at being caught in a lie and swung the giggling child about the room. To deflect her mother's anger, Linda asked, "How is dad?"

Peggy wasn't stupid and recognised the tactical change of subject.

"Sleeping," she tersely replied.

"Oh, I was hoping that I might say hello. No chance you can wake him, just for a minute?"

"You do realise your father is dying, Linda?"

Linda stopped swinging the child, holding him in midair and stared with a blank, almost insolent expression at her mother. "I know that. For heavens sake mum, I'm suffering too you know," she spat out. "It's not as if I don't care."

Peggy hadn't meant to be confrontational, but weariness combined with the stress of caring for her husband and the added few hours of entertaining a small child had taken its toll. She was spitting angry and right then, her fury descended on her youngest daughter. Later, she regretted some of the things she said, but not all. Linda's tears of shame turned to anger and hastily, she grabbed her now crying son's things and stormed from the house, calling out over her shoulder, "All I asked was for you to look after your grandson for a few hours! My God, why are you so heartless?"

Peggy, tears staining her cheeks, watched as her daughter drove the car off at speed, the tyres screeching as she thrust down hard on the accelerator.

Shaking, she made her way into the kitchen and sitting on the chair at the table, buried her face in her hands and sobbed.
From the bedroom, her husband's voice softly called out, "Peggy?"

It was late on Saturday evening when Robert Hardie parked Fiona's old Ford Escort in a bay in Cadogan Street. Dressed in a knee length, dark jacket, jeans and with a dark coloured baseball cap pulled low on his head, he made his way on foot eastwards through the Saturday night city centre revellers. Nobody took any notice of the lone figure and a little under five minutes later, he arrived at the entrance to the underpass that led from Argyle Street into the lower level railway station and also continued through to Osborne Street. He hesitated and glancing about him, his heart fell when he saw CCTV cameras located not just at either end of the underpass, but also a CCTV camera located at the exit door of an adjoining store. Quickly he made his way through the underpass and exited into Osborne Street. He was nervously surprised that a young short blonde, greasy haired girl he thought to be in her late teens, her face caked in make-up and wearing an extremely short black skirt and brown leather blouson type jacket, stood in the dark shadows of the wall, her back to the wall and a cigarette between her fingers called out to him. "Got the time mister?" she asked with a provocative suggestion in her voice, her slurred voice causing him to believe she was either drunk or drugged. Paul lowering and turning his head away, quickly mumbled "No" and then hurrying past her, aimlessly walked into Osborne Street towards Howard Street. He heard the girl half laugh and utter an expletive at his retreating back, but she made no attempt to follow him. He thought she might be a prostitute and cursed at his bad luck. Did this mean she was there every night, he wondered? A few short steps later he was in the shadowed quiet of Howard Street and hesitated, uncertain where to walk from there and glancing back, saw the young girl had walked off. A party of about eight young women were thirty metres away, walking in the opposite direction and from their raucous behaviour and dress he guessed they were a hen party. An older couple, each carrying a plastic shopping bag, ignored him as they stiffly strolled past on the opposite pavement towards the nearby public car park. A few cars passed him by, but the drivers, intent on negotiating the narrow lanes that detoured round the St Enoch Centre car park entrance, also ignored him. Turning his head back and forth his eyes searched high as he looked for further CCTV cameras, but saw none. He continued walking eastwards in Howard Street towards Stockwell Street and reaching the brightly lit and busy road, stopped and pretended to check the time on a notice at a nearby bus stop. He glanced at his watch and thought three or four minutes had passed since he'd walked through the underpass and decided to risk returning and retracing his route. He hadn't realised how nervous he was and thrust both hands in the jacket pockets to stop them from shaking. As he turned from the bus stop to walk away, a police van with two male officers travelled eastwards in Howard Street towards him and he almost panicked, his breath dying in his throat, but the officers were laughing together and seemed not to pay any attention to him. With a sigh of relief, he retraced his steps and was soon at the underpass entrance, but to his surprise, in the short time since he had walked through a chain-linked metal fence had been lowered to block off the Osborne Street entrance. He almost panicked, imagining himself caught inside and glancing through the brightly lit underpass, saw that the other end remained open and a laughing couple, arm in arm, were entering, presumably heading for the lower level train station. His watch said it was a little after ten o'clock and he presumed the shutter came down about that time nightly, guessing it was to prevent drunks or layabouts from hanging around in the underpass. His tormentor had said the man was due to walk through the underpass between nine-thirty and nine-forty-five. He glanced through the fence and gazed again at the nearest CCTV camera, pointing away from him into the underpass, and realised there was no way he could deal with the man under the cameras. If he was going to do this then he had better wait as the man exited the brightly lit underpass into the darkness of Osborne Street. He looked around and realised that if he didn't loiter too long, a nearby emergency doorway from the adjacent shop would hide him and enable him to sneak up on the man in the shadowed dark. It didn't occur to him that he had already made his mind up, that he was unconsciously planning a murder. Paul shook his head and keeping to the shadow cast by the blank rear wall of the Centre, quickly made his way back along Osborne Street and continued past St Enoch Square, keeping to the quiet of the Broomielaw as he walked to where he had parked the Ford Escort. Getting into the driver's seat, he sat for a moment or two to calm his shattered nerves.

"I can do this", he repeated over and over, willing himself to believe it. "I can do it, I can do it, yes, I can do it." Driving home, he knew that it wasn't a choice issue. If he was to stay out of jail for the murder of Fiona, he had to do it.

Chapter 24 - Sunday

Frederick didn't phone Jenny that night, but knowing like him that she would be off work on Sunday, called her just before eleven o'clock that morning. He smiled with proprietorial pleasure, recognising the relief in her voice and casually suggested that as it was such a nice day, why don't they meet later in the Botanic Gardens for a walk? He chose the location with deliberation, surmising there was little chance of meeting any of Dawson's staff there.

Jenny, later mentally cursing herself for sounding far too eager, agreed and so they set a time for their rendezvous at one o'clock at which time Frederick gallantly suggested he would treat her to lunch. "No," she hurriedly said, "I'll get a bus to the town and another bus along Great Western Road," she decided, then coyly added, "you can always run me home and come in to meet my mother?"

Taking a deep breath, Frederick tentatively agreed, but what Jenny didn't know was that Frederick had already planned their evening together, in his bedroom.

Lesley Gold's late shift had passed without too much trouble, the only hiccup being that she and Dotty Turner were detained on duty later than their two a.m. finish. The cause of their unscheduled overtime was a drunk female driver they'd arrested who not only failed to conform to the drink driving procedure at Maryhill Police Office, but in her alcohol fuelled rage lashed out with her fists at her arresting officers and managed before being overpowered to both bruise and split Dotty's lower lip with the engagement ring the young woman wore on her left hand. The cut was little more than a scratch and resulted in the woman being further charged with Police Assault. Dotty, cleaning the smear of blood off with an antiseptic wipe, philosophically commented she'd had worse cuts shaving her legs and accepted it as just another aspect of the job.

Sunday morning dawned for a tired Lesley, bright and sunny and with grumbling reluctance, she forced herself from bed to plod the streets in her continuing fitness regime. As she ran, she decided that after she had washed and changed, she would spend the first of her two days off with her parents.

In her own home, Dotty Turner enjoyed the luxury of a lie-in that was only disturbed when her son sneaked into her darkened room carrying a tray upon which rested a mug of steaming hot coffee and a plate of warm, buttered toast. Through the open door, she could faintly hear the television and guessed her daughter was glued to the BBC's early morning children's channel. Gently feeling with her right hand middle finger at her lip, she guessed from the touch it was swollen and decided to create some funny story to explain to her children why their mother was sporting a bruised face.

The school janitor Jimmy Dunlop had grown up in Second Avenue in Clydebank and throughout the years and though having moved to different areas, continued each Sunday morning to attend Mass with his wife at St Stephen's Church on the corner of Park Road. As Jimmy left the main door of the vestibule, meeting and greeting fellow parishioners, some of whom he had known all his long life, he felt troubled. The decision he had come to

about the head teacher, Gwyneth Jenkins, had been reached for personal satisfaction, but now having sat for an hour in God's house, Jimmy reflected that maybe he was being too harsh on the woman.
He stood patiently to one side of the walkway as his wife chatted with some of her friends, half listening to the gossip and nodding to passersby, when he heard his wife say, "Aye, the wee lassie was a teacher at my Jimmy's school, wasn't she dear?" and realised his wife had included him in the conversation.
"Sorry, what was that?" he smilingly apologised.
"I was saying," his wife slowly repeated, her voice raised an octave as though he was deaf, "the young woman that's missing. The teacher, she taught at your school Jimmy."
"Oh, aye right. Yes, she did. A lovely young lady is Missus Hardie. I hope she comes back soon," he nodded. As his wife turned back to gossip with her friends, Jimmy's eyes narrowed as his mind sharply focused on the face of Fiona Hardie. Unconsciously he shook his head. That young woman didn't have anyone fighting her corner at the school, he realised. Jenkins is more than happy to lie about her and sweep her under the carpet. Well, he inwardly sighed, not on my watch she won't.

In his palatial home in the Newton Mearns area of the city, Colin Davis decided to lie in late while his torn-faced and unsympathetic bitch of a wife busied herself in the dressing room for her Sunday morning tennis lesson at the prestigious club just down the road. Can't even make me a bloody cup of coffee, he inwardly raged. Struggling to sit up in bed, he grimaced at the ache in his chest and mentally surrendered, promising himself that tomorrow he would make an appointment with his doctor, guessing that his Internet check to identify his ache and burning sensation might be as he feared; a duodenal ulcer. His thoughts turned to the probable cause of his pain, preferring to believe it was the stress of work, the blackmailing shit Paul Hardie and the possible problems that might be presented by his dumping of Janice Meikle, rather than anything to do with his weight or poor eating habits.

Paul Hardie again hardly slept, his dreams invaded by nightmares that always seemed to be him being chased by faceless spectres with hands reaching out to grasp at him. Shaking, he sat up in bed and rubbed a hand across his tired face, trying again to come to terms with the waking horror that he found himself in. Wearily, he climbed from the bed, the sheets faintly smelling of body odour and long overdue a machine wash and made his way into the toilet to relieve his aching bladder. As he watched the stream hit the bowl, it occurred to him that tomorrow, bright and sharp he would present himself at the office and face down Colin Davis. He had the man by the short and curlies and was confident that he would be reinstated. His brow knitted as he

concentrated on his flow and knew that somehow, he had to organise some sort of an alibi for himself for the dirty work he was to carry out on Monday evening, though he grimly smiled, it might not be needed for if it went as Paul hoped, the evening would turn out not to be quite as straight forward as his tormentor planned. Washing his hands under the tap, he reached for a towel and realised there was none.
Glancing around him, he thought maybe today would be a good time to make an attempt to get this place cleaned up and the idea occurred to him that he might put the house on the market.

Andy Carmichael, a navy blue coloured dressing gown over his pyjamas, carefully poured the milk into Evie's bowl then sat opposite her at the small kitchen table. Evie, wearing her Peppa Pig dressing gown and nightshirt, eagerly attacked the cereal with her spoon as her doting father watched, his mind occupied by thoughts of the police officer, Lesley Gold, as he wondered just what chance a guy like him had with a good looking woman like her.

Peggy Gold answered the door to the overworked McMillan nurse who with her eyes, apologised for her tardiness and ushered Peggy into the kitchen.
"Sorry I'm late again hen, but I can't be leaving patients till their relatives arrive to let me go," she explained.
"For heaven's sake, Elsie, you're only five minutes overdue from the time that you set, not me, so don't be so silly, okay?" replied Peggy with a smile. "Here, I'll get the kettle on and you…"
"You'll do no such thing," Elsie firmly replied. "I can see how tired you are. I'll get my own tea, so you get yourself away to bed now before I have two patients to deal with," she ordered, then followed that with a raised finger, a grin and the threat, "Don't argue with me, I'm menopausal. So, I take it just the usual last night?" her eyes questioningly narrowed.
"Just the usual," Peggy nodded in agreement and leaving Elsie to it, with relief made her way to bed. She stripped off her clothes and pulling on a nightgown, folded back the quilt cover and wearily climbed into bed.
However, sleep didn't immediately come, for her mind was still plagued with the memory of the argument with her younger daughter Linda and as she lay there, she began to sob, but whether with tiredness or despair, she just couldn't tell.

A whisky induced sleep was the cause of Morris McDonald missing most of Sunday morning. During sleep, he dreamed and at one point threw an arm across to the other side of the bed and whispered, "Susan." At the partially opened bedroom door, his brother Roderick, who occasionally poked his head in to ensure that his wee brother was okay, heard the uttered name and then head bowed, gently closed the door.

Sitting comfortably with a coffee in her conservatory and staring out into the well tended rear garden, Helen Lang held the phone to her ear and listened politely as her friend Phyllis gossiped incessantly about family and work. After a few minutes, Helen managed to get a word in and posed the question that had been the real purpose of the call.
"Phil," she tactfully begun, "when you were working at that large accountancy firm in the city, Finch and company …"
"Berkley and Finch you mean," Phyllis interrupted.
"That's it," agreed Helen, "Berkley and Finch. Did you know an accountant, a man called Paul Hardie?"
Helen heard a sharp intake of breath and baulked. Had she said something wrong?
"Why are you asking about Paul Hardie?" questioned Phyllis.
"Oh, just a pal of mine came across him and mentioned his name," she smoothly lied, mentally cursing herself for not being prepared with a better excuse.
"Well," the hesitation was clear in Phyllis's voice, "if it is the same Paul Hardie and I suspect it probably is, he was a supervisor as I recall and not very popular with his team. Bit of a headcase really. Liked throwing his weight about and reminding people that he was the manager, you know the type? I seem to remember there were a number of complaints about his management style. Mostly just the usual whines and moans that we get." Phyllis paused, and Helen guessed she was trying to remember more. "If this friend of yours is a woman, I would tell her to be careful," she cautioned Helen. "He's full of himself that one. I have to admit, he's a good looking guy, tall and fair haired, but he treats every woman like a challenge. Thinks he's God's gift to the feminine gender, if you know what I mean. Oh, and he's married I think. No, I'm definite about that. He is married."
"Are you sure?" replied Helen, wondering how far she could go with this.
"Oh, yes I'm sure. I was there till October last year before I took my current job and to be honest, they weren't a bad company to work for. But you know what HR's like; we hear it all. When I was there, there were the usual stories of office romances, that sort of thing. Half of it was bullshit, if you pardon my French, but I remember there was a strong story going about that Hardie was doing a line with a woman in the typing pool. He was, as they say, the talk of the steamie. I can't remember her name, but she hadn't been long with the company and the word was," continued Phyllis, now enjoying the opportunity for a bit of gossip, "that she had come from another company under a cloud, and that she had been asked to leave because of an office

affair. A good looking young lassie, if I recall. Blonde and a bit tarty the way she dressed, you know? Anyway, it was a bit Mills and Boon at the time."
"Are they still seeing each other then?"
"No idea Helen. Certainly, it was supposed to be going on when I was there, but like I said, I left in October. Why, is it important?"
"No, it's not important, but thanks. I'll tell my pal to watch out," she smiled into the handstand and discreetly moved on to another issue, but her thoughts were racing at what she had learned and hoped the information might be of use to Lesley.

Frederick's mother Eunice Evans, just returned from the church service, waved from the window as her son turned and smiled at her then watched as he walked down the garden path to enter the car parked outside. Once she was satisfied he had driven off, she hurried to the old, mahogany cabinet in the corner and bending over, opened then reached into the bottom drawer. One hand on her stiffening back, she straightened and smiled conspiratorially at the two newly purchased glossy magazines she held in her other hand. Smiling to herself, she sat down in the large, comfortable chair and glanced at the covers of the magazines, one with a photograph of a pretty, veiled bride and the other of a proud father, holding a new born baby. Eunice knew that Frederick would not be pleased at the purchases and call her silly, but since his involvement with the young woman Jennifer, Eunice had come to hope, to pray, that perhaps one day, her dreams might just come true.

Frederick found a place to park the car on Hamilton drive near to the twenty-four hour Tesco store and hurried across the busy Queen Margaret Drive to the corner entrance gate at the Botanic Gardens.
Glancing at his watch he saw he was ten minutes early, but surprised to find Jenny already there at the gates, waiting for him. Dressed in a short, tight fitting bright yellow dress, her hair bound back by a similar coloured ribbon and carrying a small, bottle green handbag and matching coloured high heel shoes, even he had to admit that she looked quite fetching and saw to his further surprise that as he walked towards her she attracted the stares of two casually dressed, young men who passed her by. However, Frederick was also gratified to see that Jenny seemed oblivious to the men's stares and had eyes only for him and he smiled in greeting.
"Hello dear," he begun, "you look… stunning," and bent his head to peck her on the cheek.
For her part, Jenny was pleased with the compliment, but had hoped for a more passionate embrace than a brotherly kiss. "I'm a wee bit early, but the bus times on a Sunday…." she shrugged.

He held his hand up and with the other, took her by the elbow and led her through the gate into the park. "No need to explain and upon reflection, I should have travelled over to collect you," but knowing that truthfully, he really didn't relish making the trip across the city. As they walked, Frederick did most of the talking, explaining and pointing out the different fauna that blossomed along the route, turning and indicating, but in reality taking the surreptitious opportunity to watch and savour the many scantily clad young female students who abounded the area.

Jenny listened without taking much of it in, simply happy to be walking arm in arm with her boyfriend and already forgiven him for not calling last night as he promised and vowing not to even mention his lapse, lest it create some kind of atmosphere between them.

To all who passed them by, they were simply a couple walking while enjoying the too infrequent sunshine.

None of the other strollers in the park could guess that as he walked, Fredericks' thoughts were occupied by the pending event on Monday evening and that he had murder in his heart.

Chapter 25 – Monday morning

Lesley Gold yawned and lazily stretched in the narrow, single bed, at first slightly disorientated in the dark before remembering that she had spent the evening at her parent's house. The sun peeked through a crack in the curtain and illuminated the room. Turning, she saw the luminous face of the bedside clock indicated it was just after nine in the morning. She stretched again and yawned, enjoying the sensation of not having to jump out of bed and get ready for work. She had not brought her running gear, convincing herself that it had been an oversight rather than deliberate forgetfulness. Again, she stretched and rising from the bed, stood in front of the full length wall mirror that still bore the magazine stickers of her youth, most notably the 'Spice Girls' and 'New Kids On The Block'. She smiled, absently scratched at her backside and yawned again, hearing for the first time the sound of movement from the kitchen. Wandering through the small hallway, she stopped first to glance in at her father and saw that he seemed to be sleeping, hearing him snoring gently. Her mother was at the sink, filling the kettle.

"Morning love," she smiled at her daughter, "coffee?"

Lesley nodded and yawning again, scratched at her head and settled into one of the kitchen chairs. She stared at the kitchen wall clock and a thought occurred to her. "Be with you in a minute, mum."

Returning to the bedroom, she fetched her mobile phone from the pocket of her jeans, sat on the edge of the bed and scrolling down the address book, dialled a preset number.

"Hello, Jinksie?" she greeted the bar officer. "Good morning, it's Lesley. Look, can you do me a favour wee man?"
"Anything for one of my babes," he replied.
Smiling at the phone she asked if Andy Carmichael the postman had delivered the mail to the office this morning.
"Not yet," replied Jinksie, already guessing where this was going. "He usually delivers about tennish. Why, something I can do for you?"
She hesitated, biting at her lower lip then decided to plunge ahead. "When he comes in, can you give him my mobile number, please? Ask him to give me a call," then added, "I can rely on your discretion Jinksie, can't I?"
Lesley couldn't know that standing alone in the Uniform bar, the small man grinned and punched the air, knowing he had been correct, that the flowers had come from Andy the postman. Unconsciously nodding to the handset he replied in a level voice, "Of course, Lesley. I'll get it done for you."
As she ended the call, Lesley exhaled and wondered what she had just done. A sudden doubt set in and she froze. What if she had completely misread the signals? What if the wee girl, his daughter Evie had got it wrong and Andy is a happily married man? In a sudden panic, she almost called Jinksie back to instruct him to forget it, cancel her request, but stopped. Uncertainty enveloped her; the condition of the confused.
The door was lightly knocked and she turned to see her mother peering at her. "Do you want your coffee here or in the kitchen with me?"
"I'll come through mum," she replied and smiled; the decision to phone or not now made for her.

Paul Hardie dressed that morning with care, taking his time over both his grooming and his clothes. Turning back and forth at the wardrobe mirror, he was satisfied that he looked every inch the professional that he was and again, run through his head the prepared speech he had practised to finally drive home the nail in Colin Davis's coffin; the speech that would in no uncertain terms remind Davis that failure to reinstate Paul would result in not just Davis's ignominious sacking, but likely damage Berkley and Finch too. He glanced at his wristwatch, a present from Fiona's now deceased parents. Another thing that he would get rid of when this whole mess was finally concluded, he decided. Taking a deep breath he finished the coffee and made his way to the front door.

In her flat, Janice Meikle also took elaborate care that morning with her dress and make-up. Like Paul Hardie, she too was determined to remind Colin Davis that she was not a woman to be trifled with, that his dumping of her was completely unacceptable and if he wished to keep her mouth shut about his extra-marital affair with her, it would cost him dearly. As she preened in front of the wall mounted mirror, she smiled at her reflection. Her shiny blonde hair lay softly on her shoulders, the waist hugging white blouse accentuating her firm breasts and the black, pencil skirt to just above the knees alluding to her regular gym work-out. As a final touch, she decided to wear seamed, light coloured tights that highlighted her perfectly proportioned legs. Satisfied with her eye catching appearance, she made her way to the front door and like Paul Hardie, also had her speech to confront Colin Davis well prepared.

Jenny Farndale woke to the sound of light snoring and edged away from the sleeping Frederick Evans. Placing her feet on the cold floor surface in the darkened room, she gave an involuntarily shiver and glancing at the bedside clock, saw it was time she was up, dressed and off to work. As she sneaked from the bed, she reached to lift her underwear and yellow dress from the chair and glancing back at him, saw he was still asleep. Grabbing her shoes from the floor, she quietly opened the door and softly closed it behind her. The noise from downstairs indicated that Eunice was up and working in the kitchen. Jenny made her way into the bathroom and stared at her reflection in the mirror. She was angry not just with Frederick, but with herself too; angry that without too much protest, he had again persuaded her to stay the night. Her plans to have him drive her home and to introduce her mother to her boyfriend had again come second to his sexual needs. Closing her eyes, she leaned her forehead forward till it rested on the coolness of the mirror. Self-doubt ate at her. Is that all she was to him after all, a nightly shag? Yes, he had taken her to dinner; some cheap, non-descript out of the way little café just off Dumbarton Road, where the tables were covered with plastic sheets, the waitress was sullen, the floor needed swept and the food had been chips with everything. She lifted her head and again stared at her reflection. She needed some romance in her life, a man that wanted her for who she was. Bitterly as she stared, she saw herself for what she was, a plain looking woman who was so desperate for a boyfriend she was prepared to let him treat her as he wished and do to her what he wanted, without any regard for her feelings. Well, she angrily decided, no more.
It was a few minutes later that Eunice, humming along with the radio, heard the front door bang closed. Hurrying to the door, she pulled it open and looked outside, her head turning first left then right and that's when she saw the flash of yellow dress as the figure turned the corner and out of sight.

Robert Hamilton kissed his portly wife goodbye and foregoing the car in anticipation of the alcohol he intended later that evening, walked to catch the train to work. The bi-monthly day was always his favourite evening; not just for the late opening when till takings were greatly improved, but mainly for the bonus that he earned as Departmental Manager. That coupled with the social evening when he finished work and met with his few friends at the snooker hall in Stockwell Street. He smiled in anticipation, his love of the game played on the green baize second only to that for his love of his wife, bless her. Walking along the quiet residential street he sighed again, wishing that they had been blessed with children to whom he might have taught the intricacies of the game, but it was not to be. Approaching the entrance to the Hillington West railway station, he nodded cheerfully to two women who were engaged in tittle-tattle conversation and who completely ignored him, but he didn't take offence. Robert Hamilton was, if nothing else, a gracious man who simply liked people, though he would also be the first to admit there was the odd exception and Mister Evans, his salesman briefly crossed his mind. A practising Presbyterian, Robert inwardly chastised himself for his unkind thoughts. He would be horrified to know that not everyone liked him.

The overhead tannoy announced that due to unforeseen circumstances, the train was running just over ten minutes late. A collective groan went up from the gathered passengers, but not from Robert. No, as was his custom, Robert was more than thirty minutes earlier than the journey normally took and so, reading his free Metro paper, settled down on the unforgiving metal bench patiently to wait for the train. Robert did not practise nor condone tardiness and believed that as a manager, it was his duty to set his staff an example. Thoughts of his staff led him to again consider Mister Evans. The man was infuriating. For all his apparent years of experience in sales, he simply either could not or would not permit himself to interact with the customers. Why Dawson's had suffered the man for all those years, the Lord only knew. Robert inwardly sighed and knew that if the department was to flourish, he had to either motivate the man or let him go and in his heart, already knew the answer to that problem. The train arrived and Robert courteously stepped to one side to permit his fellow passengers to alight before him. As he stepped onto the platform of the train, the doors hissed closed behind him and his final thought on the issue was that Mister Evans days at Dawson's were regrettably numbered.

"You look like a dirty stop-out," Jenny's kitchen supervisor laughingly mocked her when she arrived at work, still dressed in the short yellow coloured dress. "See you're wearing a party frock there hen, so I take it you didn't get home last night then?" the older woman winked at the other kitchen girl, who giggled in agreement.

Jenny blushed and pulled the clean overall from her locker. "It just so happened that I didn't," she coyly replied. "If we get a five minute break, I'll remind you what sex is because likely you'll not remember," she added.

"Cheeky bugger," the woman laughed as she threw a dishcloth at Jenny's pretence at aloofness, then beckoned the other girl to follow her out the door. Jenny grinned in return, but then left alone in the empty changing room, her grin quickly faded. Throughout the bus journey into work, her thoughts had been filled with Frederick and his intention towards her. Her plans, she admitted had all been based on a two-sided relationship, but now she realised that it wasn't like that, not at all. Her eyes filled with unshed tears as she accepted that like the other men she had known, Frederick was simply using her for sex. Angrily she slammed the locker door closed, jumping in surprise at the loud bang it made and turning quickly to ensure that no-one had seen or heard her outburst of rage. Weakly, her body trembling, she sat down on the wooden bench and biting at her lower lip, made her decision. She had always been the one cast out, discarded like an old jacket when finished with. But this time, she clenched her fists with resolve, this time it was different. This time it was she who was doing the dumping and Mister Frederick fucking Evans was the one getting told.

Paul Hardie arrived at the underground staff car park that serviced Berkley and Finch and exiting the driver's door of the company car, nodded towards two male members of staff who first stared in surprise, then walked quickly towards the lift area. He grinned at their backs, guessing that word had got out that he was sacked and equally word would get around that he was back. Unconsciously straightening his tie, he grabbed his briefcase from the passenger seat and locking the car, followed the other two towards the lift. What he didn't know was that just a few minutes earlier, Janice Meikle had arrived upstairs at the typing pool and after signing on at her work station, was at that moment walking towards the management suite of offices to confront Colin Davis.

"Hello?" Lesley Gold answered the calling mobile number.
"Ah, hello, Lesley, it's Andy, Andy Carmichael," said the soft the voice. "Jinksie gave me your number, said that maybe I should call you?"
She smiled at the hesitancy in his voice, realising that the big guy was even shyer than Lesley had thought. "I was wondering, as I'm off today, if maybe you'd like to meet up for, say, lunch?"
There was a slight pause and for one heart-stopping instance, she thought maybe she was coming on too strong, but then he replied, "Sorry, I've a school appointment. That is, what I mean rather is that I'm meeting with Evie's teacher at one thirty this afternoon. Sorry."
She was about to tell him that it was okay, that she understood, but Andy beat her to a response as he continued, "If you're not doing anything this evening,

would you consider dinner? With me I mean? I can get Evie watched by my sister for a few hours, if that's okay?"
Lesley smiled at the phone and found herself nodding in agreement. "Yeah, sounds great. So, what have you in mind?"
Again, there was the briefest of pauses before he replied, "Do you like curries?"
"Love curries," she smiled again, curiously wondering why she was feeling so relieved.
"There's a great little place in Ashton Lane, just off Byres Road and not too far from where Evie and I met you on Saturday. Do you know it?"
"I know Ashton Lane," she replied.
"Look, why don't I book a table and meet you at the corner of Ashton Lane and Ashton Road, say seven o'clock?"
"Okay, that sounds great. I'll see you there, then. Bye," she replied and pressed the red button on the phone.
She softly exhaled and feeling a little excited, called quietly to her mother that she was off to shower.

Helen Lang had a busy morning at her department, but decided to take her lunch break in the sunshine and walked the short distance from her office to George Square where she found an unoccupied bench and opened her sandwich and bottled water. As she ate, she dialled Lesley Gold's number, but the call was diverted to the answer service. Rather than leave a message, she chose to end the call with the intention of phoning Lesley later that evening.

The sunlight streaming through the window and the sound of his mother using the Hoover on the lounge carpet downstairs woke Frederick Evans from a dreamless sleep. Yawning, he rolled over then smiled, his fingers tracing the lines in the crumpled sheets where Jenny had slept. He glanced at the bedside clock and realised that she must already have departed for work, while he still had several hours before he commenced the later shift that would take him through to the store closing that evening. Leisurely, he swung his legs out of bed, stretching his tired muscles and grinned self-consciously at his nakedness, recalling with vivid clarity the previous evening's activities with Jenny. If only she was a bit better looking, he shrugged, he might even consider continuing the relationship with her. He stood and again stretched, his glance taking in the cupboard door and remembered that he still had to dispose of his collection. He shook his head with regret, knowing that after all the risks that he took acquiring his collection, it would be difficult to part with them, but accepted that needs must. He reached for the dressing robe hung behind the door and slipping into it, pulled the door open and headed for the bathroom. He realised his mother must have heard him moving about for she called up from down stairs, her voice sounding concerned, "Frederick, are you up? Jennifer's gone to work and without breakfast. Have you two had a fight?"

He stopped at that, his face creased in puzzlement. Fight? What the devil did she mean? He leaned across the stair banister and called down to his mother's upturned face, "No, we've not had a fight. What gave you that idea?"

"Oh, it's just that she seemed a little upset when she left. Perhaps it's nothing, just my imagination working overtime," the old woman smiled at him and turned away, but in her heart she felt the dreaded fear that something wasn't quite right and inwardly prayed that her son hadn't done anything to upset Jennifer. Please God, she prayed, make an old woman happy and whatever I think is wrong, have that idiot of a son of mine get it sorted.

Morris MacDonald swallowed the two paracetamol tablets and gulped down the water, then slowly tilted his head forward to ease the throbbing pain of the hangover. His brother Roderick's hand slapped down onto his shoulder. "Here, wee man, get that inside of you, a real Scottish breakfast that is," Roderick said as he laid the plate of sausage, bacon, black pudding, fried eggs, beans and potato scone down onto the kitchen table in front of Morris then followed it with a mug of hot, sweet tea.

Morris's stomach baulked at the sight, but the strong aroma of the fry-up tickled at his taste buds and he realised he hadn't eaten a square meal for days. Tentatively at first, but within a minute he was devouring the food. Roderick sat his large bulk in the opposite chair and stared at his brother, then softly spoke. "The family will be arriving tomorrow from the Isles. Maybe today would be a good day to start getting things sorted, their accommodation and the likes I mean. Are you up to it wee man or are you happy to let your big brother make the arrangements?"

His mouth full, Morris could only nod, grateful that Roderick was there to take matters in hand. At last, he replied, "How many will we expect do you think?"

Roderick pursed his lips, his eyes narrowing and said, "No more than twenty, no less than fifteen, but we'll cope, so we will. Have no fear wee man, we'll cope. What about your colleagues at work? Will they be attending?"

Morris nodded and thought of Dotty, knowing that she would wish to be there. He laid his cutlery on the plate and took a mouthful of tea. "I expect there will be a few, perhaps four or five, I'm not sure. I'll give a friend a call later and ask, see if she will be able to ascertain who can come. It won't be a large assembly Roddy, but those who come will attend because they wish to be there."

"I'm sure you're right, wee man. Right," Roderick slapped at his knee, "finish your breakfast and then you and I will get some fresh air. I can see that a wee walk in the sunshine won't do you any harm," he grinned at his brother.

Colin Davis's secretary, a lady of mature years who had been with Berkley and Finch for as long as anyone could remember and was much experienced in preventing her boss from being disturbed by trivial issues or unannounced junior employees, stood ashen faced behind her desk when Paul Hardie arrived. Confidently pushing open the door he failed at first to see that behind the door stood Janice Meikle, her hands at her mouth, her eyes wide. Immediately, he sensed that something was wrong and turning his head form one woman to another, said, "What?"
"If you've come…" the older woman's voice broke and then taking a deep breath and swallowing hard, started again. "If you've come to see Mister Davis, I'm sorry. Mister Davis was admitted through the night to the hospital. The Western Infirmary cardiology unit," she added, dabbing at her eyes with a small lace handkerchief. "I'm sorry," she slumped into her chair, "this is just too awful. The poor man has died and such a lovely man too," she added and head bowed, began to softly weep.
Wide-eyed at the news, Paul could hardly take it in; all that planning and his prepared speech, all now for nothing. He turned to stare at Janice, but ignoring him as she also took in the devastating news. Her nostrils flared and head held high, she pushed by him without a word, the sound of her heels clicking on the uncarpeted floor as she strode off.
He turned to stare again at the older, weeping woman and wordlessly left the office, making his way through the staring faces towards the elevator that would return him to the underground car park.

At five o'clock that evening, the store tannoy system announced to its customers that the store would close at five-thirty to prepare for its '*Special Friends*', those privileged customers who held store cards and further announced that applications for this discounted privilege could be obtained from staff at the check-out counters. In the Gents Department, a quietly pensive Frederick Evans pretended to tidy the sweater counter as through narrowed eyes, he watched his manager Robert Hamilton urging his staff to tidy the shelves and re-stock them with the less saleable items that now reduced would, Hamilton hoped, entice the evening customers to take advantage of the low prices and increase the departments sale figures. In Hamilton's experience, customers, whether or not they really needed the item, were always prepared to pay for a real bargain.

"If you only knew," an excited Frederick whispered to himself, "if you only knew."

Paul Hardie sat in his car to compose himself, his thoughts reeling with a jumbled mass of doubt and uncertainty as the news of Colin Davis's untimely death struck home. His leverage gone, he frantically gripped the top of the steering wheel to stop his hands from shaking. What now, he wondered? Thoughts of the loss of his income conflicted with what he planned to do tonight, the murder his tormentor had demanded he commit. He closed his eyes in self-pity, knowing that he was losing it. The stress of the last few days, the killing of Fiona, dumping her body, the arrival of the DVD and all the time pretending to the police that he was a worried husband; all at that instant took their toll and wearily, eyes still tightly closed, he laid his head against his forearms until the shakes that coursed through his body subsided.

It was early evening when Helen Lang remembered to again call her friend Lesley. Sitting in the conservatory while her husband loaded the dishwasher, she recounted the little that she had learned from her friend Phyllis, the previous day. "So, I don't know if that's any use to you, but it seems evident from what Phyllis told me that your man, this guy …."
"Paul Hardie," Lesley reminded her.
"Yes, this guy Hardie isn't the loving husband that maybe he's trying to tell you he is. If you get my meaning," she added.
Lesley paused, chewing at her lip and then said, "You don't happen to know anyone in Berkley and Finch, do you? I mean in the HR side of the business." She could hear Helen taking a deep breath, as though considering Lesley's request and guessed Helen felt a little unsettled at Lesley's request. For an instant, she thought that maybe she had pushed the boundary of their friendship a little too far.
On the other end of the line, Helen smiled. "What you mean, my nosey wee pal is do I know anyone that can provide you with the name of this woman who was supposed to be doing a line with this guy Hardie? I take it that you have some intention of speaking to this woman? Challenging her about her relationship, I mean?"
Lesley also smiled. "That's kind of what I'm thinking," she replied, then added "Maybe a wee unofficial chat with her. Just some background information, if you like."
But then her friend replied, "Okay, but you have to understand that anything you learn about this woman can't come back and bite my pal in the pedigree chum, Lesley. You can't disclose how you came about this information. My pal would lose not just her job, but Data Protection implications might kick

in and discussing an employee with you becomes an offence, but again that's only if she agrees to speak with you."

"I know Helen and I am grateful. I don't even need to know your pal's name, just get her to call me on my mobile with the name and that's the end of it, okay?"

"Okay, I'll give her a call now and ask, but no promises mind. If she calls you then don't ask any questions. Agreed?"

"Agreed," said Lesley.

"So, how's your dad?"

Lesley spent the next few minutes updating Helen and then coyly changed the subject. "Guess what? I've got a date tonight," she told her, surprising herself with her eagerness to break the news.

"No way," gasped Helen. "Don't tell me, that big guy I saw you with at the café on Saturday?"

"Aye, Andy and the amazing thing is, I asked him out," she laughed.

"You absolute floosie," Helen laughed with her. "And he said yes? Of course he did, or you wouldn't have a date, would you?" she laughed again. "So, is it the pictures or a meal or what? Tell me."

"It's a curry place in Ashton Lane."

"He's taking you for a curry, Lesley? Not the most aphrodisiac start to a relationship is it?" Helen continued to laugh and added, "Don't forget to take some mints or toothpaste if you intend winching later on."

Both now giggling, Lesley ended the call promising to update Helen as soon as possible the next day with how the date went.

It was twenty minutes later as she was choosing an outfit for that evening that Helen called Lesley back and briefly told her, "Sorry, but my pal isn't comfortable speaking with you, Lesley, simply because she doesn't know you. But she did say that if you were to take a note of the name Janice Meikle in the typing pool, it might be of interest to you."

Peggy Gold waved cheerio to the McMillan nurse and closing the door, softly exhaled. The McMillan nurses did a remarkable job and were faultless in their care for their patients, but there just weren't enough nurses to go round and the limited time they afforded each patient only supplemented what care the family themselves provided for their loved one. She peeked into her husband's room and saw him awake, then smiling, pushed open the door and sat on the chair by his bed.

"That her away then?" he asked, his voice low and with a slight gasp.

"Aye, a lovely wee lady so she is, we're lucky to have her," replied Peggy, reaching out and taking hold of his cold, clammy hand.

"Will you try and get some rest, hen?"

"Me, I'm fine. Do I look like I need rest," she smiled at him. "Are you trying to tell me Thomas Gold that I'm worn looking?"

He returned her smile and said, "You always look good to me, Peggy. You know that," but then his body was wracked with a coughing fit. She leaned across with a tissue to his mouth, her other hand supporting the back of his neck.

"Not too long now, dear," he said as she slowly lowered him back down onto the pillow. "Sooner rather than later would be better," he added, then with a deliberate stare into her eyes, turned his head to face the row of medicine bottles neatly arrayed on the bedside table.

Chapter 26 – Monday evening

Excusing himself from the floor to make a phone call, Frederick Evans managed to catch Jenny before she left the store for the evening, but was surprised that she didn't seem pleased to see him.

"Are you all right, my dear?" he asked, "Mother said you seemed somewhat perturbed when you left the house this morning."

Jenny, hair tied fiercely back in a ponytail and still wearing the brightly coloured yellow dress, her arms folded tightly about her and head bowed, wasn't quite certain what 'somewhat perturbed' meant, but she was conscious of the other dayshift staff passing them by at the exit door and the glances that were cast towards them.

"I'm all right," she mumbled, her resolve to finish with Frederick now softened and almost gone. The teasing she had endured from her colleagues throughout the day, good natured though it had been had been intended, had sown the seed of doubt as to whether she was being too hard on him. Perhaps, she had considered, he was just not used to having a girlfriend. Maybe, she tried to convince herself she should speak up more, tell him what she wanted rather than simply follow his lead. Insist that he visit her home, meet her mother and spend a night at her place. As the day had continued, she had made her decision. She would tell him what she wanted, that if he wished to continue in their relationship, all their decisions would be mutual, by agreement and no more of this 'what Frederick wants to do, we do'. Yes, that's what she had decided, but now, having him standing here in front of her, ignoring the stares of their smirking workmates, she realised that in his own way, he was making a declaration, that he didn't care who saw them together, that they were, after all, boyfriend and girlfriend and her heart lightened. She suddenly smiled and knew that everything was going to be all right.

Frederick also smiled and reaching for her hand, the sudden doubt vanished from his mind. She couldn't know, would never realise that tonight, he needed her more than anything, but not for sex, though that was always welcome. No, he needed her to be with him this evening to alibi him so that he would never feature as a suspect in the murder inquiry that was bound to follow when his manager, Robert Hamilton was discovered dead.

Lesley was nervous, but didn't know why. I mean, she cajoled herself; it isn't as if I haven't been on dates before. As she parked her car in the adjacent car park at Ashton Lane, she swung her legs from the driver's seat out of the door and changed from her flat, driving shoes into the black coloured high heels, tossing the flats into the rear seat. Grabbing her clasp bag and black shoulder shawl from the passenger seat, she locked the door and turning, smoothed down her dress. Choosing an outfit had been more difficult than she thought. Her recent fitness regime and adherence to her diet had unexpectedly caused more pounds to be shed than she anticipated and while delighting in her new shapely form, realised it limited her wardrobe slightly. After several outfit changes, she was pleased to discover that a figure hugging, knee length deep red coloured, strapless cocktail dress that had hung at the back of her wardrobe for over a year was now, with admittedly a little tug on the zip at the side, wearable and flattered her figure. She glanced up and saw the tall figure striding toward her. To her surprise Andy, wearing an open-neck plain coloured khaki shirt, off-white chino's and a dark grey sports jacket was more handsome than she realised and almost for the first time, appreciated her friend Helen's flattering comment about him.
For his part, Andy was taken aback by Lesley's appearance. Her dark hair lay loosely about her shoulders and for a heartbeat, he felt a little intimated by her obvious good looks. Taking a deep breath, he inwardly promised that he wouldn't blow this and smiled as he approached her.
"Hi," he said and proffered his left arm. Slipping her hand through, she was grateful the awkwardness of the moment had passed so easily by his courteous act and together, they slowly walked down the cobbled Lane until they arrived at the Indian restaurant where Andy held the door open and with his hand lightly on her lower back, guided her through. "Table for Mister Carmichael," he smiled at the waiter, who returned his smile with a grin and replied "Nice to see you again Andy." The waiter took Lesley's shawl form her shoulders and then led them through the dimly lit and almost empty restaurant to a quiet corner table.
They sat and chatted as the waiter noted their drink and food orders and she was curious that like her, Andy chose a soft drink rather than alcohol. "I don't, if I have the wee one at night," he explained when he saw her surprise, then grinned as he added, "but I'm not averse to a glass of real ale now and then."

Their conversation began light-heartedly; the good weather, the ambience of the restaurant, how he occasionally popped in to the restaurant with Evie for a late lunch after work and boasted that Evie had become a firm favourite with the staff. She saw his eyes light up when he spoke of his daughter, his pride evident.

They had been sat at the table for almost twenty minutes before Lesley realised that their discussion had turned onto her. Without consciously realising she was doing most of the talking, Andy had listened as she told him of her first job straight from University, where her second class Honours degree had gained her the exalted position of office junior. Of meeting her best friend Helen who took the young Lesley under her wing, of how quickly she became bored with office work and her desire for some occupation to challenge her that finally led to the police presentation at the Career Seminar in the SECC. She spoke of her strong mother and without undue emotion, of her father who was dying and her sister Linda, with whom she had little in common. Blushing, she felt she had been rambling on, but he gallantly assured her she had not and made her blush further when, with a grin that displayed his even, white teeth, said that he could sit and listen and look at her all evening.

She confessed that quite without warning, his daughter Evie had let it slip that he was separated from his wife and quite firmly told him that had she thought otherwise, she wouldn't have dared ask him to meet with her this evening for dinner. She watched his face as he glanced away and slowly nodded, then told her that yes, he was estranged, though not yet fully divorced, that the papers was currently lodged and the petition was underway at the Sheriff Court and the only condition that prevented the full *decree absolute* was he insisted that his estranged wife Shirley kept in touch with their daughter. She sensed his underlying anger when he explained that Shirley's new partner had persuaded her to move with him to Australia and she was determined to go. As quickly as Lesley saw his anger rise, it subsided when he explained that the difficulty was telling Evie who was too young to understand. He shook his head when he confided the full divorce would likely soon be settled without Evie's mother agreeing to regular contact with her daughter, having apparently convinced herself that a complete break was in Evie's interest. He sounded sad when he added that Evie's mother would never understand what she was losing, that her own needs were always her first concern. He again half-smiled and with no apparent bitterness in his voice, explained that Shirley wasn't a bad person, but that she was shallow and could not comprehend that marriage brought responsibility, that she always sought new romance and adventure and was a woman who never wanted to grow up. A growing child, he sighed was a constant reminder to Shirley of her passing years. "In short," he said, "the only loser in the failed marriage is Evie, but I will make sure that she wants for nothing."

Lesley didn't reply, but saw in Andy a devoted father and, to her surprise, decided right then that he really was a nice guy.

The waiter interrupted to ask if they required the sweet menu, but Andy caught the slight shake of her head and smilingly declined for them both. She asked about his early years and he spoke of his upbringing in the south side of the city, his working class parents, now retired to a bungalow and whom he visited regularly. She learned he was six years her senior and preferred rugby to football. He liked real ale rather than lager and didn't drink spirits, but was fond of a glass of red wine. He had two sisters and an older brother, all of whom he got on well with and when he confided he was a favourite uncle to his two nieces, she didn't for a heartbeat suspect otherwise.

She saw Andy unconsciously stroke at his scarred tissue and her eyes betrayed her curiosity. He smiled at her and said, "Ten out of ten for not asking."

"It doesn't seem to be that old," she replied, more relaxed now that he himself had raised the subject.

Andy nodded and said, "It's usually the first thing that attracts people's eyes to me. Kind of causes more than most to be judgemental before they get to know me or how I came by it," he said, gently stroking it with a forefinger. "I have had it now for just over two years, but I'm assured as time passes it should fade even more. I can't complain. I was the lucky one. The other two guys didn't make it."

Lesley didn't respond, preferring that he tell her in his own time. He rubbed with the heel of his hand at his forehead, as though prompting a memory.

"I belonged to a Territorial Army Unit in Paisley, the Royal Engineers. I'd been with them for, oh, just over twelve, no," his eyes narrowed as he thought, "thirteen years. Weekend warriors, that sort of thing," he smiled. "During that time I was working as a Civil Engineer with a London company, though I was based here at their Glasgow office. The job was okay, good salary and excellent promotion prospects. I didn't fancy the permanence of the regular army and the TA seemed just the thing, particularly with my engineering background. It was good fun to begin with, plenty of fitness training, meeting a good bunch of guys, a feeling of belonging and then of course," he grinned, "there was the squadron bar and cheap booze. As time passed, however, with the Government budget cuts to the regulars, the TA was used more frequently to back up the regular army; first in Iraq then later and still obviously ongoing, in Afghanistan." He stroked at his scar again and wryly grinned and shrugged at the same time. "That's where I got this. I was attached to a regular unit and travelling in a Warrior infantry vehicle, an armoured car if you like, when we run over an IED. Two of the lads copped it, killed I mean, with another three of us injured. As I said, I was one of the lucky ones and got to keep not just my life, but my arms and legs too. No reason to it, just pure chance where we had been sitting inside the vehicle, when the bomb went off. I received some scarring to my neck and face, that you can see and scarring to my abdomen that of course isn't visible. It was while I was recuperating that Shirley found herself another pastime, a guy that she worked with. By the time I found out, she had moved in with him and he made it obvious to Shirley that he didn't want her bringing any baggage, so that left Evie with me," his eyes shone as he smiled, "and believe me, I got the best part of the deal."

"How long were you …" Lesley nodded to his scar.

"Just under three months. Shirley left Evie with my parents for the last few weeks, just before I got home. Anyway, the damage to my abdomen meant that I couldn't be considered operationally fit for active service and so I was discharged from the TA," he smiled again, "honourably, I may add. To cut a long story boring, I just didn't fancy going back to my old job, felt that maybe what I needed was a fresh break and took the job as a postman. What you might call a ninety-degree occupation swerve. The money isn't the same of course and there isn't the same responsibility, but I like it. Out in the fresh air each morning, early finish and I'm home every night with Evie. Oh, and I get to meet very attractive policewomen."

She smiled at the compliment, not certain how she should respond. He misread her silence as uncertainty and was about to apologise when she laid her hand on top of his and said, "Thanks. For being so open, I mean." She glanced at her watch and saw him frown, but then said, "Oh, no. I'm not that eager to go, but I was wondering who has Evie, you know, when you had to get home I mean."

"Ah, sorry, thought I was getting to the boring stage there," he grinned. "No, it's all right. Evie's with my sister and her kids at their house in Clarkston, over on the south side of the city. The cousins are slightly older than Evie and wee one loves it there and they treat her like a princess."

"But you have an early rise in the morning?"

He nodded and replied, "Yeah and you?"

"Likewise, I'm up at five-thirty for my run and then out the door to work for six-thirty."

"So," he indicated with a nod to the waiter for the bill, "we'll call it a night then, Lesley?"

She smiled and inwardly, was unable to explain her nervousness, but knew that she wanted to see him again.

On cue, the waiter placed the folder on the table and as she reached for it, Andy quickly snatched it from her. She pretended to be annoyed and reminded him that it was she who had asked him to dinner, but he shook his head and replied, "No, no. I'll get dinner and you can pay for the foreign holiday."

She softly laughed and said, "So, we're going on holiday together, are we?"

He smiled at her and slightly cocking his head to one side, stared at her as he replied, "Maybe we can discuss that at our next date, if you like?"

"I'd like that," she smiled at him.

He paid the bill and standing, took her shawl from the waiter and placed it on her shoulders. She inwardly shivered at the slight touch of his fingers on her bare skin and turning towards him, resisted the urge to kiss him. Where the hell did that come from, she inwardly panicked. Taking a deep breath, she swallowed and led the way to the door, horrified that he might have guessed the thought that had run through her head. In the cool of the night, he slowly walked her to her car, her arm again through his. They arrived at her car and she turned to face him, a sudden awkwardness between them.

"I suppose I'll be seeing you around the office then, Constable Gold."

"No doubt about that, postman Andy," she grinned at him, then felt his arm about her waist as he gently pulled her to him. She could see hesitancy in his eyes and reaching to take his face in both her hands, softly kissed him. "Look at me," she blushed, "I'm shameless. Ask you to dinner then take advantage of you."

"Wow," he said, "I can't quite believe that such a beautiful looking young woman would take any kind of interest in a dead-beat like me."

"Is that how you see yourself," she asked, serious now and her eyes narrowing, "a deadbeat?"

"Well," he replied without any false modesty, "There was a time I might have been quite a catch, but I'm not the young man I once was."

"Let me be the judge of that," she coyly replied, then pulling open the drivers door and half turning to reach the flat shoes in the rear seat, inadvertently allowed the short dress to ride up to her thighs and expose her long legs. She turned to see Andy politely looking away and smiled at his good manners.

"So, you'll call me?" she asked as she slipped on the flats.

"Definitely," he replied with a nod.

She watched him in the rear view mirror till he was out of sight and found herself grinning almost all the way home.

Chapter 27

Paul Hardie sat on the edge of the bed, almost in a daze. His world was falling to pieces around him and there wasn't a damn thing he could do about it and adding to his woes, a letter that morning officially released him from Berkley and Finch and instructed the company's Ford Focus vehicle be returned forthwith. The letter included a cheque as final settlement of his salary and the amount, he angrily saw, did little to cover that month's mortgage payment and bills. Had it not been for Fiona's monthly salary being paid into the bank, his financial situation would have been intolerable, but now that she was officially reported missing, he had no idea how much longer the council would honour her contract and pay her wage. His thoughts turned to that morning's visit to the office and the news of Colin Davis's unexpected death. He really couldn't give a shit about the fat sod, but Davis' untimely demise had not just thrown a spanner in the works; it had collapsed everything he had planned. He buried his head in his hands and tried to think of some way that he could extract himself from the situation in which he found himself. His tormentor expected him to carry out the murder this evening and his body shook at the very idea. His revulsion at the thought of carrying out the murder of a nameless man contradicted with his concern for his own problems. In his mind, he run through his plan and he knew with certainty that no matter what, he would abandon all morals and scruples if it suited his purpose.

Reaching across the bed, he lifted the black plastic handled, eight inch narrow bladed boning knife he had drawn from the wooden block in the kitchen. He stared thoughtfully at the knife, turning it back and forth in his hand and prodded gently with the needle point at his left forefinger. With a softly muttered, "Ouch!" he quickly withdrew his finger, staring with fascination at the small spot of blood he had drawn and sucked for almost a minute on the finger to stop the bleeding. He almost laughed out loud at his antics in the close-curtained bedroom where he had practised thrusting and stabbing for almost five minutes. He had felt foolish, pretending to be a threatening robber and trying to recall the action films he had watched where a knife had been part of the fighting. It occurred to him that he had somehow to secrete the knife when he was walking through the town. It wouldn't do for some nosey cop to stop him and find the knife, particularly when he was on his way back to the car or better still, he decided, quickly get rid of the knife after he had confronted this guy. For a few minutes, Paul gave this some thought and decided that rather than dress as some sort of thug, he was less likely to attract attention if he was smartly attired, guessing the police would be more interested in stopping and searching the denim or track suited pedestrians at that time of night than a man who wore a tie and suit and looked like he had some purpose to his walk. He shook his head and buried it in his hands, amazed that he had so acceptingly succumbed to his tormentors plan. Yes, he would carry-out his instruction, but there would be an added twist, he grimly smiled and standing, began to rummage through his wardrobe.

The customers, many with their arms full of carrier bags, were gradually filing out through the door that led into Buchanan Street, chattering to each other and excitedly boasting of their bargains. When at last the tannoy announced the store was now closed and clear of customers, Robert Hamilton, the Gents Department manager called his staff together and cheerily congratulated them all on a splendid evening and loudly pronounced that once again, their evening takings would be increased. "Mister Evans," he smiled conspiratorially at Frederick, if I let these younger ruffians go, would you be so kind to take both tills to the security office?"

Frederick was careful to appear eager to please and smilingly agreed, but in his mind he already imagined the bludgeoned and bloody body of Hamilton, lying dead.

It took Frederick no more than ten minutes to lodge the tills with Dawson's security officer, Peter Wylie, who grinning, handed 'Freddy' the receipt for both tills. Frederick didn't rise to the taunt, but tightly smiled, anxious to depart to meet Jenny whom he had already arranged to wait for him not at the exit door, but at the end of the lane. His planned alibi for Hamilton's murder was to then take her for a late dinner to a nearby pub that served food, though he didn't relish the thought of mixing in public with drink-sodden plebs. Later he would drive her to her own home and spend the night there with her. His small, overnight case was already packed and within the boot of his car, parked in the Mitchell Street car park. As he fetched his jacket from the male staff locker room, his heart almost skipped a beat and he stood still on hearing Hamilton's voice, bidding the security man a hearty good-evening. The sound of the heavy exit door closing caused him to exhale softly and to his surprise, he hadn't realised how tense he was. Frederick glanced at his watch and softly smiled. Paul Hardie should be in place he believed and if Hamilton carried on as he usually did, he would come upon Hardie sometime within the next five minutes. Then it would be done. He closed his eyes and smiled, unconsciously tilting his head backwards as he savoured the moment. He startled when the locker room suddenly swung open to admit two members of staff, arguing football.

Ignoring the two men and taking his time to allow Hamilton to get a good head start, he finally made his way to the exit door and smiled tightly at Peter Wylie's parting call of, "Goodnight, Freddy boy." As he slowly walked along the dimly lit lane, he could see the figure of Jenny, waiting at the end of the lane and waved towards her.

Watching as Frederick approached Jenny felt a little thrill of apprehension in her stomach. She was angry with herself that once again, he seemed to have taken control of her but at least this time, she consoled herself, her boyfriend was taking her to her home and finally he would get to meet her mum. That he intended staying the night worried her a little. No man had ever stayed over at her mother's house and though she had forewarned her mum that Frederick was coming later that evening, Jenny guessed her mother might not be happy that her daughter was entertaining a man through the night, in her room – boyfriend or not.

She smiled as Frederick quickly pecked at her cheek and taking her by the arm, led her into the brightly lit street.

All he had to do now, he thought, was remain in Jenny's company till Robert Hamilton's body was discovered and he would never be a suspect for the murder.

Robert Hamilton hummed quietly to himself as he busied about, fastidiously tidying his office desk and ensuring he locked the metal cabinet that contained not just his personal grooming items of clothes brush, shoes polish, variety of colognes and spare shirt and tie, but the confidential personnel files of his departmental staff. Tonight had been another successful sale and he smiled at the annual gratuity he expected to receive at Christmas. Already he had the money spent, in his mind planning a foreign holiday for both he and his wife. Pleased that the office was again readied for tomorrow's business, he shrugged into his coat and lifting his briefcase from the floor, switched off the internal light then with a satisfied nod, closed and locked the door behind him. He continued to hum his favourite tune as head swivelling, he walked through the dimly lit department, seeing that as was his custom, he was the last to leave the floor. He imagined himself to be the captain of his very own ship and took inward pride that he was always the last to depart. Waving as he bid the nightshift cleaning staff a hearty farewell, his smile was courteously returned, though he could not know that none of the three Polish women understood a word he said.

As he nodded to the security officer at the rear door, he stepped out into the fading light and into the lane, striding purposefully towards Buchanan Street and already savouring the waiting dram, anticipating good company, some laughs and a few hours of billiards.

Lesley Gold parked and locked her car and with high heels in one hand and clasp bag in the other, thoughtfully made her way along the brightly lit street towards the close entrance. That the date with Andy was successful, she had no doubt. That she wanted to see him again and he her, that also seemed to be assured. What niggled at Lesley was the question, was she leaping from one failed relationship into another relationship without giving time to come to terms with the break-up with Mike Duffy? But then again, she inwardly argued, Andy Carmichael was nothing like Mike. In fact, she smiled as she strolled Andy was like no-one she had ever gone out with, remembering with a blush his interest in her as he listened while she had rambled on. In

Lesley's experience, most men she had previously dated had been keen to talk about themselves and if they hadn't been cops like her, were sometimes intimated because of her occupation or boastful to impress her. As for the couple of cops she had gone out with, one being Mike and the other a number of years previously, a fellow probationer like her who had dismissed her career as a 'husband catching exercise' and had lasted just the one date. She fumbled in her bag for the main door key and pushing it open, stepped into the brightly lit close, her thoughts filled with a sudden anxiety that this time the relationship lasted more than a few months. As she made her way upstairs to her flat, she stopped on the half-landing and leaned her brow against the coolness of the tiled wall and slowly exhaled then inexplicably smiled. Sod it, she decided. If this new relationship with Andy goes tits up, then so be it. She stood upright and reaching her door, inserted the Yale key and took a deep breath. She wasn't a naive young lassie and didn't believe in fairy tales. Yes, she had recently had her fingers burned, the memory still raw and hurting, so decided that she would take the relationship slowly and as far as it would go and yes, she nodded to herself, let's just see what happens.

John Fields, known throughout Stewart Street police office as 'Gracie', parked his car on the nearby wasteland and entered the office through the main door. He waved through the glass window at the public counter to the duty Inspector in the control room to indicate that Gracie had arrived for nightshift and that he would be at his desk in the CCTV room after he popped his sandwiches into the fridge in the canteen. A few minutes later he was at his work station, nodding and smiling tolerantly as he half listened to the whining late shift operator Marie, who bleated her moans and groans while she shrugged into her jacket, anxious to be away home. "I mean, it's all right for you," she sniffed, "being gay and all. You don't have a pair of teenagers treating the house like a hotel and a lazy bastard of a husband that won't get off his arse to find work," she spat through gritted teeth.

Gracie had enough of his own domestic issues to be bothered by anyone else's, but politely nodded and tolerantly smiled, his face expressing just the right amount of sympathy while Marie droned on. Like the rest of the office, Gracie was aware that her life was an open book. As she continued to whine, his thoughts were elsewhere as mechanically, he adjusted the desk chair height and sitting down, typed in his personal code to permit him access to the system. He didn't want to be unkind, but wished that she would just get up and go and let him get on with his job.

"Right, that's me away then," sniffed his colleague as she huffily turned away.

Gracie waved cheerio and then with a sigh of relief, settled in to scan the screens in front of him.

Robert Hamilton strolled through the brightly lit Argyle Street, his thoughts occupied by the foreign holiday he planned for him and his wife. The passing pedestrians, whether alone, in two's or groups, paid no heed to the portly man who casually swung his briefcase by his side as he walked on toward the brightly lit underpass that in turn, led through to Osborne Street.
Ahead of Hamilton and standing almost motionless in the shadow of the high blank wall that was the rear of the St Enoch Centre, Paul Hardie waited with bated breath. His eyes were wide and alert as he watched for his tormentor's description of the man exiting the underpass, his hands slightly shaking and his nerves electric, conscious of the presence of the boning knife that lay in the makeshift sheath that was under his trousers and slipped into the sock on his right calf.
Just to be ready, he leaned down to reach for the knife.

It was less than five minutes later when the two, scantily clad young teenage women, one tipsy and her friend the worse the wear for drink and walking with difficulty, exited the underpass from Argyle Street into Osborne Street. They giggled as they drunkenly clung together and were laughing at their own jokes when they saw the drunken man lying face down on the ground, his briefcase lying beside him. "Hey mister," said the more sober of the two as she gently toed the man on his ribs, "You can't lie there pal. You'll get yourself lifted by the polis." The man didn't respond and the teenager again used her foot, a little more forcibly this time. "Mister!" she almost shouted and in the time honoured tradition, as drunks do when trying to assist a fellow drunk, bent over him with the intention of persuading him to his feet. Her friend who was now propped unsteadily against the wall, continued to giggle. "Mister!" repeated the helpful teenage girl and bending down to shake the man, slipped and almost fell on top of him. "Ooops," she began to laugh, now on her hands and knees beside the man, then almost immediately revulsion set in when she realised the drunk had pissed all over himself and the ground upon which he lay and the flat of her hand was in the piss and was all wet.
"Fuck!" she angrily shouted out and with disgust stared at her wet palm. But then, disgust turned to sudden suspicion as she realised it wasn't piss and that the shiny, thick substance was…. her eyes opened wide with understanding as she fell backwards onto her arse and began to scream hysterically.

Chapter 28 - Tuesday Morning.

Jinksie Peterson was, as usual, the first into the office on Tuesday morning and switching on his computer, next headed towards the kitchen to fire up the kettle and ensure the previous shift had purchased milk. More than one altercation had occurred in the recent past because there was no milk for tea or coffee in the morning, he grinned.

The back door opened to admit Dotty Turner, Alex Mason and the Sergeant, Pete Buchanan, who had all arrived together. Jinksie called out the kettle was on and returned to the front office, knowing that one or the other would fetch him through a cuppa while he dealt with the overnight correspondence and opened the front, public door.

"Any word on how Morris is, Sarge?" asked Alex.

Pete Buchanan shook his head. "The Inspector is the point of contact and I haven't spoken with him since Friday, but likely we'll hear something today, son."

Dotty said nothing, afraid that any interest she might have in Morris's welfare might be misconstrued. It worried her that she had confided in Lesley Gold, a woman that she hardly knew, but her gut instinct was that Lesley was trustworthy and wouldn't disclose Dotty's awful guilt, that she had feelings for Morris. Besides, she inwardly shrugged, Lesley had confessed her own secret and for that Dotty was grateful for Lesley's confidence in her.

The back door slammed shut and a few seconds later, Lesley entered the female locker-room. "Morning," she grinned at Dotty.

Dotty's eyes narrowed as she stared at her younger colleague. "You seem very happy for an early shift, Lesley Gold," she teased. "Either you've had sex all night or a lottery win and if you're still coming to your work, I'm guessing sex."

Lesley laughed and replied, "Not quite, but I did have a date last night."

"My God, you're quick off the mark. Dump one fella and right back out there. Good for you," and lowering her voice, though there was no-one to overhear, added, "I assume we're talking about the postie then?"

Lesley hesitated, but almost immediately exhaled, knowing that after sharing Dotty's secret, it was unlikely her pal would run off at the mouth about Andy. "Yes, well, yes," she replied, "and what a nice guy he turned out to be."

Dotty grinned. "Aye, he's a handsome big dude right enough, even with that head of grey hair."

Lesley simply nodded, curiously pleased that Dotty had seen a side of Andy that didn't include his facial scar.

"Bloody hell," Dotty continued to be impressed, "you're only here one week and already you're shagging the postie. Good for you."

"I am not shagging the postie," Lesley pretended outrage, but then smiled. "Well, at least not yet."

There was a knock then Alex Mason stuck his head round the door. "Tea up and the Sarge wants to read the bulletins in two minutes, so when you floosies are ready, eh?"

It was ten minutes later, after Dotty and Alex had departed on patrol to answer the first of that day's calls that Lesley knocked on Pete Buchanan's door. "Can I have a wee word Sarge?"

"Take a seat," he replied, dropping a report on his desk, lifting his mug and sitting back in his seat, "so, what can I do for you?"

Lesley explained her interest in the missing woman, Fiona Hardie and her feeling that something was amiss, that her husband wasn't telling the full story. She recounted her suspicions after visiting the house, but the more she spoke, the less she thought that Buchanan seemed convinced. "Look, with Morris off and you stuck here doing paperwork that kind of leaves me at the minute without a neighbour. Dotty and Alex are more than capable of handling any calls and I was wondering if I can borrow the supervisory patrol car to make a few discreet inquiries."

"And these inquiries are?"

Lesley took a deep breath and swallowed hard, knowing that what she was about to divulge could easily get result in her being disciplined. "I have a pal, someone I've known for a long time who told me that the MP's husband, Paul Hardie was having an affair with a woman at his work. I'd like to speak to this woman and try to find out if she knows anything about Missus Hardie's disappearance."

Buchanan said nothing, but simply stared at her, then shook his head and closed his eyes. "Are you telling me that you've been conducting your own inquiry outwith the parameters' of the investigation? That you've discussed an MP with a person who isn't a member of the police service?"

Lesley nodded, her face screwed tightly and too anxious to respond.

"This pal," his eyes narrowed, "is there any likelihood that she'll repeat what you've told her?"

"No chance," Lesley shook her head. "As far as she is concerned, anything we discussed is now forgotten."

They sat in silence for a few minutes and then Buchanan seemed to come to a decision for he reached behind him to the hook on the wall and tossed Lesley the car keys. "As far as I'm concerned, Constable Gold," he formally began, "this conversation did not occur. You have simply told me that you have some inquiries to make into the MP and need the car, is that understood?"

"Yes Sarge," replied a relieved Lesley, then as she stood up added, "thanks."

"Thank me with a result, now get out of here. I'm trying to work out my pension and how I'll spend it and that's something I don't want to be put at risk, do you follow me Lesley?"

She nodded and leaving the office, closed the door behind her, clutched the car keys tightly and smiled.

In the darkened room, Frederick Evans awoke in the narrow bed with a start, his head raised as he took in the unfamiliar surroundings that at first confused and alarmed him. Then he remembered. He was in Jenny's house, sleeping in the small, box room to the front of the house. He laid his head back on the pillow and let out a soft sigh. Last night had been awkward, recalling Jenny's mother's pretence at decorum when she coyly suggested that he use the spare room if he wished to stay overnight rather than as he planned, sharing Jenny's bed. My God, he thought, is the woman that naive that she doesn't realise her daughter and I are already sleeping together?

He could hear noises from downstairs and his bladder urged him to get up and dressed. Quickly, in the cold of the room he donned his clothing, regretting that unlike Jenny, he had not the foresight to pack a change of clothing and with a grimace, pulled on his day old shirt, sniffing distastefully at the armpits. He was keen to get to a radio and catch the hourly news, eager to hear of a body being found in the city centre and pulled open the door that led into the small landing. The door to the bathroom was open and after making his water and a quick wash of face and hands, with some reluctance he squeezed the crumpled tube and spread a dab of toothpaste onto his finer and worked it into his teeth.

"Frederick, are you up?" called Jenny from downstairs.

"Just coming dear," he spat into the bowl and called back then, grabbing his jacket from the room, he hurried down the stairs to the kitchen. The smell of fried food assailed him and he fought the urge to throw up. Jenny and her mother stood by the cooker in the grubby little kitchen as he entered and saw that two places had been set at the small table. "Thought you might want a wee fry-up before you lovebirds get to your work, you know?" smiled the portly woman.

Frederick smiled tightly in return, casting his eyes about the kitchen till they settled on an old radio/cassette player that was plugged in and sitting in a corner on a worktop. "Do you mind?" he asked, reaching for the dial. The weather report had just ended when the eight o'clock news broadcast commenced. His stomach almost revolted as he sat down before a plate of greasy eggs, bacon and sausage. The second item on Smooth Radio reported the discovery of a man's body the previous evening at the rear of the St Enoch Centre and carried the usual message that police inquiries were continuing. It took all his willpower to stop him from leaping from his chair, punching the air and cheering. Mister Hardie, it seemed, had followed his instruction to the letter.

Across the city, Paul Hardie had not slept all night. He sat fully dressed in a state of shock on the chair in the lounge, morosely staring, but seeing nothing. The plan had not gone as he anticipated. He hadn't meant to kill him, just rob him of his wallet. If the guy had did what Paul ordered then none of this would have happened, he would still be alive. He beat at his forehead with the heels of his hands, his mouth wide open in a silent scream. The man, whoever the fuck he was, was dead; murdered by him. He lowered his head to stare at his hand, the blood spotting still visible. With shocked horror, he realised that his clothing was also stained and he leapt from the chair, tearing at the jacket and ripping the shirt from him, the violence of his actions causing the shirt buttons to fly off as he tore at them, then throwing both items away from him across the room. His trousers too were stained and in his haste to get them off, forgot to untie his shoes and fell over onto the carpet, the trousers snagged about his ankles. He began to weep, curling up into a ball and hugging at his knees. His body began to involuntarily shake and he shivered, but not from the cold. He had killed again and this time, just as before, he hadn't meant to. Paul had thought when he held the knife towards the man that the man would be frightened and just given up and handed over the wallet. Nothing would have happened to him if he had only done as Paul told him. He didn't intend to kill the man, just rob him of the wallet and find out who he was and why Paul's tormentor wanted him dead. Paul hadn't expected the man to attack him, swing the briefcase and use it to hit out at Paul. He didn't mean to stab forward with the knife; his reaction to being hit with the case had been instinctive. He had only been protecting himself against the suddenly enraged man who was bigger built than Paul was. That was it. He hadn't really meant to stab him in the chest, but had just been protecting himself. It was the man's fault, Paul decided. The man had run onto the knife when Paul tried to scare him off by waving it at him. The man had attacked him. Of course, he suddenly realised. It was the man who was out to get Paul. Paul had only wanted his wallet. He would have been okay if he had just given Paul his wallet. The wallet would have been the clue. The wallet!
With sudden clarity, Paul remembered. He hadn't taken the man's wallet. It had all been for nothing. Now the man was dead and he was no nearer to finding out who his tormentor was.

In response to the discovery of the body at the rear of the St Enoch Centre and almost adjacent to the nearby underpass that emerges into Osborne Street, the police quickly set up a divisional murder team and sealed off the immediate area for Forensic examination. The victim's wallet positively identified him as Robert Hamilton, a fifty-eight years old manager of Dawson's Department Store in Buchanan Street who was not previously known to or recorded by the police for any crime or offence. When in the early hours of that morning the team interviewed Mister Hamilton's widow it was also quickly established that the wife did not know of any enemies her late husband had or any contact, directly or indirectly, with known criminal associates. Between bouts of weeping and hysteria, the two interviewing Detectives succeeded in obtaining a brief statement from the distraught woman and together concluded that the Hamilton's had been a happy and contented couple.

The police were unfortunate that the only two known witnesses at that time were the teenage girls who had discovered the body, one of whom was now detained at the Royal Infirmary casualty department suffering from traumatic shock while the other was still sobering up and neither of whom was able to offer anything of evidential value.

Later that morning, Detective officers designated to attend at Dawson's store obtained brief statements from senior management, who almost predictably described Mister Hamilton as a conscientious and valuable employee. In light of preliminary inquiries, the team deduced that the deceased, who had just finished work that evening and was en route to meet some acquaintances at a nearby snooker club, was the unfortunate victim of a mugging that had gone wrong. In short, he had been in the wrong place at the wrong time. As is customary, a public appeal for witnesses was issued via the local media.

The only spark of hope in the sorry incident was the belief of the Senior Investigating Officer – the SIO – that during the material time of Mister Hamilton departing the store and being discovered murdered, he had passed under a number of city centre cameras on the victim's probable route that could be trawled for any sighting of the victim or anything that might be of value.

Just after two o'clock that afternoon, a dozy Gracie Fields was awoken from his slumber by his partner Simon who brought him coffee and tenderly ruffling Gracie's dyed blonde and disarrayed hair, passed the message that Gracie was to phone his office as soon as possible.

Lesley Gold made a decision. Before she would interview the woman who worked beside Paul Hardie, she would first attend at the MP's school and speak to staff there and try to get some kind of background on the MP as an individual. The updated MP report that sat on the passenger seat beside her indicated that two of her colleagues from a neighbouring shift had already attended at the school, but their report was bland and simply concluded that nobody at the school had any idea why or to where the MP might have gone. The report included a note that they had spoken with the HT, that Lesley presumed to be the Head Teacher, a Miss Jenkins by name.

Turning into the school gate, she stopped to permit an older man dressed in council jacket and dungarees and wheeling a barrow to cross the narrow driveway as he smiled his appreciation to her. Continuing up the short drive, she parked the car and pressed the visitor's button at the front door. The secretary who admitted her seemed a little agitated that Lesley had not booked a prior appointment and nervously led her to the small reception area where she asked her to wait while the secretary spoke with Miss Jenkins. Cap in hand, Lesley smiled at the childish drawings adorning the walls, then it struck her; the silence. She thought it odd that for a school with at least a couple of hundred primary aged children that there was hardly, no she corrected herself. There was no noise at all.

"If you'll please come this way Constable," the secretary said, having almost wraith-like crept up and startled Lesley.

Shown into the head teacher's room, Lesley's first impression of Miss Jenkins was one of arrogance, compounded by the woman pretending to read a report in front of her while dismissively waving a hand at the young officer to take a seat in front of Jenkins desk. Placing the report down in front of her, Jenkins slowly took off her glasses and stared for a few seconds at Lesley before speaking. "This really won't do, Constable. I'm a very busy woman and if you require seeing me, you really should consider an appointment. Now, what is it that you want?"

Lesley resisted the temptation to rudely retort and instead smiled. "I'm making further inquiry into your member of staff, Missus Fiona Hardie, whom of course you are aware was reported to the police as a missing person."

Before she could continue, Jenkins interrupted, lifting the report again as though preparing to read it. "Don't you people speak to each other," she snapped. "I've already told some of your colleagues, we at the school have no further information. Missus Hardie left here last Tuesday and that was the last we saw of her. Now, is there anything else?"

Lesley quickly realised that this was getting her nowhere and rather than give the old bag any more excuse to be rude simply nodded and replied, "Thank you for your courtesy, Miss Jenkins. I'll see myself out." It was as she stood and turned to leave she heard Jenkins parting stage whisper of "Wasting my time."

Bristling at the comment, she decided not to retort and leaving the office, gently closed the door behind her. She stood for a few seconds to replace her cap and was about to walk out when she heard the secretary softly say, "Speak to Mister Dunlop, the janitor."

Turning, she was about to respond, but the mousey woman's head was turned away as she rifled through a filing cabinet.

Lesley exited the school main door and glanced about her. The man who had wheeled the barrow, she though must be the janitor, Mister Dunlop. As she strolled across the neatly tended grass towards him, she was unaware that Jenkins watched her from her window, curious as to why the policewoman would wish to speak to that old has-been. Jenkins eyes narrowed and Dunlop, she decided, was another name she would add to the list of personnel she wished removed from the school.
"Mister Dunlop," called Lesley as she waved. The old janitor stopped and placed the wheelbarrow down, slowly standing erect and she guessed that his back was apparently giving him bother.
"Yes, love," he smiled at her, "what can I do for you?"
From her window, Jenkins watched as the policewoman and the old fool conversed, wondering why he seemed so animated and what could be so interesting to cause the policewoman to write in her notebook. She continued to slyly watch the two, growingly increasingly angry and resolved that at the soonest opportunity, Dunlop was gone from her school.
It was almost fifteen minutes later before Lesley collected the patrol car and slowly drove through the school gates. The conversation with the old janny had been enlightening and, she mischievously grinned, in more ways than one.

Andy Carmichael pushed open the front door of Garscadden Police Office with a handful of mail and the now almost empty mail sack on his back. He greeted Jinksie with a smile, but his eyes betrayed him as he glanced past the smaller man. With a grin on his face, Jinksie shrewdly guessed that the big guy was looking for Lesley.
"She's out on patrol, on an inquiry about a missing woman," he explained, taking the mail from Andy and glancing at it.
The comment threw Andy, who then suddenly grinned. "Can't keep much from you, can we, Jinksie?"
"No you can't," Jinksie agreed as he returned the grin. "Got time for a cuppa, big man?"
Andy nodded at the invitation and was admitted through the connecting door, placing the mail sack on the floor at the chair beside Jinksie's desk while the smaller man fetched two mugs of tea from the kitchen. The next ten minutes passed in general conversation, mostly Jinksie complaining about the problems and the cost of arranging his forthcoming nuptials and then suddenly, with a cheeky grin, he said, "So, you and Lesley then. You're an item?"
"Ah," Andy felt himself blushing at the question and replied, "I hope so, but you'll be discreet, won't you?"
"Stand on me, big man," nodded Jinksie, "stand on me."

The presence of the half dozen CID officers in Dawson's spread like wildfire as the staff whispered in corners. It soon became public knowledge that Mister Hamilton, the manager of the Gents Department, had been murdered. The older employees dramatically clutched at their throats or shook their heads at the news, each vying to have personally known the poor man better than anyone else in the store while the younger staff eagerly sought more of the gruesome details. As the stories rebounded from department to department and floor to floor, they grew more salacious and outrageous, for nobody wished to believe that Hamilton was simply the victim of a robbery gone wrong. As one cynical staff member was heard to comment, "After all, there's nothing like a murder to peak people's interest, eh?"

The management response was to first gather all the departmental managers together within the illustrious boardroom for a briefing of the circumstances as they were known, where they were assured that everything that could be done, was being done. This reassurance, instructed the HR Manager, was to be disseminated among the remaining staff.

To his thrilled delight, Frederick Evans had earlier that morning been summoned by the HR Manager and almost shook with excitement when the manager gravely told him that due to demise of "the unfortunate Mister Hamilton", Frederick was required for the foreseeable future to assume the role of acting departmental manager at this difficult time. The manager took Frederick's apparent nervous disposition as shock at the tragic news and would have been appalled had he known it was all Frederick could do to refrain from jumping for joy.

"Of course, Mister Evans" continued the HR Manager, wringing his hands mournfully at the sorrowful business, though he had hardly known the dead man, "you will likely guess the CID will wish to interview your staff to elicit any detail they might have regarding the last time they saw poor Robert."

It didn't escape Fredrick's attention that the "unfortunate Mister Hamilton" was now "poor Robert" and it seemed to him that even the HR Manager was now publicly laying claim to a deep and sincere friendship with the dead man.

"Indeed. I will ensure my staff," agreed an equally grave Frederick, "will be available at any time the police choose to conduct their interviews."

It was with a light step that he returned to the department and, continuing the pretence of deep shock, gathered his newly acquired staff about him, eager for them to become aware of his new found status and insider information. "No, there is no further information," he told them. "No, there are no suspects that we know of at the minute" and then finally, "Yes, business will continue as Mister Hamilton would have wished."

Before he dismissed them, Frederick disclosed that the CID would visit the department to interview each member of staff regarding their last contact with Mister Hamilton. He could almost feel the excitement rise as they openly discussed what they knew and what they would tell the detectives. He ushered them back to their duties and watched as they dispersed throughout the department, curious that some were even smiling at the prospect of being interviewed by the CID. At last had come the moment he had longed for. Turning on his heel he walked towards the small office and using the issued pass key, unlocked the door to his very own inner sanctum. As he stepped through the door he slowly closed his eyes and could almost feel the history of the place, the decades of use by managers before him, the power and influence they wielded from the closet sized room. He opened his eyes and stared curiously at the desk, chipped at the corners, the varnish long ago faded and then frowned at the personal items that adorned the top and which he wanted to immediately consign to the bin. But that would be too premature, he decided. He must wait for a respectful period of mourning to pass before he made the office his own. Sitting in the desk chair so recently vacated by Robert Hamilton, Frederick made a pyramid of his fingers and gently caressed his chin as he sighed with deep contentment. His plan had exceeded his expectation and he resolved to make one more call to his pawn, Paul Hardie. However, this time he would simply congratulate Hardie on a job well done and promise never again to contact him. But that will be a lie he smirked, knowing that he would always retain the DVD.
After all, he smiled to himself; one never knows when one might again have need of Mister Hardie's unique talent for murder.

Doctor McPherson gently patted Tom Gold on his shoulder and even the soft touch, he saw with concern, caused the man's face to wince in pain. The old doctor sensed more than heard and turning slowly, saw Tom's wife Peggy watching him from the doorway, her eyes betraying her anxiety. He half smiled and turning back to his patient, his glance fell upon the medication and that's when he noticed. At last, he thought to himself, common sense and human decency seems to be alive and well and almost chortled at the contradiction. Taking a soft breath he stood upright, winked as he nodded at the dying man and with tenderness, played his fingers across Tom's hand in understanding.

Just like everyone else in the store, Jenny was shocked to hear of the brutal murder of the Gents Departmental manager, quickly realising he must have been Frederick's boss, but unable to recall if Frederick had ever mentioned him. The radio that blared in the back kitchen that morning repeated the story on the news hour, but so far hadn't actually named him. The sudden, playful dig in her ribs from her supervisor took her by surprise. "Does this mean your laddie gets a promotion then, hen?" she asked Jenny.

"Eh, I don't know. No, well, what I mean is, no, I really couldn't say," her voice faltered. "Maybe," she added with a half smile.

"It's extra money if he gets the job, hen and if you're planning on a wedding," the woman grinned as she played with her own gold band, "the money will come in useful."

Jenny blushed, uncertain how to respond to such a direct question. Of course, it was her dream to get married and if it was Frederick she tied the knot with, so be it. A cold shiver swept through her at the thought and for the first time since they had got together, though she could not put it into words, her female intuition caused her to doubt. Married to Frederick? Suddenly and without warning, her knees buckled and grasping the side of the large and deep kitchen sink, she almost collapsed to the floor, but for the strong, sturdy arms of her boss. "Here a minute, hen, are you okay love? Look," her concerned boss, worry etched on her face guided her to a nearby chair, "sit for a wee minute and I'll get you a glass of water." The supervisor kept one eye on Jenny as she run the cold tap and made the younger woman sip at it, calling out to another assistant to fetch the store's duty first aider.

"No, please, there's no need for that," spluttered Jenny. "It was just a wee giddy turn, Honest, I'm alright," she almost begged the woman, embarrassed and surprised at what had occurred and attempting to rise from the chair.

"Ah, time of the month is it?" said the woman knowingly with a nod of her head and one hand on Jenny's shoulder to keep her seated. The woman waved the kitchen assistant back; now that the wee turn was explained, there was no need for the first aider, she decided.

"That's it, time of the month," Jenny eagerly agreed, keen to end the fuss that now had attracted two other kitchen assistants as well as the head chef.

"Right, well I can't have you working in a kitchen if you're going to faint on me, you're a Health and Safety risk," the supervisor said with a broad wink, "so get your coat and away home with you, lassie. And don't worry about signing out either," she added. "Just leave your card and I'll see that gets done. If anybody asks, I've sent you home, okay?"

Jenny weakly nodded and assisted to her feet by the caring woman, made her way to the locker room to fetch her coat. She knew that she should be grateful for the unexpected time off, but the thought persisted. Even if he asked me, she wondered, would I say "yes" to marriage with Frederick?

Chapter 29 - Mid-day Tuesday

Constable Lesley Gold parked her patrol car in an empty bay in St Vincent Street and walked to a nearby Traffic Warden, informing the man that she was making inquiries in a nearby office and strongly emphasised she did not expect to find a ticket on the patrol car when she returned. The man didn't argue and simply nodded, assuring Lesley that as it was police business he would keep an eye on the car.

The recently sand-blasted post Victorian building located at number 239 accommodated a number of firms that included Berkley and Finch, who occupied the top three floors. Lesley presented herself to the receptionist at the desk and deciding not to bother making inquiry with HR, asked to speak with Janice Meikle from the typing pool, She politely declined the offer of a seat in the reception area, preferring to stand and pace as in her mind, she went over and over her prepared interview questions. Lesley knew that she had no direct cause to question Meikle, let alone any real evidence the woman was playing around with the MP's husband and that the presence of a police officer wishing to speak with a staff member would attract much gossip, but she figured it was best to disconcert Meikle right from the off.

Less than five minutes passed and the lift doors open to reveal a tall, slim blonde in her late twenties wearing an expensive blouse and dark skirt that Lesley guessed were not purchased off the peg. As the woman approached across the short space between them, she seemed to glide as if she knew that wherever she walked, men would watch. Lesley almost instinctively realised that Janice Meikle used her obvious sexuality as a lure and for one brief instance, doubted if Meikle would be the pushover Lesley hoped she might be. Meikle's eyes narrowed with curiosity and she identified herself in a sultry voice, her hands folded in front of her.

"Is there something I can help you with, Constable?"

"Perhaps you might feel a little more comfortable if we spoke in private, Miss Meikle."

Meikle smiled in response; her curiosity further aroused and calling to the receptionist, asked if she might use the small interview room and then led Lesley through an adjoining door that in turn led to a small room not much larger than the station kitchen. The room was furnished with a desk and three chairs; two at one side of the desk while the other backed onto the door. Tastefully decorated, Lesley guessed it was where casual visitors to the firm were dealt with. Meikle walked round the table and pulling a chair to one side from beneath the desk, slowly sat herself down and crossing her long, slim legs, stared Lesley in the eye. "Now, Constable, why exactly do you wish to see me?"

Lesley recognised what Meikle was doing; trying to dominate the conversation from the outset by opening with a question. Well, madam, she inwardly seethed, that won't work with a hard-nosed bugger like me and decided that she would go for the jugular.

"Miss Meikle, I'm making inquiry into a missing woman, a Missus Fiona Hardie. I have information you are conducting an extra-marital affair with Paul Hardie, the missing woman's husband." She watched as Meikle's face turned pale and saw the shapely outline of her throat tremble as the woman swallowed hard. Lesley guessed the last thing that entered Meikle's head was being found out and by the police, at that.

"I …I beg your pardon!" she almost cried out, standing, her hands making fists upon the desk top.

Lesley smiled tightly at Meikle's shocked face. "Perhaps you might care to sit down and we can discuss this informally, or would you prefer to accompany me to the police station to talk about it officially where we can record the conversation?"

Lesley was bluffing and silently hoped that Meikle's didn't guess that she was under no obligation to accompany Lesley anywhere. For a brief few seconds, Lesley thought the younger woman would storm from the room, but slowly to Lesley's relief, Meikle sat back down and thrust her hands into her lap to stop them shaking.

She decided to offer an olive branch and leaning forward, softly said, "Nobody at the firm need know why we're having this discussion. You can tell them whatever story you wish. All I want to know is about you and Paul Hardie and anything you know about his missing wife," and again inwardly prayed that she hadn't gotten it wrong; that Meikle wasn't in any way implicated in Fiona Hardie's disappearance. If she was, Lesley hoped she might in some way persuade her to betray Paul Hardie. She watched as Meikle seemed to wrestle over the decision, then laying her hands flat on the table and casting her eyes over Lesley's shoulder towards the door to ensure it was soundly closed, said, "Look, yes, Paul and I did have an affair, but it was over. We had a bit of a fling for a few months. Well, six months actually, but I don't know a fucking thing about his wife going missing. That happened the day or the day after I dumped him. I'm not sure." Now that the dam had burst, there was no stopping Meikle, who clearly didn't want to be involved in any police investigation into her former lover's missing wife. She sat back in the chair; her arms now folded across her chest and slowly shook her head at the memory. "What I mean is, the day he got fired from the company. When we were together, Paul was always the big man, what he was going to do, where we would live, that sort of thing." She laughed humourlessly, more of a snort than a real laugh. "He was going to divorce his wife, sell the house and, with his half of the profit, talked about the two of us getting a flat together. As if," she sniffed.

"About his wife," Lesley gently prodded, "did you get to meet her or anything?"

"No fucking way," she snapped back, all pretence of a silky voice gone and the true Janice Meikle now exposed. "All he said about her was that she was a ditsy, slovenly cow and he couldn't be bothered being about her anymore." Her eyes flashed as if a sudden understanding struck her and again, her eyes narrowed as she leaned towards Lesley. "You don't think, I mean, you can't think he's done her in or anything?"

"Why would you say that? Did her ever say anything like that or threaten to harm his wife?"

"No, no way. No." she firmly shook her head and raised her hands as though to push the thought from her mind. I don't know anything about this," she shoved back at her chair and stood up, her distress now evident.

"Please sit down, Miss Meikle," said Lesley, who remained seated, but with an edge to her voice. "Please," she firmly, but quietly repeated.

Meikle sat slowly down, her confidence now completely shattered at the thought that she might now be implicated in something over which she had no control. Her mind raced as she imagined what it might mean for her; whether true or not, she would be publicly identified as the other woman…with sudden horror, the thought crossed her mind in an instant. Had Paul done something stupid, something crazy? No way did she want involved in this. She had her own life to think about and didn't want to be the other woman who, what…. drove a man to kill his wife? Her job, her income, her flat, all would be lost and any opportunity for a fresh start gone. She had been lucky to find a position at this place as she glanced about her, when her previous firm had almost dismissed her for the messy debacle of the affair with one of their directors. Paul Hardie then Colin Davies; it seemed she was stumbling from one fucking disaster to another.

"Look," she almost pleaded with Lesley, "I really don't know anything about Paul's wife. Like I told you, we were shagging, aye, I admit that. But he promised he was leaving her and getting promoted and I thought he was someone to hold onto, but when he got sacked, well fuck. I wasn't going to hold onto a loser, was I? I had my own plans!"

Lesley recognised the desperation in the younger woman's eyes and said, "When did you last see him?"

Meikle took a deep breath and sighed, as though trying to recall. "He was standing by my car waiting for me, in the place where I park. Cambridge Street, the car park there. He wanted us to get back together, but I told him it was finished, to fuck off. No, wait," she raised a hand, "I saw him after that. Yesterday morning. Monday, about eleven I think it was. He was here, at the office. In Colin's office, I mean Mister Davies office. But we didn't speak."

"Was he here to see you?"

She shook her head, "No, I don't think so. I had gone to see Mister Davies," she almost whispered, "but he had taken a heart attack the night before and," she hesitated as if the memory was uncomfortable, "and he died. I turned around and Paul was there too. I think maybe he was in to ask for his job back. I don't really know. I didn't see him after that." She didn't think it necessary to tell the cop that she had been shagging Davies too. That was one secret she intended keeping.

Lesley nodded as though in understanding, completely oblivious to the half truth about Colin Davies. "So, Miss Meikle, in short, you have no idea where Missus Hardie might currently be or if her husband meant her any harm?"

Meikle firmly shook her head. "No, none at all," she replied.

Lesley wasn't a trained CID investigator, had never attended any interview courses, but her intuition told her that if not the full story, Meikle was probably telling the truth about not having any knowledge of the MP's disappearance. "Eh, just one final questions, Miss Meikle. Did Paul Hardie ever hit you or get angry with you or anything like that? What I mean, is, does he have a temper?"

It was just a heartbeat in time, but Lesley saw Meikle's eyes flicker. What the young policewoman couldn't know was in that short space of time, Meikle saw the opportunity to portray herself as a victim and not the harlot that, if the shit hit the fan, the press would make her out to be.

"He never actually hit me," she slowly drawled, "but that time when he was standing by my car in Cambridge Street, I thought he was going to make a grab at me." With sudden clarity, she remembered the old couple. "There was a man and a woman there. They were watching. I don't know, maybe because they were there Paul didn't, you know, get any angrier. I felt a little," her eyebrows narrowed as she considered the word, "threatened, you know?"

"So he was angry then?"

"Well," she half smiled, her confidence returning as the policewoman seemingly believed the half-truth, "I had just dumped him so he wasn't too pleased."

"Right then," Lesley slowly exhaled as she nodded and stood up, "I won't take a formal statement just now, but needless to say our inquiries will continue Miss Meikle, so I will be grateful if you don't discuss our conversation with anyone else. Is that clear?" she stared meaningfully at the younger woman.

Meikle nodded without replying. Lesley couldn't know that Meikle had no intention of discussing her relationship with anyone and already was considering a story, some lie of family bereavement to explain her interview with the cop. As she walked towards the lift that would take her back to her office, she wracked her mind for some explanation as to how the bitch of a cop found out about her and Paul; a worry that would haunt her for some time to come.

Returning to the patrol car, Lesley acknowledged the wave from the traffic warden across the road, but her thoughts were on the conversation with Janice Meikle. The interview had thrown up some new facts about Paul Hardie. For one, he wasn't the loving husband he had initially portrayed himself to be, as proven by his lengthy fling with Meikle. Lesley wasn't stupid and realised that Meikle was eager to paint Hardie as the bad guy, to cast herself as the poor, put upon woman who was afraid of his temper. But having now seen Meikle and the physical attraction she exuded and learned of the MP's description from the very helpful school janitor, Jimmy Dunlop, Lesley, now understood Paul Hardie's attraction to the buxom vamp that was Janice Meikle. That and Fiona Hardie's purchase of a pregnancy testing kit now caused Lesley to believe that Paul Hardie was a man in turmoil who perhaps… no, she stopped herself from considering any further supposition. The facts of the inquiry had now changed, as evidenced by Meikle's new information. Being dumped by his lover, his unloved wife's pregnancy as well as finding himself unemployed might just have sent him over the edge. One thing was for certain. She knew that this new information had cast a different light on the inquiry and she needed advice, if not help. Quietly excited, she settled herself into the driver's seat and starting the engine, drove towards Maryhill Office.

The news room located within the BBC's new Scottish headquarters on the south side of the River Clyde was unusually quiet that morning. Calling his staff together into the main room beside the office for one of the many "let's get our heads together" chat's, the Producer favoured, he banged the typed synopsis sheet of that day's news items on the desk before him.
"Shite, that's all that's there. Nothing worth leading unless," he cast his narrowed eyes at each of the half dozen staff, "any of you buggers have something that will make me happy? A corrupt politician, perhaps or a paedophile clergyman caught *in flagrante* maybe? I like clergyman," he smiled evilly. "They always make good television news." He peered round his staff, eyeing each one individually and then cajoled them with, "Come on now, one of you buggers must have something we can sensationalise!"
The silence was deafening until a nervous hand was raised and a junior researcher ventured, "What about the murder in the city centre? You know," she looked about her, as though seeking support from her hard-bitten colleagues, "the guy that was stabbed in the tunnel off Argyle Street?"
"Speak to me," the Producer imperiously commanded, sitting back with his hands clasped at the back of his balding head.
"The murder is number three on the list," she hesitantly reminded him. "Well, it seems the police haven't a clue at the minute. I spoke with a contact….."

"Is that the detective you're shagging?" quipped a smiling older woman sitting beside her, while the others coughed or spluttered to conceal their laughter.

"A contact," persisted the rapidly blushing researcher, "who told me that the man," she glanced down at the notes, "a Robert Hamilton, was a manager at Dawson's, you know, the department store?"

"I know where Dawson's is, sweetie," the producer smiled tightly in response and waved for the young woman to continue. At this point, he inwardly sighed as he glanced at the wall clock; any port in a storm.

"Robert Hamilton," she read again from her notes, "was fifty-eight years old, married, no children and lived in the Baillieston area with his wife. He managed the Gents Department at Dawson's and according to my contact," she hesitated, staring boldly at the older woman sitting beside her, "Hamilton wasn't previously known to the police. Once a month he would manage his department's late night opening at the store then walk the same route to a snooker club in Stockwell Street to meet some friends. Only last night, he didn't get there. He got himself murdered."

"Did your boyfriend say if the dead guy had any kind of background? I mean, was he gay, into prostitutes, anything like that?"

"No," she shook her head, "apparently this man, Hamilton, was a very decent man and right now there isn't a suspect for the murder. They, the police I mean, think it was a robbery gone wrong. Well, that's their initial supposition anyway. I was thinking," her speech slowed as though she was reluctantly disclosing her inner thoughts, "that with the Commonwealth Games coming into the city, the last thing the police and council need is a unsolved murder."

Almost as quick as a heartbeat, a decision was made. The producer slapped his hand on the desk, acutely conscious of the time-critical nature of his business. "We'll go with that as the lead story and fluff it up with maybe a follow-up piece about city centre robberies, muggings, particularly as my young and very shaggable colleague reminds us," he winked theatrically at the red-faced researcher, "that Glasgow is gearing up for the forthcoming Commonwealth Games and trying to project an image of safety and hospitality; tie it all in together with what statistics we can muster. Let's try for an eight or nine minute segment that we can pad out with an interview or two." He turned to a portly woman. "Gloria, my one true love, organise a crew. I can't see the cops permitting us access to the family at this early stage, so I want you to contact the police media mob and also the store and see if they can give us a staff member, a manager or someone in authority, to give some kind of on-camera background to this guy, the dead man I mean, okay? Send that new reporter with them, that young blonde lassie with the rather fetching tits. You know the one, her who has just recently come on board and tell them to get their arse down to Dawson's. I'm looking for the usual, so you brief them on what questions they've to ask. You might have to flimflam Dawson's management a bit; you know how sticky these bloody people can be, but you're so good at it," he blew her a pretend kiss. "And you," he nodded to the young researcher as he pulled his heavy bulk from his chair. "Good work, sweetie. Now get your tight little arse in gear and provide Gloria with statistics, lots of them and *do* try to get me a photograph of the victim, eh?"

The day began and continued to be a waking nightmare for Paul Hardie. Sleep was out of the question and every imagined sound, every vehicle outside caused him sheer panic. He lost count of the number of times he had peeked from behind the curtain in the upstairs bedroom window out into the street, watching for the police to come crashing through his door or from the kitchen window, dreading the sudden onslaught of a police tactical team covertly picking the back door lock. Too much television drama and reality programmes was taking its toll on his shattered nerves. The toilet stunk from the sour odour of vomit and though exhausted, the adrenalin rush he was experiencing kept his body alert and tense. Dressed only in his underpants and sock, the rest of the clothing he had worn, his suit, shirt, tie and even his shoes lay drying, already washed and spun dry in the machine.

The filter, his mind raced with a sudden clarity of thought. What if they check the washing machine filter? Racing and almost falling downstairs, he tripped tiredly into the kitchen and on his knees, twisted and turned at the low placed filter, unscrewing it from the machine and ignoring the flood of water that followed it, soaking the already damp and untidy flooring. With fumbling fingers, he picked at the lint and fluff embedded in the filter, his eyes straining for any tell-tale signs of blood. Still not satisfied, he stumbled over to the kitchen sink and run the filter under the hot water tap. He began to cry again, wiping his running, snotty nose on a bare forearm, the tears almost blinding him. With both hands resting on the rim of the sink, he leaned over and openly wept.

Almost three full minutes passed before Paul was again composed and he sat back onto a kitchen chair, his body now giving in to tiredness. His head was sinking onto his chest when it occurred to him he had not checked any of the radio or television news channels for information about the murder. He stood up and switched on the radio that sat on the worktop, glancing at the wall clock and seeing that the news was just a few moments away. Sitting back down, Paul drummed his fingers impatiently on the kitchen table, waiting for the end of the road broadcast. The first item on Clyde One news was the reported discovery of a man's body in Osborne Street in the city centre. Police, according to the reporter, were making inquiries and the location was still sealed off at that time. He didn't listen to any further news and switching the radio off, slowly stood up. Making his way into the lounge, he knew he was too tired to remain awake for much longer and set the television to record both the local six o'clock STV and six-thirty BBC Scotland news programmes. That done, he desperately needed to rest and flopped onto the couch, his eyes closing as he fell into an exhausted, coma-like sleep.

Dotty Turner and Alex Mason had just delivered a prisoner to Maryhill Police Office and were returning to their car when they bumped into Lesley.
"So, have car, will travel," grinned Alex. "Catch the sales up in town, did we? Get anything nice, maybe a wee cocktail dress or new shoes?"
Lesley playfully swiped at his head, missing by inches as he ducked away. Dotty stared questioningly at her friend. "You look a bit peeved there missus. Something tells me that you've had a successful mission; whatever the hell it was that you were doing. So, exactly what have you been doing?"
"I've been given the chance to do some follow-up on the MP, Fiona Hardie and guess what? Met a girlfriend of the missing person's husband," she grimaced. "Seems our Mister Hardie isn't the devoted hubby he would have us believe. I'm just on my way up to the CID to see if there's anything that they can advise."
"You think he's done her in or something?" asked an incredulous Alex. "Killed her, maybe?"
"Don't you be bandying that kind of language about, young Alex," Dotty cautioned him, her voice deliberately low. "You've read the manual, so remember your rules of evidence. We don't surmise, we act on facts, okay?"
"Okay mummy," he replied, pulling a petted lip at his tutor and then turning to Lesley, his eyes aglow, said, "I've never been involved in a murder inquiry. Can you persuade Dotty here to turn me over to you? I'd like to be there when you speak to him again."
Lesley smiled and held her hand up. "Whoa right there. Once I've spoken to El CID, you know the routine. If there is anything amiss and only if, mind you, they'll take the inquiry on and the nearest we'll get to it from then on is standing by something looking good for the media. And let's face it, young Alex," she adopted a coy voice, "if anybody's needing to look good for the camera's it's bound to be me."
"Get that woman a bigger hat size," smiled Dotty. "Right you," she pulled at Alex's arm, "back to the real world. See you later hen," she called out to Lesley.
A little cheered by the meeting with Dotty and Alex, Lesley made her way to the CID suite of offices in the building, uncertain to whom she should seek the advice from. Cap in hand, she took a deep breath and exhaling softly, walked determinedly towards the office occupied by the Detective Inspector. The door was ajar and the room empty. Lesley felt like an interloper as she

entered the office, but could see the suit jacket and short coat on the stand behind the door, so guessed the DI wasn't far and decided to wait. As she looked around the room, her glance fell on the photograph frame on the desk and leaning forward, saw the picture of a smiling woman and child she guessed was about seven or eight years old.
"That's my wife and daughter, well step-daughter really," said the voice that startled her. She blushed and turned to face the tall, craggy faced man with the three inch scar across his right cheek that stood in the doorway. "Sadie's a Sergeant over in Baird Street office and Geraldine, well Jellybean I should say," he smiled at Lesley, "she's in primary four now."
"Sorry sir, I didn't mean to…" her voice faded at her embarrassment, having been caught being nosey.
"It's all right, I'm very proud of them both," he grinned at her as he moved around Lesley to sit at the desk. "Now, what can I do for you, Constable?"
Lesley was unsure how to begin. She had not personally had previous dealings with DI Charlie Miller, though like most of the cops in the Division, she had heard the story of how as a Detective Sergeant in the city centre division, Miller had been blown up when a car exploded and though the official story was that the car experienced some sort of fuel leak, the unofficial story had done the rounds that a bomb had been set off and killed the driver, who was a known high profile Irish republican supporter from Glasgow's east end. Miller had suffered a life-threatening injury, but returned to work and almost immediately been promoted to the Maryhill Division. Those few officers that Lesley knew who had worked with Miller described him as a smart and tenacious officer who was fair with his staff, approachable and all in all, a very decent man. She hoped that Miller's decency might continue after the story she was about to relate.
"I'm actually here for some advice sir…" she began, but stopped when he held a hand up.
"Would you not feel a bit more relaxed sitting down? Constable Gold, isn't it?"
As she nodded, Miller asked, "Look, what's your first name?"
"Eh, it's Lesley, sir."
He stared briefly at the young woman and realised she was nervous. To put her at her ease, he smiled and said, "Right Lesley, this will go a lot easier if you call me Charlie, okay?" and his eyes twinkled as he stared at her. "Are you not the lassie that belted that wanker Mike Duffy on the nose?"
Lesley blushed again, inwardly thinking that story is going to follow me no matter where I go. She nodded and tried to look suitably shamefaced.
"Didn't hit him hard enough," Miller smiled at her, but didn't bother to explain that comment or any grievance with Duffy. "Now Lesley," he sat back at ease in his chair, "what can I do for you?"

She handed the MP file to him and asked him first to read through it, watching as he glanced at the cover sheet and then flicking through the updated reports on the two following pages.

"It doesn't say here that you are the investigating officer, Lesley and by all accounts, it seems to be a straight forward missing person, a woman that had done a runner from the marital home." His eyes narrowed and he stared at her. "From the entries I've read, the report has been passed from shift to shift and there's nothing to suggest anything untoward, but something tells me that you aren't here because you just can't find this woman, this Missus Hardie. You think there's something happened to her?"

She took a deep breath and began to relate her suspicions.

On the drive from the city centre to Maryhill, Lesley had rehearsed in her mind how she was going to present her suspicions to whatever CID officer would speak with her and so, began in consecutive order, telling of all the small anomalies and inconsistencies that now brought her to DI Miller's office.

The bin in the Hardie's bathroom that had been emptied and was a contradiction to the state of the small room, with paper and other debris lying about the window-sill and the shelf at the mirror.

The aromatic candles in the lounge and only in the lounge that she believed might have been lit to mask some identifiable smell. She did not allude to the possibility of the smell of blood, but left Miller to make his own conclusion from her inference.

She leaned forward, her face grim as she described the polished surface of the tiles that surrounded the fire hearth and again, stressed how this was at odds with the untidy and frankly, slovenly state of the room.

She spoke of attending at the Hardie's house and his belligerence at the police when the police called for an update on his missing wife.

Miller sat impassively as she recounted the story, speaking only to ask her to clarify some point and as she spoke, Dotty Turner's warning to Alex Mason crossed her mind; the police only deal in facts, not supposition and she suddenly felt deflated, for nothing she had said could be construed as evidence. But she pressed on and admitted that through a friend, she had discovered Paul Hardie was cheating on his wife with a workmate and recounted the conversation with the girlfriend, Janice Meikle. She saw the DI raise his eyebrows when she told how, earlier that morning, she had confronted Janice Meikle at the firm where she worked and of inveigling the admittance from Meikle that she had an affair with Hardie. She related Meikle telling her that Hardie intended leaving his wife to set up home with Meikle, or did 'till he lost his job.

She left nothing out and watched as Miller leaned closer when she spoke of Meikle's worry that Hardie had a temper and that she felt threatened when he met with her in Cambridge Street car park.

She related the conversation with the old janitor Jimmy Dunlop and repeated his description of a mousey woman who was timid and who, on the day of her disappearance, was distressed and of how the MP had confided in Dunlop she had been threatened with the sack from her job. Lesley could hardly contain the excitement in her voice when she related Dunlop's story, that he had been present when the MP's husband had confronted the Head Teacher about the MP being threatened with dismissal. She saw the DI seemed confused until she explained that Hardie could only have known of the threat to dismiss Missus Hardie if she herself had told him, but that he had categorically denied seeing or even speaking with his wife at any time that day.

Her eyes opened wide when she remembered something, annoyed she had almost forgotten to tell Miller that the husband had brought an empty pregnancy test box to the office, but there was no conclusive proof in the house of its contents and in particular, Lesley guessed, the bathroom bin where the used item would have been discarded. She added that it was her opinion that from what she had learned of Paul Hardie, he had no interest in having a child with his wife and saw Miller's eyes narrow at this. She posed the question that if the missing woman was pregnant, given the circumstances that her husband now found himself in, it was a possibility he might consider a wife he intended leaving now pregnant with a child he didn't want, to be too much for him to bear.

She finished her narrative quietly and an awkward silence fell between them. Lesley's throat was suddenly dry and she licked at her lips. Her stomach churned and she thought - no, she knew the DI didn't believe her; couldn't possibly make sense of her ranting, that the story she had related was a set of circumstances that added up to nothing. No evidence, not even a strong suspicion. Her whole body felt completely deflated.

Miller smiled tightly at her and said, "Wait here," then stood and left the room. She wasn't to know that he needed a few minutes to consider what she had told him. To her surprise, he returned a few minutes later with two mugs of milked coffee and placed one mug with a sachet of sugar in front of her. She sipped at the coffee, ignoring the sugar. His face was impassive when he began.

"First," he said, "you were out of order for involving a non-member of the police in your investigation. Secondly, it was a bad move confronting this woman Meikle on your own. You should know by now that corroboration is paramount to any investigation and let's face it. If and I mean if, your suspicions are correct, there's every likelihood that as Paul Hardie's paramour, so to speak, she might be implicitly involved in the disappearance of Hardie's wife. Thirdly, threatening to drag somebody down to a polis station when you've no evidence is a hollow threat and doesn't usually work. You were damned lucky with that one. Fourth… well," he bit at his lower lip, "there really isn't a fourth." He exhaled loudly and slowly shook his head, then asked, "Your Inspector, its Frank Cochrane, isn't it?"

A chastened young officer now, she nodded, her shoulders slumped and her heart sank as she watched him dial an internal number on his desk phone. Her stomach was churning as she heard him say, "Frank, it's Charlie Miller. I've one of your cops, Lesley Gold sitting here with me. She's brought me a wee interesting story and I was wondering if I might borrow her for a day or two?" He stopped talking to listen, his eyes narrowing then he smiled. "Okay," he nodded at the handset, "only I don't touch the stuff anymore so you can have the pint and I'll have a coke."

Replacing the handset, he stared thoughtfully at Lesley and said, "You've just cost me a beer, young lady. Right, when it comes to your investigative skills, you're a bit rough round the edges and to be honest, you've not a shred of evidence that anything criminal has occurred to Fiona Hardie. That said, married to my Sadie I've learned to trust a woman's intuition." He leaned back again in his chair, eyebrows knitted together and face suddenly now grim as he rubbed his hands together and continued, "I believe that you and I might dig a wee bit deeper into your Mister Hardie."

The HR Manager at Dawson's requested an urgent meeting with the on-site Duty Director and was called to sit with him in the ostentatious, heavily wood panelled top floor conference suite that normally was reserved for use by the Board members only.

"What's the rush?" asked the Director, glancing at his watch and noting if he wasn't away in ten minutes, he would catch the backed-up traffic jam of the M77 through to Newton Mearns.

The HR manager had little time to spare and ignoring the usual protocol of arranging coffee, came straight to the point. "I've had a call from the BBC. They wish to interview a member of staff, preferably someone from senior managerial level, to gauge the horror of poor Robert Hamilton's murder."

"Oh," smiled the Director, already planning the phone call to his wife to warn her to record the news on the television. "I suppose that means me then, seen as I'm the duty man today." He caught the HR Manager's frown and eyebrows raised slowly asked, "Or not such a good idea, you think?"

The HR Manager hesitated before replying, his worried face indicating to the Director that something was playing on the HR Manager's mind and then replied, "As you say, perhaps not such a good idea, sir."

"And may I ask why not?"

Taking a deep breath, the HR Manager said, "As you already know from the police visiting the store today, it seems that poor Robert was the innocent victim of a murder, however," he sighed "they are not that certain." The HR Manager felt comfortable calling the deceased 'Robert', having prudently pulled Hamilton's personnel file to remind him from the file photograph, what the dead man looked like.

The Director hadn't gotten to his position ignoring sound advice and with a wave of his hand, bade the HR Manager continue.

"Pure guesswork on my part, of course sir, but let's imagine Robert was not the victim of a robbery. He was, according to the police, discovered dead in a lonely lane, in a quiet area of the city. What if Robert was there for some," he hesitated, but the steely gaze from the Director prompted him to continue, "what if he was there for some nocturnal purpose; to meet with a homosexual man or a female prostitute, perhaps. What if it's later discovered that he had a life of which we knew nothing about? If we, as the management give him a glowing report as a valuable member of staff, are we not in danger of publicly admitting that we employ such persons, such deviants within our store? Such an interview might and I stress again this is only conjecture, such an interview might return to bite us squarely on our arse."

The Director, a regular church-goer grimaced, not being used to such vulgarities and particularly in this hallowed room of the long established Dawson's, where decisions made for over eight decades had made the store the success it was. He slowly nodded and said, "What do you suggest?"

Inwardly breathing a sigh of relief, the HR manager suggested a more junior member of staff be presented for interview by the news team, one who actually knew and worked with Robert Hamilton and who could be passed off as a friend and colleague, rather than a representative of Dawson's. And should the cause of the murder later turn out not to be a street robbery as is suspected, but a scandalous issue, then a member of staff could easily later be denounced as not an official spoke person for the store. "If need be," the HR Manager briefly bit at his lower lip, "someone we can quietly… dismiss."

The Director contemplated the suggestion for a few seconds, then abruptly said, "Agreed, but if as you say, this isn't as straight forward as it initially seems, it might just be preferable if the interview were to be conducted off the premises, say outside in Buchanan Street. Can you arrange that and find someone, eh, suitable?"

The HR Manager smiled. "Consider it done, sir," he nodded.

Chapter 30 - Tuesday: mid-afternoon.

Dotty Turner heard Jinksie call her name from the front office and swallowing a mouthful of tea, hurried through to the Uniform Bar to ask why

he had shouted. Jinksie stood at his desk, the telephone held in his hand with the other clamped over the mouthpiece. "It's a McMillan nurse, calling to see if Lesley is in the office. You're her pal, can you take this?"
Dotty, teeth bared and her face livid at the wee man handing her what sounded to be bad news, snatched the phone from his hand. He listened shame-facedly and heard her explain who she was and that Constable Gold wasn't immediately available and can Dotty take a message? He watched her face turn pale as she grabbed at the pen and notepad on his desk and scribbled down a phone number, before replacing the phone in the cradle.
"That was one of the nurses who looks after Lesley's dad."
"Oh, is he ….?"
"No, not yet," she replied and then as if conscious of the harshness of her words, added, "God forgive me, I didn't mean it like that." She took a deep breath and continued, "Mister Gold took a relapse, a bad one it seems and might be on the edge. They didn't want to call Lesley on her mobile in case she was driving and the nurse asked that we get her to attend at her parent's house as soon as she can."
"Will I give her a call through the control room?"
"No, I think she might still be at Maryhill. I'll give the CID a call and try to find out where she is."

Gracie Fields sat in the dungeon or, as it was more formally known, the small claustrophobic cupboard titled the CCTV Research Room that accommodated those staff who were occasionally instructed to review the hundreds of hours of recording captured throughout the city centre in a twenty-four hour period. Data Protection legislation was firmly enforced regarding the length of time that non-evidential footage could be retained and thus, when a crime or offence was known or suspected to have been captured on film, the operators were almost immediately tasked with the onerous duty of wading through the hours of footage to first identify the incident and thereafter any likely involved persons.
The first fifteen minutes after Gracie arrived at Stewart Street office was spent in the company of the Senior Investigating Officer, who provided him with a summarised brief of Robert Hamilton's murder that included the approximate time and where the victim set off from Dawson's store to the approximate time and where he was discovered. Gracie was fortunate in the time parameters set by the SIO. The victim had been seen by the store security to depart the building at a specific time that set the first parameter. The second parameter was to be set at the time the two young women discovered the victim. With such a short window, Grace, who was completely familiar with the route the victim walked, was able to recognise the locations of the relevant static cameras that recorded the victim as he

moved between them. His first task would be to identify the victim walking between the sited cameras. That done, his second task and the more difficult of the two was to identify any individual who might be walking the same route behind, in front or accompanying the victim. Of course, Gracie was acutely aware that the culprit might already be waiting at the location of the scene of the crime for the victim. The murder hinged on this issue. Was the murder premeditated or random? Did the culprit lie in wait for the victim or was it simply a chance encounter? The fly in the ointment was that if indeed the murder was premeditated, then Gracie had no clue as to what time the killer might have arrived at the location or by what route. Marking all the times and camera sites on his notepad and considering that if the culprit had arrived earlier at the location, Gracie decided on a ripple effect; first examining the footage from the known cameras within the set times and victim's route then working outwards if need be. He allowed himself an extra one hour of recording for those cameras that surrounded the location of the murder. Setting his coffee mug down on the coaster at the monitor on the desk, he settled comfortably into the padded chair, took a deep breath and begun his laborious task.

Frederick Evans mother Eunice panted a little at the exertion of hurrying to the ringing phone. "Yes? Missus Evans speaking," she formally declared, then listened intently as her excited sounding son instructed her to record that evening's six-thirty Scottish BBC television news.
"Now mother, you know how to do it, don't you? You remember what I showed you, don't you?" he sounded anxious.
"Yes dear, of course I do, but what is it all about?"
"It's just …. Look, let me go over it one more time for you. You switch on the television to the BBC news then on the SKY remote control, there's a small button that has the letter R on it. Do you remember?"
"Of course I do, dear," she tolerantly replied, almost adding that she might be in her sixties, but she wasn't stupid or senile yet. Patiently she listened as Frederick reiterated the instructions, almost pleading that she didn't forget.
"But what is this all about?" she asked again.
"I'm to be on the news," he breathlessly announced. "I'm being interviewed by the BBC news. About a colleague that was," he hesitated, then said, "killed."
"Oh dear," she placed her free hand to her mouth, "the poor man. Did you know him Frederick?"
"Eh, yes, I knew him," he replied. "Have to go now mother. Please, please, don't forget, now, eh?" and hung up.
Eunice replaced the handset and stared curiously at it. Frederick was being interviewed on the evening news? Shaking her head, she returned to the front

lounge and settled herself back into the armchair to watch her favourite afternoon soap, paused at the point the phone had rung and smiled tolerantly. Frederick had less knowledge of how the television remote control worked than had his mother.

Across the city, Jenny Farndale was in her room, feeling a little guilty at deceiving her supervisor, a woman who liked and always looked out for the younger woman. Sitting on the bed, her shoes kicked off and with her back propped up against the pillows, her arms hugging her knees, she gently rocked back and forward as she considered her relationship with Frederick. Brief though it was, she had from the outset thought he was the one, the man who would marry her. She knew now she had been foolish, swept up in the initial rush of romance and bit at her lip as tears welled up in her eyes. Her adoration began when she thought he had saved her from the bully, but like it or lump it, she now accepted that he wanted her just for the sex. It was obvious, even to Jenny, that in sexual matters he was completely inexperienced. And she blushed at the memory of the things he had done to her and, to her embarrassment, she had foolishly allowed and encouraged. She savagely shook her head at her shame. All because she believed that Frederick liked her and she hoped that he might come to love her. She wiped away the spilled tears with the back of her hand and sniffing, continued to rock back and forth. She glanced about the room and saw the peeling wallpaper at the damp spot in the top of the corner of the wall, above the makeshift wardrobe that should have been dumped years before. That and the noise of children kicking a football in the street outside was a reminder of her background. She thought of the contrast between Frederick's neatly furnished, if slightly dated home in the quiet street of elderly neighbours and lovingly tended gardens against that of her own home of ramshackle furniture, of living in an area of poorly maintained council housing, the constant hubbub of noise that ranged from quarrelsome neighbour disputes to wildly driven screeching cars, drunken fights and littered streets. Frederick had been her opportunity to leave that behind, but was she willing to sacrifice her hopes and dreams? Could she forego those dreams, the love and attention she craved from a husband to becoming little more than a second class woman in a relationship with a man whose needs would always come first? And that, she grimly reminded herself, was in the assumption that Frederick intended marriage. She laughed without humour at her foolishness, as if anyone, even Frederick, would consider marrying a shapeless, pock-marked bugger like her. The sound of her mobile phone startled her and reaching across to the small night-stand, saw the incoming caller was Frederick. She briefly considered not answering, but resignedly pressed the green button and said, "Yes?"

"Jenny," he immediately answered and she thought he sounded out of breath, "I only have a minute. Look, watch tonight's news, the BBC at six-thirty. I'm on it. I'm being interviewed. Record it if you like and we'll maybe watch it together, okay? I'll call you later."
She hardly had time to respond and didn't get the opportunity to ask why he was on the news before he ended the call. She stared at the phone then it struck her. Frederick hadn't tried to contact her at work or he'd have known she wasn't there and didn't even take the time to ask why she had to return home early. Her shoulders sank and his lack of concern added even further to her misery.

Morris McDonald sat alone in his lounge while his brother Roderick collected some grocery items from the nearby supermarket. He had refused further alcohol, preferring instead to abstain 'till after he laid his Susan to rest. He found it difficult to believe and was slightly aggrieved with himself that though such a short time had passed since her death, he was already planning for his future. His brother Roderick without whom he would not have coped, God bless him, had tentatively suggested that Morris consider returning with him to Stornoway, perhaps even consider the purchase of a croft. "After all," Roddy had reminded him, "your service with the polis was almost at an end and there is no-one to keep you in Glasgow now. Wasn't Susan just like you wee brother? A woman, and a fine lady might I add, but whose small family has moved on and there is no close contact?"
"But I have you, big brother," Morris had smiled in return.
"Indeed you have," said the giant of a man as he slapped the smaller brother on the back, "and I'll be returning to the Isles, so I want you to think about coming with me. You will think about it, won't you wee brother? After all, how can I look after you if I'm so far away?" Roddy reminded Morris that the sale of the house and his police pension would allow him to live comfortably and without the need to be re-employed, unless of course he should chose to do so.
It occurred to Morris that having reached the age of fifty-one, he didn't really need looking after, but his brother meant well and he had no desire to disillusion Roddy and his well-placed intentions. Morris liked Glasgow and the access it had given Susan and him to the theatres, the museums. Strolling in summer and winter months through the open, well tended parks and the many picture houses where he indulged in one of his favourite pastimes, the films. He liked the people of Glasgow, their diversity and the range of west end restaurants that represented the different cultures the city embraced. It was with a saddening thought that he realised that Glasgow to Morris meant Susan, whose love for her native city transferred through the years to him. With a heavy sigh he sipped at his coffee and went over again in his head the

arrangements for Thursday. Susan had been fastidious in her attention to detail and like his wife would have done, Morris wanted everything to be just perfect.

The BBC crew arrived in their large, liveried van and with previously obtained council permission, parked on the pedestrian precinct in Buchanan Street, near to the front main doors of Dawson's. In a well-rehearsed routine the driver assisted the cameraman and soundman to unload the equipment while the outside broadcast producer, who doubled as the crew's liaison and contact crewman, entered the store to seek out the HR Manager. She found him just inside the front door, waiting there with a nervous, thin faced and equally thin-haired man whom he introduced as Mister Evans, the acting manager of the Gents Department who, he assured the producer, was a friend and colleague of the unfortunate Mister Hamilton. The HR Manager had just a few moments previously in the privacy of his office, worked on his outward show of sincerity and thought he did rather well. It pleased him even further that it suited the crew to conduct the interview in the bright outdoors of Buchanan Street precinct and in close proximity to their vehicle, not just for various technical reasons but also because, as the producer succinctly put it, "If we're right there, it keeps they wee thieving bastards from knocking stuff from the van when our backs are turned."
The decision made, the HR Manager inwardly decided that, minus the expletives of course, he would simply inform the director that after some strongly worded negotiation, he successfully denied the crew access to the store and thereby hoped to impress the director with his diligence.
While the producer spoke with the HR Manager and Frederick, the raven haired young reporter Julie stood at the shaky mirror hung inside the rear of the van, combed her long hair and made minor repairs to her makeup. Satisfied or as best she could be under the primitive conditions she found herself in, she practised her facial expressions, working her jaw, smiling and frowning, again smiling and frowning for a minute or so till at last she felt ready to conduct the interview. She read again the brief notes and suggested questions provided by the redoubtable Gloria and upon exiting the van waved to a couple of elderly wifies who stood and pointed in rapt amazement at "the young lassie that's aff the tele."
Now standing in the sunshine outside the main store doors, Frederick was extremely excited, brushing at imaginary threads on his suit jacket and patting down his hair. In truth, he just didn't know what to do with his hands and wouldn't dream of putting them in his trouser pockets like a working class lout. Standing nervously in front of the camera, he glanced uneasily at the soundman wearing headphones and balancing what seemed to be a fluffy furry thing on a long pole, almost directly over Frederick's head.

"Don't worry about that, pal," the soundman cheerfully called out, "it's just an extended microphone to pick up your responses to Julie's questions." Julie, arms folded, stood watching in the shade of the van, aware that passersby were nudging each other and smiling at the television reporter, some of whom were using camera-phones to snap pictures and she practised previous advice of not getting into eye contact with the public, but to concentrate on her subject. "Mister Evans," she extended a hand to Frederick and was slightly surprised by the limp handshake that was returned. Though she couldn't say why, it briefly occurred to her that he was gay. Close friend of the dead guy, she recalled the producer had told her. Did that mean then the dead guy, she glanced at her notes, might have been gay too? Could she suggest that question to this wimpy looking guy as a possible motive for the murder? Uncertainty ate at her and she wisely decided that issue perhaps was better researched before she got herself into a libellous situation.

The interview commenced with what Frederick heard was called a sound bite, though the phrase meant nothing to him. Slightly confused, he listened as the reporter Julie said a few nonsensical phrases at different pitch levels. The soundman appeared to be satisfied for he gave her the thumbs-up and then after a backward count of three Julie asked her questions.

The interview seemed to pass too quickly for Frederick. When he thought of it later, all he could recall was the microphone being held under his chin, the young smartly dressed and very good looking woman speaking with him and he spluttering and choking on his responses. He couldn't understand why the reporter needed to hold a microphone when the furry thing threatened to descend upon his head at any time.

He did recall his shock when some young hooligans made a ribald comment to the reporter as they passed by and he heard her response, telling them to, "Fuck off, you morons," then smile apologetically as she told the cameraman to edit that piece.

He recalled saying part of his speech that he had agreed with the HR Manager, that "Robert Hamilton was a man he considered a close friend," and "poor Robert's untimely death had shocked everyone at Dawson's," and also included "even though Robert had worked at Dawson's for just over one year, he had made his mark and would be sadly missed". His triumph was almost complete when he managed to fit in his own private and practised comment, a suggestion that he hoped the HR Manager would take note of. "We at Dawson's will of course continue our work in Robert's memory and I will strive to fill the shoes of a good man and fine manager."

As the crew wound up their equipment and he made his way back into the store, he couldn't help but notice the number of staff and customers who smiled and pointed as they watched from the doors and windows and his chest swelled with pride.

The HR Manager who stood unseen behind a display, watching through a lower ground plate glass window during the time the interview was conducted, slowly shook his head as Frederick re-entered the store.

Lesley Gold returned the supervisory patrol car to its bay and still slightly shocked that DI Miller had taken her suspicions seriously, made towards the back door. The door was opened before she got there by Dotty Turner, who stared at her younger colleague. Lesley was smiling and about to boast of her success at headquarters when she seen the look on Dotty's face and her stomach tightened. She thought her legs were about to fail her and stopped in her tracks. "What's happened, what's wrong?" she demanded, yet instinctively knowing that Dotty was the bearer of the worst kind of news. Dotty guessed what must be going through Lesley's thoughts and raising both her hands to quell Lesley's worst fears, replied, "It's bad, but he's still alive. I've spoken to the boss. He says you've to head straight home to your mum. Do you want me to drive you there, hen?" By now Dotty was stood beside Lesley, gently rubbing at her arms in a display of sisterly sympathy. "Eh, no, I'll be fine. Honest. Thanks," she replied. Her mouth suddenly felt very dry and she softly exhaled, the shock of the news, though always expected these past months, still taking her by surprise. "I'll get my gear off and head over there now. Thanks Dotty," she tried to smile, but couldn't, her body tense and shaking.

It took but a minute to dump her vest, belt and cap and grab her jacket and soon she was driving from the yard, her thoughts racing, though not of her father, but of her mother needing her. The evening rush was as usual particularly heavy and though she drove speedily, her progress was determined by the volume of traffic about her. After what seemed like an incredibly long time, she arrived at her parent's house and hurried to the door, to be met by the McMillan nurse who, just as Dotty Turner did almost forty minutes previously, held up a hand to calm the visibly distraught young woman.

"He's sleeping now, Lesley," she whispered as Lesley slipped past her into the narrow hallway. "I'm sorry to have called and worried you, but we really thought he was going this time. Anyway," she half smiled, "he's rallied a wee bit. Your mum's in there with him now. Give your mum a minute or two and then we'll get you in there, eh?" With a tenderness that almost reduced Lesley to tears, the portly woman reached up and gently stroked the younger woman's cheek. "Come away into the kitchen and I'll get you a cuppa, hen. If anybody can use one, you can," and ushered Lesley through the door.

In the bedroom, Peggy Gold gently held her unconscious husband's hand. She had heard the whispered conversation in the hallway and guessed Lesley had arrived and worried at her daughter's state of mind and the fright she must have got upon receiving what must have seemed to be the worst of news. Peggy was aware the McMillan nurse had also called several times and sent text messages to Peggy's younger daughter Linda, but so far Linda hadn't responded. Peggy wanted to believe that Linda had not received the message, but in her heart knew this was not true. Linda was never beyond reach of her mobile phone and the family joke was that it took precedence over the child, more so since she had taken on the role of dutiful wife at her husband Alex's golf club's women's committee. No, Peggy inwardly seethed and angrily believed that Linda just hadn't bothered returning the nurse's calls.

Lesley Gold hadn't been gone for long from DI Charlie Miller's office when he summoned Detective Sergeant Graeme 'Sugar' Smythe to his office and once the young DS was seated, commenced by relating the story brought to him by Constable Gold.
"So boss, what do you want from my team?"
"How many jobs do you have on at the minute Sugar?" he asked.
Smythe screwed his face as he thought and replied in a soft Irish accent, "Three, if you include that static job up in Glenburn Street. That's the number one priority at the minute."
"Remind me, Glenburn Street?"
"House two up in the tenement there. The postman saw some wires leading from the electric box that's located in the outside landing. The wiring is going into the house and he thought it suspicious enough to bring it to our attention. We thought it might just be a hooky connection, you know, theft of electricity. That's pretty popular round that area. But one of my guys contacted the Board and when they checked their meter readings, they got back to us that said there's an inordinate amount of electricity being used in the close. That's when we took a wee turn up there and well, we found the wires and the smell," he grinned.
"What do you mean the smell?" Miller asked, his face registering his curiosity.
"We think it's a cultivation plant in there, a cannabis farm. The close reeks of the stuff and it's far too strong a smell for a few personal use plants. The smell is that bloody strong I'm surprised half the tenants aren't dancing in the streets and preaching peace and love to the rest of the scheme. Didn't take us long to get the authority to put a static observation post across the way in an empty flat on the other side of the road."
"Didn't any of the tenants report the smell?"
Smythe grimaced. "You know what it's like up there boss. See no evil, hear no evil and tell the cops fuck all."
"How many guys do you need for the static Ob's then?"

Smythe thought briefly and replied, "Four; two on shift and two off. There are eight flats in the building and we're still trying to identify the comings and goings at the target flat. We know who most of the tenants are now and with the postman's help, know where they are located in the building. The registered tenant of the flat did a moonlit flit some months ago. Problems with a money-lender, we hear. We just don't know who he handed the keys to. And we're still trying to sort out the odd faces. The council were considering sending their enforcement team in because the social had lost contact with the tenant and consequently the rent wasn't getting paid, but I pulled in a favour and they're staying away till we get the issue resolved. Once we've got regular visitors to the close identified that we can dismiss as tenants, we'll hit the place when we know the people using the flat are inside."

"And that leaves you, how many?"

"Eddie the new guy is on annual leave and wee Susie is on maternity restricted duties, so that leaves eight and of course, that includes me."

"If your guys on Ob's call a strike, how will they handle it if you and the rest of the team are deployed elsewhere?"

Smythe pursed his lips and replied, "Shouldn't be a problem, boss. The guys aren't daft, they know to call the duty officer and I've already made arrangements for him to gather what uniform shift is on duty and they can hit it en masse. It might be a uniform arrest, but my team will get credit when I'm putting together the monthly synopsis for the Div Comm."

His eyes narrowed. "You think there might be something in this missing woman, that her man has done her in right enough?"

Miller shrugged his shoulders and sat forward. "I really don't know, Sugar, but the circumstances are too dodgy to ignore. Young Constable Gold sounds pretty certain that something's amiss. To be honest, it might be a load of shite, but let's look at it objectively. The husband reports his wife missing and there's no previous history of her having taken off. There's an assumption she is pregnant and he's just been dismissed from his job. The MP is apparently also on the brink of losing her job, so he's lost that income too. As well as that he's been running around with another woman for almost six months." He made a slight, almost imperceptible shake of his head.

"There's something about that young cops story that makes me think this guy Hardie isn't kosher. That's why I want you and your guys to take a look at him. According to Gold, Hardie isn't known to the police, so there's no reason to suspect he'll be anyway surveillance conscious."

"You know we're pretty busy here boss. How long do you want me to give this?"

"I know how busy your team is Sugar, but humour me, okay? Let's say you commence tomorrow morning and give it, what, two days? Just long enough to get his routine. I'll square it with the Divisional Commander. He owes me one anyway," he grinned, "we saved him a pile of overtime cash last week when we solved that murder double-quick time."

Smythe got to his feet and reached for the Missing Person file. "I'll have a read of this and draw up an operational plan. Two days only, you say."

"Well, three at the most," Miller grinned mischievously and then added, "By the way, young Lesley Gold is loaned to me for a few days, so I'd like you to include her in your team." He held up his hand to cut off Smythe's protest. "Nothing too fancy, just have her in one of the cars. Make her feel that she is involved, but don't put her in a position where she's actually out there doing surveillance. She just isn't trained for that. Besides," he shrugged his shoulders again as if by way of explanation, "it's her inquiry and I'd like her to know that we in the CID are here to help. If word gets out that we listen to our uniform colleagues, it might go some way to improving departmental relations round here. Savvy?"

"Savvy boss," Smythe wearily replied and then, almost as an afterthought, said, "Is she the cop that punched that loudmouth Duffy?"

Miller grinned and nodded.

Smythe returned his grin and left to draw up his plan.

The subject of the two detectives' discussion, Paul Hardie, had just showered and dressed in clean, but wrinkled clothing and boiled the kettle for coffee. His appetite had gone completely for though he hadn't eaten in over twenty-four hours, he didn't feel at all hungry. Taking his coffee through to the lounge, he sat in front of the plasma screen and switched it on, tuning to the Scottish Television channel and waited restlessly for a few moments for the evening six o'clock new bulletin. The radio news broadcasts had told him little, other than the police were investigating the discovery of a man's body, believed murdered. He knew from watching news bulletins through the years that unlike their southern neighbours; the Scottish Police gave very little information away unless they were seeking the public help and even then, the sour-faced bastards always had a copper sitting by the relatives of the victims, presumably to prevent the wrong thing being said and important information being divulged.

He watched dull-eyed as the studio bound reporter opened with a story from the Scottish Parliament and unconsciously sneered at the pettiness of local politics. The second item almost took him by surprise as the grave-faced anchorwoman revealed that earlier today the body of a man was discovered at the rear of the St Enoch Centre in Osborne Street, in Glasgow city centre. As Paul listened intently, the woman named his victim as Robert Hamilton, a fifty-eight year old departmental manager at Dawson's store in Buchanan Street. "Robert Hamilton," he softly whispered to himself, almost in

wonderment, the name sounding strange upon his lips as though the very saying of it could somehow conjure up a memory of what the man looked like. It had all happened so fast he just didn't get the opportunity to take in the man's face. The report finished without anything further and
He settled back, vainly trying to recall what the dead man, the man he murdered, looked like.
He switched the TV channel to the BBC and disinterestedly watched the end of the UK news. The Scottish BBC news, to his surprise, opened with the murder and he leaned forward as the anchorwoman led the story.
So engrossed was Paul thinking of what he had done that he didn't immediately realise that the screen had changed and now showed a younger woman standing holding a microphone, her face grim as she said, "…was employed within the Gents Department of Dawson's and worked here in Buchanan Precinct. I have standing here with me one of Mister Hamilton's colleagues, Frederick Evans. Mister Evans," the reporter turned towards a thin faced man in his late thirties or early forties, standing ill at ease, his eyes straining against the bright sunshine and his straggly hair slicked over to hide a balding pate. The camera panned across to encompass both the reporter and the man in the shot. "I understand you were a close friend and colleague of Mister Hamilton? You must be very shocked by the dreadful news."
"Indeed," he solemnly nodded as he agreed; his voice nervously pitched an octave higher than usual. "Robert was a dear man, very well liked and highly thought of among his colleagues here at Dawson's."
In the background, an incredulous Paul, his eyes wide and face frozen, listened to the faint sound of bagpipes being played in the background of the interview. But it was the man's voice as he continued to speak that caused Paul to react in shock.
It was a voice that Paul had heard before, a voice that he could not forget, a voice that daily filled his thoughts.
It was the voice of his tormentor.

Chapter 31 - Tuesday Evening.

Peggy Gold hugged her daughter, but insisted that Lesley go home. "Look love," she gently held her in her arms, "I now that you got a hell of a fright today. My God, didn't we both, but dad's still with us, at least for now. When," she swallowed hard, almost reluctant to say it, "when the time does arrive, there will be time enough to be together, but for now, you've got a job to do. I don't want you hanging about here like a bad smell," she smiled at her daughter, desperate to lighten the moment. "I'm sure you're bosses will give you the time off when you need it, but now is not that time, understand?"

Lesley could only nod, yet the guilt of leaving her mother again to cope with her ailing father persisted.
"But before you head off," her mother took her by the arm as she led her into the kitchen, "tell me about this date you had the other night."

The evening viewers of the STV news included Jenny Farndale, who watched in wonder at Fredrick's short performance on national television. Her brow creased with confusion. She couldn't remember having seen the man that was killed, probably because he didn't use the staff canteen, but she knew who he was only because now that she thought about it, she recalled Frederick moaning to her about his boss. That's what confused her. She didn't understand why Frederick would describe the man as his friend.
"He looks good on the TV, your boyfriend, doesn't he hen?" her mother, sitting on the opposite chair, broke into her thoughts. "The promotion he got at his work, does that mean he gets more money?" she then asked, her voice betraying her as she sighed with longing. Jenny's mother asked for nothing from her children but their time and didn't get much of that. A daughter who six years previously had gone through a civil wedding ceremony in London and called to say she was married and staying down there and who made the occasional phone call home to whine about her life. A son who immigrated in his teens to New Zealand and married over there and who now had his own family and seemed happy to forget his Glasgow roots. A second son with a criminal record for thievery and drug abuse and was now banned from his mother's house.
Jenny had long ago accepted that it fell to her to make her mother's one ambition come true; to have at least one child on whom she could rely to permit her to perform the one role she most desired, to be the Mother of the Bride. No pressure then, she inwardly sighed.
"He might be the one then, hen?" her mother asked, her eyes wide and curious.
"Aye, I suppose so," Jenny automatically answered, half listening and distracted as to why Frederick would say such a thing, because it wasn't true. The more she thought about it, the more she remembered. Frederick just didn't like his boss, he hated him. So why would he say he was Mister Hamilton's friend?
But Jenny knew why. In her heart, she had always known. Frederick simply said what suited Frederick and if it suited him to call Robert Hamilton 'friend', then that's what he would say, just as it suited him to call her 'girlfriend' when she knew, had always known, that it also wasn't true. She stared intently at the screen as the news programme continued, afraid that her mother would see the tears that welled up and threatened to engulf her.

Feigning a coughing fit gave her the excuse to rise from her chair and leave the room. She hurried upstairs and with a sob, threw herself onto her bed.

Dotty Turner arrived home to the tantalising aroma of cooked food, the meal bubbling away nicely in the slow cooker, the table set and her two kids in their own bedroom's. Her daughter was diligently studying and her son pretending to study, but instead was speaking softly on Skype to his new, dark-haired girlfriend and blissfully unaware that his mother had peeked her head into his room, smiled and gently closed the door. Downstairs, she hugged her parents, thanked her mother for preparing the dinner and waved cheerio as they drove off. In the privacy of her bedroom, she stripped off her police issue polo shirt and kicked the cargo pants towards the laundry basket. Her underwear and navy blue socks followed the pants into the wicker basket. Deciding on a relaxing bath before putting the dinner on the table for the kids, she turned on the taps in the en suite. Naked now, but for a huge, pink bath towel wrapped around her, Dotty run a hand in the water to test the temperature of the drawn bath. Too hot, she thought and while it cooled, thought about texting Lesley Gold, just to check on how her new pal was doing. The brief message sent she sat on the edge of her bed and thought again of Morris McDonald, wondering how he was faring with the ceremony so close on Thursday. Her mobile phone in her hand, she had a strong urge to call him, but resisted the temptation and bad-temperedly threw the phone onto the bed. Dotty flopped backwards onto the mattress and closing her eyes, lay for several minutes, her mind blank and enjoying the sense of nothingness, an almost weightless sensation of being totally at peace, the quiet of the house permitting her to imagine being single again with no responsibilities, no need to get up and feed the kids, but to just lie there and slowly breathe in and out, in and out, in and out.
The moment passed when her daughter shouted, "Mum, when's dinner ready?"
She smiled at the call and realised with a certainty that even if no man ever again entered her life or her bed, she would never be truly alone.

Frederick was eager to get home and fervently prayed that his dim-witted mother had remembered to record the interview. Stepping from the bus, he quickly made his way home and almost ran the final few yards to his gate. He fumbled impatiently with the front lock and pushing the door open, ignored his mother's cheery greeting as he hurried into the lounge. He saw with relief that though the television was switched off, the light on the SKY box beneath the set indicated the set was recording. A panicked thought crossed his mind that his mother was recording the wrong channel, but switching the television on he saw that yes, she had did exactly as he had instructed.

"Would you like your dinner on a tray, dear?" said his mother's voice from the doorway, slightly miffed that her son had completely passed her by when he arrived home.

"Ah, yes please," he replied, distracted as he operated the television control and settled into the comfy chair facing the set.

With his mother in the kitchen preparing his meal, Frederick literally drooled over his brief television appearance but to his surprise, the interview cut short before his final, practised comment and no-one heard his promise to strive to fill Robert Hamilton's shoes. Suddenly enraged, he felt a sense of betrayal and his hands clenched into fists. He cursed loudly, using expletives that he had only ever practised when in bed with Jenny. His mother, hearing the bad language, hurried through to the lounge, her face white with shock.

"Frederick!" she called out loudly.

He turned towards her, his face contorted with anger and for a heartbeat as she stared at her son, Eunice Evans felt afraid; a vivid and horrid memory of her husband's evil temper sweeping before her eyes.

As suddenly as he had erupted, Frederick calmed and sitting back in his chair, said "Sorry mother. The interview, it wasn't as I had planned."

Eunice cautiously approached and with a tentative hand, gently stroked at his shoulder and replied, "I saw it live, Frederick. I thought you did very well, under the circumstances. Losing your friend in such a horrible way, I mean."

"My friend?" he stared back at her in surprise. "Oh, you mean Hamilton. Yes well, I suppose so," he added.

Lesley Gold arrived home, a little calmer but still felt guilty at leaving her mother at this worrying time. She switched on the kettle and fetched the ringing mobile from her jacket pocket. "Hello?"

"Hi Lesley," said Andy Carmichael, "thought I'd give you a wee call. See how you're doing."

She couldn't know that it had taken Andy a full ten minutes to pluck up the nerve to phone her. The last thing he wanted was to come across as being too intense.

"Andy," she breathlessly replied, "nice to hear from you. How's Evie?"

The question took him by surprise, but pleased him. "She's great, toe-rag that she is. I had her at the swimming this afternoon. She gets formal lessons once a week, but the wee bugger was thrown out of the pool by the instructor for jumping in when she should have been listening. Can you believe it? Five years of age and already red-carded."

Lesley laughed and asked how Evie took the ban.

"She wasn't fazed at all. It was me, as we say in Glasgow, that was black affronted. So," he continued, "how's your father doing?"

"Ah, he took a turn today. We thought we had lost him," she said, her voice almost breaking.

Andy sensed the hesitation and said, "I'm guessing things are not going that well, then?"

She felt the tears prick at her eyes then roll down her cheeks and bit her lip, unable to reply. The fright and tension following the news she had received earlier in the day was kicking in and she felt weak, an emotional wreck. All she wanted was to curl up into a ball and weep.

He heard her take a deep breath as she tried to control her emotions and said, "Look, my sis's got the wee one this evening. I know you live in Crathie Drive. What's the number there? I'll jump a taxi and come up. I'll make the tea and hold your hand, if you like. Trust me, I'm a postman."

She laughed through her tears and sensed he was being kind, that he had no intention of taking advantage and took a deep breath. "Number fourteen, flat three," she finally gasped, her voice quivering.

"I won't be long," he replied and cut the connection.

He was true to his word and arrived within fifteen minutes. Casually dressed in a brown cord jacket, bottle green polo shirt, dark brown chino's and wearing brown brogues, he pressed the outside buzzer and stood back from the main door to allow her to see him from the window. She had washed her face, brushed her hair and changed from her uniform into a fresh, lemon coloured sweater and pale yellow coloured knee length skirt. She tried to smile, tried not to cry, but the sight of him at her door caused her to blink rapidly and she burst into tears.

It felt natural when he held her close to calm her as she sobbed against his shoulder. He gently stroked the back of her head and soothed her with soft words. The moment passed and she relaxed, then with a trembling lip and a soft smile, looked up at him and said, "Maybe we should close the door."

Paul Hardie was breathing rapidly and so excited that his hands were now shaking. He re-run the news item again and again, listening intently to the voice of the man whose name he read on the ribbon beside the BBC logo. 'Frederick Evans, Co-worker and Friend', it read. He glanced at the notes he held in his hand, the notes he had scribbled down after his tormentor's phone call and read 'well-spoken, polite voice' and 'a little high-pitched'. He had marked a question mark against the word 'condescending'. For the man's age he had scribbled anything between thirty and fifty and glanced again at the paused screen. Yes, he hadn't been far wrong with the age, maybe about forty, he thought. Pressing the button that allowed the interview to continue, he turned up the sound and listening intently, heard the faint strain of bagpipes being played in the man's background. His notes read that when his tormentor had last called, he thought he had heard a busker playing nearby,

with a question mark against the notation and had also written, perhaps in the city centre. He smiled without humour at the television and used the control to pause the interview as the camera zoomed in on the face of Frederick Evans, who was in mid-speech. Paul leaned forward and with his fingertips, traced Evans face on the screen. In his mind, there was no doubt.
"Got you, you bastard," he venomously said through gritted teeth.

"Jenny, did you see the news? Did you see me being interviewed?"
Jenny swallowed hard and holding the mobile phone tightly to her ear, softly answered in a monotone voice, "Yes, Frederick. I watched the news."
His excitement was such that he did not notice her dull reply and continued to relate the interview, his account differing from what she had seen; he describing himself as confident and assured while she recalled his nervous responses to the reporter's questions.
"So," he confidently breezed, his voice lowered in innuendo, "fancy coming over tonight and we'll, eh, celebrate?"
His schoolboy invite suddenly disgusted her and her hesitation must have confused him, for he then asked, "Jenny, are you there?"
"No, Frederick, I mean, yes, I'm here, but no, I can't come over tonight." She wanted to ask him, to scream at him, why did you say Robert Hamilton was your friend? Why don't you ask how I am, why I left work early to come home? Why don't you treat me as an equal? Why do you use me then treat me as though you're ashamed to be seen with me? Her courage again failed her and she lied; the easy option.
"Not tonight Frederick, I have my, eh, you know, woman's thing, you know?"
Frederick really didn't know about 'women's thing' and recoiled in disgust when he recalled it meant some kind of bleeding. Better to let her get it over with before he has her back over to his house, he decided, then said, "Yes, yes, of course. Perhaps you can phone me when you're, ah, finished. It's about a week, isn't it?"
A week, she inwardly raged, her knuckles whitening as she clutched at the phone. I'm no fucking use to him for a week. She took a deep breath and forced herself to be calm, then replied, "Yes Frederick, about a week. Goodbye."
She pressed the end button and dropped the phone onto the bed beside her, too upset even for tears.

Chapter 32 - Wednesday Morning.

Lesley Gold woke before the alarm activated and fumbling at the switch, saw the digital clock read five am. She lay back and deciding to forego her usual morning run, pressed her hands against the sides of her head and thought of Andy, embarrassed that she had broken down like that in front of him and wondering what he must think of her. He had stayed till almost midnight, making her tea and toast and sitting with her while she rambled on. She blushed at the memory of things she had confided. She had sobbed like a baby, snotters and all and through her tears admitted that having accepted her father was going to die she constantly was worried sick about her mother. She blushed again with shame when she recalled her mood changing from anguish to anger and going off on one about Linda; that she determined to have it out with her sister later the next day, after she finished work. Andy had listened patiently, at first without comment, and tactfully suggested that she might consider making use of her police training, dealing with her sister in a calm and professional manner as though Linda was a witness or someone like that. "Then, if you start off reasonably, you can be more forceful if you feel the need to be. However, start off with all guns blazing and you've nowhere to turn to and it's difficult to come back down from that height. Confrontation isn't a starter; it's always the last resort."

His reassuring presence and common sense had finally calmed her and she accepted the wisdom of his advice, promising him that no, she wouldn't tear her sister a new one, that she would not even contact her, but concentrate on helping her mother through this difficult time of their lives. "After all," Andy had added, "it's your sister's loss if she doesn't contribute at this time in your parent's life, something she'll need to go through regretting for the rest of her life."

Privately, Lesley didn't believe Linda would be regretful about anything that didn't immediately impact on her own social and domestic circumstances, but didn't want to argue with Andy. He'll learn soon enough, she thought and then inwardly startled. She was already thinking of him as a permanent feature in her own life.

"And I'll be here to help you, if you need me," he had said, holding her close as together they sat on the couch in her lounge. At the door as he left, they embraced and he kissed her and she realised that part of her didn't want him to leave. The awkwardness of the moment passed and making excuses they half laughed as they joked about their respective early rises for work, the next morning.

She had hurried to the window and waved as he climbed into the taxi, feeling a little foolish, like a teenager ending thier first date.

Now, the day had dawned, she no longer felt the shadow of darkness and despair and rising, remembered that she wasn't on duty at Garscadden, but was to travel to accompany the Divisional Surveillance Team at Maryhill on their new operation, targeting Paul Hardie.

Paul Hardie had experienced another sleepless night. Try as he might, he could not erase the memory, even for a short time, of the face that haunted him, the face of the man on the television, Frederick Evans. Through the dark hours he planned his encounter with Evans, imagining a hundred ways that he would make the bastard pay for ruining his life. In his tired and confused state of mind, Paul accepted no responsibility for the way things had turned out; even the death of Fiona, he now settled at Evans door. He wandered into the kitchen, muttering to himself about the revenge he would plan for Evans, the stress of the previous week, the lack of sleep and nourishing food all taking its toll on both his physical health and mental well-being. He stared at the wooden knife block on the worktop, at the empty slot where the boning knife should rest and remembered; the knife was gone, bloodied and abandoned. But there were other knives in the block, he wickedly grinned, enough to deal with Mister fucking Evans. He arched his back and stretched his neck, the tiredness overtaking his aching muscles and in a moment of rationality, realised he needed to sleep, even if only for a few hours, that if he was going after Evans, he had to be alert. He turned and went through the door and headed for the bedroom. The very idea of sleep was already working its magic and wearily, he climbed the stairs to the bedroom.

Stewart Street police office was coming alive as the nightshift bade first good morning and then, after the handover, cheerio to the incoming early shift. Among the early starts was Gracie Fields who grabbing a coffee, made his way back into the 'Dungeon', settling himself into his chair and yawning as he switched on the DVD player and monitor. While the machines fired up, he settled back to study his notes from the previous day, cross referencing the details and descriptions of the male and female pedestrians who had in some way or another caused him to be suspicious. The tentative list numbered almost two dozen, but throughout yesterday's shift, he was unable to associate any of the individuals directly with the murder or indirectly near to the location of the crime. In his mind he was confident that once he had gone over the list and watched each of the individuals again, he would narrow and likely discount most if not all of them.
A collateral success of Gracie's retrospective and detailed observation of dozens of recorded hours identified a male and female partnership that had been sought for mugging young women in the city centre. While this was a minor coup and would result in the known pair later being arrested, the timing of their street robbery placed them some distance from the murder locus and ironically provided them with an indisputable alibi that they were committing a crime elsewhere.
It was twenty minutes later that Gracie's eyes narrowed as he watched the fifteenth number on his list. That peculiar, unaccountable feeling he

occasionally experienced again tickled at the back of his neck. He stopped playing the DVD, wound it back a few minutes and leaned forward to peer at the monitor, seeing the figure that hurried underneath the CCTV camera located on the north side of Argyle Street near to the Radisson Hotel. The camera's arc was relatively wide and mounted on a lamp-post covering the junction of Argyle Street and York Street. The figure seemed to be a man wearing a short coat who hurried, but within a short distance looked twice over his shoulder as though fearing pursuit. Gracie knew it wasn't uncommon for punters walking the city centre streets late at night to be a little anxious, but something in the man's gait seemed odd. He knew from the camera's positioning it was a fixed camera and guessed the man's behaviour had been missed because the duty operator Marie had likely concentrated her attention on manoeuvring the zoom cameras that scanned the clubs and pubs that abounded the Sauchiehall Street area. Marie was well known by her colleagues to favour this area late at night, making no secret of her desire to catch some unsuspecting celebrity, out of their face with drink or drugs, being flung out of a pub or club or caught in some compromising situation. Gracie had his own view on her indiscreet voyeur issues and heard a whisper that management were ready and waiting for the opportunity to dump her. As he watched the recording, the man turned into York Street and almost immediately stopped, looked about him and then for no more than a second or two with his back to the camera, stooped at the side of the road and was again quickly on his way walking south in York Street. Uncommonly for him, Gracie swore under his breath, frustrated that there were no CCTV cameras located further down York Street to follow the man's route and no cameras sited where the street exited at the junction with the Broomielaw. But the man's behaviour when he stooped puzzled Gracie. The operator regretted he hadn't the use of the camera at the time the man stooped, but was now merely watching a recording. Time and time again he rewound the recording and watched the same few seconds till at last he was convinced. The man had dropped something at the side of the road and Gracie's guess was that whatever was dropped went down a drain. Unconsciously smiling at this small success, he reached for the phone and dialled the murder inquiry SIO's internal number at the incident room.

"Boss, its Gracie here" he was smiling in anticipation. "I wonder if I might ask you to pop down to the Dungeon for a minute."

Tony the van man, sitting in the darkness of the battered, scraped and dented white coloured Transit peered along the road to where the grey coloured Focus was parked outside the mid-terraced house at number nineteen. The Focus was faced towards the rear of the van, parked fifty metres from it and giving him a clear and unobstructed view of both the car and the front door.

With patience he waited, feeling bloated and regretting the late night curry and two cans of lager from last night's dinner. He sipped at the coffee from the flask and sighed, debating with himself whether or not to tackle the ham sandwiches his wife had prepared or keep them till later. It was a decision every surveillance officer faced; wolf the food down and run the risk of the target suddenly appearing to spoil the enjoyment of the grub or waiting and hoping the target settled down somewhere for an hour or two. His grumbling stomach won the argument and with a "Bugger it", unwrapped the tinfoil. As he chewed he maintained his vigil on the house's front door. He had no concern about the target departing via the rear lane, aware that Jan, a fellow team member, was sat there with the young lassie that had previously dealt with the targe,t in an unmarked vehicle covering the lane's exit and who could identify him, if he took off on foot. Though he had no photo of the target, Tony's was the easy task. Any guy fitting the physical description getting into and driving off in the Focus was presumably going to be the target. During Sugar's briefing earlier that morning, the operational order had been clear. The next two days, three at the most was a baby-sitting job, follow, observe and record only. The target, this Paul Hardie was a suspect only, not a career criminal and was unlikely to cause the team any surveillance problems, but that didn't mean they could relax. Sugar, to the team's embarrassment, had reminded them of the recent fiasco when in two separate incidents in one day, the previous week they had been burned by two members of a local drug team. "We weren't so much burned as scorched to a fucking cinder," he had scornfully said and suggested the team use the two days as a training exercise, but with the advantage of having the use of a live target. Tony licked his fingers and screwing the cup back onto the lid of the flask, screwed his face tight as he noisily farted and sighing with relief, settled down to watch for the target.

Frederick Evans arrived early for work, a small yellow carnation plucked from his mother's flower bed in his jacket lapel. He had given it much thought and was of the opinion that if he demonstrated his eagerness and willingness to be first to arrive each morning, such loyalty and enthusiasm would soon be recognised by the management and his status as temporary Departmental Manager might be that bit closer to the position being made permanent.
With a cheery wave and good morning to the departing night cleaning staff, he clocked in and made his way to the first floor. The predominantly Polish women glanced at each other in surprise, wondering if the skinny little man with the bad attitude and who usually ignored them had been given a personality transplant. Shaking their heads and muttering between themselves

at the unusual behaviour of the idiot weirdo, the women clocked off and went wearily home.

Frederick entered the Gents Department and with anticipation, rubbed his hands together. The staff, his staff, he smiled again, were not due to commence work for another fifteen minutes and that, he was certain, would give him plenty of time to clear all of Robert Hamilton's little knick-knacks from the desk in the office. Reaching below a counter he collected two empty shoes boxes and in the office, set about his task. Once that was done he opened the plastic bag he had brought with him and laid out the new stationary items he had purchased from the newsagents shop near to the Central Railway Station. Satisfied, he slowly sat in the chair, hands flat on the desk and savouring the moment, sighed with contentment. His thoughts turned to Paul Hardie. He had promised Hardie that once Robert Hamilton had been dealt with, as he so effectively had been, that Frederick would destroy the DVD and Hardie need never fear hearing from him again. But, he inwardly smiled, that had been before Frederick realised how valuable a commodity Mister Hardie had proven to be. He sat back in the chair, his fingers making an arch as he contemplated what other tasks Hardie might be persuaded to complete that would further Frederick's ambition. Glancing about him, it occurred to him that the position of manager of the Gents Department might suit him for a while, but when he proved his worth to his senior management, when they finally recognised Frederick for the brilliant and insightful man he knew himself to be, perhaps other opportunities might become available if certain senior staff should also meet with unfortunate accidents.

Lesley Gold, hair tied back and wearing jeans, hiking boots and navy coloured sweater and with a light black nylon anorak folded in her bag, sat in the passenger seat of the unmarked Renault saloon with the female driver. The woman called Janet or Jan for short was roughly about Lesley's age and, from her accent, Lesley guessed she originated from Fife or somewhere on the east coast, that seemed to be confirmed by her habitual use of the exclamation "eh?" at the end of her sentences. Jan wasn't previously known to her, other than by reputation and from what little she had heard, Jan was dour and not given to social niceties. It probably didn't help that Lesley had once heard some of her male colleagues describe Jan as having a face like a stuntman's knees. The drive over from Maryhill to their location had been made in uncomfortable silence. Lesley had been instructed by DS Smythe to accompany Jan to monitor the lane at the rear of 19 Borden Road in the unlikely event the target, Paul Hardie left on foot. As the only officer in the team who could positively identify Hardie, Smythe with some reluctance

agreed her presence on the 'plot', but with the strict instruction she did not leave the vehicle for fear her lack of training compromised the operation.
Jan pressed the switch to lower the driver's window and bringing a carton of cigarettes from her bag, said "Mind if I smoke?" the comment being the first she actually acknowledged Lesley being in the vehicle. Without waiting for a reply, Jan stuck a cancer nail in her mouth and lit it. Lesley took the question to be a statement of intent rather than a request and merely shook her head, acutely aware she was the spare part in the bridal honeymoon suite.
"So, what's your story," asked Jan, blowing smoke through the partially open window and turning in the seat to face Lesley.
"What do you mean?"
"You're the cop that busted Mike Duffy in the mouth, aren't you?"
Once more Lesley shook her head and thought, here we go again. It would be a long time before anyone forgot that story, if ever. She sighed and simply said in reply, "His nose, actually. I was going out with him, he fucked about with another woman and I smacked him one. End of."
Jan pursed her lips and with sisterly accord, nodded. "Good for you, hen, eh," she responded and turned to blow more smoke through the window.
The ice broke, or as near as damn broke, Lesley asked, "DS Smythe, how did he get the name Sugar?"
Jan chuckled, and flicked dropped ash from the front of her blouse and shrugged to make her back more comfortable in the driver's seat. "Well, therein lies a story," she continued to grin. "You'll likely noticed he's not a bad looking guy and young looking too, as well as being full of it, the Irish blarney I mean. Apparently a few years back, before I knew him anyway, when he was a DC at Baird Street CID he got a successful result to a housebreaking inquiry and recovered some family heirlooms for a middle-aged woman, a spinster so the story goes, eh? Seems the woman was very grateful and she became besotted with him and constantly called and visited the office to see him. The rumour was he ended up riding her, but never admitted to it, eh? Anyway, the old bird kept bringing him sweets and cakes, using any excuse to be near him, called him her 'Wee Sweet Man', so the office dubbed him Sugar, you know, sweet? From what I heard, the only one that didn't get the joke at first was Sugar himself. Anyway, the name stuck and he's been Sugar ever since, eh?"
As she finished, Lesley saw Jan's eyes narrow and reaching to press a button on the steering wheel said, "Four-one-nine, roger," then turned to Lesley and pointed to the small, flesh coloured hearing aid in her ear. "That was Tony in the van. No change at the house."

Frederick was the talk of the store. His Warhol 'fifteen minutes of fame' resulting from his brief appearance on the national news overtook the gossip of Robert Hamilton's murder and wherever Frederick went, staff pointed and nudged each other as he passed, some nodding and keen to be noticed by the stores very own celebrity. Acutely aware of his new found status, with uncommon graciousness he joked with and slapped his male staff on the back, commented on how lovely the ladies were looking and for that morning, was the very epitome of junior management. Customers, aware from the media reporting of the murder of a Dawson's staff member, were shocked to discover that the victim was the former Departmental Manager, but consoled by staff who eagerly pointed out the temporary manager as the man who had appeared on national television. A few customers used the death of Robert Hamilton as an excuse to converse with the minor celebrity that was Frederick, such conversation providing those customers with an item of gossip to later share with their cronies. On behalf of Dawson's, Frederick accepted the condolences with solemn and respectful thanks, but wished the HR Manager was present to witness how well the temporary manager represented the store at this troubled time. As if by magic, he turned from shaking an elderly woman's hand to find the HR Manager standing behind him. With a tight smile, the manager beckoned Frederick follow him to the small office. When both were closeted behind the closed door, he informed Frederick that in the interim, Fredrick would continue to act as temporary departmental manager until an appropriate time had passed when the position would, as company rules dictated, be publicly advertised.

Frederick was aghast and his face turned chalk-white, having presumed the position would naturally fall to him as senior salesman and as first choice for temporary manager.

"It doesn't quite work that way, Mister Evans," the HR Manager smoothly said, unaccountably enjoying the skinny wee bugger's discomfort, "as a long serving employee you will naturally be aware that we at Dawson's only wish the best of the best and hence we will seek the best qualified for the position." To soothe Fredrick's hurt feelings, the HR Manager sighed as he added "You of course have every right to apply for the position, just like everyone else and we will, of course, take into consideration your current role. However in the meantime we can't have a rudderless ship, can we, so in the interim you will continue to act as temporary manager."

Frederick swallowed hard. His whole being wanted to shout and scream at the man, at the unfairness of it all, but he simply asked "How long before you advertise?"

"I should think some time within the next four weeks. We can't after all be seen to be heartless," the man half laughed, "I mean, with poor Robert not yet buried, can we?"

After the HR Manager left, Frederick sat down heavily in the chair, his face still pale and his knees shaking. After all he had done, all he had planned, all he had hoped for, now this. Tears welled in his eyes and his body shook. He savagely shook his head. I will not cry, he decided as he clenched his fists tightly. I will not cry. His anguished despair turned to hatred and the focus of that new hatred was the HR Manager, the bearer of the bad news. In an instant, the HR Manager was transformed from Frederick's route to promotion to the obstacle that denied him his rightful position in the store. But obstacles had been dealt with before, he gritted his teeth and that thought led him to again consider Paul Hardie.

Across the city, Tony in the now fetid smelling rear interior of the van, worked hard at staying awake. There had been no movement to report from the house at number nineteen other than what seemed to be a postal delivery, Due to the way the houses in the street bevelled in a soft arc rather than a straight run, he could see the front door and just make out the house windows, but not if the curtains were open or closed. He was about to consider requesting a team member perform a walk-past to check the curtains when a man suddenly appeared from the door, turning to lock it behind him. Startled from his thoughts, he depressed the microphone button and softly said, "Standby, standby, male exiting the property. Tall, maybe about five ten to six feet, fair hair, not too long, wearing a what looks like a black leather jerkin type jacket, dark trousers, probably jeans. Standby, that's the male now getting into the target vehicle driving seat, standby. The vehicle now off, off and towards me," his voice raised a pitch as he spoke. He then said, "Convoy?" as he sought confirmation that the team had heard his broadcast. In numerical order, the four cars including Lesley and Jan's vehicle, acknowledged the broadcast. The surveillance car, strategically situated in Chamberlain Road, was the first to sight the target vehicle and smoothly turned to follow when the vehicle drove south towards the junction at Southbrae Drive. As the follow continued, radio traffic was kept to a minimum with the double-manned eyeball car continuing the commentary. During a break in the eyeball driver's transmission, and contrary to the previous instruction about Lesley getting out of Jan's car, Sugar Smythe ordered that at the first opportunity Jan was to get Lesley into a position to positively identify the driver as the target, Paul Hardie. Jan acknowledged the instruction and turning to Lesley, said, "If we get out of the car, follow my lead. Don't get out of my sight. I'm wearing a radio harness, you're not, so stay close and watch me at all times, savvy?"
Lesley, caught up in the excitement of the follow, nodded, her mouth dry and her body tense, a thousand questions racing through her head. All other thoughts were forgotten as she listened to the commentary, concentrating on the unhurried voices that emitted from the speaker hidden under the front dashboard. As the convoy turned onto Crow Road, the lead vehicle turned off

into an adjoining street to permit the back-up vehicle to take the eyeball position. Intent on her driving, Lesley saw Jan deliberately drive their vehicle to be caught behind a slow moving bus. "Don't want to get too close now, do we," she turned to grin at Lesley.
"I thought I was to identify if it was Paul Hardie?"
"Yeah, I know, but we'll do that when he's exited the target vehicle. I'm not going to drive alongside him so you can get a look, am I? Remember, hen, he's seen you too so the last thing we need is a show-out, eh?"
As they drove eastwards, gradually approaching the city centre, Lesley's mobile phone activated. Glancing at the screen, she didn't recognise the calling number and a shiver of apprehension went through her.
"Hello?"
"Lesley, its Sugar. Have you any idea where he might be headed?"
"No, none at all other than the only thing I can think of is his office is located in St Vincent Street. I can only guess he might be visiting there, but I know he was sacked so whether or not he intends going to see his former girlfriend or he has some other business, to be honest, I really don't know."
"Okay, the office and his bird. If nothing else, that's worth bearing in mind. We'll see how it goes," and without a further word, concluded the call.
Almost immediately she heard Sugar on the radio asking permission to break-in to the eyeball's commentary. The permission granted, he reminded the other three cars that Hardie worked in St Vincent Street and that might be a possible destination.
By now, the target vehicle was being driven eastwards on the Clydeside Expressway and another change of eyeball car indicated from the commentary that Sugar was driving. As his soft, Irish brogue relayed the target vehicles speed and location, it seemed even to Lesley that Hardie was unaware he was being followed. She risked a question to Jan.
"What happens if he stops, to park I mean?"
Jan skilfully manoeuvred the surveillance car round an old, small and heavily loaded flatbed truck that seemed ready to discharge its untidily laden cargo of junk onto the highway, before answering. "We all find somewhere to park up and get the footmen out as soon as possible. If the target exits and moves away from the car, they'll take him on and we sort the cars out into positions where we can sit and watch the target vehicle, though it need not always be in line of sight. What I mean is we get ourselves into a position we can take it on if he moves off again, regardless of which direction, savvy?"
"Yeah, I get that," replied Lesley. She surprised herself at how exciting she found the surveillance follow and wished that Jan would somehow or other, manoeuvre their car into a position to take on the target vehicle.
As the convoy progressed towards the city centre, it seemed that Hardie had no intention of visiting his former office. For one, heart stopping moment,

Lesley thought the convoy was compromised when the soft voice of the driver of the eyeball car related that he was sitting behind the target vehicle at a red light in Renfield Street, but then they were off again and she listened as the target vehicle first went through the lights into Union Street junction then turned left into Argyle Street.

"Fucking coffin dodgers," swore Jan when two elderly women, seemingly oblivious to the traffic, suddenly waved to a friend across the busy road and without regard to their safety, shuffled into the road in front of their car, causing her to sharply slam on her brakes, then she turned and broke into a grin. "They must be worth at least forty points," she laughed.

"It's a left, left, left into Mitchell Street, that's Mitchell Street West I mean," the eyeball man corrected himself as he shouted across the radio, then added more sedately, "Footman out."

Jan, still driving in Union Street, drove through the just turned red light at the Argyle Street junction, ignoring the angry sounding horn and two fingered salute from an irate bus driver. "Right, look for somewhere to dump this," she told Lesley.

Lesley was confused, but being relatively familiar with the area, realised that Hardie had nowhere to drive from the narrow lane, that the only place accessed from the narrow street, that was really no more than a wide lane where he had driven, would be the Mitchell Street Car Park. "He's going to park the car," she burst out.

"You think so, Sherlock?" replied Jan, her voice oozing the sarcasm she was noted for. She drove the surveillance car the short distance in Jamaica Street into Howard Street and turned into the multi-storey car park there. Through the barrier, she stopped in an empty bay and switched off the engine.

A slightly chastened Lesley decided to keep her mouth shut and listened as Sugar deployed the footmen to converge with the eyeball car footman and requested an update as soon as possible. Then he said, "Four-one-nine, take your pal to where the target can be seen. We still need confirmation."

Jan acknowledged the instruction and unclipping her seat belt, turned to Lesley and said, "Okay, hen. You're on."

Paul Hardie didn't know what his next move would be. All he did know was that he wanted to see his tormentor, this man Evans and he would play it by ear from then. What was certain in his mind was that Evans would suffer; that he would pay for all that he had done, for causing him to kill Fiona, for Paul losing his job and Janice leaving him. And for the dead man too. In his fragile state of mind, Evans was the cause of all his misery, all his woes. As he made his way from the car park towards Buchanan Street, the casually dressed man wearing the baseball cap and carrying the small rucksack on his back, kept pace five metres behind Paul through the busy Mitchell Lane, all the while whispering into the covert microphone attached to his shirt lapel.

In the Gents Department, Frederick Evans had come to a decision. He would make another phone call to Hardie and warn him to expect further instructions. He guessed that Hardie would protest, perhaps even threaten, but as long as Frederick held the master copy of the DVD and Hardie had no idea how to identify him, he was safe; safe and in complete control. He stalked from the office, slamming the door behind him, ignoring the young assistant who approaching with a smile stopped dead in his tracks at the morose expression on Mister Evans face. Turning to a colleague, the assistant's face fell as he whispered, "Back to bloody normal, then." Frederick decided on the stairs rather than the down escalator and pushed open the door.

Paul Hardie slowed his step as he approached the main door to Dawson's department store. It had suddenly occurred to him that though he had already decided the fate of his tormentor, he realised that he couldn't just abduct him from a store full of staff and customers and drag him through the city centre streets to his car. For one, if Evans resisted, if he screamed and shouted it would undoubtedly attract the attention of the police and the knife he carried in his inside jacket pocket would surely get him locked up. As if for the first time he looked up and saw the CCTV cameras attached to the building walls. A cold chill spread through his body. What if the cameras had caught him on Monday night, moving through the city centre? What if they …. ?
The realisation that he could be identified brought a sudden reality to his situation, an awareness of what he intended doing. He stopped walking and stood still, glancing about him, aware that the police could be watching him right now. But how could he tell? On a bright morning like today, there were literally dozens if not hundreds of people milling about and walking in the precinct. Paul looked intently at those passing by, but saw nothing other than shoppers, businessmen and women, teenagers hanging around or standing talking. On the far side outside a shoe shop, a busker played bagpipes, the strains of *'Loch Lomond'* rending the air as the kilted piper tapped his feet to the music. Paul's throat was suddenly dry and he felt faint, his lack of food and the sleep deprivation finally taking its toll. He staggered to a nearby wall and stood against it for support. His head was down and he didn't notice the slightly built suited man pass within five metres, who walked quickly towards a public telephone booth situated in the centre of the precinct.

The surveillance officer had been joined by a female colleague and as they stood closely facing towards each other, their arms about the others waist and smiling as lovers do, his eyes were cast over her shoulder and he spoke into the covert microphone.

"No idea Sugar," he said. "Just stopped dead, looked up and now he's just standing there. He looks ill, if you ask me. What do you want us to do?"

"Maintain contact," replied Sugar in his ear. "Our pal will be joining you shortly. I want absolute confirmation he is the target and we've still to get that, okay?"

"Roger that."

"Right, we're just two women out shopping, eh?" said Jan, handing Lesley a large shopping bag from the car boot that was padded out to appear full. She slammed the boot lid down. "Two of the guys have the target standing in Buchanan Street precinct. All we'll do is give him a pass by with a wide berth, just enough for you to make him as the target, understood?"

Lesley nodded and wanted to comment she wasn't stupid, but didn't need the confrontation with the sour faced Jan.

It took but a few minutes to walk the short distance to the precinct and all the while, Jan, leaning close into Lesley and smiling like some old friend, related the update that the target hadn't changed position, but was still static.

Entering the precinct, Lesley walked arm in arm with Jan who counted down then squeezed Lesley's arm to indicate where the target stood.

Her stomach churning, Lesley saw Hardie backed against a wall, his head down, but in no doubt it was him. Quietly she whispered, "It's him," and heard a blank-faced Jan, who staring at Lesley, say into her microphone, "Confirmed target is correct, Sugar."

She listened as Sugar relayed her information to the rest of the team, then her face brightened and then tugged gently at Lesley's arm. "Right, while we're here anyway and he doesn't seem to be going anywhere soon, let's nip in to this shop. There's a pair of shoes I want to see, eh?"

Frederick dialled the number again, but for the second time the answer machine with a woman's voice, the dead woman he presumed, activated and with a shaking hand he slammed the handset down. He realised he was acting in anger, that he hadn't prepared any kind of script to read to Hardie and forced himself to be calm. He argued with himself that perhaps he was acting in haste and that he should think this over before using Hardie again.

Behind him, the man who leaned against the wall stood upright and slowly walked towards the main door that led into Dawson's.

"He's on the move again Sugar," said the surveillance officer, now walking hand in hand with his female colleague behind the target, "Looks like he's heading towards Dawson's store."

In the surveillance car parked in the designated disabled bay in Queen Street, the driver flashed her warrant card and a big smile at the parking attendant and politely told him she was engaged in police work and she would be gone in ten minutes. The attendant walked off, muttering under his breath at the liberties the polis took with their fucking warrant cards. The driver listened to the footman's report, noted the targets movement towards Dawson's, then timed and wrote it in the team log.

Paul Hardie pushed through the heavy glass doors and from previous visits to the store, knew the Gents Department was located on the first floor. He made his way towards the escalator, unaware of the young man wearing the baseball cap and carrying the backpack who watched as he followed him into the store. Nor did Paul notice the young woman holding the man's hand, nor did he see her hold the door open to admit the skinny man, who walked discourteously past her without so much as an acknowledgement of her manners.
The young woman held her tongue, because she was working, but she watched the man hurry towards the stairs and muttered, "Wanker" under her breath.
Paul guessed that Evans, who had taken over from Hamilton, must work in the Gents Department and arrived on the first floor with no idea what he intended doing. If Evans saw him first, he would undoubtedly recognise Paul from the DVD and hide. If Paul saw Evans first, he wondered how he would handle it. The knife in his jacket pocket felt as large a sword and he unconsciously touched the bladed weapon with his hand through the leather material, taking unusual comfort by its presence.
To anyone who noticed them, the surveillance man and his colleague were just another couple shopping in the store, chatting together as they browsed in the Gents Department. What no-one could guess was the man was giving a running commentary on his target's movements while the woman simply mouthed as though speaking in reply.
"He's not shopping, we're certain about that," said the surveillance officer, smiling down at the woman as he astutely added, "but he does look like he's searching for something or someone."
Frederick pushed through the door that led from the stairwell into the shop floor and hurriedly made his way to the office.
Across the floor, Paul was pretending to inspect a row of sweaters on a rail when he saw his tormentor and froze.
The surveillance officers both saw the target's head snap up and noted the change in his demeanour. They saw his head swivel to watch something or someone that was out of their vision and then, for some unaccountable reason

they were unable to fathom, he abruptly strode away and headed towards the escalator.

It was too public, Paul decided. Too many witnesses for what he intended. He would wait till he saw Evans leave the store then somehow, though he hadn't worked it out yet, force him to Paul's car and take him somewhere quiet. Yes, that was how he would do it. He would wait till his tormentor was alone and get him then.

Jan listened in her earpiece to Sugar's snapped instructions and instructing Lesley to stay in the shop out of sight meantime, hurried to get an eyeball on the main door of the store. She watched as the target exited the doors and then curiously, he hurried across the precinct to a shadowed doorway where he stopped and leaning against the wall, turned to watch the store. He's sussed the footmen inside the store was her first thought and was waiting for them to follow him out. "Sugar," she quickly said, "tell the footmen to remain where they are, now."

Sugar complied without questioning and then returned to speak with Jan, who told him of her suspicions.

"He's watching the door? Bugger it. I'll get them to stay there meantime."

Jan knew that Sugar now had a decision to make. If the target had made the footmen, there was little choice but to end the surveillance. The standing rule for the surveillance team was 'better to pull out than show out'. Less than a minute later, Sugar spoke in her ear. "The footmen tell me it's not them, Jan. The target saw someone in the store and they're happy that's who he must be watching for. They're going to exit in thirty seconds. If he reacts, to them, we'll know for certain, so watch and report immediately what happens, savvy?"

Jan acknowledged and almost thirty seconds later, with bated breath she saw her colleagues emerge from the store and hand in hand, eyes only for each other, stroll off into the precinct.

To her relief, the target didn't budge or appear to give them a second glance. "Sugar, the guys were bang on. Whoever the target is watching, it isn't us."

DI Charlie Miller was at his desk when he took the phone call from Sugar Smythe. He listened as Sugar related the unusual circumstances of the Target, Paul Hardie's movements that morning.

"Missus Hardie was a teacher, wasn't she boss?"

"Yeah, primary teacher," replied Charlie, "and the girlfriend worked beside him at, wait," he flicked through the copy MP report on his desk, "at some mob called Berkley and Finch in St Vincent Street. So Sugar, what's your next move then?"

Sat in his vehicle parked in a bay in Queen Street, Sugar explained that the team had no other option than to sit tight and try and identify who the target was looking for, then once that was established, endeavour to find out why. They both kicked a few ideas at each other with Sugar suggesting maybe the target suspected his missing wife had run off with someone from the Gents Department, that he intended following this individual to try and locate her. Miller disagreed, reminding Sugar that if Hardie suspected his wife had done a runner with another man, or he grinned into the phone, "To be politically correct, another woman, then why didn't he just inform the cops when he reported her having gone AWOL, rather than have us repeatedly call on him while we to try and locate her."

"Pride, maybe?" replied Sugar.

Miller sighed and said, "This guessing isn't getting us anywhere. Right, we'll go with your decision and sit tight on him for now. What time does the store close?"

"Six o'clock the doors shut, so I'm guessing all staff will be out by half past. That means overtime, boss."

"Okay, okay, I get the hint. I'll square it with the Div Com," then, almost as an afterthought, asked, "What about your passenger, Lesley Gold?"

"She's hovering about with Jan at the minute. Will I send her up the road? She's done her bit, identified the target for us."

Miler paused as he thought about it, then replied, "No, not yet. If your target's static meantime, keep her with you and she can sit in when you and the team have your de-brief for the day. It's her inquiry so I'd like her to be here later for the wash-up."

"Will you be hanging on then?"

Miller smiled into the handset. "My missus is on back-shift and the wee one is at her grannies', so yeah, I'll be here to put the kettle on."

Miller hung up then stroked lightly at the scar on his cheek. Why the hell, he wondered, does Dawson's ring a bell?

The morale of the floor staff at the Gents Department that afternoon plummeted when a red-faced Frederick returned to the floor, his face betraying his mood. A leak in the HR department about the hunt for a new manager got round faster than a woman with a new credit card. As one, the floor staff groaned, envisaging a horrible time till the new man or woman was appointed while fervently praying it wouldn't be the torn faced Freddy. As if aware of the change in attitude, Frederick took his meanness out on the staff and pounced on the least issue, finding fault with a dropped hanger, a sweater incorrectly folded, a suit wrongly sized in the rail, an assistant standing talking to another; all merited a rebuke and a warning that he, as temporary manager, had the authority to discipline and recommend suspension without pay. The staff walked on eggshells, heads down and hushed, and clock-watched till the magic hour.

Outside in the precinct, Sugar's team settled down to that which they did best, surveilling both the target and the front doors and like the staff, also waited patiently for closing time.

Paul Hardie was getting cold and he wanted to pee, but the overriding need was to watch his tormentor leave the store and follow him to where they could be alone, even if that meant following Evans to his home. His attention never waned from the door and when six o'clock arrived, he saw the last of the customers being ushered through the doors. At twenty-five minutes after six, he was dismayed to see the two security guards lock the doors from inside and the inner lights dim, then switch off. A frustrating thought occurred to him. The staff didn't exit via the customers doors, but must leave via another door.
Watching from almost eighty metres away, the surveillance officer with an eyeball on the target also reported the closing of the store and that the target seemed a little confused and was walking one way, then another.
Paul clenched his fists with frustration and turning on his heel, began to walk towards Mitchell Street and his car, unaware of the shadowy figures that watched and reported his every move and the cars that began to drive towards his vehicles location.

After Jan dropped her at the front door of Maryhill Office, Lesley made her way to the CID suite. The DI was just entering his room, a sheaf of papers in his hand and waved her along the corridor towards him. "I've just heard from Sugar. Hardie's travelling home, so once he's housed, the team are calling it a day and they'll head back to the office. Have you and the guys had anything to eat yet?"
"I haven't," she replied, "but some of the team managed to get some grub at the plot.
"Good, you get yourself across the road to the shops and grab a sandwich or something and then meet me in my office. When you've got your grub, meet me here and we'll have a quick chat while the team are putting their equipment and the cars away."
Five minutes later, seated across the desk from him, Miller quizzed her as to her thoughts on why Hardie would be staking out Dawson's store?
Lesley shook her head. "There was no mention of Dawson's in the MP report and to be honest, I have no idea at all why he would have any interest there."
"Definitely no suggestion the MP might have had a fancy man tucked away somewhere?"
"No, none at all and from the discussion I had with the janny at her school, it seems highly unlikely."

His face wrinkled in thought and he said, "Dawson's, Dawson's. Why is it that the name sounds so familiar?"

"I had the same thought earlier," repeated Miller. "Maybe you're thinking of the TV news yesterday? The man who was murdered? The body discovered in the Central Division? He worked at Dawson's I believe." Miller suddenly startled, his eyes opening wide. No, he thought, that's too big a leap. Nevertheless, it wouldn't do any harm to check. "Lesley," he smiled at her, "Can you give me a minute or two? Grab yourself another coffee from the canteen and as soon as the team are in, gather them together in the briefing room and tell Sugar I'll be down, but first I want to make a phone call."

Chapter 33 - Wednesday Evening.

Eunice Evans had always been a tolerant woman. God knows, hadn't she enough to put up with living with her husband? When the front door slammed behind him, she knew that Frederick was in one of his black moods and it was wise to tip-toe about the house rather than incur his sullen attitude and sarcasm. It's not as if she was getting on in years, she unconsciously touched at her hair, for after all sixty-six wasn't considered these days to be old. She startled at the sound of the bathroom door being slammed upstairs and sighed. He hadn't mentioned his girlfriend Jennifer for a few days and she worried that maybe the short lived romance was over. If indeed it was, then it would be a great pity, for Eunice longed for a marriage and perhaps even a grandchild. On that train of thought and while she tried in vain not to consider it, a marriage might also mean peace and quiet and that perhaps Frederick would move out and find his own home. She thought briefly of Jennifer, such a nice girl, pleasant and polite and not at all like the naked women in those magazines that he kept hidden from his mother. She glanced at the ceiling, hearing the sound of his footsteps returning to his room and the door noisily closing. Sitting in the kitchen chair, her hands folded in her lap, it occurred to her how nice and quiet the house would be if Frederick weren't here, if he would only move out. Feeling guilty, she hurriedly dismissed the thought from her mind. Of course, she would miss him, miss his company, but again sighed when she realised that other than mealtimes, they didn't really sit nor do anything together. To all intent and purposes, Frederick was simply boarding in the house. Yes, she accepted he contributed a token sum to the household budget, but adding the money from her husband's work pension and her own state pension together and with no mortgage, she had no real financial worries. She certainly wasn't affluent, but neither was she poor and Frederick's meagre contribution wasn't that necessary, though she would never admit that to him. No, she slowly shook her head; Frederick wasn't a burden on her but, she sadly admitted, neither was he a source of pride.

Back home again, Paul Hardie slammed the front door behind him and smacked the heel of his hand off his forehead a half dozen times. He couldn't believe how naive he had been. Of course, a store the size of Dawson's would have a staff entrance, but why he hadn't considered it, he didn't know. The only success he had today was that he now knew his tormentor worked there, in the Gents Department. He took off his jacket and hung it on the row of hooks on the wall, remembering to remove the kitchen knife from the inside pocket and made his way through to the kitchen. The red light on the answer machine was blinking and he pressed the play button. There were three new messages. The first two callers didn't leave a message, but the third caller was a man who without leaving his name, said he was calling from Berkley and Finch to inquire when Paul intended returning the Focus, stressing that failure to do so would result in the consideration of legal action to recover the vehicle. "Fucking never, you wanker!" he screamed at the phone. His rage wasn't really directed at the caller, but at his own failure earlier in the evening at missing his tormentor leaving the store. He stood with his hands on the worktop, his body shaking and head throbbing. Again he wondered how he could have been so stupid and began to laugh. The laughter turned into hysteria and his hands still gripping the worktop, he crumpled weeping to the floor.

Jenny Farndale had spent a miserable day at work. Her kindly supervisor, under the impression that her kitchen assistant was still feeling poorly, considered sending her home again, but Jenny protested she was fine and the woman didn't press the issue.
There had been no contact from Frederick. Nothing, not even a text message nor did he pop into the canteen for a meal or even a cuppa. Her whole being wanted to stand up for herself and end it with him, but the fear of again being alone, left on the shelf as her mother frequently reminded her, just wouldn't go away. Her supervisor had jovially hinted at her new man now doing his acting manager, but Jenny's face betrayed her unhappiness and the woman decided that was a subject best left alone. The supervisor also took the time to gather her other staff about her and quietly whisper that none were to mention the weasel Freddy Evans and threatening the younger two with physical harm if they tried to tease Jenny about him.
The long day's shift finally came to an end and collecting her coat and shoulder bag from her locker, Jenny slowly made her way to the rear staff exit. Half of her wished to bump into Frederick, speak with him and tell him how she felt while the other half dreaded meeting him and a possible confrontation. It was as she was clocking-off she overheard two young men, oblivious to her standing behind them, discussing Frederick.

"If he gets the job, we're all fucked," moaned the younger one, stamping his card in the machine. "The word is though that he's not popular with the management, so fingers crossed, eh?"

"Anyone else from the department in the running?" asked his friend.

"No, not to my knowledge, but let's face it, it doesn't matter who gets the manager's job, they can't be any worse than that wee bullying shite," and laughed as he pushed through the door.

Jenny was stunned, but not at what the two men had said. It was the younger one's perception of Frederick, recognising him for what he truly was; a bully. Almost as if her mind had been made up for her, she stamped her card and pushing through the door, inwardly sighed with relief. Walking along the lane, though her lips trembled, she felt like a weight had been lifted from her shoulders.

No matter what he said, no matter how he might plead, Jenny was done with Frederick.

The atmosphere in the surveillance team briefing room was light and the patter bandied among the team was coarse, but good-humoured. Lesley, seated at the side of the room, had the feeling that some of the comments and hilarity were meant to impress her and caught more than one of the male members of the team giving her a second glance. Sugar Smythe entered with a folder in his hand and called for quiet, ducking a rolled up newspaper that was flung his way from the back. Sugar grinned and fined the thrower fifty pence for the day's kitty. Jan leaned over to explain to Lesley the kitty was fifty pence's and pound coins kept in a large tin that was collected from the team as fines if, during surveillance operations, any of the team made some sort of balls-up's. Once a month the money then paid the bulk of the bill for a team curry and piss-up. "And believe me," she then added with a low snarl, discreetly nodding towards a female colleague, "some of us regularly balls-up."

"First things first," Sugar waved the team to shut up. "No movement yet up in Glenburn Street, so the guys on Ob's there will continue meantime."

Sugar again called for silence at which point DI Charlie Miller entered the room, a sheet of paper in his hand, and a respectful hush fell over the team.

"Evening girls," grinned Miller to the team, who replied with hisses and boo's. "Good Op today, Sugar tells me though I understand the missing wife's not been returned to her husband yet?"

"He can have mine," Tony the van-man offered with a grin.

"Settle down you lot," ordered Sugar, with his own grin.

"Right," continued Miller, his face now serious. "You might have wondered why the target, Paul Hardie visited Dawson's today or who he saw in the Gents Department at the store that caused him to leave in such a hurry. I also understand from your observations he staked the place out. Frankly, we don't have a definite clue as yet. However, thanks to a timely prompt from our very own Lesley there," he pointed towards her, "it set me thinking. Likely you will have read the newspaper reports that on Monday evening, an employee of Dawson's," he glanced down at the paper in his hand, "Robert Hamilton was discovered stabbed to death near to an underpass just off Osborne Street. Coincidence so far you might think. Well, let me continue. I'm not long off the phone with the SIO in charge of the murder inquiry and it seems the victim was not just employed at Dawson's, but was employed as the manager of the Gent's Department."

Lesley's mouth opened in shock and as she looked about her, saw the team were also taken by surprise. The atmosphere in the room was electric.

"According to the SIO, there is no current suspect, no motive and no evidence. However, one of the CCTV operators at Stewart Street, Gracie Fields, a good guy who is known to me," Miller added, "did a bit of work on the DVD recordings of that night and came up with a figure dumping what later proved to be a knife down a roadside drain in York Street. The knife is recovered and Forensics is able to confirm it is the murder weapon. Regretfully, no fingerprints or any DNA of the culprit were found on the knife. However, while the SIO reports the CCTV footage isn't particularly good, it is strongly believed the figure is male. The circumstances of the murder would suggest, and this is speculation only at this time ladies and gentlemen, that given the location of the murder and where the knife was dumped, it is unlikely that it was a robbery gone wrong, therefore the SIO is now working on the presumption the murder was a premeditated act. In short, someone set out to kill Hamilton."

"Are you suggesting, boss," said Jan, "that our target, Paul Hardie is the killer?"

"No Jan, I'm not saying that at all, but what I am saying is that a set of circumstances have been presented to us as follows. What we have is a target brought to us by our colleague Lesley there who she suspects might somehow be implicated in his wife's untimely disappearance or, at the very least, being unhelpful as to why or how his wife went missing. Regretfully, there is no hard evidence to corroborate Lesley's suspicion, but her cop instinct was enough to persuade me to authorise an operation against Hardie, savvy?"

Jan nodded in understanding while Lesley inwardly breathed a sigh of relief. Throughout the day, she had worried that her suspicions might have been a waste of time, but now it seemed Miller did believe and had backed her from the start.

"As you all know," Miller continued, his hands held open as he spoke, "your observations on Hardie took him to the very place where he apparently sees someone in the location where a recently murdered man worked and this causes him to rush from the store and stake the place out. Coincidence again you may ask? I think not," he dramatically concluded, clapping his hands together with a slap.

"In short, ladies and gentlemen, the SIO at Stewart Street has requested we continue to monitor Hardie meantime. He will conduct his investigation on the little he has while we," he grinned, "you lot that is, stick with Hardie."

"Does that mean we're on twenty-four hour round the clock Ob's boss?" asked a bearded, grizzled faced team member from the back seat.

"No, not at the minute Joe, you mercenary bugger," Miller smiled then shook his head. "Remember, there is absolutely no evidence at this time to connect Hardie with the Central Division's ongoing murder inquiry. All we have as I said is a peculiar, yet extremely interesting coincidence. So, what if we hypothesis and consider his actions to be nothing other than a worried husband searching for his wife? Consider this. What if Hardie suspected his wife was a regular shopper at the store and simply turned up on the off-chance of seeing her there? Reasonable, you would agree? Alternatively, what if he thought she had been seeing someone working there and decided just to watch for her entering the store? Again, you would agree a reasonable assumption? However, what if," he held his hand up, "and this isn't a criticism, but what if the person you guys thought Hardie saw today in the store was his wife and he was watching for her leaving?"

There was a murmur of disbelief at this statement and a few of the team shook their head's, for they had to admit they had concentrated all their effort on the target and none could truthfully say they had been watching for the MP, although all had seen her photograph in the briefing file.

"I know it sounds a bit farfetched," admitted Miller, "but the point is at the minute, we've no evidence otherwise and so we go with what we know. As far as the SIO at the Central is concerned, this is a tenuous crossover with our operation and his murder. Needless to say, should anything develop, we'll then consider merging the inquiries, but I stress, for the time being we concentrate on Hardie and finding his wife."

"Boss," interrupted Sugar, "just to diverse slightly, what about our Ob's in Glenburn Street?"

"Can you work with what you've got here? I know that you guys," he waved a hand at the room, "aren't a full team, but I need you to cut the cloth to suit or at least for now."

"I can work with the numbers here at a pinch, yeah and we have the advantage that so far, Hardie doesn't seem to be surveillance conscious, but it might mean incurring more overtime."

Miller hesitated for a few seconds then said, "Let me speak to the Div Com. If I can squeeze some money out of the pot, I will. In the meantime, do the best you can. Thanks guys, I'll let you get on with it Sugar," he clapped the DS on the arm and nodded to the team as he left the room.

Sugar turned to his team. "Okay, it's got a little more exciting now, so let's break for this evening and we'll assemble here six-thirty in the morning."

As the team shuffled to their feet and made towards the door, Lesley's phone activated with a text message. Glancing at the number, she recognised her mother's mobile, hurried to a corner and pressed the button, but the message simply read: *Dad comftble. Dnt be worrying abut 2nite. Giv me a phne wen u can. Mum xx*

"Everything okay?" asked Tony the van man as he passed her by and touched her shoulder.

"Yeah, yeah, it's fine," she replied, then under her breath added "so far."

Andy Carmichael sat beside his daughter on the couch in front of the television as she cuddled into her father, engrossed in her favourite characters in 'The Adventures of Jake and the Neverland Pirates'. He held his mobile phone in his hand and thought about whether or not to call Lesley. Last night had surprised him more than he realised. When he received her call and went to her flat, he hadn't known what to expect. Finding her there upset and on the verge of tears brought about an inner urge to protect her, tell her that everything would be fine and soothe her as he did his own child. She had been vulnerable, yet trusted him enough to be the one she called and it was partly that decision by her that caused him to realise that, crazy as it seemed in such a short time, he had feelings for her. She liked him, he guessed and the date they had been on, the first in years for him he wryly grinned, was the best evening he'd had for as long as he could remember. He was in no doubt he wanted to see her again, but knew that theirs wouldn't be a straight forward relationship. For one, he looked down and tousled Evie's hair, he was bringing baggage with him and though she had been kind and thoughtful when speaking of his daughter, he didn't know how Lesley might feel about having another woman's daughter in the relationship. Evie would always be a part of his life, a major part and anyone, Lesley or whoever, would need to accept that. It worried him that in such a short time, he had come to think of Lesley as a long term commitment and it also worried him more that if Evie got to know Lesley and it didn't work out, the effect a failed relationship might have on the small girl. He glanced at his daughter and the clock on the small table by the TV and figured she had another twenty-five minutes before bed, then startled when the mobile phone in his hand went off.

"Hello?"

"Catch you at a bad time?" asked Lesley.

"Eh, no, just sitting here with Evie, watching some pirates getting the better of Captain Hook."

"Right," Lesley slowly replied, her voice betraying a little uncertainty, "I'll probably need that one explained later. Look, I've just finished work and I've not been home yet, so I'm a wee bit smelly. I've half eaten a rotten sandwich and right now, could eat a monkey dipped in fat. I'm thinking of treating myself to a chip supper. Would it be too forward of me to ask if I can pop up and maybe share some chips with you and the wee one?"
She took his surprised silence for hesitancy and was about to speak again when Andy said, "We'd be delighted to share your supper with you, wouldn't we Evie," he glanced at the upturned and curious face of his daughter.
"Okay," she replied, trying not to sound too relieved, "I know you're in Kingsborough Gardens, what's the number?"
"Number forty-eight. We're on the second floor. Press the button on the nameplate at the front door and I'll buzz you in. I'll get the kettle on."
"See you in fifteen minutes, bye," she said and hung up.
"Who was that daddy?"
"That," he couldn't stop smiling with pleasure and yes, he inwardly admitted, with some delight, "was Lesley, who is bringing you and me some chips. Right, let's get some plates and the tea ready, eh?"

Sitting on the edge of his bed, Morris MacDonald stared at the wall, his mind blank. His brother Roderick had wanted to stay at home with Morris and keep him company on the eve of Susan's service, but Morris insisted Roderick go out, get himself a drink and let Morris have some quiet time alone to reflect on tomorrow. With reluctance, Roderick agreed, but only if Morris promised to phone his big brother if he later changed his mind and wished to grab a pint.
Tonight Susan laid at rest in the funeral home and from there the cortege with both brothers, in the company of her elderly aunt and sister, would depart at nine-thirty in the morning for the ten o'clock service at Dalnottar Crematorium.
The arrangements had been made to Morris' satisfaction and there was nothing more to do. His suit was neatly pressed, her favourite yellow coloured tulips were ordered for delivery to the funeral home and all that remained was for him to get a good night's sleep for tomorrow, he sighed, would be a very long day.

While others throughout the city went about their own business, Frederick Evans sat in his bedroom quietly smouldering and seething. The more thought he gave it, the more convinced he became that the HR Manager had set him up, used him and was now discarding him like so much rubbish. Well, Frederick wasn't for having any of it. The idiot just didn't know who he was dealing with. He would show him that Frederick Evans couldn't be fucked with. The more he imagined the revenge he would plan for the man, the more excited he became. He considered phoning Jenny, but that would take too long for her to get across the city to him and he needed some relief now. Switching on his laptop, he signed into his private account and selected a mobile phone recording he had filmed in the canteen, one of his favourites; two of the tarts from the lingerie department touching and pushing at their breasts as they discussed brassieres and completely unaware that he had watched them. As the brief recording concluded, Frederick resumed from the start and while it played, fetched his cardboard box from behind the water heater in the cupboard and with shaking hands, spread the stolen underwear on the bed. He lay on the bed and closing his eyes, thought of Jenny as he fondled himself.

Chapter 34 – Thursday Morning

It wasn't cold, but the day dawned with a slight drizzle of rain and just the right weather for a funeral, thought Morris MacDonald. He shaved and showered with care, knowing that all eyes would be on him at the service, wondering how he would cope with the stress of saying a final farewell to his wife. Downstairs, he could hear Roderick banging about and guessed his big brother was preparing a hearty breakfast in preparation for the long day and the wake that lay ahead of them both. He smiled as he towelled himself dry, remembering that was Roderick's answer to every problem. A full stomach and a dram always seemed to make things that much easier, he would say. Less than five minutes later, though he hadn't relished the thought of food, Morris went downstairs and found the appetising smell of bacon that wafted from the kitchen assailing his taste buds and reminding him that he hadn't eaten well for several days. Taking the precaution of donning a full length apron over his clean, white shirt, he settled himself at the table in front of Roderick's multi-calorie cure for all; bacon, sausage, black pudding, potato scones and two fried eggs, surrounded by a generous dollop of beans and a large mug of tea at the side.
"Get that down you, wee brother," the big man's lilting voice softly said as he clapped a heavy hand on Morris' shoulder and sat opposite at his own full plate. "I want you to be the strong man today, as our lovely Susan knew fine well you to be. No matter how you feel, no matter what soothing and kind words are said, you will stand upright with your head held high, for all will know that Susan MacDonald had a fine and loving man as a husband. A man that cared for her in the darkest days of despair and who loved her as no other could. I am very proud of you, wee man. I am proud to be your brother, to be your family and so very proud to have been Susan's family too."

He paused and looked away, then in a voice shaking slightly with emotion, said, "Now, eat up and don't be letting good food go to waste."
Morris stared at Roderick and with trembling lips, softly smiled as the first of the day's tears slowly trickled down his cheeks.

Peggy Gold stood up from the armchair at the sound of the car drawing to a halt outside. Her husband snored softly and glancing at the clock, she realised with surprise that she had slept for a full four hours. Her neck ached from the uncomfortable position and she massaged it as she opened the front door to admit the McMillan nurse who quietly slipped past her. The portly nurse held up a paper bag with six breakfast rolls and whispered, "Straight from the bakers down the road, so they should still be warm," and guessing that her patient Thomas was still asleep, tip-toed into the kitchen.
Peggy filled the kettle and gave the nurse a report of Thomas's night, admitting that she had a full four hours sleep. The nurse frowned and replied, "Peggy, you've had so little sleep these last months that four hours must seem like a luxury and you've conditioned yourself, hen, to think that four hours is enough, but it really isn't. Now, I'm not going to argue with you, but here's what's going to happen. I'll check first on our laddie through there and then make you a quick roll and bacon and a cuppa. In the meantime, I want you to get yourself a quick shower and get into bed. I'm here to midday before my next patient. Like it or lump it, you need to grab sleep when you can, no matter what time of the day."
"You're a bully," Peggy tiredly smiled at her.
The nurse flashed a grin at her and said, "You should hear what my man calls me," then ushered Peggy towards the bathroom while she checked on Thomas.

Lesley Gold had again been neighboured with Jan and sat with her in the surveillance car as they pulled up at the location they had occupied the previous day. A light drizzle of rain fell onto the front windscreen. Jan reached for the hidden switch and, in sequence with the other surveillance cars, informed Tony the van man they were in position. That done, she and Lesley settled down to share a flask of coffee the now more sociable Jan produced from a backpack that lay on the rear seat.
"Get up to anything last night?"
"No," Lesley shook her head, "just visited a friend and his daughter for a couple of hours then went home and crashed. I couldn't believe how tired I was."
Jan smirked. "The shift cops think that all we do is sit about in cars all day and I suppose in a sense, they're correct. This job is about eighty per cent sitting on our arses waiting on something happening or someone moving,

then about ten to fifteen percent following a target and about five per cent actually dealing with the bad guys. I know it sounds boring, but the time sitting about can be just as strenuous and wearing as actually going out and walking or driving about a beat."

Lesley thought she was being defensive about her team and the role they played and was about to respond, when Jan continued.

"It's all about attitude, getting the right person who can adapt to this kind of police work, because it doesn't suit everyone. Then again," she glanced at Lesley and then quickly looked away, but not before Lesley caught her, "you also need to be physically suited for the job, eh?"

"And you think I might not be?"

Jan shrugged. "To be honest, no," then quickly raised her hands, "but let me explain. I'm not talking about your fitness or anything. The male psyche is that most guys like women, yeah?"

Lesley, curiosity aroused, nodded.

"Look at you, slightly above average height for a woman, good looking," and she raised her hands again, "and I'm being honest here, not predatory, okay? Anyway, let's say you're a surveillance officer and your part of a team following a guy down the road. He turns and sees you and guys being guys, has a second look because he thinks you're attractive. Then maybe half an hour later, sees you again. Does he think coincidence? If a target's at all surveillance conscious, then he won't accept it as coincidence. He's made you as a cop, following him. Effectively, you are now burned for the rest of that operation."

"So, you're saying all surveillance officers should be plain or ugly?" then almost immediately took an inward sharp breath.

"No," Jan smiled tolerantly, "what I'm saying is we should be nondescript. Look hen, I know I'm no pin-up, though admittedly if I do say so myself, I scrub up okay, eh?"

Lesley inwardly thought, but without malice, that Jan should keep telling herself that.

"I have to admit though I'm not the kind of woman that guys instantly remember, savvy?" Jan added with a touch of regret in her voice.

"But you're telling me I'm attractive?" Lesley grinned at her.

"I'm saying you're too good looking for surveillance," blushed Jan, but grinning herself and continued "I'm not hitting on you, you stupid bugger. Anyway, how did we arrive at this conversation? Oh yeah, I was explaining …."

"Complaining you mean," interrupted Lesley, still grinning.

"Okay, complaining then about cops and how they see us in the surveillance team. I sometimes think the uniform guys think we're a bunch of lazy gits."

"You're wrong, you know," Lesley shook her head. "If there is that

perception among your team, then it's a mistaken perception and probably because there's a streak of jealously among some of the uniformed guys. Most cops would like a turn at what you guys do. Maybe you should speak to Sugar and ask him to consider what I'm doing, you know, accompanying you on an operation. Maybe like a week's secondment for cops, but nothing too responsible. Perhaps consider participating in a static Ob's or something along those lines. It would give the uniformed guys some kind of idea of what your team do, you know?"
Jan didn't reply, but seemed thoughtful, then nodded and said, "That might not be a bad idea. I'll run it past Sugar and see what he says."
Over the hidden speaker, Tony the van man updated with a "No change" and added the Target's car was in position outside the front door.

Jimmy Dunlop unlocked the main gates that led into the primary school and was pushing the second gate back into its locking position when the car drew up and stopped beside him. The driver's window was lowered and a hand emerged with the forefinger crooked to beckon him over.
"Mister Dunlop," said the Head Teacher, Gwyneth Jenkins as he bent towards the window, "I am not satisfied that the main driveway to the school entrance is as clean and tidy as it should be. Be sure to deal with the matter as soon as possible."
Before the elderly janitor could respond, Jenkins pressed the accelerator and sped away. Jimmy took a deep breath and was about to utter an oath under his breath, but then his eyes narrowed in surprise. Just briefly, his nose wrinkled and he smiled in understanding, for the air suddenly smelled of mint sweeties.

Dotty Turner returned from dropping her children at school and laid out her navy coloured, skirted suit, crisp white blouse and underwear on the bed. She run a cloth over her black patent shoes and phoned to confirm with her parents they would collect the kids after school, all before she took her shower.
As the water cascaded over her, her thoughts were filled with Morris and how he was feeling, then chastising herself for being so stupid. Of course he would be devastated and nothing anyone would say, least of all Dotty, could be of any comfort to the man. She placed her hands flat and leaned her forehead against the glass panel, resigning herself to accepting that her love for Morris was unrequited, that he must never know how she felt. She took a deep breath and began to soap her body and shampoo her short, blonde hair.

Paul Hardie had visited the depths of despair, had survived the downward plunge and now he was healed. He no longer needed sleep for his body was cleansed. He had overcome exhaustion and hunger and mastered both.
His body needed nothing, no nutrients, no rest; nothing other than revenge. Revenge would bring peace.
He knew now who was responsible for all that had happened to him. He knew now with certainty the man who was to blame - his tormentor, Frederick Evans.
He sat in the armchair, unshaven and unwashed, his hair in disarray and not at all like the man who had once been the smart and presentable Paul Hardie of old. He sat with his legs splayed holding the six inch knife in one hand as he gently stroked the serrated edged blade with the fingers of the other hand. He lifted the knife against his own cheek, felt the cold metal against his skin and imagined drawing the blade down his tormentor's cheek, the bright crimson blood flowing and the terror he would inflict. He smiled and closed his eyes, his head thrown back drawing a sharp breath as he envisioned the knife being slowly and carefully pushed into Frederick Evans body. Paul would stare into his dying eyes and remind Evans that it was he and not Paul who was responsible for Fiona's death; Evans who had cost Paul his promotion and his job; that it was he and not Paul who was responsible for killing the man Robert Hamilton and it would be he and not Paul who was the architect of his own death. Yes, he smiled and vowed to tell Evans that it was all Evans fault. Yes, everything. His eyes narrowed, but maybe not the bit about Janice Meikle. That was down to Colin Davis and he stopped smiling. He couldn't remember that bit, couldn't remember killing Davis. He frowned and tried to recall. Davis was dead, yes, he was sure about that, but did Paul kill him? Did it matter, he suddenly grinned. The bastard was dead and Janice would be his again. Janice. His thoughts turned to her and he remembered she had betrayed him with Davis then dumped him like he was a bit of shit on the sole of her shoe. He gritted his teeth; suddenly angry and not realising he was gripping the sharp blade in the palm of his hand. She was responsible too; Janice and his tormentor, Evans. They were in it together, he now knew. They had laughed behind his back, made him do the things he had done. Together they had done him over good and proper. He snarled, his eyes blazing as he decided when he had done with Evans, he would then deal with Janice.
His hand felt wet and he glanced down at the bright, glistening blood dripping between his fingers onto his trousers and sighed. He'd better get that cleaned, he thought, get rid of the evidence and his eyes were drawn to the tiled hearth and with a cold shudder and sudden clarity, he remembered. Paul did not know, could not realise that sleep deprivation, hunger and his guilt all colluded to confuse and bewilder him, that reality and his

imagination were causing him to become disorientated, to merge fact and fiction and to create a hallucinatory world where he was the victim.
In Paul Hardie's perception of reality, he had little choice but to make amends for others failures and this would commence today, with the killing of Frederick Evans.

Paul Hardie's intended victim thought about not going into work and considered feigning some illness or other, but still the need to dominate the other staff in the time he had remaining as the temporary Departmental Manager, was overwhelming. He must make his mark, he decided; demonstrate to the senior management that he was the tough and ruthless Departmental Manager that Dawson's required, no needed, he unconsciously nodded; the kind of manager who took no shit from the staff, the junior employees, he inwardly scoffed; the kind of manager that had made Dawson's great, a leader in the retail industry. Wearily, he rubbed at his eyes and stared into the bathroom mirror. Through the sleepless and restless night he had convinced himself that the stumbling block in his quest for promotion was none other than the HR Manager. In his mind, the man needed to be hurt, destroyed completely and Frederick couldn't achieve that from home. No, he had to be in the store, watching the HR Manager, getting to know him, working out how best he could set Paul Hardie upon him.
And when the stumbling block was removed, who would dare stand in Frederick's way then.

Inspector Frank Cochrane stood with Alex Mason outside the waiting room avoiding the drizzling rain that beat upon the glass roof of the overhang above them, when Pete Buchanan pulled up at the Dalnottar Crematorium car park. Buchanan parked his vehicle and walked towards both men, turning when he saw them wave to Dotty Turner who had just exited the driver's door of her vehicle while the Bar Officer Jinksie Peterson got out of Dotty's passenger door.
"I might just start a wee rumour about them two," Mason quipped to Cochrane as he nodded to Dotty and Jinksie and then swallowed hard when Cochrane drew him a sharp, disapproving look.
"Boss, Alex," Buchanan nodded to the two men and to a group of other officers, all like Buchanan out of uniform and attired in sober suits and coats, some with hands in pockets while others grabbed a quick fag.
"Not a bad turn-out," said Cochrane.
"Aye, Morris is a well liked man, though I have to say that in the twilight of his career, quite a lot of his peers will be unaware of his wife's death otherwise I would have expected a larger turn-out. All the same, as you say boss, not a bad crowd."

Dotty and Jinksie joined them under the overhang and the small group shuffled together just as the hearse and the large saloon following it appeared at the top of the driveway.

"Did Lesley not make it?" asked Jinksie, turning his head back and forth, his eyes searching for her.

"She's on a wee job," replied Cochrane, "working with the Divisional Surveillance for a few days. Besides in fairness she didn't really know Morris that well and I'm sure probably didn't know his wife Susan either."

A hush fell among the group as the hearse drew level with the overhang and disgorged the undertaking staff who in a practised movement, surrounded the hearse and readied the coffin for carrying through to the Place of Rest. The doors of the saloon, stopped immediately behind the hearse, were opened by a staff member.

Dotty's heart skipped a beat when she saw Morris step out of the car and she turned away, fearing that someone would see in her eyes the compassion and affection she held for the solemn faced man.

As he passed by his colleagues, they reached out to shake his hand or simply to touch his arm or shoulder.

The group were invited to follow Morris and the big man they assumed to be his brother Roderick, into the building and did so, filling the pews nearest to the front.

Sitting three rows to the rear, Dotty stared at Morris's back, his head bent down and a shame overwhelmed her that even at this sad time, with the man's wife lying in her coffin not more than ten metres from her, Dotty could think of nothing else but her own happiness; a happiness that she now accepted would be forever denied her.

"Standby, standby, standby," said Tony the van man over the radio, the urgency in his voice snapping the dozing and relaxed surveillance officers to their senses. "Target exiting his front door and now locking the door. He's wearing the same clothes as yesterday, wait," said Andy, the tension in his voice evident, "now putting on a dark coloured baseball cap and he's holding something in his left hand. No, wait. His left hand," there was a definite pause before Tony went on to say "it looks like it might be bandaged, over." One by one, the surveillance team drivers acknowledged the information, but before the last car was similarly able to acknowledge Tony, he cut in with, "That's the target to the Focus, in the driving seat and he's off. Same route as yesterday, over."

Jan turned to Lesley, the fag now cast out of the partially opened window. "Time to play, eh?" she grinned.

He hadn't thought it through, had no real idea what he intended or how he was going to go about it. All he knew was that today his tormentor Frederick Evans was getting what he deserved. At first he drove recklessly and was soon on Dumbarton Road towards the city centre, then passing through a red light at the junction with Crow Road, narrowly missed colliding with a bus turning onto Dumbarton Road. The near collision brought a moment of sanity and he realised if he wasn't careful, he would attract the attention of the cops and slowed down.

"Bloody hell," the voice over the radio was almost frantic. "The bugger ran a red light and nearly got blindsided by a double-decker. He's off and we're stopped at the red light, over."

"Remember your radio procedure," said the calm voice of Sugar Smythe. "We'll catch him up along Dumbarton Road. Four-one-nine, are you in a position to get in front of him? Possibility is he's returning to the Mitchell Street car park, over."

"Roger, will try, over," responded Jan.

The next few minutes were, as Lesley later recounted, hair-raising and she deliberately avoided speaking to Jan, worried that any conversation might distract her from her driving as she wheeled the car through the side roads of the west end to avoid the main Dumbarton Road. On occasion Jan edged the car through red lights to the fury of other drivers and blithely ignored the Highway Code as well as the traffic laws in her aim to beat the Focus to Mitchell Street. As the radio broadcasts continued, it seemed certain they had achieved their goal and abandoning the surveillance car in an empty bay Union Street, raced round on foot to the entrance of the car park where a few minutes later from a shadowed vantage point, they saw Paul Hardie drive the Focus through the barrier. With a smug grin, Jan winked at Lesley as she radioed the convoy to inform Sugar they had the target parking his car and awaited him exiting the car park door.

Caught up in the excitement of Jan's harum-scarum driving, Lesley felt an aftermath sense of relief that Hardie hadn't gotten away and reckoned the five per cent Jan had earlier spoken of was worth the hours sitting in the car and the nerve-wracking drive through the city.

"Here he comes, stay back," warned Jan as they watched Hardie quickly exit the car park door and at a discreet distance, followed him to Buchanan Street precinct.

The drizzling rain caused the pedestrians in Buchanan Street to keep their heads down as they walked and a man wearing a baseball cap who strode quickly attracted little attention.

The elderly woman wearing the scarf and bright yellow coloured waterproof jacket exiting the sports shop, the present for her grandson in the plastic bag she carried clutched in her hand, collided with the man and was about to apologise, but the smile froze on her face and she flinched when she saw the man's eyes. She had been retired for almost eight years, but the eyes were the giveaway. In her long nursing experience, she had seen eyes like those of the man's more times than she could recall. The brief, angry seconds he had stared at her were enough for the woman to recall a forgotten skill, a skill acquired dealing with such men and women for over twenty years.

The eyes of the man indicated to the elderly woman one thing and one thing only; madness. Not the revengeful madness of a man wronged, not the angry madness of the husband who catches his wife *in flagrante delicto,* but the madness that creeps up on an individual and takes them not just to the edge, but over the long drop thereafter; the madness of the insane, the dangerous insane.

Then the man was gone, hurrying on into the drizzling rain.

He knew now that Dawson's had a rear staff door and this time, he snarled as he walked, Evans wouldn't get away from him or from justice, his mind shouted at him. He wouldn't get away for all the hurt he had inflicted upon Paul nor from the deaths he had caused nor the lives ruined. As he walked Paul unconsciously touched at the knife under his jacket in the makeshift sheath he had fashioned from the paper towel cardboard tube. It reassured him and he felt happy that he had the foresight to bring it, for he could think of no other way that he might induce his tormentor to come with him to the place of reckoning.

"He's not stopping in the precinct, over," reported an anxious Jan, now confused and wishing that some back-up footmen would hurry along to assist in keeping pace with the target.

Lesley had not been fitted with a radio earpiece or body set and mindful of the few but important hand signals Jan had shown her, obeyed Jan's instruction to walk three to four metres behind her colleague, keeping Jan in her view and trusting the surveillance officer would keep sight of the target.

"He's onto Argyle Street and walking west towards Mitchell Street, over," said Jan into her collar.

Jan was confused. Hardie had not given Dawson's front door a second glance, but walked straight past. Was he now returning to his car, she wondered?

"He's into Mitchell Street and northwards towards the car park, over."

Of the forty or so mourners who had attended the ceremony to lay Susan MacDonald to rest, just over twenty accepted the invitation to participate in the wake that was to be held within the bowling club in John Knox Street in Clydebank. As was appropriate, the widowed Morris, his brother Roderick, Susan's sister and the slightly confused elderly aunt arrived first at the venue. With the aunt seated, a sweet sherry clenched in her arthritic hand and ably attended to by Roderick, Morris and Susan's sister greeted the arrivals at the inner door to the hall and accepted their condolences, their handshakes and their hugs. As the hour progressed and after the obligatory sandwiches and sausage rolls had been consumed, the tea and coffee drunk, the drams, the vodka's, the wine's and the gins were liberally dispensed and when they took effect an almost light-hearted atmosphere swept through the small gathering. Some might have called it Gallows Humour, but laughter soon rang through the function room as stories were bandied about of Susan's stubbornness, her graciousness, her devotion to her husband and her voluntary work with Yorkhill Children's Charity that continued till the disease ravaged her body and confined her to the house. Gradually as time passed, the small numbers dwindled as some left to return to work, Susan's sister tearfully to return the aunt to the nursing home and soon the one table comprised of Morris, Roderick, Pete Buchanan, Alex Mason, Jinksie and a quiet Dotty Turner, who through the day had discreetly avoided contact with Morris for fear she would disgrace herself and embarrass him.

"You're not thinking of coming back, I hope," Pete Buchanan, now slightly the worse for wear, shook his head as he addressed Morris. "I mean, with the time you've left to do, you could easily see that out through your bereavement leave, Morris. There's no need for you to be rushing back," he repeated.

"I'm not sure what I'm going to be doing, Pete. Naturally, I'll need to come to terms first with what's happened. I know, I know," he held up a hand as if to stave off comment, "we've all known that Susan wouldn't have survived her illness, that it was a question of time. But it still came as a shock, you understand?"

The group as one solemnly nodded and a silence lay across them all.

"I'm trying to persuade the bugger to sell up and come home with me," growled Roderick, playfully cuffing his younger brother softly on the back on his head.

Sat beside Roderick, Dotty had to stop herself from crying out and hurriedly excusing herself from the table, made her way to the ladies toilet. The door closed behind her and she stood leaning over one of the enamel washbasins, staring into the mirror. It had taken all her courage to stay with the group, all her will power to stop from crying out that he needn't leave, that he would always have friends here, that she would always be there for him.

"Jan, stand down, I have the target in sight, over," said the voice in her ear. With a relieved sigh she watched as Hardie turned to her right out of her sight and, stepping into a closed doorway, she clenched her fist, knowing that Lesley would see the sign and stop where she was. "Target's walking slowly in Mitchell Lane, it's a stop, stop, stop," said the voice. Jan turned back to where Lesley stood against a wall, her eyes wide and uncertain. Jan nodded for them both to walk back towards Argyle Street and whispered Hardie was hovering at a lane that led to the rear of Dawson's and probably to a staff entrance. "We've been on him too long anyway," she continued, "so let's get back to the car and we'll sit there till we know what he's up to."

DI Charlie Miller listened as Sugar Smythe reported by phone what had occurred.
"So Sugar, what do you think? That he's back doing his own Ob's on Dawson's, but this time he's watching the staff entrance?"
"Seems to be that way boss. I'm relatively confident that he's got some sort of agenda regarding a member of staff, but what that agenda is, I can't say. However, young Danny got close to him with a walk-past and says that Hardie seems to be dishevelled; untidy I mean and with a couple of day's growth on his face. Oh, that and he's now sporting a bandage on his left hand. Danny says it didn't seem to be a proper bandage, just something that he has wrapped round his hand. Can't say of course if it's genuine, but Danny doesn't think it's concealing anything, like a weapon or that."
"What's your next step, then?"
Miller heard a long drawn out sigh before Sugar replied. "No option, boss. We'll sit on him and see what happens and try and identify who it is that interests him in Dawson's."
"So he didn't go into the store this time?"
"No, just walked round it. If you ask my opinion, I think he was looking for the staff entrance. According to wee Jan, he completely ignored the main doors."
"Right, stick with it and keep me apprised of any developments. Oh, by the way, I spoke with your guys in Glenburn Street. There's no movement there."
"Thanks boss, speak later."

Dotty pee'd, washed her hands and face, brushed her hair and taking a deep breath, opened the door to the corridor. She didn't expect Morris to be there, standing with his back to the wall. "That's a bad habit you have there, Constable MacDonald, hanging about ladies toilets," she smiled with more humour than she felt.

Morris nodded and simply stared at her. "I'm not going anywhere, Dotty," he said at last, speaking softly and clearly and surprised how little the alcohol had affected him.

Her mouth was suddenly dry and her throat felt tight and she didn't trust herself to speak. The silence between them was almost unbearable and then he continued, "The last few years, the time we've worked together I mean, I've guessed or known rather, how you feel about me."

She tried to protest, but he held his hand up. "I'm not a man that would lie or intentionally hurt anyone. Not Susan and certainly not you and I would never, ever encourage you or give you false hope. I know how hard it is for you, how hard it's been I mean, with that scoundrel of a husband abandoning you and those lovely kids of yours. I know how little social life you have had," he shook his head, "I know better than most what difficulties you have had to overcome. Look," he stood upright, feeling suddenly awkward, his head turning to ensure they were alone, his hands flailing and his tongue running across his lips, his mouth suddenly dry as he sought for the right thing to say and the words not coming as he had practised. "This is a bad time for me, for both of us. All I'm trying to say, Dorothy, is that I'm not leaving Glasgow. I might not be back at work, but that doesn't mean I'll be out of touch. I need some time to get my head together, some time as I said earlier, to come to terms with losing Susan. But I will get on with my life. I will continue living, of that I'm determined." He suddenly grinned. "Am I making any sense here at all?"

She smiled at him, the tears coming easily and she didn't try to stop them. "You called me Dorothy. In all the years we've worked together, you've never called me Dorothy."

"Hey you two," Roderick suddenly appeared at the corridor door, his accent more pronounced by drink, "I just put another round up at the bar, so you buggers get yourselves in here, will you now?" He stared from his brother to Dotty, his face suddenly confused. "Have I missed something?"

"No, big brother," Morris reached over and gently drawing Dotty to his shoulder, he walked her to where Roderick stood and with an arm about each, he led both her and Roderick back into the function room. "You've missed nothing. Dorothy and I just agreed on something that hasn't been open to discussion," then to satisfy his brother's querying look, formally added "polis business."

Chapter 35 – Late on Thursday Afternoon

He found a closed doorway from where to watch the lane, a distance of no more than ten or fifteen metres away and gave him a clear view down the lane to where he thought the rear exit for Dawson's was situated. Though the light drizzle continued, it was light enough to clearly identify anyone coming from the lane. He hadn't been there for long when a steady stream of people, shift workers he imagined, began to appear.

The staff leaving Dawson's didn't give the man in the baseball cap a second look. It wasn't uncommon for husbands and wives, boyfriends and girlfriends to wait on their spouses and sweethearts, in the lane.

The team were on edge. Every five or ten or fifteen or thirty minutes, in fact, at no determined time, an employee or pair or group would depart the lane, presumably having exited Dawson's staff door. At each departure, the surveillance officer Danny, who had sight of the target, would see Hardie jerk upright in apparent anticipation and Danny would alert the team to "Standby", only to then mutter "Stand-down" into his microphone at another false alarm, his voice becoming more laconic at each new disappointment. Sitting in his car in Jamaica Street, Sugar realised the false alarms were becoming monotonous and the team were becoming distracted and distraction, he knew from bitter experience, led to mistakes. "Look sharp, people," he broke into the wavelength, "this guy is here for a reason and the reason is still to appear. Let's not …."

"Standby, standby, standby," snapped Danny, his voice excited now. "Target on the move walking towards a male figure, wearing a raincoat, about five feet six inches tall," he got no further with his description, but continued "Target now engaging male in conversation. Standby," he repeated as with uncertainty, he peered at the two figures.

Frederick had seen the man approaching him, scruffily dressed with one of these cheap, American type caps on his head, pulled low presumably because of the rain he thought. As he got a little closer, Frederick warily slowed his walk and was about to change direction to avoid the layabout, but the man made straight towards him. He saw the man hadn't shaved and detected a faint smell of body odour from him. He was about to tell him to fuck off, that Frederick had no change to give to dossers when to his surprise, the man said, "Mister Evans, how nice to finally meet you."

Frederick's apprehension at being accosted turned from shock to horror to abject terror, realising in that split second that the dosser wasn't what he had thought, but the man from the DVD, the man he had watched kill his wife, Paul Hardie. He stood rooted to the spot and felt his stomach churn and bowls tremble and he squeezed his arse cheeks together, fearing he might mess himself. His mind screamed at him to run, to shout for help, but Hardie had closed in on him and bending slightly over, stood almost nose to nose. Such was Frederick's fear and timidity he could only stare at Hardie in helplessness as his worst nightmare was now a reality.

"I want you to come with me," Paul softly replied, his voice low but full of unspoken menace, his eyes boring into the eyes of his tormentor.
"Please, don't hurt me," Frederick's voice begged in almost a whisper.
Paul had no need to touch the little shit, realising instinctively that not only did he tower physically over the smaller, slighter Evans, but such was the intimidation he exuded it was enough to make Evans comply without actually grabbing a hold of him. To reinforce his complete control, he leaned into Evans and in turn, whispered back to him, "In my jacket pocket, I have a knife, a very sharp, pointed knife, just like the knife I used to kill your friend. The friend you made me kill. Do you understand?"

Danny the footman watched the two men standing together, wishing he could hear what was being said, but of course fifty metres distance didn't lend itself to anything other than visual Ob's. However, they seemed to know each other, he guessed and relayed his opinion back to Sugar.
"Is there any suggestion or indication of Hardie being aggressive with this guy or anything like that Danny?"
"No nothing like that, Sugar. As I said, they seem to know each other. They're still talking away there. Two women have just passed them from the lane and I'm guessing if he works there, then they're co-workers of the wee skinny guy. The women didn't give the target or the wee skinny guy a second look. I suppose if the wee guy was worried, he'd have probably said something or walked away, eh?"
"Aye, likely you're right, over."

Frederick could only nod, too terrified to do anything else, his full concentration on Paul Hardie's eyes and so intent with his own safety he didn't even see the two curious women pass him by.
"If you try to run, if you try to speak to someone, if you try to fuck me about, just remember this. I have nothing to lose. I will take the knife and stab you to death, understand?"
It took all of Frederick's willpower to stand upright, not to faint. His legs shook and he fought hard to contain his bowels. His body shook with fear and he wanted to cry, the tears threatening to explode from his eyes.
"We're going to walk together, you and me, just two pals, to my car that's parked in the Mitchell Street car park. It's not too far. Will you cause me any problems?" Paul hissed at his tormentor.
Frederick could only nod, too afraid to look away as his captor's eyes bored into him. Then he whispered, "Please, don't hurt me. I won't tell anyone. Please."
"Just do as I say," replied Paul, enjoying the sensation of power he felt and now leading him gently by the arm as they slowly began to walk along

Mitchell Lane towards the car park. He thought it wise to reassure Evans to prevent the smaller man from crying out for help and added, "You will not be harmed," but knowing that he was lying, that he had every intention of hurting his tormentor and making him pay, and pay and pay and pay.

"Standby," said Danny the footman, "standby. Both target and the male now towards the car park, over."
"Who the fuck is this guy he's met," fumed a puzzled and suddenly worried Sugar as he turned to his startled neighbour. "What's their connection?"

In the car beside Jan, Lesley had a thought and quickly phoned Sugar on his mobile.
"What!" he almost exploded in her ear and caused her to think maybe it wasn't such a good idea calling him.
"The guy Hardie just met, he's just left the store, yes?"
"Yeah, I suppose so," mumbled Sugar, "what's your point?"
"I expect there will be security on the back door, so will there be any value in Jan and I nipping into the store's staff exit to ask who the skinny guy was that just left within the last five minutes?"
"Do it," Sugar decided.

Pete Buchanan had imbibed far more of the golden nectar than he meant to and wisely deciding to abandon his car 'till the following day, asked at the bar if the staff would kindly fetch him a taxi. "Oh, and taxi's for these drunken buggers too, please," he added, still the Sergeant and assuming a parental responsibility for his guys and drunkenly trying to work out just who was going where.
"Just one taxi will do," countered Dotty at his elbow, shaking her head at the grinning barmaid as she turned and patted Buchanan on the back. "If you can drop young Alex off, he's on your route, I'll get the MacDonald brothers and Jinksie up the road." She shook her head at Buchanan's questioning look and added, "I've been on the soda water and lime, you drunken bum."
"Right," slurred Buchanan, eyes glazed and trying hard to focus on the blonde head that seemed to be bobbing about in front of him. "That's us sorted then, eh?"
Dotty smiled and softly exhaled, happier than she had felt for a long time and replied, "Aye, that's us sorted."

In the poorly light car park, Paul took a firmer grip of his tormentor's arm and hurried him up the stairs towards the Focus on the second level. Shafts of light from the openings in the concreted walls of the building illuminated them as they made their way to the car, but no police officer was there to see

that the casual walk from the store to the entrance door had now become a forcible dragging by their target, of the smaller man,
"Where… where… where are we going?" Frederick finally found his voice. Paul ignored the question, not trusting himself to speak, his nerves tortured by the excitement of what he had planned when what he really wanted to tell the little shit was, 'We're going where nobody can hear you scream!'

Sugar Smythe was in a quandary. The target had met with an unknown male and returned to the Focus. Nothing in the two men's body language or at least, nothing his guys could determine, suggested anything other than a straight forward meet. The problem was both had made their way to the target's Ford Focus and Sugar had a decision to make. Send a footman in to watch both men if the meeting was to be held within the Focus or the building itself and risk compromising the operation, or trust to his instinct that both men will be departing in the car to travel elsewhere. After all, he told him himself, it might be that the target was simply giving a pal a lift home, but Sugar knew in his head this wasn't so. "Right," he flipped the switch on the steering wheel, "Danny, cover the exit of the car park. Let's know when it's an off and convoy, we'll take them wherever they go, over." One by one, the other cars acknowledged other than the crew of four-one-nine who were just entering the rear staff door at Dawson's.

Peter Wylie, seated at his security desk with the early edition of the 'Glasgow News' in his hand, was nodding cheerio to a couple of the staff, who held the door open as Lesley and Jan entered.
"Evening ladies," he greeted them and then frowned, his eyebrows knitting together and held his hand up ready to point. "I'm sorry, this is a staff entrance, the main doors…" but he got no further as Jan held up her hand with her warrant card displayed for him to see.
"Wee inquiry mister, eh, Wylie," she read from his name badge. "Within the last ten minutes, a man departed from the store, probably an employee," and gave Wylie a description of the man who met with the target."
Wylie glanced about him and in a low voice, said, "I'm ex-job myself, retired from the Central Division here. I'm not supposed to give out information on staff. Supposed to refer inquiries to the HR people," but glancing about him again, said, "That sounds like Freddy Evans or Frederick as he likes to be called. He's a wee stuck-up shite, so he is."
"Whereabouts in the store does he work?"
"Eh, since that guy Hamilton was murdered at the beginning of the week, Evans has been doing his temporary departmental manager, but the word is he hasn't a hope in hell of getting the job. Not a popular man is our Freddy."

Wylie stopped speaking when a male member of staff appeared and stamped his card, giving the officers a curious look before pushing through the exit door.

"Do you have an address for Evans?"

"No hen, I'd need to refer you to the HR for that and if I'm thinking right you're not wanting Freddy to be aware you have a wee interest in him, eh?"

"Right, thanks," replied Jan and turned to leave, but Lesley raised a hand to stop her and asked, "Evans, is he married or anything? I mean, straight? Doesn't have a male friend that might meet him from work or anything?"

Wylie seemed puzzled then nodded in understanding. "Aye, I think he's straight. He was supposed to be seeing a wee lassie for a while from the kitchens, Jenny Farndale, but she's already away home," then leaning in as if disclosing a confidence and in a low voice, added, "I don't think Freddy has any pals. I'm not kidding you ladies; he's a right weird wee guy. Won't even look at you let alone give you the time of day. No, if you want my opinion, he's a right Nigel Nae Pals."

"Thanks," smiled Lesley and touched with a forefinger at the side of her nose. "You'll keep this to yourself, eh?"

"Stand on me," beamed Wylie, his curiosity killing him, but too long in the tooth to start asking why the polis were sniffing about Freddy Evans. Time will tell, he inwardly sighed and took comfort that he would be able to boast he was the first to know.

In the lane outside, Lesley saw Jan's head jerk as she listened to a transmission in her earpiece and then, her face displaying puzzlement, said, "The Focus has just been driven from the car park, but it's only the target in the car. There's no trace of the other guy, this man Evans." She turned to Lesley and suggested, "Maybe you should give Sugar a call and update him with what we've learned, eh?"

In the claustrophobic darkness, Frederick Evans lay in terror, his trousers sodden at the crutch where his bladder had released its contents. He was curled into a ball, his hands gripping both sides of his face as over and over, he whimpered like a child, "Please don't hurt me, please, please."

Tony the van man was starving. The pieces his wife had prepared for him long ago were scoffed, the flask of coffee finished, last night's edition of the 'Glasgow News' read, its cryptic crossword completed and the bloody rain was obscuring his vision through the rear window. As he glanced again into his piece bag, he saw there remained one Mars Bar and the bottle of water and those, he miserably realised, would have to do him till the operation was stood down. He listened to the transmissions from the team and his eyes narrowed. He was familiar with the area the target was driving through and unless he was mistaken about the direction of the follow, it sounded to Tony that the target was en route back home. He checked his camera equipment was set and ready to go, made himself more comfortable and then settled down to watch the roadway outside number nineteen and await the arrival of the Focus. With a sigh and finally giving in to temptation, he hungrily tore the wrapper from the Mars Bar.

Andy Carmichael delivered a sleepy Evie to her grandparents in time for dinner, but declined their generous offer to stay and eat with them. His parents were a Godsend and for the umpteenth time, wondered how he would have gotten by if they and his sister and her husband hadn't been around to help with caring for his daughter. His retired parents were particularly good at coming over to the flat when Andy had the early morning shift starts, to care for Evie and get her out to school, but now and again, he thought it a good idea to have their granddaughter stay overnight with his folks and give his parents that little bit of a lie-in. Besides, he knew Evie loved being there and was fussed over and well cared for. Yes, he grinned as he made his way back towards his flat, he was a lucky man in a number of ways.

His thoughts turned to Lesley and her visit the previous evening. She hadn't stayed long, but the very fact she had arrived at all was, to Andy, an indication that like him she was keen to continue their budding relationship. He had a feeling, just a feeling, that last night if Evie hadn't been at home with him, things between Andy and Lesley might have gotten a little heated. That worried him a bit, remembering that it had been some time since he had enjoyed the favours of a woman and the last time, so long ago that he hardly recalled, was with his ex-wife. As he walked, he realised that he was smiling, thinking about Lesley. It crossed his mind that his lack of recent sexual experience might hinder him, but hoped that she would understand if he wasn't as romantically confident as perhaps she expected him to be. He glanced at his watch and wondered what she was up to now that Evie was at his parents overnight and he had, what the guys at work joked was 'an empty'. When she arrived last night all she had said about her day was she had assisted a plain clothes unit with something, but hadn't elaborated and he guessed whatever the inquiry was, it must be sensitive. He arrived at his close and making his way upstairs, thought about sending her a text message, just in case she finished work early and was at a loose end, but then remembered her father was very ill and thought perhaps she might instead make her way to her parents home for the evening. Still, he convinced himself as he inserted the key in his front door, it might not do any harm to send a text message, just to say hello.

Last to leave the plot, Lesley and Jan at Sugar's instruction, had firstly and briefly scouted the area to try to find the skinny man, but without any luck. Now Jan drove fast, but competently as she strove to catch up with her teammates, but then slowed to a more sedate speed as the radio broadcasts seemed to indicate it now seemed certain Hardie was heading towards his home.

"Where do you think the other guy, this Frederick Evans, went to?" asked Lesley.

Jan, a cigarette stuck between her lips, turned her head slightly to blow smoke through the partially opened window and brushed irritably at the ash that blew back onto her jacket.

"No idea," she mumbled, negotiating the car around a stopped bus, "but I'd love to have been a fly on the wall listening to what they two discussed, eh?"

"The target vehicle is now turning into Chamberlain Road. He's all yours Tony, over," said the voice on the radio.

"Roger," acknowledged Tony, preparing himself to snap a few photos as the target exited the vehicle.

"There's still nothing to suggest that Hardie has done anything to his wife," said Jan, stopping the vehicle in Munro Drive and switching off the engine, "though I have to admit, meeting the guy from Dawson's is one hell of a coincidence with what we now know about the murder in the Central Division, eh?" Jan inhaled deeply on her fag. "Got any plans for tonight, then?"

"No, nothing planned," replied Lesley, but already having decided to visit her parents and spend time with her mother. She didn't tell Jan simply because Lesley didn't want to have to drag out a lengthy explanation of her father's illness, preferring to keep such family issues confidential.

"Me, I've a hot date," grinned Jan. "A guy I met hill-walking last week. I'm seeing him in the town for a drink later tonight. Think I might get lucky, eh?" she grinned again.

"Target vehicle now drawing up outside number nineteen, target vehicle stopped and the target out of the vehicle," drawled Tony's voice.

"Target opening the boot of the car and reaching in…bloody hell," Tony almost screamed across the air. "He's pulling a guy out of the boot! There's a guy been in the boot of the vehicle and the target is dragging him into the house," then almost as an afterthought, said "Over!"

Jan stared wide-eyed at Lesley, her mouth hung open and the cigarette stuck to her lower lip then, her face expressionless, she said, "Well, that's tonight's shag well and truly scuppered, eh?"

Chapter 36

The rain had finally stopped and darkness was descending when Peggy Gold waved goodbye to Doctor McPherson and watched him walk down the path to his car. As she glanced at the garden, so lovingly tended to by Thomas, it occurred to her that she should be out there tomorrow if the fine weather returned, to mow the grass and pull some weeds. She waved as McPherson drove off and continued to stand at the doorway, in her mind's eye seeing Thomas in his garden clothes, the old white floppy hat she had bought him in Benidorm atop his head as he worked away at the flower bed, always with the optimistic suggestion that if she wanted to join him or would prefer to put the kettle on, it was her choice. She smiled at the memory, knowing it was his bare-faced hint that she fetched him a cuppa as he laboured. Standing with one hand on the wrought metal railing, she closed her eyes, enjoying the sensation of peace and quiet and the smell of the slightly damp, but warm air. She thought of her daughter's; Lesley who had sent yet another of her frequent text messages to say that she might be delayed at work, but would try to get there later in the evening and Linda, whose one phone call that day had begun asking if her mother was able to look after her grandson and who had abruptly hung up when Peggy tried to explain it wasn't possible.
"I mean, it's not as if I ask you regularly," Linda had sharply complained. "If you choose not to see your only grandchild, that's your decision, mother." Peggy had not sought an argument and was too tired to engage in yet another fight with her youngest daughter. It was only later, when she had sat down with a coffee in the kitchen to compose herself that she realised not once had Linda asked after her father.
Her thoughts were interrupted by a fit of coughing from the bedroom and turning she closed the front door and called out, "Coming darling. I'm here."

DI Miller, sat at his desk with the phone pressed to his ear, listened with increasing incredulity as Sugar Smythe related Tony the van man's observations. "So there was a guy hiding in the boot of the car and from the description, probably this man Evans?"
"Well, boss, from what Tony described, it wasn't so much hiding as being forcibly dragged from the boot. It sounds more like abduction."
"Let me get this straight, Sugar. The target, this guy Hardie, met with another man who seemed to be in conversation with Hardie. Both are then seen walking calmly towards the car park in Mitchell Street and at that time there was nothing to suggest the man was being forced to accompany Hardie, yeah? Your guys lose sight of them at that time and," Miller hurriedly staved off a complaint, "that's not a criticism, okay? I know how hard it can be following a target on foot. So to reiterate, Hardie is seen driving off alone then when he arrives at his house, the van man sees Hardie dragging a guy, probably this Evans character, from the boot of the car. Correct so far?"

"Correct boss," sighed Sugar, feeling slightly out of his depth and more than happy to unload the burden on to Miller.

"I take it your guys are still plotted about the house and there's no likelihood of Hardie getting out of there unseen?"

"Correct boss, but saying that, if he sneaks out the back door and keeps low, there's no lighting there and he obviously knows the topography of the area, so he could slip past us in the dark."

"But that would suggest he is aware there is surveillance around the house. There's no suggestion your team has been burned by him, is there?"

"No boss. I'm happy that we're not compromised," replied Sugar, unconsciously crossing his fingers and toes as he made the statement.

Miller run a worried hand across his brow and knew that tonight was going to be a long night. "Right, here's the plan. First, we don't know what the connection is between Hardie and this man, whom we suspect is Evans. I'll get the late shift CID from here to knock up the security at Dawson's and get some background on Evans, if nothing else, a home address and photograph and in the first instance, try to confirm it is him that Hardie has in the house, savvy?"

"Got that boss," replied a relieved Sugar.

"Secondly, we don't know if the man, let's call him Evans to make it easier, if this guy Evans is at any risk from Hardie. However, if your man Tony is right, it seems that Hardie was none to gentle getting Evans out of the car, yeah?"

"According to Tony, it seemed that way, yeah"

"So, from Tony's observations, if it is abduction as you suspect and if indeed that is the case then we need to get in there and establish if Evans is at risk, yeah?"

"I agree boss, yeah."

Sugar heard Miller exhale loudly over the phone and then Miller said, "Okay, Sugar. Here's what I believe. The circumstances seem to indicate there is a possible threat to life and if not life, then certainly Evans safety seems to be at some sort of risk. That leaves me no choice but to inform the Div Com and we'll need to get an armed response team down there to back you guys up."

"Isn't that a little extreme, boss? I mean, bringing in the armed back-up?"

"I've no choice in the matter, Sugar. The Force's Standing Orders quite categorically state where there is a presumed threat to life, we are obliged to meet that threat with the appropriate response, though God knows what the Div Com will make of it. Look, you're the commander on the ground right now. How do you feel if I run the whole thing past the Div Com before I make that decision, if that makes you feel any better?"

"How long will that take?"

"About as long as it takes me to apprise him with a verbal update. He's still in the building. He's got a Community Council meeting so let me get on to him and I'll get back to you as soon as I have a decision, okay?"
Right boss," replied an increasingly anxious Sugar.
"One more thing, Sugar, any update, get me on my mobile."

Sugar broke into the team's radio channel and in a short, concise narrative, related his conversation with Charlie Miller, ending the transmission with a warning that everyone must stay alert that under no circumstances was the target to depart the house without being spotted.

Agnes McClafferty peered from the brightly lit rear lounge window into the darkness of the lane behind her mid-terraced house, her sense acutely attuned to any movement since the theft of her and her daughter's knickers from the washing line. The baseball bat that lay within handy reach of Agnes's puffy hands had cost her two pounds at the Saturday's Fruit Market car boot sale for just such an emergency.
"I'm telling you, there's someone out there," she whispered to her daughter who, bored with her mother's incessant suspicion, suggested it might yet again be the neighbour's cat.
"It's no the cat," said Agnes, comfortable that with no visitors in the house, she could drop the Bearsden accent. "I'll bet it's that cheeky bugger from across the lane, him whose wife has run off with another man."
"You don't know his wife left him for another man," her daughter scoffed, wishing her mother would shut up and let her get on with her studying.
"Well, if I was his wife, I would bloody well leave him, I can tell you, girl," she sniffed over her shoulder, remembering how the sod had rebuffed her and just because she was being nice to him as she continued to stare into the darkness in the vain hope of catching the thieving bastard sneaking about her garden. As she watched, a ginger cat suddenly sprang from the top of a bin onto the ground and stared defiantly at the large woman before huffily disappearing through a gap in the hedge.
"Wee shite," whispered the startled Agnes under her breath and continued to peer into the darkness.

The Divisional Commander, Chief Superintendent Willie Ormond had been looking for some operational reason to avoid attending the Community Council meeting with its petty complaints and bumptious self-righteous councillors, but never in his wildest dreams could he have imagined being handed an excuse like the story his DI, Charlie Miller had just related.

"Bloody hell, Charlie, is this a wind-up? You're telling me that because of one of my cop's suspicions about the husband of an MP, we might be looking at a possible abduction?"
Miller, sat in the chair in front of Ormond's desk in the Div Com's office, nodded. "It seems that way boss."
Ormond, gray haired and a thick, grey moustache, had been a copper for just over thirty years, was well respected and not only among his peers, but by those officers he commanded.
"Right," he exhaled, "Obviously the buck stops here, so I'll take charge and I'll make the decisions on recommendations made by you and the man on the ground, that's DS Smythe, isn't it?"
"Aye sir, Sugar."
"Okay, Charlie, based on the information that you are currently in possession of, do you have any thoughts or plans on what you intend doing?"
"As I've said, we really don't know for certain what if any threat this guy Evans …."
"The guy you think is Evans, you mean?"
"Yeah," Miller glanced at his watch, "hopefully that will be firmed up quite soon, but in the meantime we'll call him Evans. If he is at threat, we need to establish that and sort the situation out."
Ormond held up both hands, palms towards Miller. "The last thing I want on my patch is a hostage situation, Charlie."
"I'll try to avoid that kind of scenario, boss," grinned Miller, then his face became serious. "What I'm about to propose might not be to your liking, but it might get the situation resolved quickly."
"And that is?"
"The young cop that set the ball rolling, Constable Lesley Gold; she's smart and keen too. She might be persuaded, with a colleague of course, to knock on Hardie's door in the pretence of doing a follow-up call about his missing wife."
"Sounds a bit dodgy, Charlie," replied Ormond and then cocked his head slightly to one side, his eyes narrowing and continued, "Lesley Gold? Isn't she the cop that punched….?"
Miller grinned as he interrupted, "Some would say the sod deserved it, boss."
"Aye, well, maybe I shouldn't know about such things, but it's nice to hear about a lassie that can stick up for herself," replied a poker-faced Ormond, the father of two daughters who were both going through the angst of teenage years and, due to all sort of boyfriend issues, causing their father a few sleepless nights.
"Anyway, if young Lesley's up for it, she and her partner needn't go beyond the doorstep. It might be enough to establish if there is something amiss in that house. While they've got Hardie on the doorstep, I understand from

Sugar there's no lighting in the rear of the houses that backs onto a common lane, so I can have some of the surveillance at the back of the house to see if they can spot anything through the window. Either way, we haven't lost anything by that approach and the best we can hope for is that it turns out to be a huge false alarm."

"Aye, a false alarm that will take a chunk out of my overtime budget," sighed the fiscally conscious Ormond. "Right," he nodded, "I'll remain here in the control room where, I assume, they have access to the surveillance team's channel, yes?"

"Yes boss, you'll be able to monitor what's happening and of course, I'll get myself down there and take over from Sugar. The poor sod's probably wetting himself at the responsibility," he grinned again.

"One more thing, Charlie, the young lassie Gold and whoever you choose to neighbour her to this man Hardie's door. Extreme caution at all times. Their safety is paramount as far as I'm concerned. I don't want any of my guys getting themselves hurt, understood?"

"Understood boss," replied Miller as he left the room.

Eunice Evans invited the two very polite and well dressed men into the lounge and offered tea or coffee, her face betraying her curiosity. She was both thrilled yet a little anxious at the presence of the detectives.

"So, Frederick is your son and resides her with you, Missus Evans? Is he at home just now?" asked the older man.

"Yes, Frederick is my son," she smiled hesitantly, "but he's not returned this evening from work, officer. Has anything happened to Frederick?" she raised a hand to her throat.

"Not as far as we know, Missus Evans. We're still making inquiries regarding his whereabouts," smiled the detective, "so you weren't anxious when he didn't arrive home at his normal time this evening?"

"Well, no, not really. He has a girlfriend or at least, I think they are still romantically linked," she lowered her voice as though confiding a great secret. "Still," her eyes wandered, "I haven't seen Jennifer these last few days so, well, you know what young people are like," she smiled.

It didn't take much for the detectives to persuade the old lady to permit them to search her son's room, though she did insist that she accompany them, explaining, "He's that fussy, you know. Usually locks the door when he goes to work, but doesn't know that I have always had a spare key," then added with a sigh, "must think the blinking place cleans itself."

While she stood guard-like at the bedroom door, the detectives gave the place a quick glance and not only discovered Frederick's sordid little pile of magazines at the bottom of his wardrobe under the woollen pullover, but also couldn't fail to see the laptop on the desk.

"Into computers is he, your son?" smiled the younger detective to Eunice, shuffling the magazines back to where he found them and pretending he hadn't noticed their titles.

"Yes, he likes to think he is," she replied, but her eyes warily followed the older man as he fetched a cardboard box from behind the water heater in the small cupboard. She saw his eyes narrow and then his head snap up as he glanced at her, a forced smile on his face. "Just odd's and sod's in here then," he said, but Eunice could see it in his eyes. The man was lying.

"What have you there, officer?" her voice trembled a little and though she couldn't possibly have guessed at the box's contents, she knew in her heart it was something very bad.

The detective, a kindly man who took no pleasure in delivering bad news, took a deep breath and his voice now grave, replied, "Missus Evans, I think you and I might go downstairs now for that cup of tea, eh?"

Eunice Evan's son had never known such fear. Sat cross-legged on the floor in front of the armchair in his damp, suit trousers with sticky tape now stuck across his mouth to stop his whimpering pleas for mercy. He could not guess that the roll of tape had previously been used to seal the bags containing Fiona's body. He sat with his hands in his lap, bound by tape at the wrists and facing his nemesis who towering over him, was seated in the armchair, legs akimbo and his bandaged hand on the arm of the chair while the other hand dangled the knife towards Frederick.

Paul had made his tormentor remove not just his coat and jacket, but his shoes and his shirt too, though insisted the tie remain as he used it as a lead to make it easier for Paul to pull his tormentor through the house. He had not bothered tying his tormentor's legs, knowing that the little skinny man was too frightened to escape or do anything other than shake with fear. Now his tormentor's torso had more than a dozen little, blood-stained pinpricks that he had inflicted with the needle point of the knife, taking satisfaction from each whimper of pain that the knife induced. He had never known such a feeling of power over another human being; even his rape and sexual domination of Fiona had not been as exhilarating as what he now experienced. His madness did not mask his perception that his tormentor was fully compliant to his every whim. He wondered how long he could play with his tormentor, what injuries he could inflict before he killed him. It occurred to him that his tormentor might not be fully appreciative of why Paul was hurting him. Perhaps, he thought, he should explain the wrongs the man had done to him, the hurt he had caused Paul. Yes, he would tell him and he would know and understand why Paul had to first hurt him and finally, to kill him. He smiled down at his tormentor, as a god would smile upon a lesser being.

By arrangement, Charlie Miller met with Sugar Smythe and Lesley Gold in the rear of a marked police transit van in Helensburgh Drive, handy to respond yet far enough away from the target address not to cause any suspicion to Hardie or nosey neighbours.

Lesley felt a little humbled at being instructed to attend what was presumably a management meeting to discuss the situation, yet realised she wouldn't be there unless she had something to offer, but couldn't guess what that would be.

Miller instructed the transit van would be the command vehicle from where he would take charge of the incident and quickly outlined his plan and also assured Sugar that Miller taking charge did not in any way reflect on the junior officer's ability to handle the incident. Honour satisfied, an inwardly relieved Sugar acceded control to the DI and then Sugar and Lesley listened intently to the plan suggested by Miller.

As he spoke, Miller's mobile phone activated and both Sugar and Lesley watched as his face first registered surprise, then heard him say, "Note a statement from the mother and no, don't put the old lady through that. If need be, she can be shown the items at another time. Bring a photograph with you and meet me in Helensburgh Drive. It seems more than likely, but I still want positive confirmation that the man in the house with Hardie is Evans, okay? Also, send your neighbour with the laptop to Pitt Street. There should be an on call IT Forensic officer. I want that laptop examined pronto and anything of value downloaded as evidence. Oh, and tell your neighbour to stay with the laptop for continuity of evidence and he's to call me as soon as he has anything, Okay? Well done, mate," he said and concluded the call.

That done, Miller turned to Sugar and Lesley and grinned. "It seems our Mister Evans has his own sordid little secret. The guys I sent to Evans house discovered a box hidden in his room, full of ladies underwear. Unless I'm reading it wrong," he continued to grin, "Mister Evans is a knicker-knocker."

Lesley startled, recalling the visit she and Dotty Turner made the previous week to Austen Road and quickly recounted the circumstances of the theft. Miller was unfamiliar with the local area and asked Lesley to describe the location of the house relative to where the theft of the knickers occurred.

"Austen Road is the row of mid-terraced houses that backs onto Borden Road," she said, her voice rising with excitement. "It seems pretty odd that knickers are stolen from the house that backs onto Hardie's house, doesn't it sir?"

"Odd? Bloody well more than odd, young Lesley," Miller shook his head as he raised a hand and began counting off on his fingers. "So, what have we got?

One, Evans is a knicker-knocker. Two, knickers are stolen from the house across the back from the home of a woman who, coincidentally, is reported missing the following day. Three, the MP's husband who, according to what you learned Lesley, is a philanderer with a bit on the side. Four, a man who at first seemed to be totally unconnected meantime with Hardie is murdered in the city centre; a man who it now seems worked at the same place as Evans who, coincidentally, has now assumed the murdered man's managerial position. Does that now infer a possible connection between Hardie, Evans and the dead man? I believe so," he firmly stated.

"Number five, the MP's husband Paul Hardie meets this evening with Evans, bundles him into the boot of his car and drives him to Hardie's home address. So, what does that add up to? Is Hardie getting some sort of revenge for the disappearance of his wife? Are Hardie and Evans colluding together in some sort of scheme? Was the murdered man part of this scenario?" He frowned at his colleagues and slowly shook his head. "I'm guessing and putting together a jigsaw puzzle that just doesn't seem to fit together and getting nowhere fast, aren't I?"

"Problem is boss," said Sugar, "until we sit these guys down and interview them, we're no further forward. If our surveillance of Hardie is anything to go by, I'm confident that they have no idea the police are aware of their relationship. If we hit them now, we might just catch them literally, with their pants down."

Miller and Lesley laughed together at Sugar's unintentional analogy. He started at them curiously and then he sniggered. "Oh, yeah, knicker-knocker and pants. Very funny, you pair of comedians."

Miller turned to Lesley. "You're sure about this?"

"Absolutely, sir," she nodded.

"Right then, Sugar, pick your best man and let's get it done."

Agnes McClafferty had tired of her nightly watch at the rear window. The two old pair of pants she had hung out as bait was still there, on the washing line. It occurred to her she might have to bring them in before the neighbours thought she was a slovenly cow for leaving them out there all week.

Frederick Evans didn't understand. How could he be held responsible for Hardie's wife's death? He didn't kill her. All he had done was watch her husband kill her. And who the hell was Janice what's her name? And why did Hardie think that it was Frederick's fault that Hardie lost his job? He wanted to shout and scream that he was innocent, plead that he be set free, that he wouldn't do it again, ever, but the tape was tightly bound to his mouth and though his fingers weren't bound, he daren't lift a hand to remove it, not while Hardie rambled on and held the knife in his hand.

Paul stared down at the cowardly little shit. He couldn't decide whether to stab his tormentor in the body or use the pointed blade to stab him in the eyes. Either way, he frowned, there would be a lot of blood and he was fed up cleaning the blood off this floor. Blood on the floor, he thought? Then he remembered. Evans had killed Fiona, hadn't he? Not that it really mattered, for Paul had tired of her anyway. Her constant moaning and then she got herself pregnant. His eyes narrowed as he continued to stare at his tormentor. Fiona was pregnant? Was it his tormentor, he wondered that got Fiona pregnant? He snarled and pricked his tormentor again with the tip of the knife; just one more reason the little shit had to die.

Frederick twisted, but couldn't avoid the point of the knife piercing his skin. He grimaced in pain and threw his hands up to protect his torso, but this action caused Hardie to feint with the knife and then stab down lightly at Frederick under his raised arms.

Paul laughed at his tormentor's futile attempts to avoid justice and knew then that if he was going to kill his tormentor, it had to be now.

In his state of mind, in his insanity, Paul Hardie had become the most dangerous individual the police are called upon to deal with; the individual with no conscience and no regard for his own fate or the fate of others.

Chapter 37 – 19 Borden Road

The surveillance team, now ably assisted with uniformed colleagues who at a discreet and unobtrusive distance maintained a cordon on the roadways about the area from the target house, were apprised of the plan on their radios by Sugar.

Two Armed Response Vehicle's, each crewed by two highly trained armed officers wearing black one-piece jumpsuits, Kevlar body armour, helmets and armed with Heckler Koch short barrelled sub-machine guns as well as their personal issue Glock handguns at their waist, had abandoned their vehicles some distance away and been led to the house by their surveillance colleagues; two of the male officers to the front of the target house and crouched in shadow a short distance from number nineteen, while the other male Constable and the supervisory female Sergeant had been situated with Danny, a surveillance colleague, in the darkened lane to the rear of the target house. Miller had met and briefed the four armed officers and informed them that while there was no suspicion the suspect Paul Hardie was armed with a firearm, their presence had been required because there was a reasonable belief Hardie might be threatening danger to life, one Frederick Evans. In short, Miller regretted, the threat was unspecific and the danger unknown. The Sergeant had grimaced, but knew Charlie Miller from old and later quietly and out of Miller's earshot told her officers, that was what it was all

about. "Trusting your instincts and the good people we work with," but also reminded them that if they had to take the shot, to make sure it's righteous. The team waited anxiously, aware that everything now hinged on Tony the van man who had immediate control of the network. Steadily and professionally Tony relayed his colleagues approach to the door at number nineteen, at which time Tony would pass control to his teammate.
Paddy, the press-ganged volunteer who accompanied Lesley, would then assume control when the target answered the door. It was, as the stocky built Paddy was later heard to comment, "The dry mouth, sweaty palm and tight bum cheeks bit of the operation."

Paul Hardie leaned his head back and closed his eyes. He wanted to savour this moment, savour the joy of exacting his revenge on the tormentor who had caused Paul so much grief.
Frederick stared up at the man who held Frederick's life in his bandaged and knife wielding hands. The sudden thought that he would jump up and escape run through his head, but to do so, he quickly glanced, he would first need to get to his feet and then leap over the long, outstretched legs that were on either side of him. That and Frederick's own legs were cramped from sitting cross-legged for what now seemed to be an interminably long time on the floor. But where would he run to, he wondered?
Paul opened his eyes and bending his head down, stared evilly at his tormentor. He gripped the knife tighter.

Agnes McClafferty decided to have another wee peek into the back garden before she went to bed, just to make sure the thieving bastard hadn't visited when she was fetching her sweet sherry from the near empty bottle in the kitchen. The glass held daintily in her huge hand, she cocked an ear and listened at her daughter's music from upstairs, satisfied that the moaning faced wee bugger wouldn't be downstairs complaining that her mother was having another tipple. "After all", Agnes giggled to herself as she sipped at the glass and murmuring again in her adopted Bearsden accent, "a half bottle of an evening doesn't make one an alcoholic now, does it?"

Lesley banged on the door, her chest tightening as she worked to control her nerves and wishing she had first taken the opportunity to pee. Standing beside her, Paddy gave her arm an unobtrusive, but encouraging squeeze and breathing slowly, got ready to deal with whatever was about to occur and whispered into his microphone, "That's the door getting chapped now, over."

Paul startled at the knock on the door and placing the knife tip at his tormentor's face, hissed, "Move from here and I'll slice this fucking nose off, understand?"

In total terror, Frederick nodded and folding his shaking hands into his sodden lap, stared down at the floor, praying that he satisfied the madman that he was going nowhere.

In his arrogant belief that he completely dominated the smaller man, Paul arose from the chair and stepped over him, vowing that when he had dealt with the caller he would finish this once and for all. He made towards the lounge door and turned to stare at his tormentor, reminding him, "Move and you're dead."

Frederick, his back to Hardie and mouth still taped and head bowed low, could only nod vigorously to indicate he understood.

Agnes McClafferty pulled aside the curtain and stared into the darkness, then stared again, her nose pressed against the window pane and the sherry from her glass spilling onto her fat hand. Yes, there was someone out there, someone moving in towards the back garden across the lane.

The ARV sergeant and her colleague moved silently along the lane, slightly behind the surveillance office Danny who had volunteered to approach the rear of the house and endeavour to see inside. The two armed officers, kneeling in the shadow of the garden's dividing brick wall, watched as Danny crept up to the lighted window. On a hunch, he gently tried the back door handle, only to discover the door was locked and decided to raise his head to the window sill. Grimacing, with frustration, he saw that the curtain seemed to be pulled tight together and denied him the opportunity to see inside the room.

Paul Hardie pulled open the door, his face contorted with rage when he saw it was the nosey police woman and a bearded man who was probably another nosey copper.

Lesley was about to apologise for calling so late, but before she could open her mouth, she saw the knife held in Hardie's hand.

Paul saw her eyes open wide and he knew the police were in league with his tormentor, that they had come for Paul.

Frederick Evans had to overcome his terror of Paul Hardie if he was going to get out of this and his fear gave him a strength he didn't know he had. With his hands still bound at the wrists, he turned onto his knees and pushed himself to his feet, his body colliding with the armchair as he did so, but his

legs felt rubbery from sitting so long. Hands outstretched before him, he stumbled towards what he thought must be the kitchen door.
He had to get away, hide somewhere, anywhere away from Hardie.

Agnes McClafferty gave a deep throated roar and snatching the baseball bat from where it stood upright against the lounge door, snatched open the rear door that led into the garden and in her slippered feet, rushed out into the darkness, the baseball bat clutched in both fists as she began to raise it above her head.

In an instant and maddened at being disturbed from taking his revenge on his tormentor, a wide eyed Paul Hardie decided that he would first stab the nosey policewoman to death then kill his tormentor and raised his knife to thrust downwards at the bitch.

The two ARV officers dressed entirely in their black outfits and in the shadows of the lane, were concentrating wholly on the surveillance cop Danny, kneeling below the house window, and didn't see the whirling Dervish wearing what looked like brightly coloured curtains approaching from behind until the large figure flashed past them growling with a bloodcurdling snarl.

Paddy, a long in the tooth beat man who had served for a number of years in the Possil area of Glasgow, saw the gleam in Hardie's eyes and instinctively knew the knife would be used. He grabbed at Lesley's jacket and hauled her out of harm's way then raising his left arm to deflect the blow, almost immediately realised he wasn't fast enough, that he was too late.

Frederick ignored the tape over his mouth and in the semi-lit kitchen, his fingers tore desperately at the handle of the back door, but realised with horror the door was locked. Crying now, the tears spilled down his cheeks and his whole body shook with desperation. In the partial light that flooded through the door from the lounge, he saw the key in the lock. How could he have missed it? He twisted at the key and pulled frantically at the door, banging against a worktop and cringing as he noisily knocked over some dishes onto the floor. With relief, the door swung open and shoeless, he run into the coolness of the moonlit night, the garden path lit by the shaft of light that streamed through the door behind him and marked his escape route to the lane beyond.

Tony the van man watched tensely as the door opened and then aghast, saw the young woman cop being pulled by Paddy then falling to the ground and what looked like Paddy wrestling with someone, presumably the target. "Assistance required at the door, now!" he screamed into his microphone.

In a heartbeat, Paddy knew he had been too slow and watched almost in slow motion as the knife arced down and sliced through his jacket, feeling the sharp blade bite into his left forearm. He heard a scream and didn't immediately realise it was he who had screamed.

The two ARV officers, just metres from the target's front door, saw the female cop fall down and hearing the male officer scream, rushed forward with their short barrelled sub-machine guns pointing forward.

Lesley, now pulled off balance and fallen onto her backside, watched in horror as Hardie struck Paddy on the arm with the knife. Instinctively, she seized the opportunity to kick out with her right foot through Paddy's legs and with more luck than design, struck Hardie on his right knee with the heel of her walking boot. Hardie grunted at the unexpected pain and releasing his hold on the handle of the knife that was stuck and protruding from Paddy's arm, stumbled backwards into the narrow hallway. Paddy, no longer grappling with Hardie, fell backwards on top of Lesley, a crimson fountain of arterial blood from his wound spurting over them both.

At the rear door, Danny the footman, crouched beneath the lounge window, heard through his earpiece Tony the van man's call for assistance then stared in shocked surprise as the figure of a shirtless man snatched open the rear door and arms outstretched, wordlessly fled past him. As he snapped his head around, a large figure in a bright, multi-coloured billowing dress, holding a big stick above her head, came through the open gate and ran down the narrow garden path towards the man screaming at the top of her voice, "I'll teach you to steal my fucking knickers, you pervert!" then, as a dumbstruck Danny and the two ARV officers watched helplessly, the figure struck the man squarely on the head with the thick stick.

In the rear of the transit van, Charlie Miller sat with the young, uniformed Constable driver and held his hands in his head as the operation went apeshit. He listened open-mouthed as the cries for assistance and an officer down continued with an almost immediate call for an ambulance, shrieked through his headset. Miller fought hard, resisting the urge to call in to the channel and demand a situation report, a sit-rep, trusting that the team, who worked so well together, would coordinate their resources and get help to whoever was injured as quickly as possible. With mounting apprehension, he heard one of the ARV call signs, he didn't know which one, shout into the radio that they were entering the target premises in pursuit of a suspect. Dear God, he silently prayed, let this work out okay.

The two ARV officers entered the narrow, but brightly lit hallway as they had been taught in textbook formation. 'Tic-tac' was the nickname for the drill as one officer covered the other, who moved forward, then repeated the manoeuvre; both men breathless with tension, their fingers on the triggers, mouths wide to aid their hearing and their hearts beating rapidly in their chests as adrenalin coursed through their bodies.

In the darkness of the rear garden, Agnes McClafferty watched in horror as the small man stared wide-eyed at her in shocked surprise, teetered slightly, reached for her then collapsed in an untidy heap at her feet. She couldn't be sure, but the shirtless man seemed to have something covering his mouth. It was then that she heard the shout and turning, saw two wraiths, both dressed in black and wearing helmets with guns pointing at her and screaming for her to drop the weapon. Weapon, she wondered? She had almost forgotten she was holding the bat and was about to explain when both the figures together dropped to one knee and screamed again they were going to shoot her if she didn't do as they said. Whether it was the excitement, the best part of a bottle of sherry or the shock, she wasn't certain, but the next thing she knew everything went dark and she collapsed in a dead faint.

Paul Hardie, clutching his damaged right knee where the bitch had kicked him, stumbled back into the lounge to discover that his tormentor was gone, that even though Evans had promised he wouldn't move, he had gotten away and now Paul had to find him again before he could kill him. He stared at the empty space, at the pool of urine where the skinny wee man had wet himself and realised that Evans had planned the whole thing; that he must have arranged for the coppers to come and distract Paul so that he would get away. That was it then. The polis were working with his tormentor and now the bastards were after him and all he had tried to do was get justice for his poor Fiona and all the bad things that had happened to him. He began to weep and the days of tension, the sleep deprivation and lack of nutrients finally took their toll. He collapsed sobbing onto the arm chair and wished Fiona was here to make his dinner and that things could just go back to how they had been.

Lesley saw the ARV officer's move into the house after Hardie and pushing Paddy off her, shoved the ashen faced man into a sitting position. She could heard the sound of running feet, but her full concentration was taken by the knife lodged in his arm and in the light that shone through the door from the hallway, she could see the bleeding was heavy and dark red. Guessing an artery had been cut or severed, she sat astride him and gasped, "Sorry," to the ashen faced Paddy, raised then punched her fist into the underside of his arm where she guessed his artery would be in an attempt to quell the flow of blood to the wound.

"Fuck me, first I'm stabbed then you set about me too?" he half laughed and grimaced as the pain shot through him.

Almost immediately, Tony the van man arrived at the run and unceremoniously pushing Lesley out of the way, but only enough to permit him to get into his teammate, and cried "I'm a first aider, hen. Keep the pressure on and I'll deal with the blood-flow, okay?"

It seemed to Lesley an age had passed as they both worked on Paddy, but within a few minutes, if not seconds, other officers were in attendance and she was roughly, but not unkindly, pulled to her feet as someone took over her position, then she was led to a nearby surveillance car and seated on the passenger seat with her legs on the roadway and form somewhere, a blanket procured and thrown over her shoulders.

"Sit there and don't you be moving," ordered Jan, her face pale in the street lighting and a fag dangling from between her lips. "You're in shock, hen, so just breathe easy, eh?"

It occurred to Lesley it might be easier to breathe if the Fifer refrained from blowing cigarette smoke into her face, but kept her tongue still, realising Jan was trying to be kind.

Inside the house, the two ARV's stared at each other and wordlessly, in a well practised manoeuvre, one kicked open the lounge door and both quickly advanced into the room, their weapons sweeping a covering arc in front of them. They found the target sitting on an armchair, weeping like a baby, but kept their weapons trained on him as they screamed, "Show us your hands, now!"

Paul could hear someone shouting at him, but he didn't care anymore.

While one officer maintained a weapon on the target, the other placed his sub-machine gun under his neighbour's foot, then keeping out of the arc of fire, moved toward the target and roughly dragged the now pliant Paul to the floor. To both the ARV officer's relief, the target didn't struggle as the arresting officer pinned the target's wrists at his back with flexi cuffs.

They turned to find the ARV Sergeant stood in the kitchen doorway grinning and who said, "Nicely done boys." Removing her Kevlar helmet and running her fingers through her hair, she added, "Dear God, what a fuck-up, eh?"

CHAPTER 38 – The Aftermath

Charlie Miller, sitting beside the uniformed Constable, arrived in the police transit van just as the ambulance pulled up. Getting out of the vehicle, he stood to one side with his hands in his pockets and watching the paramedics go to work on Paddy. It occurred to Miller that if he hadn't given up the booze in favour of family life, he would have sunk more than a few halves after tonight's debacle.

"Boss," Sugar Smythe acknowledged Miller's presence as he sidled up to him.

"What's the damage," asked Miller, then nodded at Paddy who grinned and gave him the thumbs up, "apart from the obvious, I mean?"

Sugar took a deep breath. "Bit of a story about the guy Evans. He's badly injured I'm afraid."

Miller closed his eyes and shook his head. "So we were too late, Hardie tried to kill him then?"

"Eh, not quite, boss. Evans was battered by a neighbour from across the back. A big woman with an even bigger stick, I'm afraid."

Miller stared at him. "I'm not going to like this, am I?"

Sugar shook his head. "Some woman that we think lives across the rear lane. We think it's the woman that got her knickers stolen, the one that Lesley Gold mentioned, remember? Anyway, she's in custody at the minute."

"So, she gets her knickers pinched and tries to murder the thief? Is that not against the law or something?"

Sugar paused and couldn't tell if Miller was being cynical, joking or had lost it.

A CID car was driven into the newly established cordon that had been created by the hastily summoned uniformed officers who were valiantly trying to hold back nosey neighbours, alerted by the commotion of the preceding fifteen minutes.

From the car stepped the Div Com, Willie Ormond. It was the nature of the man that his first concern was his injured officer and he made his way towards Paddy, who was being stretchered into the ambulance, his injured arm held aloft by Tony the van man.

"So, Paddy, you think you're getting some sick leave out of this, do you?"

Paddy grinned in appreciation at the levity, but was too weak with shock to respond.

Ormond patted him gently on his good arm and watched as the paramedics closed the rear doors and the ambulance made off, its blue lights illuminating the narrow street. Within a short distance, they all heard the sirens activate as the ambulance hit the traffic on the main roads and headed towards the casualty department at Gartnavel Hospital.

"Bit of a rum doo, then Charlie," said Ormond, taking Miller by the arm and leading him to a quiet spot. They stood close together, hands in pockets and spoke softly, neither man wishing to be overheard.

Miller shook his head and replied, "What can I say, boss. It all went to shit faster than we anticipated. As planned, the two cops, Lesley Gold and Paddy went to the front door, but before there was any dialogue, they were attacked by the target, Paul Hardie who apparently carried the knife to the door with him."

"Where's Hardie now?"

"He's in custody, still in the house. I haven't had the opportunity to speak with him yet, but according to Sugar, he's raving and not making any sense. Sugar's of the opinion he's gone off his head and suggests that first thing, we get a doctor to examine Hardie."

"Any trace of the wife in the house?"

"The team have made a cursory search, but no trace, nothing to suggest she's in there. The guy Hardie abducted, this Frederick Evans, and we're quite certain that it was abduction, he tried to flee through the rear of the house when our ARV guys went through front door." Miller sighed as if he had trouble believing it himself. "Seems that young Danny from the surveillance team was with two of the ARV officers at the rear when Evans burst out the door, but a woman from across the back, some woman that had her knickers stolen …"

Ormond's eyes narrowed as he stared in surprise.

"I know, I know, you couldn't make this up, believe me. Anyway, this woman, a big lassie by the sound of it, came running up the garden path and clubbed Evans on the head. She was shouting something like "steal my knickers" and calling him a pervert. We don't know if she was previously acquainted with Evans, so that's something we'll need to find out." He shook his head and continued, "Evans took one blow to the head, but it laid him out and though the first indication was that he was a goner, he's now en route to the Neuro at the Southern General Hospital in Govan. According to the paramedic who attended him, he thinks Evans won't survive; something about his pupils being too dilated and his eyes filled with blood, anyway, the paramedic's the expert so I won't quibble."

"What about this woman who hit him?"

"She's in custody. According to the ARV Sergeant, she fainted after she hit Evans just as they were arresting her at gunpoint. Seems she's a big woman and they had a hell of a job getting her onto a stretcher. Apparently she came to went berserk, slapped an ambulance man and they had to restrain her with handcuffs."

Ormond clapped Miller on the shoulder and leaned close.

"Listen Charlie, this is going to be a long night for everyone. Right now I want you to prioritise and your first job is getting the team together for a very, very short debriefing back at the office and I am emphasising short, understand? I am aware how capable you are, so don't take this the wrong way. Get this place," he waved to the house, "sealed off and stood by with some uniforms and ensure the Forensic are in there first thing tomorrow morning. In the meantime, charge this man Hardie with the abduction on what we know so far and the woman, the neighbour, charge her with assault and we'll reconsider tomorrow morning, okay? Statements and everything else can be dealt with tomorrow. What I want is the team fresh and ready first thing. They're too tired tonight and too shocked by the events to effectively put the whole story together. Right, I'm off to Gartnavel to find out how Paddy is doing." Ormond paused for breath and staring at Miller, asked, "There's something else on your mind, isn't there?"

Miller softly laughed and shook his head. "No, nothing boss, but I'll tell you this. I can feel it in my bones; this isn't the end of the inquiry, not by a long chalk."

Lesley Gold, her jacket, jeans and blouse soaked in Paddy's dried blood, sat in the surveillance car still wrapped in the blanket. She was being driven by Jan not to Maryhill Police Office, but under strict orders by Charlie Miller to go home and get herself cleaned up. As an aside to Jan, he told her that if there was no family or friends immediately available, she was to stay with Lesley overnight. "No problem," the Fifer had replied, but hoping instead that she could contact someone for Lesley and get back to the office to be involved in whatever was happening there.

"Eh, is there someone I can call for you, hen?" she asked as she drove, fingers mentally crossed and wishing to be anywhere but staying overnight with Lesley.

"No, honestly, I'll be fine," Lesley protested, equally dreading the thought of spending what remained of the evening in Jan's company. A few minutes passed as both strived for some mutual conversation and then to Jan's relief, Lesley said, "Yeah, maybe," and dialled Andy Carmichael's number.

Chapter 39 – Friday Morning.

Friday morning broke bright and sunny and the ever optimistic citizenry of Glasgow once more convinced themselves that summer really was beginning after all. Across the length and breadth of the city, dayshift for many was commencing - for some, it was a welcome morning; for others, not so welcoming.

DI Charlie Miller was roused from almost four hours of uninterrupted sleep by his stepdaughter Geraldine, who carefully balanced a plate of warm toast in both hands as his wife Sadie followed the little girl into the bedroom with a mug of hot tea.
"Bad night?" asked Sadie, but already knowing the answer, for if Charlie got in really late, he always used the spare bedroom rather than disturb his wife. He rubbed at his face and grinned at the redheaded wee girl while reaching up to receive a kiss from Sadie.
"Bit of a bummer," he wearily replied.
"You said bummer," giggled Geraldine and pointed to him, the other hand across her mouth to register her pretend shock.
"So I did, bad me," he playfully slapped at the back of his hand.
"It's gone seven-thirty, so I've laid out your things for when you've showered," smiled Sadie and taking their daughter by the hand, left Miller to finish his tea and toast and reflect on the enormous undertaking of collating all the evidence that had been and was still to be gathered before submitting his final report to the Procurator Fiscal.

Paul Hardie sat in the cell, rocking back and forth mumbling to himself. He refused all offers of newspapers from the turnkey, indeed ignored the man completely and his breakfast of roll and sausage and hot sweet tea lay untouched on the plastic tray.
In his mind, he was betrayed by everyone. When he got out of here he'd find his tormentor and this time, he vowed, he would kill Evans before he answered the door to the police.
Outside the cell, the civilian turnkey stared at the prisoner through the eyehole in the door and turning to the young probationary police officer who had drawn the short straw and sat in the chair by the cell door, grinned and made a rotating motion with his forefinger against his head. The officer smiled weakly in return, knowing that with this idiot working in the cell block area, it was going to be a long shift.

The Sister called the young Staff Nurse to her and together they left the ward for the relatives Waiting Room. "It will be good experience for you," she assured the nervous young Nurse. "There's going to come the time when you will have to do it yourself, so you might as well come with me and we'll see her together."
The Sister paused outside the Waiting Room to give her time to adopt what she believed was a solemn face, then pushing open the door, went and sat beside the old woman, reaching for and taking the woman's hands in her own.

The Staff Nurse thought the Sister was being too theatrical, but stood silently, her hands folded neatly in front of her and wishing she would just get it over with and let the Staff Nurse get away to her break.

"Missus Evans," began the Sister, "I'm so very sorry to be the bearer of such bad news…."

The Forensic team greeted the Constable who stood guard at number nineteen and donning their protective clothing and masks, moved their equipment into the hallway. They began their ritual with the obligatory tut-tutting at what they perceived to be a complete contamination of the crime scene by the flat foots who were vastly overpaid while they, all degree men with a fistful of additional qualifications, were left to find the evidence the bloody CID always seemed to overlook. Their usual collective whine over, they began their painstaking search of the mid terraced house and it wasn't too long before they discovered what they perceived to be a pathetic attempt to clean the blood from the tiled hearth. "Chalk another one up to the top team," sang out the delighted Team Leader as the three men gave each other pretend 'high five's'. The sample of blood diligently obtained from the hearth was bagged and tagged and set among the few pieces of evidence the Team had collected. However, to their unmitigated delight, when the Forensic team switched on the television and DVD player, they found to their shock what seemed to be the most important evidence that any of the three men had ever discovered. With unparallel haste, the Team Leader phoned DI Miller at Maryhill CID and as he watched the screen, related to the DI what seemed to be in the Team Leader's opinion, if not a murder, then certainly a very serious assault and all, he excitedly added, recorded on DVD. As the three Forensic officers watched the scene unfold, three pairs of eyes simultaneously drifted from the screen to the tiled hearth as all three men simultaneously arrived at the same conclusion; the likely source of the blood staining.

The shift at Garscadden Office, like officers throughout the rest of the Division, received partial news of what had occurred the evening before in Borden Road. The officers stood about Jinksie's desk, listening as he read the summarised version from the Divisional twenty-four hour bulletin and it didn't take a genius to work out that their very own Lesley Gold was one of the team involved. After much persuasion, Dotty Turner was tasked to phone Lesley and find out what had happened. "Maybe later," Dotty replied, refusing to be bullied into phoning right away. "If Lesley has been involved in the incident, it's likely she will have been up half the night, so no way am I am not going to disturb her now, okay" she raised a hand to indicate that was the end of the matter.

At the civilian bar, Andy Carmichael quietly laid the mail on the counter and slipped away unnoticed, preferring not to be seen and feeling privileged that Lesley had called him last night and so very glad that he was first in her thoughts when she needed someone.

It was just as she and Alex Mason were about to depart the office to go on patrol that Dotty Turner was called by Jinksie through to the Uniform Bar to receive a phone call.
"Gentleman says he spoke to Lesley Gold and asked for her, but I explained she is on another duty at the minute and I was wondering if you might take the phone call."
Dotty nodded and taking the receiver from Jinksie, said "Hello?"
She listened as the man hesitatingly explained that he was speaking the other day to Constable Gold and wanted to know if Constable Gold might be interested in some information?
Dotty again explained Lesley was on duty elsewhere and asked if she could assist, while indicating to Jinksie to pass a message pad and pencil. As she listened she wrote down some details. "Don't you worry, sir," she smiled at the handset, "I'll see that gets attended to personally, be sure of it."

Paddy the footman was the hero of the hour. The team had phoned the ward and left a message to let him know that after they had sorted out statements and other issues, they would attend en masse to harangue and pester him. The duty Staff Nurse, wise beyond her years and herself married to a police officer, noted the call and assured DS Smythe that when his Constable was awake, she would pass the message, but post-op she warned Sugar, could mean he might be unconscious for the best part of the day.
"So Staff, are you able to say how bad the wound is? I mean, will it affect him returning to duty or anything?"
"Sorry, DS Smythe, you know that I can't officially give out that information to anyone who isn't a near relative," the Staff Nurse coyly replied, then glanced about to ensure she would be overheard, said "but hypothetically speaking, I'd guess if he's a golfer or any kind of sportsman, it's reasonable to assume he should be back playing within a couple of months, okay?"

Lesley Gold felt guilty that it was Paddy wounded in Paul Hardie's attack and not she. "Survivor's guilt," suggested the all-knowing, all-wise Jan when the following day, Lesley confided her feelings at Maryhill Police Office.
"Let's get into the briefing room and get this over with," added Jan, as she ushered Lesley along the corridor, "and let's just be grateful that Paddy isn't too bad. The surgeon apparently said there's a good likelihood he'll make a one hundred per cent recovery and use of the arm, eh? Besides," the

pragmatic Jan further added, "the old sod will milk his hero status, you wait and see."

The surveillance team, unusually for them, sat quietly discussing the previous night's event and Lesley was gratified to see that none apparently held her responsible in any way for Paddy's injury. Indeed, the reassuring winks and pats on her back went some way to cheering her. She didn't not know that her instinctive kicking out at the suspect Paul Hardie, in defence of Paddy, was witnessed by Tony the van man, as well as both the ARV officer's and all three in their own time had related her action's to their surveillance colleagues.

The door opened and the four ARV officers led by the Sergeant, entered the room, closely followed by Sugar Smythe. Once the four ARV officers were seated, the door again opened to admit Charlie Miller and the Div Com, Willie Ormond.

Ormond called upon the team to stay seated where they were and in short, terse, sentences he began by saying he would leave the wash-up of the incident to DI Miller. However, Ormond felt he had to speak to the team and with a smile and gesticulating with his hand encompassed the ARV officers, to convey not just his own thanks, but congratulations on a job well done. To her embarrassment, Ormond pointed out that had it not been for the well-founded suspicions and tenacious initial inquiry conducted by Constable Gold, the crimes committed might well have gone undetected. Ormond rounded up by quite firmly stating that when DI Miller was finished with the team they were to take the remainder of the day off to gather their thoughts and, with a final smile, if they cared to return to their respective homes via Gartnavel, to try not to get Paddy into any more bother.

Miller thanked the Div Com and as Ormond left the room, turned to the team. "First thing, Frederick Evans died earlier this morning at the SGH, so I want you guys to get your statements down on paper. You know what you need to do and I won't teach a granny to suck eggs, savvy?"

The team nodded as one. Miller paused to gather his thoughts, before continuing. "As you will have guessed from the feedback emanating from the cell block downstairs, the suspect Paul Hardie has been examined by two doctors for both medical and psychiatric evaluation. Some time later today, at the instruction of the Fiscal, Hardie will be conveyed to and sectioned under the Mental Health Act in the State Mental Hospital at Carstairs." It didn't escape his attention that some of the team looked dubious, perhaps considering that Hardie was faking his mental illness and so Miller added, "It doesn't matter what we think, guys. The experts have given their opinion and either way, Hardie will be locked up. At the minute he is charged with the abduction of Frederick Evans. There is enough Forensic and surveillance evidence to substantiate that charge. You might also wish to know that in the course of the Forensic examination of the house, a DVD was discovered that we assess was filmed on a phone owned by Frederick Evans. Evans's phone and laptop are currently undergoing Forensic IT examination and will undoubtedly corroborate the assessment it was he who filmed the DVD. I'll add that the laptop also contained filmed items that seem to indicate Evans was a voyeur of women." He paused again and licked at his lips. "As for the DVD, it's pretty graphic, if poor quality, but it shows Hardie back-handing his wife, the missing woman Fiona Hardie and knocking her to the floor. On the film, that admittedly is quite short, she doesn't get up again and Forensic have discovered an attempt was made to wash blood from the area where she fell. Unfortunately, we are unable to say how much blood was spilled, but it is reasonable to assume it's hers and it's being checked against DNA we found in the house. It seemed from the film the punch was enough to render her unconscious. Regrettably, the DVD does not indicate if she later became conscious and there is strong suspicion the blow that felled her might also have been fatal. Tony?" Miller pointed to the raised hand.

"Has Hardie admitted killing her or anything, boss?"

Miller shook his head. "The brief interview I was able to conduct before the doctor's put a stop to it was a bit strange and I'm not kidding, by the way," he sighed and shook his head as if in disbelief. "Hardie insists it was Evans that killed his wife, Evans that killed the man in the city centre, Robert Hamilton and basically, Evans was responsible for all his problems and blamed him for nearly everything. I half expected the Kennedy assassination to be in there too."

"So the murdered man in the town, this guy Hamilton, it was Evans who killed him?" asked Tony.

Miller shook his head. "No, the SIO for the Hamilton murder confirmed an hour ago the knife recovered from the street drain that was used in the murder is part of a set we found in the kitchen at Hardie's home. Forensic also discovered some blood spatters on a dark jacket owned by Hardie, hanging in his cupboard and the blood matches Hamilton, so it's more than probable Hardie murdered the man Hamilton. Suffice to say, the SIO is satisfied Hardie is the culprit and the murder inquiry is being wound down, as we speak. Evans didn't actually commit the murder," Miller slowed his voice as he stressed the comment. "However it doesn't mean he's off the hook for the murder, that he wasn't implicated. Evan's mother thinks at the time the murder was committed he was out with his girlfriend. I've sent a couple of my guys to trace her to confirm that and eliminate Evans from the actual deed, as it where." Miller glanced at his notes. "The SIO and I are both of the opinion and agree an assessment that Evans, who apparently was an ambitious though not very nice man, witnessed Hardie kill his wife and recorded it on his mobile phone, then somehow coerced Hardie into killing Hamilton. Why? Like I said, it's open to conjecture, but the assumption is that Evans wanted Hamilton's job. The irony is the SIO discovered in the HR files at Dawson's, that Evans wasn't even close to being considered for Hamilton's job, though according to Dawson's HR Manager, Evans believed himself to be next in line. To placate him and because of his long service, Dawson's made Evans the interim manager, but it was just a temporary appointment."

To the amusement of some of his team Danny asked, "What about the mad woman from over the back, the big woman that bounced the bat off Evans head?"

Miller smiled and shook his head. "That's one for the Fiscal to make a decision on. At the minute, Missus McClafferty has been charged with serious assault, but on the instruction of the Fiscal, she has been released *pro loco et tempore* until such times a decision has been made regarding Hardie and the Crown Office sorting out who is being charged with what. Needless to say, once a lawyer gets her story and twists it, she'll likely put forward the defence she was rushing to arrest a thief, her knicker-knocker I mean. Whether she will be convicted or a plea entered, I really don't know, unless," he smiled, "any of you guys have a suggestion? What, no takers? Right then, so moving on." He pointed to Jan's raised hand.

"I'm not quite following this boss. Hardie and Evans, they were working together, then?"

"We don't know for certain Jan and the only guy that can confirm it is gibbering like a madman," he stopped, frowning at the sniggers from the team, "forget I said that. What I mean is Hardie just isn't making any sense and it's up to the shrinks to tell us if he ever will. Our priority was and remains trying to find Hardie's wife." He rubbed at his forehead with the heel of his hand and continued, "However, from the DVD that is recovered, I'm of the opinion that Missus Hardie is dead. I think we're looking for a body. The Media Department at Pitt have already run a story about her being missing and with the Div Com's permission, I intend asking them to put out a further appeal, but I feel in my bones it'll be a waste of time."

There was a knock at the door and a civilian support officer put his bald head round it. "Sorry, Mister Miller," then his glance took in Smythe. "Sugar, that's a call from the officers on Ob's at Glenburn Street. A van with three guys has turned up and apparently they're away into the close and the Ob's want to know if you and the team are available to hit the flat?"

Sugar turned a pleading eye to Miller, who grinned and said, "I'll let the boss know that you and the team have a wee thing to attend to before you take the day off, eh?" then stood to one side as the team rushed to the door.

Lesley Gold hesitated, uncertain whether or not to join them, but the decision was made for her when Miller waved for her to sit back down and came to sit with her.

"I just want you to know, Lesley that you did a cracking job. Your instinct came through, but as I said earlier, there is a strong likelihood your MP, Missus Hardie, is dead. Difficult to accept I know, but you did the best with what you knew and you can take some comfort that her husband didn't get away with it."

"So, what's next sir?"

Miller shook his head. "It's just a question of time. Missus Hardie's body will turn up and we'll close the inquiry, but in the meantime, she remains a missing person. Her husband's unlikely to divulge what he did with her body, that is, if he ever accepts he is responsible, but charges for the murder of Robert Hamilton, the abduction of Frederick Evans and, added to that, the charge of attempted murder of a police officer will ensure Hardie is unlikely to ever be released. Whether Crown Office will have the balls to go for the murder of his wife without a body, that's a decision they'll need to take and personally, I think it's highly unlikely, given the charges they can already prove. In short, they'll take the easy course and Missus Hardie will remain missing meantime. In the interim, Hardie will probably be detained indefinitely under the Mental Health Act and if he is later deemed fit for trial, he faces those solemn charges that will remain libelled. No," he shook his head, "Hardie won't be going anywhere in the near future. Now, you," he smiled and clapped her on the shoulder, "take the Div Com up on his offer and get away home. When you're back on duty, come and see me and we'll have a wee chat about how you think your career should progress, okay?"

The old janitor straightened slowly, one hand on the yard brush and the other massaging his painful back. The sound of a car door closing caused him to turn his head and he watched as the Head Teacher Gwyneth Jenkins started the engine and drove down the driveway towards the school gates.

Jenkins ignored the janitor, believing him unworthy of an acknowledging nod as she passed him by and slowed the car at the gates before turning left towards the main road. She had travelled a mere fifty metres when she saw the marked police car parked at the side of the road, a police woman standing behind the car, her hand raised to stop Jenkins vehicle. Puzzled, she slowed and stopped the car and, as the short blonde haired officer approached, wound down the window.

"Yes!" she snapped at the delay, "what is it. Why have you waved me down?"

"Constable Turner," Dotty gritted her teeth at the driver's attitude and forced herself to be professional as she leaned down to the open window and

introduced herself. Her eyes narrowed and her nose twitched at the strong smell of peppermints. She stared at Jenkins, her right hand waving to summon Alex Mason who appeared from the other side of Jenkins car to join her at the driver's door. "I am in receipt of information that the driver of this vehicle," she theatrically paused and smiled "and that seemingly would be you, madam, has consumed alcohol and as such, I will require you to take a roadside breath test."
Standing beside the school gates watching the police at Jenkins car, Jimmy Dunlop chuckled and whistling his favourite tune, finished brushing the leaves from the driveway.

Chapter 40 – Saturday Morning

Peggy Gold was exhausted, but though she tried to remain awake, sleep overcame her and she fell into an almost state of unconsciousness, her head awkwardly resting on the armchair. She awoke with a start to find her husband lying with his head turned towards her, his lips trembling and his eyes glistening with tears.
In the spare bedroom, their daughter Lesley slept fitfully, her dreams punctuated by nightmares of a faceless man stabbing at her as she ran from him through a large, cavernous shop, her soundless screams ignored by passers-by. She woke with fright and shivering in the cold of the room, her head aching and saw the time on her phone read almost eight-thirty on that Saturday morning. She sat up and rubbing at her head, reached for her mother's dressing gown and wrapping it about her she made her way into her parent's room.
She realised almost immediately her father was dead.
Her mother knelt beside the bed holding her father's hand in hers, a handkerchief pressed against her nose and lips as she stifled her sobs.
Lesley fell heavily to her knees beside her mother and wrapped her arms awkwardly round her as she leaned her head against her mother's shoulder, but no tears came and she could not understand why.

Early that morning by arrangement, Robert Hamilton's widow was visited by the police Family Liaison Officer who was accompanied by the inquiry SIO. Sitting with the widow and female detective in the comfortably furnished lounge, the SIO patiently explained that though they had arrested her husband's killer, it was unlikely he would stand trial and explained the killer was now incarcerated in the State Mental Hospital, adding that she could take comfort in that it was unlikely the man would ever again be released into society. Throughout the visit, the widow sobbed inconsolably and he worried

that the woman didn't understand what he had told her and instructed the female detective to remain with the widow for as long as necessary.
As he later drove towards his office, the SIO knew it wasn't the result he had hoped for, but he had to be satisfied a bad guy was off the street, regardless of how it had been accomplished.

The receptionist at the surgery knocked on Doctor McPherson's door and informed him that Lesley Gold had called to report her father Thomas had died and would he attend at the house to certify the death?
McPherson instructed that his waiting patients either be cancelled with a new appointment or if they preferred, transferred to one of his partner's list for that day. As he pushed up from his desk, he inwardly said a silent prayer for the repose of the soul of Thomas Gold and grabbing his worn old valise, hat and coat, made for the door.

Jenny Farndale stood at the garden gate, feeling like an interloper intruding on the grief of Frederick's mother and fearing the reception she might receive when she knocked on the door.
The detectives who had visited her the previous evening at her home had been curt, the older one almost rude and while the older man had sat with her in the lounge, the younger one persuaded her mother to move into the kitchen, telling her they needed to speak to Jenny alone and closing the door on the anxious woman. She saw them looking about the room, the older man's mouth turned down as though he thought himself above being in her home while the younger one's eyes conveyed a regret at his colleagues behaviour. The older man, the Detective Sergeant he had said, swept the chair with his hand before he sat down, grimacing as if he thought it might soil his trousers. He didn't smile and he wasn't polite and he scared her. He did all the talking and wanted to know if Frederick had been with her on Monday evening. She had started to ask what was it about, why had they called at her home, why they wanted to know about Monday night, but the Detective Sergeant abruptly interrupted her with, "Just answer the question, hen, or we could do this down at the local station."
The implied threat had been enough and Jenny, never in her life having argued with any man, meekly submitted to the bullying and told him of Frederick and she going to the multi-cinema on the corner of Renfrew Street and West Nile Street, describing the film they had seen and with nervous fingers as they watched her, searching through her handbag for the ticket stubs. They both seemed satisfied and on a sheet of paper attached to a clipboard, the older man wrote down her name, her age, her address, her occupation and what she guessed was a statement. Then he told her to sign the form on the clipboard and it was only as they left, he turned towards her

and almost with a sneer told her Frederick was dead. But he didn't call him "Frederick", he called him her "fucking boyfriend" and the Detective Sergeant sounded glad he was dead. The younger Detective didn't interrupt his boss, but glanced back as he walked along the garden path and politely nodded as he caught her eye.

And now here she was. She gripped her handbag tightly and swallowing hard, nervously knocked on the door. She took a deep breath and stepped back, fighting the urge to turn about and walk away, but the door was yanked open and Eunice stood there, her face chalk white and tearstained and a handkerchief clutched in her hand. "Jennifer," she gasped with surprise and for a heartbeat, Jenny thought she had made a mistake, coming to the house. But then Eunice opened her arms and wrapped them about the younger woman as she buried her head against Jenny's chest. Instinctively, Jenny hugged Eunice to her and, stroked her gray head as she looked past the smaller woman into the hallway. She thought again of the changes she could make to the house if she lived there and for the first time in a long while, smiled contentedly.

Blissfully unaware, she could not know then, as she returned Eunice's hug, that Frederick's careless disregard for sexual protection had already taken seed in her womb.

Between them, Doctor McPherson and Lesley persuaded and half carried the exhausted and distraught Peggy to her own room where together they laid her on the bed. Lesley fetched a quilt cover from the hallway cupboard and laid it across her mother, but as she turned to follow McPherson from the room, he raised a hand and quietly said, "Stay with her. I just want to tidy up in there." It didn't occur to Lesley to question what he meant nor did the remark seem untoward and was immediately dismissed from her mind as she pulled up a chair to sit with her mother.

In Thomas's room, McPherson walked round the bed to the small table and lifted the two painkilling medicine bottles. His elderly eyes narrowed as he stared at the contents of each bottle in turn against the overhead light. He smiled and softly muttered under his breath, "Brave girl, Peggy. Well done, you brave, brave girl," then gently patting the shoulder of the deceased man, quickly went into the bathroom where with a sigh, he poured the remaining contents down the toilet bowl and flushed them away.

Needless to say, this story is a work of fiction.
If you have enjoyed the story, you may wish to visit the author's website at:
www.glasgowcrimefiction.co.uk

The author also welcomes feedback and can be contacted at:
george.donald.books@hotmail.co.uk

Printed in Great Britain
by Amazon